MORE WINNING PRAISE FOR WIL MARA'S
THE DRAFT

"*The Draft* is a fascinating novel about what can go on behind the scenes in an NFL front office—the intrigue and maneuvering. It is terrific reading for the fan who wonders how these trades and deals are made."

—Ernie Accorsi, general manager of the New York Giants

"A smartly crafted and highly engrossing novel about deals, decisions, and desperation in the world of pro football. The characters are marvelously drawn, and the writing is razor's-edge sharp. If you are a fan of this game, then *The Draft* is one book you absolutely must read."

—Peter Golenbock, author of *Landry's Boys*

"There couldn't be a better time for a book like Wil Mara's *The Draft*. It gives fans a glimpse into parts of the NFL that they wouldn't see otherwise. I was very impressed by Wil's attention to detail, and by the great storyline he created. As a former player, I can honestly say he really nailed it. The emotion, the excitement, the suspense—everything is right here. I was amazed."

—Jon Harris, defensive end and first-round draft pick of the Philadelphia Eagles, 1997 NFL draft

ALSO BY WIL MARA

WAVE

THE
DRAFT

WIL MARA

St. Martin's Paperbacks

This is a work of fiction. All of the characters, organizations, and events portrayed in this novel are either products of the author's imagination or are used fictitiously.

THE DRAFT

Cover photo © Michael Grecco/Workbook Stock

Library of Congress Catalog Card Number: 2006045767

ISBN: 0-312-94779-8
EAN: 978-0-312-94779-8

Printed in the United States of America

St. Martin's Press hardcover edition / October 2006
St. Martin's Paperbacks edition / September 2007

St. Martin's Paperbacks are published by St. Martin's Press, 175 Fifth Avenue, New York, NY 10010.

10 9 8 7 6 5 4 3 2 1

FOR MARK DAVID CHALLIS
AUGUST 4, 1964–JANUARY 21, 2000

"A long December . . ."

ACKNOWLEDGMENTS

THE IDEA FOR THIS BOOK AND THOSE THAT WILL FOL-low came about in late 1997, and in the near-decade since then, many individuals have invested their time, energy, and faith to help me turn that idea into a reality.

My family, of course, has been there from Day One. My wife, Tracey, and my three girls—Lindsey, Jessica, and Jenna—continue to drive me ever higher. They are my shining stars, my glowing beacons of hope and happiness. (And having a wife who is also a diehard football fan is just as sweet as it sounds.) Similarly, my mom has never wavered in her belief that these books would one day puncture the tough membrane of big-league publishing. I needed that reassurance on many occasions.

My editor, Pete Wolverton, and my agent, Tony Seidl, are both terrific guys, and I am grateful for their support and counsel. The fact that they were willing to take a chance on these books is, in itself, astonishing. I could not have found two better men in this business for such an effort. They are gridiron fans in their own right, and I believe readers will find many good things from the three of us in the years ahead. I'd also like to thank Joe Rinaldi, publicist extraordinaire, for the time and effort he has devoted to this project.

My father-in-law, Walter "Butch" Bartlett, helped in countless ways. A former coach in his own right, he got things moving by introducing me to an old friend named Bill Parcells. And on a sunny day in 1998, Bill was kind enough not only to invite us both to Jets' camp, but also introduce me to several key members of the organization. In the years that followed, I was able to turn to these people to gather up the kind of information that made all the difference. Nothing beats firsthand, insider knowledge; nothing.

One of the other people I met that day was Chris Redmond. He was there for me in the early development of the story, taking me behind the scenes and answering countless questions. Similarly, Milton Love, who is still with the Jets and climbing through the ranks (and rightly so), has been a reliable ally and an all-around good guy.

Another good guy I met through this seemingly endless process has been Matt Israel. We connected through a mutual friend—James Farrior, formerly of the Jets and now of the Pittsburgh Steelers (who, as I write this, are still celebrating their victory in Super Bowl XL)—and have remained pals ever since. Time for another steak dinner and a few cigars, I think . . .

In the league proper, I cannot thank anyone more than Leslie Hammond. Her patience, openness, and cheerfulness have been priceless. Whatever I requested, she gave, and without a fuss. I am so grateful to her that I cannot possibly quantify it in mere words. She is, truly, as good as it gets. Also from the NFL, Mark Zimmerman has been there from the beginning and has contributed in countless ways.

So many players, coaches, and executives shared their time and knowledge, too—Curtis Martin, Anthony Becht, John Hall, Vinny Testaverde, Wayne Chrebet, Jon Harris, Fred Baxter, Mo Lewis, Frank Winters, Bert Sugar, Gil Brandt, Bill Polian, Ernie Accorsi, Marv Levy, Terry Bradway, and the aforementioned Maurice Carthon and Bill Parcells . . . the list is endless. And in the world of sports journalism, ESPN's John Clayton and WFAN's Chris "Mad Dog" Russo patiently answered my bothersome little questions. Their generosity overwhelms me.

And for anyone who's not on this list but should be, it's

only because you arrived too late in the game for us to make the editorial change—please know that you still have my gratitude. As always, any errors in the text are mine and mine alone. My deepest thanks and eternal good wishes go to all who helped get this book on track. To paraphrase, I get by with a lot of help from my friends.

AUTHOR'S NOTE

The story you are about to read is one of fiction. It never happened anywhere, at any time. The principle characters are therefore also fictional. They were gathered from the dust of creativity and are not intended to reflect real people, living or dead.

You may notice, however, that there are some passing references to actual people and places. Former quarterback John Elway got a few lines, as did Jets running back Curtis Martin. The aforementioned Bill Parcells, future Hall of Fame coach, and Maurice Carthon, currently of the Cleveland Browns, are mentioned as well. But as I said, only in passing. They are not crucial to the story, as you will see. And then there's the factuality—details about the draft, the Collective Bargaining Agreement, the headquarters of the Baltimore Ravens in Owings Mills, and other things. I have done my best to make wise decisions concerning where to cross the line from fiction to nonfiction (and vice versa). This had to be done on a case-by-case basis. But here's the thing—this is *not* a work of nonfiction, nor is it meant to be. For example, I state in the prologue that a man named Quincy Pressner nearly led the Rams to the Super Bowl at the end of the 1988–1989 season. But anyone who bothers to check the Internet or a good sports almanac will quickly discover that the '89 championship game was a 20–16 barnburner between the 49ers and the Bengals. The Rams did manage to eke out a wild-card berth with the second-best record in the NFC West, but they lost to the Vikings in the first round, 28–17. And there was no one on the team that year by the name of Quincy Pressner. For that matter, as far as I know, there has *never* been anyone in the league by that name.

The point is this—you will only tie yourself in mental knots trying to figure out where fact meets fiction in this book. It is first and foremost a story, not a source of reference. Many of the details offered here are the product of hours of research; interviews, phone calls, and 'Net surfing until my eyes were swollen. I attended three NFL drafts—in 2001, 2002, and 2006—and have three full notebooks and hundreds of pictures as a result. Former New York Jets general manager Terry Bradway, a true gentleman, gave me an entire morning of his time so I could assail him with questions. But it's still *fiction*. Enjoy it at face value. Don't write letters saying you couldn't find any information on Quincy Pressner or an agent named Freddie Friedman. Think of the events that transpire as having taken place in some kind of alternate reality, similar to ours but not a mirror image.

All sports fans have their fantasies.

—Wil Mara
February 20, 2005

PROLOGUE

WITHIN THE EERIE QUIET OF WASHINGTON, D.C.'S, RFK stadium, with more than fifty thousand Redskins fans watching in disgust on an otherwise clear afternoon, Rams quarterback Quincy Pressner crouched down behind his center, hands open and ready, and began the count.

The play he'd chosen was an obscure one, from last year's book. But the guys would remember it. They used it only once before, and it worked so well that they'd joked about it in the locker room afterward. It wasn't a "trick" play; Coach Jessel didn't care much for those. But it was unorthodox. It required the quarterback to pitch the ball to the tight end, who then pitched it back after the quarterback ran behind him, to the right flank, to create the illusion that he was going to sacrifice himself as a blocker. It gave the receivers on the opposite side more time to get downfield. It was a tough diagonal throw, across the center of activity and usually off balance. But a good arm could manage it. Pressner's execution of it last season was flawless, and he was even better now.

He stretched the count as long as possible, hoping to draw one of the defense lineman offside; another five yards certainly wouldn't hurt. He knew these guys were dying to get at him. His own line had played immaculately all day, protecting him with Secret Service fanaticism. They wanted this victory, wanted it like they'd never wanted anything before. Some of them had been here for ages, waiting. Mitch Walken, the left guard, had been a part of the Rams' organization for nearly twelve years; his entire career. He'd been thinking about retiring, had mentioned it to a few writers and some of the guys on the team. No one wanted him to go, but he was growing weary from the lack of postseason appearances. Now the dream was within reach. Pressner knew how hard he'd play. He had a sense of that with all his teammates. He had always been able to accurately gauge the mood of the men at his command.

The ball came up, its cool leather sliding between the calloused skin of his large palms, and he took off like a rabbit. He faked left, then swiveled right and tossed the ball to Aaron Howard, the quiet tight end who would be making his third straight Pro Bowl appearance in a few weeks. Pressner ran behind him, turned, and started downfield. The Redskin defense fell for the con and followed the ball. When it came back to Pressner, the defense slammed on its collective brakes and tried to adjust, but two of them slid to the ground. In those critical seconds they became nonfactors in the play. When Pressner saw Sammy Greene's hand waving wildly on the far side, he tossed the ball over the mayhem and watched as Greene brought it into his lap and, alone and unthreatened, slow-jogged the remaining fifteen yards into the end zone. It had been pathetically easy—and this was against the defending Super Bowl champions during the first round of the playoffs.

A few isolated cheers emanated from the crowd, but otherwise the frustrated silence maintained. There were boos, of course, as the defense got to its feet, many of them with their hands on their hips and their heads low. They weren't used to this type of humiliation, but Pressner had been shredding them all day. A wunderkind, some of the papers called him. The next Namath, the new Unitas. One reporter wrote, "He has the athletic grace of a champion thoroughbred, and his ability to read and disassemble defensive schemes is somewhere in the freakishly genius category. Just his third year in the league, and he's leading his team on a march to the Lombardi Trophy like none before."

Pressner glanced up at the scoreboard—Redskins 7, Rams 34. Period: 4. Time Remaining: 01:47. It was over.

He lingered on the sidelines with his helmet on, distantly aware of the praise being heaped upon him by his coaches and teammates. *Brilliant performance, Quince. Just amazing. Super Bowl for sure. Next stop for you, Canton, Ohio.* He couldn't bring himself to share in their jubilation, for reasons he kept to himself. He knew they'd noticed his "off" temperament all day. Some had asked about it. He made excuses but didn't give answers. No one needed to know.

He scanned the enormous crowd, taking in the moment. Then he closed his eyes and breathed deep, catching the sounds and scents and committing them to memory. He was nearing the top of the mountain, he knew. The other games would almost be a formality. Washington was their toughest opponent, and he'd eaten them alive. Two more, and then the big one. The chance to make history—the first black quarterback to lead his team to a Super Bowl and then win it.

Except . . .

The clock ran down and the game ended. Feeling somehow detached from it all, Pressner followed his teammates back onto the field to shake hands with the enemy. Some of them passed along comments that he certainly wouldn't be sharing with his young son. But most were valiant enough in their defeat, wishing him well in the battles ahead.

As Pressner headed into the tunnel, he spotted the three men standing off to the side, their backs to the wall. They were smiling pleasantly enough in their tailored suits, three sanctimonious agents of righteousness who moved in a little pack as if sharing one mind. They watched him as he entered the darkened corridor. At first he pretended not to notice. Then he made eye contact and, unable to resist, flashed the "V" sign. Their smiles fell as if on cue, and the smallest of the them looked like he was capable of homicide. No one else noticed the exchange, but for Pressner it would be his last great victory.

Nearly four hours later, when the full moon was glowing like a pearl in the clear northern sky, Pressner walked alone to his car. He opened the door and tossed his bag in the passenger seat, then paused. He looked back at the stadium, its lights glowing majestically around the rim, and he was suddenly fully aware of the magnitude of what was happening to him. This time the tears broke free, streaming down either side of his young face. He took a long, hard look at the world that he wanted so desperately to conquer—one that he would no longer be part of in a few brief weeks—then got into his Cadillac and sped away.

At that moment, the legend that eventually evolved into myth began.

1

SEVENTY-NINE-YEAR-OLD PHYLLIS SMITH KNEW IT was dangerous for her to be driving. The medications had robbed her of the privilege. She was frequently tired, and her reaction time was slow. Nevertheless, she *had* to get to the supermarket. If that new caregiver—the one with the two kids and the sleazy-looking boyfriend—had come early this morning like she'd been asked, this wouldn't be necessary. Nearly a year had passed since she was last behind the wheel. She still had the hulking black Mercedes Don bought her. She knew she should've surrendered her license at some point, but she couldn't bring herself to do it.

The images in the street were fuzzy at best. She could see colors and make out most shapes, but details were impossible. It was fairly busy already, the sun coming up, people moving about. All that really mattered, she had convinced herself, was the car ahead of her. She could more or less make out where it was since her depth perception wasn't too bad. She simply kept back a good distance and drove slowly.

The dizziness began as she approached the intersection where Light Street met Pratt. At first it felt similar to the pleasant numbness associated with being slightly drunk. Then it heightened to a gentle swirling sensation. After that, she would say later in a deposition that precluded a sizable payout from her insurance company, she couldn't remember a thing. It all happened so quickly.

There was only one vehicle sitting at the intersection that fateful morning—a blue Jaguar XJ6. A beautiful machine but unremarkable in this affluent Baltimore suburb. The driver wasn't looking in his rearview mirror. If he had been, perhaps he could've reacted in time. Instead he was fingering through his CD collection, trying to decide whether to go with Randy Travis or Clint Black. Maybe even some of that Bruce Springsteen stuff everyone around here liked so much.

Meanwhile, Jack Harris, a carpenter from nearby Glen Burnie, was on his way back from Home Depot, where he'd picked up a load of railroad ties. He had the window down, elbow out, and was whistling to Johnny Cash's "I Walk the Line." He'd come down Pratt hundreds of times. He knew the intersection was dangerous, knew there'd been dozens of accidents there. But that didn't make him slow down as he approached it today. Seeing that the light was green, he didn't give it another thought.

Phyllis Smith's tiny body slumped over the wheel when she lost consciousness. The Mercedes swerved crazily for a moment, but not sharply enough to avoid the Jag. Upon impact it lurched into the intersection, giving Harris no time to react. On pure reflex he tightened his grip on the wheel and jammed the brake. The tires screamed, burning on the pavement. His truck swung to the left, and the back end began to drift forward. But the distance required to avoid the collision just wasn't there. In fact, Harris would realize with great irony much later on, the accident probably wouldn't have been half as bad if he'd just stayed on course. He would have smacked the Jaguar in the rear, spinning it sharply but probably leaving the driver relatively unharmed. As it turned out, the bulk of the impact delivered by a payload of railroad ties was absorbed by the Jag's door and, unfortunately, by the person on the other side of it.

When it was over, a horn was blaring and someone was

screaming. Harris looked up but couldn't see anything because of the white smoke blowing from his radiator. He checked himself quickly and found no signs of injury. His arms were already aching—the punishment for the understandable reaction of tightening his muscles—but there didn't appear to be anything broken or otherwise out of place.

There was no way the other driver could have been as lucky.

Trembling, he got the door open and stepped outside. He was faintly aware of a crowd beginning to form along the fringes. He could feel their eyes on him and suspected that some of them were already forming their judgments. Big guy, plaid shirt, swollen belly. *Probably a drunk. Typical.*

He started toward the crumpled Jag, then stopped. The tinted window was gone and the driver was nowhere to be seen. But the blood was there—a dark red stain down the side like cranberry juice.

"Oh Christ . . ."

Now the *real* terror came. Harris hadn't been in an auto accident since he was a teenager, driving his father's sky blue Chevelle in the rain. The tires lost touch with the road, and the car fishtailed into a pair of garbage cans. He wasn't hurt and no one was with him. But he was petrified at the thought of what his father would do. As it turned out, the old man was pretty teed off but mostly thankful.

Many years had passed since then, and Jack Harris had developed the common assurance that auto accidents happened only to *other* people. You saw them on the news when they were particularly bad, read about them in the paper, or heard of them at the local diner. But they didn't happen to *him*. They were part of a different reality, nothing to do with his. He was fifty-four, after all. Far too old and too wise to get into that kind of a mess.

The blood running down the wrinkled metal, however, transmitted a different truth. *My God,* Harris thought, *this is really happening.* That's someone else's blood trickling down the side of the damn door like rainwater. Something about the *movement* of it made it all the more unbearable.

He willed himself forward, determined to do something useful. As he got to the door he saw the driver for the first time. It was a fairly large young male dressed in a jogging suit. He lay on his side across the front seats. He sort of looked like he was sleeping. His clothing sparkled with bits of glass.

Harris heard several sirens in the distance. For some reason it made him think that he shouldn't move the victim. He went around to the other side, where he found more blood, spattered on the inside of the window. At this point he began crying—something else he hadn't done in ages—and reached for the door handle. To his surprise it released, albeit with a protesting creak. He brought the door back gently, took one look at the driver's face, and froze.

Any of the other people standing nearby would have recognized the guy just as quickly. Now the situation shifted from unreal to surreal. *This can't be right,* Harris thought. But of course it was—some people really did win the lottery, whereas other got hit by lightning. Those were the extreme ends of reality's spectrum. No explanations, no sense or significance. Sometimes things just *happened.*

And for whatever reason, on this bright and chilly morning in April, Jack Harris, master carpenter and father or three, drove his beloved Ford pickup into the side of a dark blue Jaguar occupied by Michael Bell, the starting quarterback of the Super Bowl champion Baltimore Ravens.

IRONICALLY, THE SAME DAY BEGAN VERY QUIETLY FOR jon sabino, the Ravens' general manager. He awoke at the usual 5:00 A.M., showered, shaved, put on khaki slacks (almost standard for NFL front-office personnel) and a polo shirt bearing the Ravens' logo. He moved about quietly so as not to wake Kelley, his wife of eight years. Then he went in to check on their two-year-old daughter, Lauren. She was lying peacefully on her side, wearing a tiny Ravens T-shirt and hugging a stuffed tiger. Her blanket, a hand-knitted gift from one of Kelley's college friends, lay nearby; Lauren had a habit of uncovering herself during the night. Sabino pulled it over her and brushed away the soft brown hair that had spilled onto her face.

It was still dark when he stepped outside. Dark and cool, but not cold like April could sometimes be in Maryland. The moon was full, casting everything in an eerie neon glow, and the North Star shone brightly. After he locked the door and reset the alarm, he paused for a moment, as he did every morning, to admire his neighborhood. It was an American paradise—a world of castles and glistening lawns and BMWs.

Jon had earned a scholarship to the University of Maryland, where he majored in business administration with a minor in sports management. He also played football and baseball, but he was realistic enough—even though the admission was a bitter one—to know he did not possess the natural skills required to be a pro in either.

Nevertheless, upon graduation with honors, his love of sports led him to seek a position with a pro team. The general manager of the Washington Redskins admired his determination and gave him an entry level position assisting the scouting staff. Jon worked like a dog over the next four years and eventually became a full-fledged scout in the northeastern region. The logistics of the job could be brutal—eighteen-hour days, traveling for weeks on end, living in hotel rooms, eating in restaurants, watching one talented-but-not-quite-talented-enough player after another while trying to maintain focus and freshness.

In spite of the strain, it was at this phase of his career that his true gifts began to emerge—it didn't take long for the Redskins to realize he was a natural at judging and evaluating others. The players he recruited weren't flashy or dramatic, but the steady and reliable quality was there. An unusually high percentage of his recommendations ended up being drafted and making starting squads. Two even became Pro Bowlers. Jon's philosophy of placing such a high value on character was somewhat uncommon, but his reasoning was irrefutable—football skills are easier to teach than integrity. As a result, his recruits were more mature, more disciplined, and more driven, and thus hurdled the kind of barriers that stopped most "flash-in-the-pan" talents cold. Coaches liked working with Jon's picks, administrators liked dealing with them, and the fans loved them.

Jon moved through the ranks quickly, becoming Washington's head scout when he was only thirty-four. The politics within the non-public side of the NFL, he quickly learned, were brutal, but he learned how to play that game, too. It was all part of the competitive nature of the league. He made few enemies and had a knack for knowing when to be invisible. He fit in and became part of the greater dynamic. Soon other teams were scouting *him*. He was eventually offered the position of vice president of player personnel with the newly ordained Ravens. The Ravens' leadership was looking to fill some key roles with youthful, energetic individuals. It was not only a step up but an opportunity for him to return to his hometown. Since the Redskins didn't have a similar position to offer, they reluctantly let him go.

The Ravens weren't exactly a new team, but in fact the transplanted incarnation of the Cleveland Browns. In 1984, the Baltimore Colts moved to Indianapolis in the middle of a snowy March night. Then, in 1996, Art Modell, the Browns' owner at the time, was offered a sweet deal from the city of Baltimore. Modell uprooted his organization and headed for the East Coast, rechristening his club after the classic poem "The Raven" by Baltimore resident Edgar Allan Poe.

Hopes ran high until it became obvious the former Browns, who had struggled through the '90s thus far, didn't fare much better as the Ravens. In their first season they won only four games, suffering from overall mediocrity and the oppression of not one but two powerful rivals—the Broncos and the Jaguars. They didn't show much improvement the following season, either, winning only six games as they landed in last place in the AFC Central.

During those inaugural years, two keys developments

took place—Jon displayed tremendous ability as an evaluator of talent and as an administrator, and the Ravens' current general manager, Harry Colby, displayed tremendous ability as an incompetent idiot. He was a petty, power-crazed bureaucrat who insisted on having final decision over all personnel matters even though his experience in that area was minimal. He rarely heeded the advice of his underlings and even ignored the recommendations of his coaches, some of whom were veterans. The fact that most of the staff couldn't stand him didn't help much, either. So, at the end of three straight losing seasons, Modell showed Colby the door. His replacement, it was decided, would be the popular forty-two-year-old Sabino.

Jon inherited a bitter, war-weary group of players, front-office personnel, fans, and local sportswriters. The latter crucified him even before he made his first decision. And those who had toiled in the organization for years and were hoping to take the next step up the ladder began circling like vultures, watching for signs of vulnerability, waiting for a huge screwup so Jon would make a quick exit.

But he kept a level head and didn't take any of it personally. He understood the frustration and wanted to see the team succeed as much as anyone. He had studied the strengths and weaknesses of other teams through the years, collecting information that would be useful when this day came. He allowed himself the typical freshman mistakes and learned valuable lessons from each one.

He soon came to learn that the title "general manager," like most other titles in the NFL, was without clear definition and ambiguous at best. Some GMs were businessmen, others were football men. Some had strong skills in marketing and promotion and would busy themselves with issues concerning everything from merchandising to ticket sales, whereas others knew the X's and the O's. Some did a lot of the front-office hiring, others delegated it. Their duties varied from team to team, and the best ones focused on their strengths.

Jon decided to take this sensible route. Knowing his pedigree was in football personnel, he brought in good people to take care of the things he didn't know rather than allow pride to rule the day and try to be a renaissance man. To some this was a sign of weakness. He hoped the men who had been largely responsible for bringing him here would interpret it as a sign of honesty, a dignified attempt to put the team's interests before his own. He kept tabs on what was going on, but he allowed his directors to direct and didn't meddle. And as his understanding of the pro football universe and his place in it began to crystallize, everything turned around.

In the first season under his guidance, which included a new head coach, two new scouts, a handful of new trainers, and even a new videotape librarian, the team went 7–9. Not a miraculous record, but a step in the right direction. The more fair-minded writers took note of the fact that a number of the players Jon had either signed from free agency or acquired through the draft were making significant contributions. One, a guard that Jon plucked from the third round, not only made the starting team but was elected to the Pro Bowl. Another, a defensive back, made the second team that same year. Even the most skeptical observers had to admit the Ravens were getting better.

During his first off-season, Jon knew his central priority was improving the team's offense, and in a slick free-agent maneuver that would eventually grow to historic proportions, he managed to lure hot young quarterback Michael Bell away from what seemed like a done deal with the Denver Broncos. It was on that day, the talking heads determined, that the Ravens became a force. Bell, who'd spent his first three seasons with the Jaguars, had developed into a dynamic and confident leader with devastating pass accuracy and a slippery quickness that would have made Fran Tarkenton proud.

The next year the Ravens leaped to the top of their division with a 10–6 record and a wild card spot in the playoffs. Unfortunately their fledgling team was still too inexperienced to handle the pressures of playing on that level, and they were eliminated in the first round by the Jets. But they were on a roll, and the fans and media were rolling right along with them.

In Jon's third year, the Ravens made their statement. Completing their offense with a high-priced wide receiver and a pounding, powerhouse fullback, they stomped their way to a 9–0 record before losing their first game, by a field goal, to the Patriots. Two more losses to Miami and Tampa Bay completed an unbelievable 13–3 record and home advantage throughout the playoffs with a first round bye. Now Jon's name was being freely intermingled with the word "genius." His gift for creating powerful chemistries was no longer deniable. *Sports Illustrated* ran a nine-page article on him—"Savin' the Ravens: Are They Losers Nevermore?"

In spite of the fact that the team stalled on the road to the Super Bowl by losing 24–17 to the Broncos in the AFC Championship Game, one thing was clear—the Ravens were headed to the top. Less than a week after the season was over, experts across the nation were picking them as next year's favorites.

Their faith was well placed—in an unforgettable march to the championship, the Ravens' defense allowed fewer points in a single season than any other team in league history while compiling their second 13–3 record. Then they hurdled three playoff games and authored a 34–14 Super Bowl victory over the Buccaneers. The next season they reached the top again, crushing the Panthers 42–7.

Only six other teams had won back-to-back Super Bowls—the Steelers, the 49ers, the Cowboys, the Dolphins, the Packers, and the Broncos. And *none* had managed a third. Many said it couldn't be done; it was impossible in the free-agency era. Free agency had, after all, been implemented to arrest the development of dynasties. But somehow, it appeared, the Ravens were building one anyway. Either enthusiastically or bitterly, the fans and the media were forced to admit Baltimore looked like the best team again. A third straight championship was within reach, and Jon wanted it more than anything he'd ever wanted in his life. It gave legitimacy to everything he'd ever done, justified all the hard work and years of toil he'd invested. It would lend solid, undeniable credibility to his "genius" tag and silence the few remaining doubters once and for all. His detractors were running out of things to say, his colleagues were boiling in their own jealousy (which, Jon could not help but admit, he enjoyed tremendously). To do something great in professional sports was one thing. To make *history* . . . well, that was something else. Sometimes just the thought of it kept him awake at night.

Best of all, it was *possible*—the core of the club was still together, they were all still young enough to remain in top form, and there had been no changes to the coaching staff or even the front-office personnel. The chemistry remained; it looked very much like the Baltimore Ravens were on their way to making history.

After all, only a cruel twist of fate could stop them.

THE RAVENS' OFFICES WERE LOCATED IN A MAGNIFI-cent modern facility in the Maryland suburb of Owings Mills, a twenty-minute ride from the stadium. They were well secured and off limits to the public.

At the front gate, Jon waved to Gary Stone, the Ravens' head of security. Stone possessed a deep loyalty to Jon, who hired him. They had been classmates in high school and kept in touch when they went to separate colleges. Stone joined the FBI shortly after graduation and traveled overseas for a few years. When he returned to the states, he left the agency to be a private investigator but found the work distasteful— too many sleazy divorce cases—and wanted out. Jon heard about this and happened to be looking for someone reliable and experienced to work for the team. He wanted either ex-military or ex-FBI, which was common criteria when it came to security positions in the NFL. Stone was the perfect choice.

They briefly exchanged small talk, then Jon pulled through the gates and into his space near the front of the main building. Access required a security code on a keypad.

Once inside, he turned everything on, then went to a small locker room reserved for the coaches and front-office echelon. It was similar in appearance to any scholastic locker room, with rows of steel boxes, wooden benches bolted to a tiled floor, and a set of showers.

Morning workouts had been part of his routine since he was a teenager. They were common not only to the players but to everyone who worked for an NFL club. The prevailing attitude throughout the league seemed to be that workouts were the proper way to start the day. They certainly were for him. A good workout provided the stamina he needed to get through the demanding twelve-to-sixteen-hour days without those sloggy, low-energy periods. And the solitude afforded him the opportunity to collect his thoughts and focus on current priorities.

After he showered and dressed, he returned to his paneled office. It was less dramatic and luxurious than one might expect for a man in such an exalted, high-profile position. It was relatively small, with a walnut desk and a computer, a few framed photographs of Kelley and Lauren, and three large windows overlooking the practice field. There was no wet bar, no cabinet humidor filled with Cuban cigars, no plush deep-pile carpeting. Most general manager's offices were like this one. Contrary to common belief, high-ranking team executives weren't pampered by any means. The only true luxury item Jon had was a new Volvo sedan, and even that was leased by the team. If a GM wanted toys, he had to buy them himself.

Early April was draft time, and for a general manager that meant *busy.* As Jon got into his comfortable leather swivel chair, he remembered how he used to think when he was a kid, like any other ordinary fan, there was very little activity in a professional football club during the off season. It didn't take him long to realize this was dead wrong, especially for the administrators. Pro football had its "down time," but in positions like his it was only for a few weeks at the end of spring. Early September could also bring a simmering once everything was in place and attention turned to the players

and the game. When that was over, however, a very different
game began. This was the game the fans never saw and
barely heard about. Perhaps it wasn't as glamorous, but it
was just as tough, just as competitive, and the stakes were
just as high. A young athlete's entire future was decided by
the stroke of a pen. Millionaires were made in afternoon
meetings. The power was tremendous and, for some, cor-
rupting.

Preparation for each year's draft was particularly demanding. Technically the process began years before, when
the scouts were reviewing players early in their college ca-
reers. By January, a team would begin to assemble their draft
board, which was usually nothing more than a collection of
names on a wall. These were the players a team deemed capable of playing in the pros. Of the tens of thousands of college players in the country, a mere two hundred or so would
be considered. A team had to base their choices on two
factors—what they needed, and what was available. It was
nothing more than a guessing game, plain and simple. In
most cases, someone other than the head coach made the final personnel decisions, but usually that person conferred
with his coaches when determining his teams most urgent
needs. If a coach utilized a system that required a large tight
end who could block, then such a tight end became that
much more valuable in the draft. Putting together the final
draft list was in part a slow process of elimination. Beyond
the board of college prospects, a team would also assemble
boards of both semipro players and those who were of pro
quality but, for one reason or another, were not playing for
any team at the moment. And, as with the college boys, each
pro team had staff whose job it was to keep the information
on all such players fully updated.

Jon took a heavy folder from his desk. On the first loose-
leaf page was a neatly handwritten list of the Ravens' desired picks, arranged in order of preference. The desk was
usually locked as a standard security measure—insider information on a team's draft was worth a small fortune and
treated like a military secret during wartime. This year, how-

ever, he doubted anyone would be interested. Due to last year's second Super Bowl victory, the Ravens naturally had the last pick in the draft's first round. By that time most of the surprises would be over and most, if not all, of the premium talent would be gone. Every now and then a gem would slip into the lower rounds, but those cases were rare and usually the result of a player who greatly exceeded expectations rather than an oversight on the part of the scouts.

Jon tuned his radio to a '70s station and reviewed the list for what seemed like the hundredth time. There were two, actually—a "wish list" made up of players he'd love to get but didn't expect to, and then a "reality list," which he was studying now. He was still comfortable with it, sure that the player at the top would be available when their turn came. That player was Bryan Engler, a tackle from Florida State. The Ravens weren't in desperate need at that position, but the coaches felt they lacked depth. One of their present tackles, Craig Little, would probably retire in the next year or two, and Frank James, another veteran in the same position, was also mumbling about calling it quits. So they needed to think about his replacement. Engler, if they could land him, would fill the role nicely.

Jon was thinking about the next player on the list, a wide receiver from North Carolina State, when the phone rang. Surprised, he glanced at his desk clock: 7:04. Odd that anyone would be calling this early, he thought. It wasn't often they had business so urgent that it needed attention at this hour.

"Hello? Oh, hiya, Tommy. What are you doing up at this hou—what's that? No, I haven't put on ESPN yet. Why?" When Jon heard and absorbed the fateful news, his stomach tightened. He asked if it was a joke.

It wasn't.

2

MICHAEL BELL'S HOSPITAL ROOM WAS QUIET EXCEPT for the mechanized, rhythmic hiss of the respirator. Jon quietly stepped inside and shut the door. Bell's bed was surrounded by an array of high-tech medical equipment, the centerpiece of a macabre tableau.

Bell lay flat on his back with dozens of tubes and wires slithering over his body. Jon came alongside him, externally devoid of expression but internally battling several unpleasant emotions. The ribbed, opaque tube running from Bell's mouth was particularly disturbing for some reason.

Jon had become friends with some of the players, and Bell was one of them. He'd invited him into his home, introduced him to his wife and let him play with his daughter. Bell was charming in a roguish, naughty-little-boy sort of way. Women loved him, men wanted to be like him. He had two distinct sides to his character—the dirty side that wanted to drag every beautiful woman he saw to bed, and the moral side that sometimes succeeded in overriding the other. It wasn't hard to understand why so many people were fascinated by him. He was larger than life in every sense.

It seemed surreal to see him lying there, unmoving and helpless. A recognizable face that had appeared in countless magazines and newspapers, and on television. This hulking figure of a man—six foot five, which was a good size for a quarterback—who seemed nearly indestructible on the field, was now as vulnerable as a baby. He probably wouldn't believe it, Jon thought. They were all like that; it was a quirk of the breed he had long grown used to. The average pro player was treated like a prince everywhere he went. He was young, healthy, and rich. The last thing he worried about was his mortality. Many of them did think they were indestructible.

The door opened and a man in white lab coat came in. He was tall and slender, perhaps in his early fifties. He wore large round glasses and suffered a common form of pattern baldness that had already cleared off the top of his head and was working its way down.

He came forward with a smile and held out his hand. "Good morning, Mr. Sabino. I'm Joshua Blackman."

"Nice to meet you."

They turned to Bell together. "He looks like he's in pretty bad shape."

Blackman nodded, but the smile remained. "He is, right now. But it could have been much worse. You know about what happened?"

"I heard on the way over."

"He received a great deal of the impact directly, with only that thin metal door for protection."

Jon shook his head. "He preferred sports cars over SUVs. If he was in a big Ford Expedition, this never would have happened."

Most NFL players drove sport-utility vehicles, and not simply because they could fit into them more easily. They were contractually bound to maintain peak physical health, and the average SUV protected them from potential road injuries. It was hard enough staying healthy during the course of a game.

"If he was an ordinary man," Blackman continued. "I doubt very much he would have survived." Then he added, "Getting hit by linebackers all those years was probably the best preparation he could have had."

"I'm sure he'll be glad to hear that when he wakes up," Jon said. When he realized the seriousness of what this implied, he added, "He *will* wake up, won't he?"

Blackman nodded. "I don't know if anyone's told you, but he's not just unconscious—he's in a low-level coma right now."

"He's what?"

"I know, 'coma' is a scary word. But don't let it be. Most people have been conditioned to believe a coma is about the worst state you can be in short of being dead, but that's a myth. Sometimes a coma is the brain's way of protecting itself. Often patients are chemically induced into temporary low-level comas to aid in the recovery process." Blackman looked back at his patient. "Mr. Bell still reacts to most of the conventional stimuli, and he's been moving around and making sounds."

"So he'll come out of it?"

"I can't make such a prediction with hundred percent certainty, but I'm as certain as I can be."

"How long?"

"I'm guessing anywhere from two days to two weeks."

"Any damage to his head or . . . you know, his brain?"

"Not that we can tell, but it's still early. We'll be running tests on him in the coming weeks, though. Many of them, I'm afraid." Then he added, "I think you should know the coma is only one of the problems. Maybe the least of them."

"Oh?"

"He'll wake from it eventually, but he sustained some injuries elsewhere that concern me very much."

"Such as?"

"Well, he has four broken ribs, one of which punctured his right lung. He also has a broken right leg and two broken fingers on his left hand. But what really concerns me is his spine."

"His spi . . . No, don't tell me—"

A slow, confirming nod. "The lower portion sustained severe trauma." He paused, and the question that lingered between them was so obvious that neither bothered to articulate it. "There's a small chance he won't be able to walk again."

Jon looked back at his star quarterback. "My God."

"But it's highly unlikely. Again, because he's in such good physical shape . . . I just want to prepare you for the worst. But it's still too early to tell. The next forty-eight hours are crucial."

"Okay, okay." Jon shuffled for a moment, hands in his pockets. "Uh, look, doc. About this coming season. Any chance he'll—"

Blackman might've laughed, but he didn't—he was absolutely stonefaced. "No, no way at all."

Jon's shoulders sagged. It was the reply he dreaded most.

"There is absolutely no way he'll be able to play this season. That would be impossible. Next season . . . maybe. But this year, no way."

Jon stared at Blackman for what seemed like a long time, unable to pull his eyes off the man who had just told him that his team's chances of making NFL history were basically over.

AS HE BREEZED THROUGH THE HOSPITAL'S HALLWAYS he focused on just two things—Bell's long-term health, and the team's quarterback situation; his thoughts ping-ponged from the personal to the professional. When he emerged from the paired glass doors in the emergency wing and was nearly trampled by a herd of reporters, photographers, and cameramen, he jerked back as if shaken from a dream.

Damn—I should've known. When anything like this happened, of course the press would be there. They were nothing if not reliable. Of course they'd show up for this.

Impromptu press conferences were one of the more unpleasant aspects of being a general manager, but it went with the job. By their very nature they were sheer chaos. You had no time to prepare, so it became something like a skeet shoot. The most seemingly innocuous remark could turn into tomorrow morning's headline. Players suddenly resented you, colleagues were giving you the cold shoulder, owners were screaming. Sometimes you came in and found your office locked and your personal effects in a box in the hallway.

The questions came fast and furious. A dozen voices babbled at once. Early on Jon found this daunting, even a little frightening. But he had learned through experience and from talking to other GMs to simply relax, listen, and sift through the cacophony for the three or four points the writers obviously considered most important. Even though they were a group of individuals, they often functioned as a single, organic unit.

"Jon, how is Mike Bell?"

"How's Bell doing?"

"What's the state of Michael Bell's health?"

He felt uneasy without the protection of a podium, so his hands went into his pockets. He scanned the crowd briefly, noting and naming each face. Everyone was familiar; same old group. They weren't friends, but they weren't really enemies, either. They were acquaintances, professionals with a job to do. A lot of Jon's peers considered the media a necessary evil, but he hadn't reached that point yet (although he feared he would someday). You couldn't really be buddies with any of them, he felt, but you didn't have to hate them, either. You just needed to be careful.

His first thought was how much he should reveal. This instinct was automatic now; part of his training as a high-ranking team executive. Everyone within an NFL club was instructed, either directly or indirectly, on what should and should not be discussed with the press. That was why so many phrases and comments came from the same template—*I have the utmost confidence in him and what he brings to the table* or *We have as good a team as anyone, and as good a chance of making the Super Bowl as anyone.*

"I spoke with the physician a short time ago, and it appears Michael is in pretty rough shape."

"Can you be more specific?"

"Right now he's still unconscious and has multiple injuries to his arms, legs, chest, and back."

That came out well, he thought. Specific enough to satisfy their curiosity and remain completely truthful.

"Will he be ready to play this year?"

It took Jon only a nanosecond to decide honesty was best here. There was no point in taking any other approach—the facts would leak out one way or another. His prudence told him to hedge, but he knew damn well the hospital people would talk.

"Uh, no. His doctor has made it clear that there's no chance of him playing this season."

The ones who brought notepads scribbled this down. The rest held out their microphones and microcassette recorders.

"So then his injuries must be pretty serious?"

"I can't really give any specifics yet."

Jon searched their faces. As he expected, some looked skeptical. He wasn't surprised—it sounded like a bullshit response. It sounded like he was hiding something.

"We'll know a lot more in about two days. The doctor said the next forty-eight hours will be critical in determining his long-term health. Until then, I don't want to speculate."

A kid who looked to be in his early twenties nudged his way to the front of the crowd. "Are you being truthful about that," he asked with a crooked smile, "or are you saying it just because the draft is coming up and you don't want to lose any negotiating power?"

The moment Jon saw Bobby Verlucci, he expected a dumb question. How this guy still had a sportswriting job was a mystery to him. Jon considered him brash and arrogant, hopelessly ignorant, and under the peculiar impression that interviewing someone was synonymous with harassing them. No question was too scandalous, no topic too sensitive. A real First Amendment hawk. Dealing with Verlucci was like dealing with *The National Enquirer.*

"That question is so idiotic I won't even dignify it with a response. Next."

Verlucci's eager gaze faded. He was embarrassed, but the discouragement was temporary. Jon knew he'd be back and in a vengeful mood next time. Losers like him always kept score.

A handful of other questions were tossed out—considerably more reasonable than Verlucci's—and Jon answered them frankly and honestly. Nothing too difficult, nothing unexpected. Then Patti Sheridan raised her hand. Jon spotted her and smiled for the first time all day.

Patti was the only woman in the group; always had been. When she first arrived on the scene just over five years ago, everybody figured she'd be eaten alive. A female writer in the exclusive boys' club of sportswriting? No way. Admission for new *males* was rare. The old schoolers were particularly offended by her audacity. To them she was a symbol of the modern age. This simply wasn't the *place* for women. Couldn't she understand that? Surely she was pursuing it only to make a statement for feminism and liberalism, and for the fun of getting under their collective skin.

In time Sheridan *did* work her way under their skin—by evolving into a first-rate journalist. She churned out penetrating and insightful articles in a direct, objective style that readers loved. Then the stories about her past began to surface—mother died when she was a child, father committed suicide, raised by grandparents who were barely able to take care of themselves, paid her own way through college. Perceptions began to change. Gone were the days when no one would share their notes with her or invite her to dinner after a big event. She became a full-fledged member of the club, the little sister with dozens of big brothers. And God help you if you pushed her around.

Jon admired her grit and made a point of giving her at least one nod during each conference. He knew it was a wise investment—she didn't ask Verlucci-type questions. But she did often ask tough ones.

"Patti?"

"With Michael Bell out for the season, what are you going to do for a quarterback?"

"Yeah, are you going to enter the McKinley Sweepstakes now?" another reporter added. "Is drafting Christian McKinley your only option?"

A third said, "If so, are you eager to get back into the ring with Brendan Cavanaugh?"

Jon knew the Cavanaugh Question was coming, yet hearing it still made his stomach knot. *Do these guys ever forget?*

"I'm sorry, guys, but right now I just don't have that many answers for you," he said, disappointed that he couldn't give Patti something better. His response received a collective groan from his audience.

Within minutes he was in his car, speeding back to Owings Mills.

IF YOU ASKED TEN DIFFERENT PEOPLE AROUND THE league who, if anyone, hated each breath that kept Jon Sabino alive, all ten would, without hesitation, give the same reply—Broncos general manager Brendan Cavanaugh. Cavanaugh was sitting as his desk when the phone rang. On the wall across from him was a huge team logo flanked by smaller photos of Denver's greatest players—John Elway, Terrell Davis, Shannon Sharpe. All were inscribed.

Cavanaugh glanced at the number on the caller ID and decided to let his assistant get it. She was stationed in a small antechamber next door.

"Hello, Brendan Cavanaugh's line. Yes? Hold please. I'll see if he's in."

An attractive brunette's face appeared in the doorway.

"Are you here?"

"It's Corwin, right?"

"Yes."

Cavanaugh shook his head. *Not that little bastard.*

"He'll just call back if I don't talk to him now. All right, put him through." He cursed and picked up the receiver. "Hello, Don."

"Cav? That you?"

"Sure is. What can I do for you?" The fake smile alone

was a struggle. It wasn't easy being friendly to a man who'd said so many negative things about your team through the years. But a general manager had little choice. Tell a writer to piss off and you left yourself wide open. At the very least they would report that you "refused to comment," which was interpreted as an admission of guilt anyway.

"Well, I'm calling to get your take on this whole Bell issue."

"Bell issue?" It came out so sincere he almost believed it himself, as if Corwin wasn't really the third scribbler to call in the last hour. "You mean the car accident?"

"Yeah, what do you think about it?" Corwin's phlegmy voice made Cavanaugh's skin crawl. He could almost *smell* the old man's halitosis.

"What do you mean?"

"Well, without Michael Bell, the Ravens' chances of reaching that hallowed third Super Bowl are next to nil. That must put a smile on your face."

"A man was in a car accident that left him in a coma," Cavanaugh replied, sounding pious. "If that puts a smile on your face, then you need professional help."

He was pleased with how that came out. It might have been a little self-righteous, but the point was inarguable.

"But let's face it, Cav—chances are the Ravens won't reach that third Super Bowl now, and that'll keep them out of the history books. In fact they'll probably have a pretty rough season. You must get some satisfaction out of that."

"I'm not concerned with the Ravens right now. The draft is less than two weeks away, so I'm concerned with the Denver Broncos."

A BS response if there ever was one, and a seasoned vet like Corwin would certainly realize that. But it was all he was going to get.

"What about Christian McKinley? The rumor is Sabino will be after him now."

"Rumor? What rumor? I didn't hear that. Who told you that?"

"I'm sorry, I can't reveal my sources."

Greatest alibi the press ever had, he thought. It had given them license to get away with damn near everything.

"It doesn't matter. What Sabino does doesn't affect our plans."

"But I heard you guys are also after McKinley."

Cavanaugh smiled. "Sorry, I can't confirm that. You know—can't reveal my sources."

He was being an asshole now and he knew it, but what the hell. It was worth it.

"If it's true, though," Corwin went on anyway, "then it's kind of a general manager rematch, don't you think?"

"I wouldn't think of it that way, no. Whatever Sabino does is Sabino's business. If he does something that affects us, we'll deal with it then."

"But what about—"

"Don, I gotta cut it short. Alderman just walked in."

He replaced the receiver without waiting for Corwin's response. Then he rose and went to the doorway.

"I'm not here for the next hour, okay?"

"Okay."

He shut the door and slumped into his chair. He leaned back and thought about Corwin's remark—*It's kind of a general manager rematch, don't you think?* They never forget, he reminded himself. *Never . . .*

The incident occurred almost five years ago and centered around Bell. Five long years, but it might as well have been last goddamn week. Bell had started his NFL career with the Jaguars, drafted from the third round out of LSU. He had tremendous potential but was wild and undisciplined on the field, often leaving the pocket early and attempting throws Johnny Unitas couldn't have made on a good day. The consensus among coaches was that he might be able to function as a starter if given the proper attention. But the average NFL team wasn't as quarterback-friendly as it used to be. Only a few were willing to invest the time required to develop a quarterback properly. It was assumed Bell would land a starter spot on some perennial .500 team for a few years, then fade into obscurity. It was a familiar pattern.

At the start of his third season, however, he showed up for minicamps in near-perfect condition and requested a shot at the starting job. Skeptical at first, the coaches finally relented and discovered they had a very different Michael Bell in their midst. His decisions were more mature, his throwing was more accurate. He scrambled only when necessary and had learned the value of sliding before being tackled rather than try to plow through defenders. With increased skill came increased confidence, and with that came a more natural leadership. By the end of the preseason it was obvious he had taken possession of the team, so the coaches gave him the nod and never looked back. During the regular season he amassed staggering statistics and shattered team records. The following season was even better as he carried the Jaguars to their first playoff appearance in ages.

When that season ended he was an unrestricted free agent. His contract had been so structured because, in plain truth, the team never expected him to amount to much. Since his rebirth they had put out feelers to see if he'd be interested in a new deal, one that would give him more money up front while keeping him in the organization. But his agent, Jerry Wahlberg, always declined. The general feeling was that he planned to shop Bell's services around to assess their market value.

Which is precisely what Wahlberg did. In the quarterback-poor NFL it came as no surprise that his value turned out to be very high indeed. Six teams beyond Jacksonville expressed interest, all with handsome long-term offers featuring huge signing bonuses. One of those teams was the Denver Broncos.

The man who represented Denver at the time was Brendan Cavanaugh, their new general manager. He was in the job only six months, backed by eight years of NFL experience along with his MBA for Northwestern. He had a reputation for two things—brilliance and ruthlessness. Some said he was still a bit too inexperienced, including sportswriter Don Corwin. Also too young, too brash, and too cocky. An Ivy League rich kid who had stepped on too many toes and cut too many throats to get to the top. But those were his detractors, and there were always a few. The people who knew him best had no worries. He was careful, he was cautious, and he was calculative. Like watching a great poker player at the table, Cavanaugh's were certain he could pull off the deal.

Cavanaugh knew he was in a sweet position to put Bell in a Bronco uniform. The team had had some rough seasons, finishing no better than 8–8 in the last five years. Their head coach was one of the NFL's finest, but the front office had been too money conscious during his tenure, developing a reputation for low salaries and in turn routinely losing their best players to free agency.

The upside was that they had plenty of room under the salary cap when Bell became available. That put Cavanaugh in a very attractive position; so attractive in fact that he was sure he would cut the deal. He never came out and said as much, but he couldn't resist implying it in his blind desire to rub the writers' noses in his all-but-certain conquest. Consequently the Denver fans came to believe Bell was already theirs. What began as a distant hope evolved into a sure thing. With this new and brilliant quarterback would come a new era in Broncos history. There was talk of the playoffs, and in some bars and backrooms even the words "Super Bowl" were uttered. With Bell at the helm, it seemed reachable.

Then Cavanaugh walked into his office one morning in late February, turned on ESPN, and discovered Michael Bell had been signed by the Baltimore Ravens. He stood in the cool of his office, blinking in disbelief as the report rolled out on the screen. And like any great poker player who had just suffered a bad beat, he replayed the hand in his mind many times, searching for the spot where it all went wrong.

The reaction by others was horrific. Phillip Alderman, the team's principal owner and president, was clearly pissed. He didn't come out and say so because it simply wasn't his style. He was a refined, gentlemanly type who thought it disgraceful to allow your emotions to grow beyond your con-

trol. But Cavanaugh knew it. Everyone did; even the guy
who emptied the garbage cans in the locker rooms. Alderman was leading the charge to build a new and better Bronco
team, and he wanted Bell in the worst way. "Whatever it
takes," he'd said to his young general manager, in whom he
had repeatedly expressed overwhelming confidence. "Just
get him." The quarterback was the starting point to any offense, and the one Alderman wanted had slipped away. Who
knew when such a gem would become available again? His
plans would have to wait now. He barely spoke to Cavanaugh for the next three weeks.

The sportswriters, on the other hand, had plenty to say.
Corwin, for example, joyously reminded his readers of his
many predictions about the "inexperienced rich boy," conveniently forgetting that almost all of the other dazzling acquisitions that had led the Broncos back to prominence had
been Cavanaugh masterstrokes. He implied instead that Cavanaugh's reputation was based a few freak acquisitions that
just happened to work out—isolated moments of sheer luck
that were parlayed into an overblown career. The fans
weren't quite as cruel, but a few called into the sports-talk
radio stations and demanding Cavanaugh's demotion. Once,
when Cavanaugh was recognized as he drove home in his
black Porsche, he was pelted with beer cans, some of them
full. Such was the murderously competitive nature of the
National Football League—not just on the field but on every
level.

The furor died down eventually, but the media never forgot or forgave. Every time Bell led the Ravens to victory,
someone would mention it. Cavanaugh rarely made it
through an interview without hearing about it. After Baltimore won their second straight Super Bowl and the camera
panned to a smiling Michael Bell carrying the Lombardi
Trophy above his head as his teammates rode him on their
shoulders and confetti fluttered around him, Al Michaels,
one of the greatest football commentators of all time, said,
"The Denver fans must be *livid*."

But Cavanaugh survived. He survived and went on to

make other deals, most of them superb. He was ultracompetitive by nature and never quite got over his one miserable defeat. He desperately wished the whole Bell affair would be forgotten; an unpleasant chapter in his personal history that would fade away in time.

But now Jon Sabino was going to join the race for Christian McKinley. He would throw everything he had at it. And Sabino had a lot. Deep down Cavanaugh knew he was a bona fide genius. But so was he. What the press reported was part of a different reality. Maybe the fans believed everything they read, but what they read was rarely the whole truth. He knew he was just as good as Sabino; better in some ways. And others knew it, too. Plus, he was a lot older now—older and considerably wiser. The sting of that singular defeat was still surprisingly sharp. With the kind of supermasculine motivation that possesses everyone who devotes their life to the NFL—whether on the chessboard that lies between the goalposts or in the boardrooms and bedrooms beyond—Cavanaugh's desire to crush his opponent's ego and humiliate him, if for no reason than to even the score, suddenly shifted into overdrive. If he failed this time, he knew, it would be all over. Maybe he wouldn't be out of a job, but his respectability would be history. The fans had forgiven him once, albeit grudgingly, but they wouldn't do it twice. Same with the press. Even now, he knew, they were hunched over their laptops, rubbing their hands together as they waited for the saga to unfold. This would be his sweet revenge . . . or his final defeat. And the latter could not happen. It simply wasn't an option.

As the phone rang yet again, one thought blinked in his mind—no matter what it took, he had to get Christian McKinley.

JON LISTENED TO THE RADIO ON THE SHORT RIDE back to the offices. The talking heads were already at it, speculating about the team's next move. The naysayers conveniently reappeared after an almost three-year absence, squawking about how the Ravens were no longer this year's Super Bowl hopeful, just as they had predicted, etc. Some-one cut in with a sound bite from the meeting outside the hospital. Jon heard his own voice crisply and clearly, and he marveled at the speed with which technology made news re-porting possible these days. He'd spoken those words not more than fifteen minutes ago. Incredible.

He also got some information on the old lady who'd caused the accident. She was shaken up and had a bruised sternum from the impact with the steering wheel, but ulti-mately she'd be okay. He shook his head at the irony. Just like a drunk driver, *she* was the one who didn't get hurt. She claimed not to remember any of it. That was the final touch, Jon thought. Her insurance company would handle the legal end of things, and she'd just walk away. If only his quarter-back had been so lucky.

He was thankful there were no more reporters waiting when he arrived. Must've gotten their fill for the day, or at least for the morning. *Is it still only morning?* He checked his watch—11:05. The day wasn't even half over yet. He shook his head and got out of the car.

The offices were buzzing. People moved through the hall-ways at a speed that was almost comical. Phones rang, paper spilled out of the fax machines, the copier ran nonstop. It seemed like a typical American business center, but then that's exactly what it was—a business. In spite of their indi-vidual burdens, each person found a moment to glance at him. Their expressions belied a mixture of fascination and pity.

He turned toward his office but was stopped by his secre-tary, Susan Schiff. Schiff never smiled, spoke only when necessary, and wore horn-rimmed glasses with thick plastic frames. Some referred to her as "Susan Stiff" or just "Stiff." In spite of her almost complete lack of personality, though, she was about the most organized and efficient individual that Jon had ever seen.

"The others are waiting for you in number two."

"Who's in there?"

"Mr. Connally, Coach Blanchard, Kevin Tanner, and Dr. Mendel."

"Anyone else expected?"

"Not that I'm aware of."

"Okay, thanks."

The Ravens' conference room was, like Jon's office, surprisingly modest. The centerpiece was a long table with a white Formica top. A markerboard ran the length of one wall and featured ghostly remnants of past scribblings. Lavishly framed photos of noted gridiron figures hung on the others like dead members of a gentleman's club. Visitors were invariably drawn to these, whereas the staff paid them no mind.

The others were standing in a cluster at the far end when he came in.

"Sorry we couldn't be meeting under better circumstances," he said as he took a seat.

The first question came from Connally. Peter Connally was the Ravens' current owner. He'd made his first fortune simply by inheriting over twenty million from a beloved aunt. That got him into the financial elite, but the respect came some years later when, through his own smarts and mettle, he parlayed the original twenty into more than a hundred when he jumped into the world of satellite television long before any other investors would touch it. He last reported net worth was well over half a billion, with interests ranging from rare coins and gems to publishing, restaurants, hotels—and professional football. He had longish silver hair and large, round eyes, the combination of which gave him the vague appearance of a mad scientist. Born and raised in provincial Vermont, he still possessed a crisp New England accent, not to mention a New Englander's no-nonsense approach to life, especially business. His bottom line was simple, and ruthlessly enforced—get results or get out.

In spite of working for Connally these last few years, Jon hadn't made up his mind about the man. He had the same powerful business intuition that had brought fortune to most of the other owners, but considerably less charm and charisma. One day he could be patient and refined, even charming, and the next he was brash and uncouth. Art Modell, the previous owner, had run the team like a business but understood football, whereas Connally ran the team like a business, period. Sometimes he would show what appeared to be a genuine interest in the game, other times he behaved like a nervous accountant, obsessing over every penny.

"How does Bell look?" Connally asked.

Jon shook his head. "Not too good. He had tubes and wires running all over him, and a bandage on his head that looked like something on a mummy. But the worst part was the complete lack of movement. I mean . . . he *looked* dead."

The others flinched. "Christ," Tanner said in a whisper. Kevin Tanner, a jovial, bearded, heavyset individual, was the Ravens' salary cap expert. He'd been a mathematics whiz at Princeton, and one needed to be nothing less to understand the cap's vast complexities. He was, along with Gary Stone, one of Jon's closest friends in the organization.

"Yeah, it was awful. Have any of you spoken with Dr. Blackman yet?"

They all nodded. "We just had a conference call with him in here," Mendel said. Alan Mendel was a stoic older man with fine hair and steel-rimmed glasses. Aside from being the Ravens' head physician, he was also an associate professor of sports medicine. And like other team physicians, his opinions carried tremendous power.

"So you know the details, the coma and everything?"

"Yes, Blackman went over the case with me." Mendel shook his head. "Not good."

Connally said, "So, no chance of Bell playing for us this year?"

"None whatsoever."

"What about the following year?"

"We'll have to wait and see," Mendel replied. Everyone translated: *He might not be able to play again, period.*

Jon folded his hands. "Well, while we're waiting for him to get better, we should think about what we're going to do for a quarterback in the meantime."

"Good idea," Blanchard said. His trademark gravelly voice had evolved over nearly forty years of screaming and yelling at talented young men, a few of whom he came to love as if they were his own sons. "However, I don't know how many boys are out there who can get the job done." Cary Blanchard had been the Ravens' head coach for five seasons; twenty-six in the NFL overall. He was another Sabino acquisition—Jon admired him for years and silently vowed to acquire him if he ever got the chance. Blanchard had retired at one point but was hinting through channels that he might return if the right offer came along. Jon went out of his way to make that offer.

"Okay, let's examine the simplest route first," Jon said. "Promoting from within. I'm assuming this isn't feasible, right?" He turned to Blanchard.

"Right."

"Neither of the two backups can get it done? No chance whatsoever?"

"Well, Nate may have the years," Blanchard began. "but he isn't going to get it done. Sure, he's a real professional. He keeps his mouth shut, studies the playbook, and is always ready. That makes him ideal for emergency situations, and he can jump in on a moment's notice. But he's like an aging racehorse—he can't handle the long runs anymore. He's a stopgap. He's a great teacher and a great soldier, and I'd like to keep him around for another year, maybe two if he doesn't retire. But there's just no way he can go a whole season, not with those knees. If worse came to worse we could do it, but making the playoffs alone would be a miracle. Forget the Super Bowl. No way he can compete at that level."

"What about Clark?"

Blanchard said, "He's likely to stay right where he is—third string. He's not going to amount to much, I'm afraid. He's got great physical assets, but mentally he's not sharp enough. He is exactly what he appeared to be when we got him—a typical sixth-round pick. He showed a little promise and a willingness to work hard, but he'll never be a Dan Marino or a Steve Young, or even a Michael Bell. He gets too frightened out there. The pressure unnerves him. The great ones feed on it, whereas he folds. It's a shame, too, because he's a really nice kid. But I think we've given him all the chances we can. We've been patient, we've been supportive, but he apparently doesn't possess the potential we thought we saw." Blanchard shook his head. "So promoting from within won't work."

Never one to dwell on a hopeless situation, Jon moved on. "All right, what about free agency?"

"That could also be a problem. From what I've seen, there's not much out there."

"What do you think of that kid from the Bengals— Jarden?" Jon asked. "I believe he's available."

"He not a very accurate passer," Blanchard said, "He's quick on his feet, but we have a solid front line right now, so that's not as important as it might be. And he's been ruined by a lot of bad guidance. It would take us a whole year just to erase the bad habits he's picked up."

"How about Cory Doleman?"

Blanchard said, "He fumbles a lot; more fumbled snaps than anyone I've ever seen. And he has issues with attitude, too. One time, I heard, he didn't show up for practice because one of his dogs was sick." Blanchard shook his head. "No, he wouldn't make it here. At least not with me."

"Kensley?"

"Great promise coming out of college, and he was pretty good in his rookie year. But then everything fell apart for him. He couldn't make the tough throws, couldn't read the defenses. Just one of those things." Blanchard tapped the side of his head. "Something snapped up here and he never recovered. It happens."

Connally ran a hand over his silver mane. "There must be somebody." Then he snapped his fingers. "Doug Birch!"

The others laughed. "Shit," Blanchard said. "I'd have to seriously consider retirement if we got that desperate."

Connally was genuinely puzzled. "I don't understand. I thought he was good."

"He is," Jon said. "He'll never make it to the Hall of Fame, but he's very capable."

"So what's the problem? He's available, right?"

"Yes."

"But that's because no one wants him," Blanchard added. "Talk about attitude problems. He makes Doleman look like a saint."

"He's that bad? So bad that no one wants him in spite of the shortage of talent at quarterback?"

"Someone will take him eventually," Jon said, "if not now, then later in the year, as the injuries pile up. But not this early. He's a troublemaker. He's prone to temper tantrums and creates tension in the locker room. He's the first one to point a finger when something goes wrong, but never at himself. And the worst part is, he doesn't have nearly enough talent to justify such an attitude."

"If he did, he wouldn't have to be that way in the first place," Blanchard added. The others nodded.

"That's right. Maybe it's insecurities. I don't know, I'm not a psychologist. All I know it he's more trouble than he's worth, even with the quarterback situation being what it is."

"Okay," Jon said, "then it looks like we're down to making a trade or drafting someone."

"And trades are uncommon in this sport," Connally said. "Right?"

"That's right," Jon replied. He had to admit he was impressed with the way Connally had applied himself in recent months to learn as much as he could about the way the league worked. In the years prior, he seemed to regard his team as little more than one of his many investments. But when it began paying off—namely in the form of those championships—his interest intensified. Suddenly he wanted to know everything he could about professional football.

"If a team is eager to let a player go," Connally continued, apparently eager to show off his newfound knowledge. "It's probably because that player can't do the job. It's rare that they'd release someone who was genuinely contributing."

"The only time that happens," Tanner added, "is when there's a salary cap or contractual problem."

"And player-for-player trades are particularly rare. Both teams have to know exactly what they're getting."

"The real bottom line is this . . ." Jon said. "No team in their right mind is going to trade a good quarterback anyway. Not now. They're just too scarce. Teams will release other good players before they sacrifice a prime quarterback. So I think a trade is definitely out of the question."

Connally leaned back and folded his arms. "Seems to be a seller's market."

"It is," Jon replied. "And that brings us to our final option—the draft, right?"

"And there aren't a great many choices there either, are there?" Connally said. It was more of a grave pronouncement than an inquiry.

"No there aren't," Jon said. "Not this year."

"Just one decent choice, in fact."

"Yep, just one."

"And the media has already been asking about him."

"I'm not surprised," Blanchard said.

Jon looked directly at him. "Is McKinley good enough?"

"Oh, yes."

"He can fit into your system?"

"I believe so."

"And he could start this year?"

"I have no doubt. Barring some devastating injury, you're talking about a future Hall of Famer."

No one in their right mind would question Cary Blanchard's evaluation. He'd been around too long, seen too much, coached too many. He'd cultivated dozens of great players, two of whom were already enshrined in Canton. His word was gospel. And Jon was the only other person in this room who knew he was contemplating retirement, permanently this time. If he did in fact win that incredible third straight Super Bowl, he'd hang up his clipboard and headset and take the fast track to Canton. Jon would miss him tremendously—as would the rest of the organization. When that happened, assistant head coach Grant Palmer would take the reins. While Palmer certainly had the faith and respect of the entire staff, players included, he was not Cary Blanchard. Without Blanchard acting as the linchpin, at least a handful of the assistant coaches would seek jobs elsewhere, too. Dave Leibler, the genius behind the mind-boggling defensive schemes, would almost certainly be offered a head coaching position somewhere.

"He's got all the assets—speed, strength, accuracy, quickness, intelligence," Blanchard continued. "He's everything they're saying he is. He's fearless on the field, with that magic 'X factor' that makes him a little bit more than human. He's the best new quarterback to come along in ages."

Connally asked, "And what would it take to get him?"

All eyes turned to Jon.

"A lot," he said. "A real lot."

"Is it possible? Do we *have* a lot to give?"

Jon shrugged. "I have no idea. I haven't looked into it. I have to take a good hard look at our roster tonight. We'll have to have another meeting first thing tomorrow. I'll need all of you to evaluate our assets from your individual perspectives. McKinley will go with the first pick, I guarantee it. So we have to move from last to first. I'm not sure it's ever been done. Hell, up until this morning we all thought this draft was going to be a snap."

"And it's less than two weeks away," Tanner pointed out.

"Yeah, thanks."

"Sure. There's something else to be considered, too. And this isn't going to make it any easier, either."

"What's that?"

"As far as the cap is concerned, things are getting pretty tight for this year. However . . ." He looked around the room. "We could free up plenty of space if we released Bell now."

They all looked uncomfortable, even Connally—a man who had terminated hundreds, maybe thousands of employees in his lifetime.

"For the time being," Jon said, "We'll have to put him on

the NFI." The others nodded. NFI stood for "non-football injury" list. When a player was placed there, he was not entitled to any compensation but his contract was still valid. Often it was nothing more than a holding place until a more concrete decision could be made. "After that I guess we'll have to release him, if it really will be impossible to keep him and sign the whiz kid at the same time."

He looked to Tanner, who shook his head. "There's no way we can keep both of them. And it won't be any better next year, either. We'll lose at least half a dozen guys to free agency. It had to happen sooner or later. It's a miracle we've kept this squad together as long as we have. Easton, Simmons, and Sawyer are definitely going to shop around, and I'm sure they'll get hefty offers."

"All key members of the defense," Blanchard muttered. There wasn't much disgust in his voice, but there was enough. Unlike a lot of older coaches, Blanchard had successfully transitioned his thinking when the era of free agency began. He understood the new rules and made the necessary adjustments. But he never liked them. Not just because they made it harder for a coach to maintain continuity on his roster, but also because they discouraged loyalty and rewarded greed. Teamwork and coherency were set aside for the pursuit of the dollar. Athleticism lost out over capitalism. For a man who had spent much of his career during the gridiron's golden era, it was a bitter pill. He could play by these rules, but he couldn't stand them.

"That's right," Tanner continued. "And there are a few offensive starters who'll probably be gone, too."

Blanchard shook his head. Connally asked, "So you're saying it's now or never?"

Tanner shrugged. "Pretty much. I don't want to sound melodramatic, but let's face it—it'll be a helluva long time before we see another chance to win a third consecutive championship. A *long* time. We'll be paying for the guys we have now for a while."

"So it *is* now or never."

"Yeah."

Connally stood up—a familiar sign that he was done.

"Honestly, gentlemen, that's fine with me. I don't give a whit what happens after this season. We'll worry about that when the time comes. But for now, I want it understood that I want this third championship. I want it for the team, for the fans, for myself—and I want it so we can write the Ravens into the history books. You can argue with merchandising, you can argue with ticket sales, and you can argue with the building of new stadiums, but you cannot argue with history. I've got big plans for this organization, and they'll be a lot easier to execute if we have the prestige of a third Super Bowl victory behind us. I was counting on it—and frankly, I still am."

He walked over to Jon and put a hand on his shoulder.

"Get it done, but don't give away the *entire* farm. At least not this year."

Jon realized he was once again being asked to do the impossible.

"Sure, no problem," he said.

3

THE FOLDER WAITING ON HIS DESK AFTER LUNCH
was enormous, particularly considering it had been assembled in just a few hours. But then there was plenty of printed material on the incredible Christian McKinley. The Ravens had a man whose primary job was to keep records on all the players who weren't Baltimore Ravens. Jon insisted on creating this position when he took over as GM. He knew a team had no chance of being competitive if it focused only on the players it already had. If, for example, a better kicker than theirs suddenly became available, he wanted to know about it. Or if a college kid they deemed draftable wasn't picked by any other team, Jon wanted to bring him in for a workout.

In the case of McKinley, gathering information wasn't all that tough. There was plenty of printed material available, as he was already more famous than most of the players who were already in the league. Jon put his feet up and flipped back the cover.

McKinley's smiling face jumped out at him from the cover of *Sports Illustrated*. He was black, handsome, large, and muscular. You couldn't tell much else from the picture. He wore a novelty jersey with a large question mark where the number would normally be. The headline read, "Who Will Win the McKinley Sweepstakes?" He had a ball tucked into the crook of his arm.

The article opened on a two-page spread that featured a closeup of McKinley's face plus the headline, "Wanted: Christian McKinley. Money No Object." It began—

> In a quiet antechamber just off the locker room at Michigan, Christian McKinley sits in a folding chair wearing nothing but a white towel. His hands are laced together under his chin in a pose of deep contemplation. He looks up, notices me standing there, and flashes the disarming smile that has become so familiar to his fans. He offers his hand and a warm greeting, and within seconds I have almost forgotten that I am in the presence of the young man being touted as the first great athlete of the twenty-first century . . .

Characteristic of *Sports Illustrated*, it packed a great deal of solid information into a relatively small space. It covered McKinley's playing abilities, both physical and mental, plus his background, both academic and personal. There were quotes from his family, friends, coaches, teammates, and opponents. It was a standard "introductory" article, a way of presenting the much-heralded prodigy to the rest of the world now that he was about to finish his college career and break onto the national scene. Jon remembered the piece; he'd read it a few months ago. Back then he thought about what a battle there would be to get McKinley and was thankful he didn't have to take part in it.

Behind the *Sports Illustrated* was McKinley's BLESTO report. BLESTO was an organization created in 1963 to gather information on thousands of college players each year, then offer it to the teams that subscribed to its service. The acronym stood for "Bears, Lions, Eagles, Steelers Talent Organization." Most other NFL teams jumped on the BLESTO bandwagon eventually, but for reasons of tradition the name was not changed again.

The goal of a BLESTO scout was to assemble a complete picture of each player, from basics such as height, weight, stats, past injuries, and speed in the 40-yard dash, to more abstract characteristics like strength, quickness, explosiveness, durability, character, general intelligence, and the ability to get along with teammates. The scout used a grading scale from 0.0 to 4.1, with 0.0 being the highest. Once all attributes were evaluated, the numbers were averaged into a final, overall grade. In BLESTO's history no player had ever achieved a perfect 0.0, but some came close. Among the elite class that managed to stay under 1.0 were John Elway, Tony Dorsett, and Troy Aikman. The lowest ever, 0.4, was achieved by O. J. Simpson while at Southern Cal in 1968.

And by Christian McKinley.

Jon shook his head as he reviewed the report—Arm strength, 0.3. Quick release, 0.5. Accuracy, 0.3. Field Vision, 0.4. The worst score, for his quickness in setting up before the throw, was 1.2. Still well above average. And the name of the scout who filled out the report was Bud Grant. Jon knew Grant well. Former director of player personnel for the Tennessee Titans back when they were the Houston Oilers. As tough a sonofabitch as there ever was. He played a major role in the acquisition of such legendary talents as Earl Campbell and Warren Moon. He never let kindness or pity cloud his judgment, which is why many trusted him. If a player didn't have it, Grant said so. And he wasn't saying Christan McKinley didn't have it. If anything, he was using these numbers to say this kid was going to be the next Joe Montana.

0.4.

Jon had seen thousands of BLESTO reports and never came across a player who'd achieved less than a 1.5. He never thought he would, either.

There was a stat sheet provided by Michigan. Jon had seen this before, too, but hadn't paid any attention to it. The numbers were surreal:

PASSING STATISTICS

	ATT	COMP	PCT	YARDS	TD	YD/ATT	INT	LG	GM/AVG	RATING
FRESH.	240	122	51	1854	19	7.1	8	68	212	121.34
SOPH.	277	149	54	1966	20	7.7	8	76	227	134.29
JUNIOR	297	169	57	2012	24	8.7	9	81	245	151.44
SENIOR	322	212	66	3055	28	9.3	11	87	276	164.55
TOTAL	1136	652	57	8887	91	8.2	36	78	240	142.91

RUSHING STATISTICS

	GP	GS	NO	YARDS	AVG	TD	LONG
FRESH.	10	8	91	531	5.8	6	101
SOPH.	10	10	98	512	5.2	7	68
JUNIOR	10	10	111	577	5.2	8	75
SENIOR	10	10	101	589	5.8	8	82
TOTAL	40	38	401	2209	5.5	29	81.5

There was another sheet provided by Michigan, covering personal points. It was intended primarily as filler for the writers; fan magazine material. But Jon always made of point of reading through it. You could learn a lot about a person from the most seemingly insignificant details.

His father had been a college coach for more than thirty years. He still was, in fact, and had been part of six national championship teams. Christian carried his high school team to the state championship while maintaining a B average and holding down a part-time job. He was a cool, confident leader on the field, displaying a maturity beyond his years. His teachers said he worked hard and never caused any problems. So his character, it appeared, was as attractive as his playing abilities. He really was, in so many ways, the perfect quarterback.

Jon released a deep breath, forming his lips into a little

circle as if he were blowing out a candle. This was going to be a struggle, and a costly one. And after it was all over, would he still have a job? This was a real issue. If he didn't get McKinley, a lot of people would be disappointed. The NFL had a low tolerance for failure, past glories notwithstanding. The "What have you done for me lately?" mentality was omnipotent. And if he did get McKinley, perhaps the price would be so high that the team would have to let him go to save face. Someone had to be the fall guy, and politics had to be considered. The list of people who'd kill to have his job was a mile long.

He put all the papers and articles and other material back into the folder. McKinley was still smiling at him from the cover of *Sports Illustrated.*

"You're gonna get me fired, you sonofabitch," he said, wanting to laugh but finding little humor in the fact that was probably at least half right.

4

PETER CONNALLY DIDN'T COME TO THE SECOND MEET-
ing in the Ravens' conference room the following morning.
Each of the other four—Jon, Kevin Tanner, Cary Blanchard,
and Alan Mendel—came with his own set of notes and papers, and each with his own point of view, which was exactly
what Jon wanted. He had the power to do this deal without
outside approval or input, but he wouldn't. It would be fool-
ish not to use their experience and their wisdom as a re-
source. He also preferred to rule by committee rather than
dictatorship.

He unzipped his folder and removed his printout of the
team's roster, which he kept on a spreadsheet on his PC, plus
that of upcoming draft picks.

After handing copies around, he said, "OK, let's figure
out what we can give up in order to get our man. We gotta go
from last to first in the draft. No problem right?" The others
grumbled.

"As you know, the first overall pick is currently the property of the San Diego Chargers. Let's face it, Skip has a lot
of work to do over there."

RAVENS ROSTER

#	NAME	POS.	HT.	WT.	YRS.	COLLEGE
3	Terry Butler	K	5-11	205	6	Virginia
8	Michael Bell	QB	6-5	210	5	LSU
11	Scott Clark	QB	6-4	208	2	Brigham Young
12	Nate Brown	QB	6-4	207	10	Penn State
13	Steve Russell	P	6-1	205	5	Kansas State
20	Milton Love	S	6-2	211	3	Troy State
21	Paul Ellis	FB	6-1	235	4	Tennessee
22	Chris Redmond	S	6-0	209	8	Illinois
23	Greg Buckley	CB	6-1	199	9	Western Illinois
24	Harold Rowling	CB	6-1	203	3	Michigan
25	Thomas Rhodes	CB	6-0	205	7	UCLA
26	Pete Wolverton	S	6-2	220	4	Iowa
27	Lawrence Dixon	RB	6-1	202	3	Virginia
28	TJ Matthews	RB	6-0	200	5	Wisconsin
29	Herb Axelrod	S	6-1	217	6	Northern Arizona
30	Buster McDaniels	RB	5-11	201	7	Mississippi
31	Walter Bartlett	CB	6-3	201	2	Kansas State
32	Aaron Holloway	RB	6-1	205	2	Florida State
33	Nick Wakefield	CB	6-0	201	R	Auburn
34	Andre Jenkins	S	6-1	214	R	Temple
51	Brian Northbrook	LB	6-2	240	4	Arkansas State
52	Elliot Easton	LB	6-3	243	6	Wake Forest
53	Brett Savage	LB	6-4	250	11	Washington State
54	Earle Webster	LB	6-4	244	2	Purdue
56	Larry Townsend	LB	6-6	247	5	Alabama
57	Ryan Mason	LB	6-5	242	2	Baylor

(continued on next page)

RAVENS ROSTER (continued)

#	NAME	POS.	HT.	WT.	YRS.	COLLEGE
60	Derrick Gorden	C	6-4	312	4	Penn State
61	Jared Cope	G	6-2	310	8	Georgia Tech
63	Matt Israel	G	6-1	312	4	Miami
66	Barrett Blake	C	6-3	305	R	Stanford
67	Jason Freemont	LC	6-6	277	7	Texas Tech
68	Shaun Erickson	G	6-1	320	7	Michigan
69	Scott Montgomery	G	6-3	324	11	Illinois
70	Frank James	T	6-4	263	5	Rutgers
71	Keith Kubat	T	6-5	277	3	Hofstra
74	Craig Little	T	6-6	302	9	Maryland
80	Ryan Hart	TE	6-4	250	7	Kentucky
81	Anthony Jennings	WR	6-4	209	6	Mississippi
82	Jordan Patterson	WR	6-1	203	R	Kentucky
84	Sam Sargent	TE	6-6	261	3	West Virginia
85	Raymont Carter	WR	6-1	198	2	Troy State
87	Darry Bailey	WR	6-0	200	5	North Carolina St
88	Tony Kramer	WR	6-0	211	3	Notre Dame
89	Kevin Curtis	DT	6-3	274	R	Rutgers
90	Corey Holbrook	DE	6-4	277	9	Syracuse
91	George Kontoleon	DT	6-2	303	2	Purdue
92	Donald Harper	DT	6-3	310	8	Florida State
93	Jon Harris	DE	6-6	281	3	Virginia
94	Dexter Simmons	DE	6-3	280	7	Wisconsin
95	Tony Seidl	DT	6-5	280	5	Miami
96	Alan Hill	DE	6-3	274	R	Temple
97	Howard Sawyer	DT	6-4	277	6	Iowa
98	Ted Forrest	DE	6-2	276	4	Texas A&M

RAVENS DRAFT PICKS

YEAR	PICK	NOTES
Current	1st round/32nd overall	
	2nd round/44th overall	Rec'd from Bills for 4th- and 5th-round picks from this year
	2nd round/64th overall	
	3rd round/96th overall	
	6th round/192nd overall	
	7th round/224th overall	
2007	1st round	
	2nd round	
	3rd round	
	4th round	
	5th round	
	6th round	
	7th round	
2008	1st round	
	2nd round	
	3rd round	
	4th round	
	5th round	
	6th round	
	7th round	

Skip Henderson started with the Colts in the 1950s as a gofer, and through the years was also an equipment manager, scout, film analyst, assistant coach, head coach, and, ultimately, general manager. He retired in 2001 but was lured back by the Chargers largely because he was close with the family that owned the team, and because they needed nothing short of a wizard to bring the organization back to glory.

"He's rebuilding almost from scratch. They've been struggling for a long time—seven straight losing seasons. It was no surprise to anyone when they booted their GM, director of player personnel, *and* their head coach halfway through last season. They have every right to the first pick, but it will only provide them with one player. If they trade it, however, they can get considerably more. I'm guessing this is Skip's plan. He's been given carte blanche to do whatever needs to be done. In fact, if what the media is reporting is true—about other teams bidding for that pick—then that's exactly what Skip is doing. He's trying to parlay the guarantee of acquiring Christian McKinley into a huge payoff. So let's try to determine which of his needs are most urgent, and how we can satisfy them."

"So we'll definitely be using players in this deal rather than picks?" Tanner asked.

"Yeah, we'll have to use both. I don't see where we have much of a choice. Established players will be more valuable to Skip than picks. I'm not talking about giving up a lot. Just a few will make all the difference. We've got great depth here, so I think we can sacrifice a handful of guys. Of course we'll use draft picks as the bulk of our currency, but I don't see how we can pull off this miracle without throwing in some established talent. To that end, I've asked Cary to sort through the roster to determine, if I may be blunt for a minute here, who can go. And from you, Kevin, I'll need some quick cap assessment."

"No problem."

Blanchard handed around his own copies of the roster, organized per Jon's criteria—

RAVENS ROSTER W/NOTES FROM CARY BLANCHARD

#	NAME	POS.	HT.	WT.	YRS.	COLLEGE	NOTES
11	Scott Clark	QB	6-4	208	2	Brigham Young	CAN TRADE
20	Milton Love	S	6-2	211	3	Troy State	CAN TRADE
23	Greg Buckley	CB	6-1	199	9	Western Illinois	CAN TRADE

(continued on next page)

RAVENS ROSTER W/NOTES FROM CARY BLANCHARD (continued)

#	NAME	POS.	HT.	WT.	YRS.	COLLEGE	NOTES
30	Buster McDaniels	RB	5-11	201	7	Mississippi	CAN TRADE
32	Aaron Holloway	RB	6-1	205	2	Florida State	CAN TRADE
33	Nick Wakefield	CB	6-0	201	R	Auburn	CAN TRADE
34	Andre Jenkins	S	6-1	214	R	Temple	CAN TRADE
51	Brian Northbrook	LB	6-2	240	4	Arkansas State	CAN TRADE
53	Brett Savage	LB	6-4	250	11	Washington State	CAN TRADE
61	Jared Cope	G	6-2	310	8	Georgia Tech	CAN TRADE
66	Barrett Blake	C	6-3	305	R	Stanford	CAN TRADE
67	Jason Freemont	LC	6-6	277	7	Texas Tech	CAN TRADE
69	Scott Montgomery	G	6-3	324	11	Illinois	CAN TRADE
71	Keith Kubat	T	6-5	277	3	Hofstra	CAN TRADE
82	Jordan Patterson	WR	6-1	203	R	Kentucky	CAN TRADE
84	Sam Sargent	TE	6-6	261	3	West Virginia	CAN TRADE
89	Kevin Curtis	DT	6-3	274	R	Rutgers	CAN TRADE
90	Corey Holbrook	DE	6-4	277	9	Syracuse	CAN TRADE
92	Donald Harper	DT	6-3	277	8	Florida State	CAN TRADE
96	Alan Hill	DE	6-3	274	R	Temple	CAN TRADE
12	Nate Brown	QB	6-4	207	10	Penn State	PREFER TO KEEP
26	Pete Wolverton	S	6-2	220	4	Iowa	PREFER TO KEEP
28	TJ Matthews	RB	6-0	200	5	Wisconsin	PREFER TO KEEP
31	Walter Bartlett	CB	6-3	201	2	Kansas State	PREFER TO KEEP
57	Ryan Mason	LB	6-5	242	2	Baylor	PREFER TO KEEP
85	Raymont Carter	WR	6-1	198	2	Troy State	PREFER TO KEEP
91	George Kontoleon	DT	6-2	275	2	Purdue	PREFER TO KEEP
98	Ted Forrest	DE	6-2	276	4	Texas A&M	PREFER TO KEEP
3	Terry Butler	K	5-11	205	6	Virginia	STARTER—DO NOT TRADE
8	Michael Bell	QB	6-5	210	5	LSU	STARTER—DO NOT TRADE
13	Steve Russell	P	6-1	205	5	Kansas State	STARTER—DO NOT TRADE
21	Paul Ellis	FB	6-1	235	4	Tennessee	STARTER—DO NOT TRADE
22	Chris Redmond	S	6-0	209	8	Illinois	STARTER—DO NOT TRADE

(continued on next page)

RAVENS ROSTER W/NOTES FROM CARY BLANCHARD (continued)

#	NAME	POS.	HT.	WT.	YRS.	COLLEGE	NOTES
24	Harold Rowling	CB	6-1	203	3	Michigan	STARTER—DO NOT TRADE
25	Thomas Rhodes	CB	6-0	205	7	UCLA	STARTER—DO NOT TRADE
27	Lawrence Dixon	RB	6-1	202	3	Virginia	STARTER—DO NOT TRADE
29	Herb Axelrod	S	6-1	217	6	Northern Arizona	STARTER—DO NOT TRADE
52	Elliot Easton	LB	6-3	243	6	Wake Forest	STARTER—DO NOT TRADE
54	Earle Webster	LB	6-4	244	2	Purdue	STARTER—DO NOT TRADE
56	Larry Townsend	LB	6-6	247	5	Alabama	STARTER—DO NOT TRADE
60	Derrick Gorden	C	6-4	312	4	Penn State	STARTER—DO NOT TRADE
63	Matt Israel	G	6-1	312	4	Miami	STARTER—DO NOT TRADE
68	Shaun Erickson	G	6-1	320	7	Michigan	STARTER—DO NOT TRADE
70	Frank James	T	6-4	263	5	Rutgers	STARTER—DO NOT TRADE
74	Craig Little	T	6-6	278	9	Maryland	STARTER—DO NOT TRADE
80	Ryan Hart	TE	6-4	250	7	Kentucky	STARTER—DO NOT TRADE
81	Anthony Jennings	WR	6-4	209	6	Mississippi	STARTER—DO NOT TRADE
87	Darryl Bailey	WR	6-0	200	5	North Carolina St	STARTER—DO NOT TRADE
88	Tony Kramer	WR	6-3	211	3	Notre Dame	STARTER—DO NOT TRADE
93	Jon Harris	DE	6-6	281	3	Virginia	STARTER—DO NOT TRADE
94	Dexter Simmons	DE	6-3	280	7	Wisconsin	STARTER—DO NOT TRADE
95	Tony Seidl	DT	6-5	280	5	Miami	STARTER—DO NOT TRADE
97	Howard Sawyer	DT	6-4	277	6	Iowa	STARTER—DO NOT TRADE

Everyone studied it for a few moments. Blanchard poured himself a glass of ice water and took a long sip. Jon leaned back in his chair and twirled his pencil. Tanner's eyes moved through the list with an almost computer-like fervor as he did some quick calculations. Mendel, predictably, showed no reaction.

"Okay," Jon said finally. "This looks like about what I expected. Alan, would you like to start? Any comments?"

The doctor ran a hand over his carefully combed hair. "Well, I see you've got Montgomery as a possible trade. I don't know if he's going to be particularly attractive with that ACL tear he suffered two years back. The resulting bad knee doesn't allow him to make quick, pivoting movements like he used to. Since the anterior cruciate ligament aids in limiting the joint's mobility, that tear was the equivalent of ten years' movement in a matter of seconds. And he's lost a step from age, too. The combination of that and the tear, I imagine, would hinder his trade value."

Jon nodded. "I understand. His main value to Skip, I figured, was as a veteran. Almost like having an extra coach around. It's no secret that Scotty wants to go into coaching after his playing days are over. And he's got the basic skills, too. Right, Cary?"

"Yeah, I'd say so. The boys love him, and he knows when to be tough on them. He has many natural leadership qualities. He could do it."

"Okay," Mendel said. "Just giving the medical angle."

"Anyone else?"

"Buckley, the cornerback." Mendel said the kid's name with the same marked indifference that Jon always found irritating, as if each player was a product rather than a person. But it was more than that—he sounded like he was mildly disgusted by them, by the idea that he had to actually care for them. His lack of a "bedside manner" was well known around the organization.

"The broken collarbone?"

"It healed well enough, but he has pain from time to time. And there's evidence that it affected him psychologically. I've seen him protecting it on the field. Sometimes it seems as though he doesn't want to hurt it again, so he'll hold back. A classic case."

"His numbers are still decent," Blanchard countered, almost defensively.

"Yes, true," Mendel replied without so much as glancing up from the roster. He had it flat and neat on the table but wouldn't touch it, as if doing so might lead to some prolonged illness.

"He's still useful to the right team," Jon said. "Anyone else?"

Mendel shook his head. "No, I think that's it."

"Okay, good. Kevin? What do you see here?"

Tanner was still scanning, his eyes darting from name to name.

"Brian Northbrook's situation could be a problem," he said. "That gigantic signing bonus we gave him. It was $1.25 million, which is quite a bit for a guy who ended up on the bench."

"He's in his third year with us, right?" Jon asked. "So that means we've already paid out $500,000 of that bonus money, leaving $750,000."

"Right," Tanner said. "And with the way the cap works, we'd have to continue paying a quarter of a mil each year until the fifth and final of his contract. And that's guaranteed money. But if we unloaded him now, the payment schedule for the remaining bonus would accelerate, and we'd have to count it all against the cap *this* year." He sighed and shook his head. "If only this was baseball, where the team that *picks up* a guy is responsible for paying out parts of his contract. . . . No such luck in our world."

"And how bad is our cap situation again?" Blanchard asked, even though it was common knowledge that he had little interest in the business side of the team.

"Like an overstuffed garbage bag about to split," Tanner said. "This would push us right to the edge . . . unless, of course, we waited until after June first. Then, as you know, the acceleration rule wouldn't apply, and we'd be allowed to spread the rest of that money over the next two cap years."

Jon nodded. "Okay, if it comes to that, I'll see if Skip's willing to wait. Who else might be trouble?"

Tanner scratched his beard. "Well, we know Lawrence Dixon's heading for renegotiation. Remember all the incentives we stuck into his rookie deal? They're coming back to haunt us now. Hell, I'm not complaining that he turned into such an amazing player. But, if you recall, most of those incentives were categorized as NLTBEs—Not Likely to Be Earned. That being the case, we figured they'd never count against the cap since only LTBEs would have cap impact. Then TJ goes down in Game Six of that year and Lawrence comes in. Next thing we all know, he's piling up historic numbers, taking over the starting position, and—worst of all, from my little world—he's passing each of his cash incentives like a racehorse. And the more he does this, the more hits our cap takes."

"But he cannot go," Blanchard said, "if that's what you're suggesting. He's absolutely essential."

"Oh, I know that, Cary," Tanner told him. "I know we couldn't win another championship without him. I'm simply saying his incentives are troublesome enough from a cap perspective. But his contract also ends this year, and he and his agent have been very tolerant of the last one. Now that he's proven himself, he's going to want more guaranteed money next time around. The problem for us is fitting him into the whole scheme with McKinley here, too."

Jon massaged his temples. "Well, this was all part of the plan," he said. "Hold everything together with Silly Putty and bubble gum until we get that third championship. I don't think any of these problems come as a surprise."

"After this year," Tanner added, "our cap situation will explode. We'll be lucky to hold onto anybody. And they know it, too. Easton's in the prime of his career, so he'll be shopping himself around. We'd have to cut him anyway, because, with the way we back-loaded his contract, we'll owe him more then six mil next season. Same with Jennings. He took the league minimum in the first year he signed with us, so next year his base salary will count three million against the cap." Tanner leaned forward and tapped the table with his pudgy finger. "At this exact moment, we are more than eight million over the cap for next season. Of course, we can relieve that burden simply by cutting a lot of guys after the June first deadline. But we still have to pay all those amortized signing bonuses. Those alone will count more than twelve million against the cap next year, even with the cap's annual increase per the Collective Bargaining Agreement." He shook his head. "Like Peter said, it really is now or never. Next year, we'll be lucky to even *have* a full team."

"With that in mind," Mendel said, surprising everyone by

jumping into a conversation that had nothing to do with the medical angle, "how are you going to afford McKinley even if you get him?"

Tanner, who had turned to Mendel and was nodding to indicate he was thinking the exact same thing, said, "We'll be forced into a rebuilding phase. Which, while that might be good for us financially, would be a nightmare, I would think, for McKinley. Cary, am I wrong about that?"

Blanchard cleared his throat. "No, that's correct. You see this happen all the time—a team that's strapped for cash loses all their good guys because they're forced to cut them. Then, when the purse strings loosen up, they start rebuilding slowly. The players who are there at the beginning of this phase go through hell, especially the good ones. They never reach their potential because they're surrounded by subpar talent. And quarterbacks, I hate to point out, suffer the most. If you can't afford to protect them with a good front line, they take a beating. A lot of potentially good kids have been ruined this way." He looked at Jon in earnest. "And McKinley might be one of them. He's fantastic, Jon, but there's no way he'll be able to perform to his peak without some of our guys. Without Israel and Erickson at guard, without James and Little at tackle, he's going to be either on the run or on the ground. If we *do* need to rebuild—and it looks very much like we will after this year—then we should try to first keep our offense together."

"Which is a shame, because most of the biggest cap problems we have lie with offensive guys anyway," Tanner added. Blanchard shrugged as if to say, *What do you want me to do about it?* Tanner replied with a shrug of his own.

"Okay," Jon said, "I'll have to figure all that out when the time comes. But at least we're starting to see some shape of things to come. First things first, though. We need to get Christian McKinley here and on this team so we can have a realistic shot at that third championship. That's the objective for this season. And to do that, we have to acquire that first pick from Skip Henderson. That's our focus at this precise moment." He held up the resorted roster Blanchard provided. "Cary, are you sure you're comfortable with the segmentation you provided here?"

"As sure as I can be, under the circumstances. As long as you don't get rid of any of the starters, we should be able to make it."

"And Kevin, aside from Northbrook, no one else will give us cap pains in the immediate future if we let them go?"

"No, not from the trade part of this list. And like I said earlier, cutting Bell would help. It's not a nice thing to do, but . . . it'll help."

"So noted. Alan?"

"I don't have anything to add beyond what I've already stated."

"Okay, good. What we have to do next is figure out Skip's greatest needs, and put together an offer he can't refuse." He returned to his folder and extracted another small pile of photocopies—San Diego's current roster. Handing them around, he said, "This will be the key to getting the deal done, and the decisions we make now will have a tremendous effect the future of this team." He shook his head, almost dizzied by the enormity of it.

"Let's get started."

A FEW HOURS LATER, DURING A STRANGELY QUITE moment that felt like the eye of a hurricane, he stood by his office window, sipping coffee and thinking about the previous season. If he concentrated hard enough, he could envision the teams on the field. He could hear the roar of the crowd, the tinny echo of the stadium speakers. The excitement was almost tangible. The mood, the frenzy . . . all of it. All part of the addictive experience that was the NFL.

But that was in the fall, not now. Right now the field would be empty. No players, no fans, no coaches. Not even a lone security guard. Nothing but pools of rain and bits of trash. Jon had always been fascinated by the abruptness with which each season ended. One minute you had the circuslike atmosphere of the Super Bowl, the next . . . nothing. Like the falling of an ax blade. The players went home and the locker room became an unlit stage set.

He returned to his desk, picked up the phone, and tapped in the number Susan Schiff had written on a blue Post-It. It rang twice, then a pleasant female voice said, "Good morning, Skip Henderson's office."

"Hi, this is Jon Sabino of the Baltimore Ravens. Is Skip available?"

"I'll check, please hold."

The sound of a roaring crowd provided the backdrop to an enthusiastic male voice giving instructions on ordering tickets, merchandise, and fan club memberships. Jon wondered how the media would react if he joined San Diego's fan club.

Then a new voice, with a raspy Southern accent, cut in— "Hey, Jon Sabino, how are you doing?"

"Good afternoon, Skip. Or I guess I should say good morning to you."

"That's right. It's not even ten o'clock out here yet. How are things back East?"

"Well, not so good," Jon said. "Not so good."

"No, I guess not. To be honest, I was wondering when you'd call."

Jon smiled again. Skip was letting him know that *he* knew the tight position he was in, just so there wasn't any confusion on that point.

"Well, I had to take care of some preliminary business beforehand. But here I am. I wish this could be a social call, but circumstances dictate otherwise."

"Yeah. It's a real shame what happened to Bell. A real shame."

"Tell me about it."

"How's he doing?"

"We're not sure yet. We'll know more in a few days."

"It looked pretty scary when they brought him in."

Jon rose and began pacing. He wasn't able to sit still for long periods. "It sure did."

"I remember when I first heard about Dale Earnhardt. He

was unconscious when they brought him in, too. I remember saying to Debbie, 'That's not a good sign.'"

"No, usually it isn't." *He's digging for information*, Jon thought. Trying to obtain clues as to Bell's long-term condition so he could better position himself for the negotiation. If Bell's career were over, the pick would be even more valuable. Asking for such information outright would be a breach of etiquette, so he simply disguised it as concern. Jon had little doubt that Skip truly cared about Bell's health. But he also cared about the San Diego Chargers, and Jon understood this. It was his job.

"So look, I'm not going to dance around the point here. I think you know why I'm calling."

"I'm guessing it has something to do with that big fat pick we've got."

"Correct."

"I figured as much."

"Yeah, you and every sportswriter in the country. There's no sense in playing games, Skip, so I'll just ask outright—one, are you willing to part with the pick, and two, if so, what are you hoping to get for it?"

This was merely a courtesy question. He was already well aware that Henderson had been shopping it around.

"Well, I'll tell you—I *am* willing to give up the pick. For the right deal, I certainly am."

"And, if I'm not mistaken, a few other teams are interesting in it as well. Am I right?"

"You are."

"The Chiefs, the Seahawks, the Broncos, and the Texans, I believe."

"You are well informed."

"It helps to read the papers."

Skip laughed—a big, hearty Texas guffaw. "That's a fact. Look, what I plan to do is this—I will inform the team that offers the best deal that they're in the top spot. Then I will tell the other interested teams, but I won't reveal any specifics. When this whole thing is all over, I'll make all the information available so everyone knows I've been playing it straight. Sound okay to you?"

By leaving out the names of the players and teams involved, it was impossible for an interested bidder to contact another one and sway their decision or conspire against the seller.

"Fine."

"Good. For the moment, then, the Chiefs are in the top spot. If the draft started right now, the pick would be theirs."

"Okay."

"Now, as for what I'm looking to get, well . . . why don't you tell me what you have in mind, and we'll take it from there?"

Jon took a deep breath. "Okay, sure. I sat down with a few other guys around here—Blanchard, Kevin Tanner, you know, the usual suspects—and we tried to get a fix on what your greatest needs were. We've gone through your roster pretty exhaustively, and we believe we've put together an excellent package offer."

"I'm all ears."

"All right. First, concerning the upcoming draft, you can have our first four picks. That's the last pick of the first round, two picks in the second round—forty-fourth and sixty-fourth overall—and our third-round pick, which is ninety-sixth overall."

Jon paused for just a moment to gauge Henderson's reply. None came.

"As for established talent," he went on, "we've surmised that you've got some rebuilding to do. In fact, if you don't mind my saying so, it looks to be quite a bit."

"Yep," Skip replied, "that's no secret. We're in bad shape."

"Okay, so, with that said, our offer will cover both sides of the ball. On offense, we'd like to give you running back Aaron Holloway, who is only in his second year and is quite good; rookie center Barrett Blake; tackle Keith Kubat; and guard Jared Cope. Kubat is a solid third-year man, and Cope is a first-rate veteran. He'll bring a lot of seniority to your team."

Another pause as Jon waited for some reaction. All he received this time was a murmured, *Mm-hmm. . . .*

"On defense, we've got third-year safety Milton Love; veteran linebacker Brett Savage; veteran end Corey Holbrook; and rookie end Alan Hill."

Now that the package was complete, Jon was sure Henderson would be so blown away by it he'd have to call 911 for emergency cardiac treatment. It was, by far, the most generous deal he'd ever made. According to Kevin Tanner, it was one of the most generous in league history. There was no way Skip could say no. *No way.*

"Well, I'll tell you, Jon, that sounds like a pretty good deal. But I'm afraid it won't turn the trick."

Jon stopped pacing. "What's that?"

"I'm afraid it's not comparable to what I already have on the table from another bidder."

Jon scanned the roster quickly and picked out a name almost at random.

"What if I included Buster McDaniels, our other running back? That'd give you a nice backfield combo."

"No, I don't—"

"And our sixth-round pick, too?"

"No, that won't—"

"Wait a second, Skip, let me ask you something."

"What?"

"Have you already dealt this pick? Am I doing all this just for laughs?"

"Holy Jesus, no!" Henderson replied with a chuckle. "Not at all, son. I wouldn't play games like that. No, the pick is still very much available."

"Then I don't understand. It seems like this package we've put together is—"

"Headed in the wrong direction," Henderson said.

Jon paused again. "In the wrong direction? We're offering—"

"I need defense, Jon. Plain and simple. That's where I'm

going to start. You've outlined a nice package, but it's not what we're looking for."

"Defense? Only defense?"

"For now, yes. We went over and over this point on my end, and we decided that's the best place to start our reconstruction. If we can focus on keeping our opponents from scoring, maybe we can win a few games, even with this lousy offense, with just one or two touchdowns. We've got a solid kicker, and our quarterback isn't too bad. We need some linemen to protect him, but what we really need is a defense. That's what wins championships, right?"

Jon was back at his desk, scanning the roster and flipping through pages of data. *Sonofabitch*, he thought bitterly. *They've been an offense-oriented team all these years, and now he's taking them in an entirely new direction.* And every other team Skip had ever worked for had been offensive-minded, too, so Jon thought he had a good read on the matter. *Dammit . . .*

"Right, right. Okay, forget all the offensive guys I just mentioned. Take the five draft picks, plus Love, Savage, Holbrook, and Hill, and I'll add Buckley and Northbrook, too."

"Jon," Henderson began, speaking like a patient father, "Northbrook's a dud. And you can't afford the cap hit his accelerated bonus would give you."

Jon Sabino was stunned that Skip knew this so quickly. He'd only been there a few weeks.

"And Buckley's not a performer. Nine years in the league and he's had one Pro Bowl season. He's slow and a bit too small for a cornerback. I'm sorry, Jon, those two additions don't help."

"What about the first four I mentioned? Savage, Holbrook, Hill, and Love?"

"Savage and Holbrook are old-timers. I'd get a year out of them if I was lucky. And Hill's a rookie. I don't need rookies. Milton Love, though, he's got promise. I'll take him off your hands."

"So I guess you wouldn't want Harper, either."

"That's right. Send him to the retirement home."

"Okay . . . what about Bartlett?" Jon pleaded, sliding down to from the "can trade" section to the "prefer to keep" area. He was hoping he wouldn't have to do this at any point. Now, only ten minutes into the first call, it was unavoidable. "He's in great shape and probably our best backup. A tremendous cornerback with a real future."

"Mmm . . . I agree. Now *that's* a good offering. I'll take him in a heartbeat."

Jon smiled. "Good, so we've got a deal?"

His heart sank when Henderson chuckled. "No, not quite yet."

"Huh?"

"The picks don't do me any good, either, Jon. We already have other draft picks this year, remember? I can't use picks—I need *players*. I need guys who can perform *right now*. First of all, your draft picks are so low that each kid we took would be a gamble. That's wasted money as far as I'm concerned. Second, the Hewlett family wants results immediately. And frankly, so do the fans. If this team doesn't turn around quick there's going to be a rebellion in this town. That's why I was brought here—to get things moving. If I go back to Carlton Hewlett, Sr., and say, 'Well, we're thinking of building up slowly, through the draft,' he's going to send my ass out the door so fast my clothes'll have to catch up with me."

Jon felt the situation was drifting beyond acceptable boundaries. A package that looked so good fifteen minutes ago seemed like a pile of crap now.

"Well, you can use those draft picks to deal higher up and get better talent. You could make trades with other teams for—"

"No, that's your job," Skip said flatly. "I'm not going to get into that whole mess when I've got other teams already offering me real talent. Jon, you're a terrific GM. One of the best in the business. So I don't need to point out that you have to offer a comparable deal if you want to compete in this situation. Offensive players and low draft picks are not the answer."

Jon studied his list of defensive players. "We just don't have that much to offer in the defensive area. You're telling me the Chiefs do?" Like all good general managers, he was familiar not only with his own roster but those of other teams in the league. "They haven't had a good defense in ages. What are they offering, their whole starting squad?"

"No. In fact, they're not offering much off their own list at all."

Jon was dumbstruck; a reaction he didn't experience often. He sat in his black leather chair and stared into space as a gaudy pendulum clock with a swinging Ravens logo marked off the seconds on the wall behind him.

"You mean they're doing deals with other teams?"

"You got it."

"Good God . . ."

Henderson snorted a little laugh. "I know, it's pretty amazing. They must really want this pick. And, just so you know, the Texans and the Seahawks have been doing the same thing. I don't know about the Broncos. I haven't heard from them in a while."

Jon was barely listening. His mind was swirling with the manifold implications of what Skip just said—multiple teams making multiple deals with multiple other teams in an attempt to put together the best defensive package in order to secure one draft pick. It was enormous; potentially historic in its proportions. And he knew he had no choice but to get involved in it.

"Uh, okay, Skip. Okay . . ." He swallowed into a dry throat and grabbed a nearby sheet of paper. He didn't know what was on it; it could've been the original copy of the goddamned Gettysburg Address for all he cared. He flipped it over, took a pencil from his cup, and began scribbling.

"I'm jotting down everything we just talked about. I'm making notes here, making notes. I'll try to get something together for you, and soon, of course."

"Sounds good."

"Sorry about the first misstep. I had no idea."

"That's all right. Good luck."

"I don't suppose you're willing to tell me who the Chiefs—"

"No, I can't do that."

"I didn't think so. Okay, thanks. I'll be calling back shortly."

"Talk to you then."

He hung up the phone and kept scribbling. Suggestions, ideas, calculations—stream-of-consciousness stuff, free thinking and totally devoid of structure. He had to open his mind, search outside the box; *way* outside. This was going to be a challenge and a half. Totally unexpected, totally infuriating, and totally unavoidable.

After fifteen minutes he stopped writing and reviewed his notes thus far. It was at this moment that a helpless, slipping-away feeling came rushing in. He began to fully realize what would be required in order to put together just the right package for Skip Henderson, and it revealed an ugly and wholly unavoidable dimension to his forthcoming negotiations—most of the teams he'd be dealing with were tired of the Baltimore Ravens and their current reign of terror. The NFL was supposed to be in its glorious Age of Parity, where all clubs were created equal and everyone had a fair shot at the big prize. In an industry where it was everyone's singular goal to prove they were better than everyone else, consistent winners became targets; objects of jealousy and hatred. Behind every pat on the back was the seething desire to crush and bury. Behind every line of friendly praise was a hunger to destroy with as much humiliation as possible. A lot of people were gunning for the Baltimore Ravens, and not just for the players, either—for Connally, for Blanchard, and, in particular, for Jon Sabino. Other teams were tired of hearing about the "genius architect" and the "Oracle of Owings Mills." It was bad enough after the first Super Bowl, and downright depressing after the second. But when the chatter began about how the team was the overwhelming favorite for a third, Jon knew this was coming. His organization would face numerous battles not just on the field but off it, because you were allowed to win once, but not twice, and certainly not thrice. Three straight times was an affront. It was swaggering without the need to actually swagger. And with all the fanfare and praise and adulation he had personally received—including his own posters, trading cards (the first time in pro sports history a front office person received such recognition), and half-hour weekly radio show—Jon knew he'd be targeted.

His original plan was to take it all in stride, survive behind his thick skin, and then, if and after they did indeed win a third trophy, be sentimental and good humored about all of it when the whole thing fell apart next season. That much was inevitable, and he and everyone else in the league knew it. Next year didn't matter, because the party would be over and the league would reacquire its default form.

All that mattered was now, and suddenly it looked as though the ride wouldn't be as smooth as planned. He had no choice but to descend among the ranks of people who hated his guts. Individuals in other organizations who, now that the word about Bell and the desire to acquire McKinley was undoubtedly seeping out, were giggling maniacally as they loaded their proverbial rifles and prayed that Jon Sabino, resident miracle worker of the historic Baltimore Ravens, called them up personally to beg for help. Maybe not everyone was of this mind-set, but Jon knew some of them were. And he was sure he would find out over the next few days who those people were. In fact, he was quite certain he'd discover *many* interesting and enlightening things over the next few days. For all the years of struggle and the sacrifices he'd made to reach this point, he was quite sure this was going to be the most difficult and unpleasant experience of all.

He took a deep breath, massaged his temples, and went back to his scribbling.

THE NEXT TWO HOURS FLEW BY, AND THE RAIN HAD picked up and was now spattering against the windows. Jon didn't seem to notice. He just kept staring at the roster, already sure there was no way to build an attractive defensive offer for Skip from what was already there. At one point, however, he ventured into the "don't trade" area, mostly as an exercise in theoreticals. It was his job, after all, to consider all possibilities, and using guys in this category *was* an option. He did have the power to do it. Blanchard would hit the ceiling, but Jon still had final say.

His eyes kept getting stuck on one name in particular. The guy was a wide receiver; nothing to do with defense and therefore, at least to the uneducated observer, of no use to Skip Henderson and the San Diego Chargers. But Jon knew more. He knew the guy was a favorite of Henderson's, knew the old bastard admired him. He had, in fact, tried twice to acquire him—once when he was the Cardinals' offensive coordinator, and once when he was GM of the Jaguars. Yes, Jon thought, he might be useful at the right moment. His offensive pedigree notwithstanding, he just might be a factor in the deal.

But Blanchard would go through the roof.

And so would the fans. Remember that he's a fan favorite, too.

It wouldn't be the first time he'd made a deal that left the fans screaming for his head. When he first took over as general manager, he found himself unable to avoid cutting Dwight "Roast Beef" Reynolds. Reynolds was a lineman with a barrel chest and a heart of gold. He earned his nickname when he once bragged to the press that he could eat an entire roast beef in one sitting, and then proceeded to do just that during a live taping of a local sports talk show. He was a devoted family man with a charitable organization for kids ("The Roast Beef Club"), and once even spoke out viciously against Maryland's governor for cutting funding to a program that gave athletic equipment to elementary schools in underprivileged areas. The fans regarded him as a god.

The problem on the field, however, was that he had long passed his prime. He still had tremendous strength, but his speed and reaction time had diminished. The sound of thousands of fans chanting his nickname after he recorded yet another sack was heard less and less. Coordinators didn't double-team him any more. He became injury prone and once missed half a season. Clearly it was time to let him go, but the previous hierarchy didn't have the heart to do it.

When Sabino finally mustered the courage to bring him into his office and deliver the bad news, "Roast Beef" just smiled and said, "I was wondering when you'd finally get around to doing this." The fans, however, weren't so forgiving, even after Sabino and the coaches decided to keep Reynolds around as an assistant coordinator.

Jon remembered this story, in detail, as he stared at the tantalizing name on the roster sheet.

"No," he murmured softly. "No . . . Susan?"

Schiff appeared in the doorway.

"Yes?"

"Could you please get me printouts of the rosters for the other thirty-one teams?"

She hesitated. "All of them?"

"Yes, I believe there are still thirty-two total. Unless you know something I don't."

"Uh, sure."

"Thanks."

A dull throb flared in his head; the first stage of what he knew would grow into a whopper of a migraine. He glanced down at the name one more time, then shoved it to the back of his mind.

Unless there was no other choice, there was no way he would even consider trading Darryl "DB" Bailey.

SPORTS CARDS PLUS HADN'T HAD A DAY OF BUSINESS like this in years—maybe ever. The line ran down the sidewalk to the far end of the strip mall. The show was only supposed to go from one o'clock to three, yet three had passed nearly a half hour ago.

The store's owner, Pat Lanigan, had sore cheeks from the all-day smile. Bailey's appearance fee had been twenty-five thousand, and Lanigan had already made that back and then some. He stood next to the star with his hands clasped together, greeting each new face as cash register sounds echoed joyfully through in his mind—*cha-ching*! Bailey wasn't just a football player, he was a bona fide celebrity. Lanigan decided it wasn't due merely to his remarkable skills as a wide receiver. He was, as it turned out, as nice of a guy in person as he seemed to be in the media. It didn't always work that way, Lanigan knew. The PR machinery in the NFL was huge and powerful. But that didn't seem to be the case with Bailey. He could see why the fans loved him.

The man on Bailey's other side was his public relations agent, Mark Coleman. He to adopted the hands-together-feet-slightly-apart posture, making him and Lanigan look like a pair of unusually cheerful Secret Service agents. Coleman checked his watch, then leaned down and whispered in Bailey's ear.

"It's just about three thirty, big guy."

Bailey was seated behind an enormous table covered with memorabilia that was waiting for his signature to magically make it more valuable. He looked up and evaluated the crowd.

"What about all these people, Mark? You wanna tell them to go home?" A few of the fans who were nearby overheard this exchange. Bailey looked at Coleman and smiled. "You got a hot date or something?"

Everyone laughed and the tension evaporated. "No, it's just that I'm supposed to let you know when, uh . . ."

"It'll be time to go when everyone gets what they came for. Right, folks?"

The fans cheered. Coleman smiled and shook his head. He was used to abrupt schedule extensions when it came to Darryl Bailey.

During this warm-and-fuzzy moment, one fan reached over and patted Bailey on the shoulder, sending threads of pain in every direction. He grimaced, which everyone noticed, then covered it by coughing. "Oh man, when is this cold going to die?" he mumbled, and was relieved when it appeared as though everyone bought into the illusion.

It would be another hour and a half before they got out of there. Bailey would sign hundreds of items—from conventional stuff like footballs and jerseys to weird things like people's everyday clothing or parts of their body. One girl, for example, asked him to sign her right arm, which he happily did. And a six-year-old boy who was also a baseball fan apparently grabbed the wrong item off his shelf at home, so Darryl ended up writing his name over an eight-by-ten of Cal Ripken, Jr.

The limousine Lanigan had provided dropped Coleman off first. Once he was gone, Bailey stretched his long, lanky frame across both seats. He felt like talking with someone, and he considered called Jon Sabino. It wasn't common for players to be chummy with their GMs, but it did happen from time to time. DB liked Jon. He had a good reputation, and other players liked him, too. In that indefinable way, he had become acceptable within the brotherhood of the players' network. Darryl liked his sense of humor, and he knew Jon was smart as shit, so he turned to him for advice on matters both personal and professional. They'd gone out to dinner a few times, and Jon and Kelley had gotten on well with his girlfriend, Bernadette. Jon seemed to approve of her, and DB was surprised at how he seemed happy about this.

He tried Jon's office phone but got no answer. *If he's not there, he's not anywhere,* DB thought. So, instead, he chatted with the driver, whom he recognized from past journeys, and listened to an NBA game on the radio. There was cold beer and hard liquor in the little fridge, too, but he ignored it. The novelty of being in a vehicle that had a refrigerator and three telephones had worn off years ago. This was everyday living now.

His house was like something from a glossy magazine on the rich and famous. The paired iron gates at the front swung back slowly, allowing access to a gently sloping cobblestone driveway. The limo pulled around to the front step, and before Bailey got out he tipped the driver with a fifty and signed two more items for the guy's kids. The driver, in turn, silently wished all the people he carted around were more like Bailey.

The house was large and stately, with colorful landscaping and tall Roman columns. Bailey worked the key into the lock and went in. After disarming the alarm system and checking the answering machine, he went to the kitchen and downed two glasses of orange juice. Bernadette would be over in a little bit. They were supposed to go out for dinner. That meant another limo, another driver, and probably more autographs, too. It didn't bother him. He'd been in the league long enough to know he should enjoy it while he could. Ten years after he retired no one would want his autograph anymore.

He poured another glass of juice and walked into the living room. He went to the sliding door that led to the sundeck

and overlooked the bay. The city of Baltimore was miniatur-
ized in the distance. He loved this view, had always loved the
water. He had a condo in Key West that he visited a few
weeks each year. The rest of the time he rented it. It more
than paid for itself.

When he first realized there was someone sitting on the
couch behind him—the stranger's image was reflected in the
sliding door's glass—his heart jumped and he spun around.
The visitor had a dark green suit that bore a muted shine, a
small fortune in gold jewelry, wraparound sunglasses, and a
broad smile.

"How've you been, DB?"

"Damn, Cory, you scared the shit out of me!"

Cory Fletcher rose and came toward him with a grin. "Is
that anyway to talk to an old friend?" Fletcher threw his
arms around him, slapping him vigorously. He wasn't quite
as tall as Bailey, but he was wider across the shoulders and in
the same excellent physical condition.

When they separated, Bailey said, "How the hell'd you
get in here? This place has more alarms than the White
House."

Fletcher strutted back to the couch and picked up his
drink from the glass coffee table. He apparently had helped
himself. Bernadette couldn't possibly be home, Bailey
thought. If she saw Cory Fletcher, the only drink she'd give
him was a few ounces of battery acid in the face. Bailey's
eyes went to the front door, which was partially visible
through the hallway. Fletcher didn't know much about
Bernadette Redmond, but Bernadette knew about Fletcher.
One of the vows Bailey made when they met was to be completely open and honest about his past. No lies, no coverups.
When Bernadette came along, he told her everything. Told
her about the drugs and the drinking during his colorful
youth in LA, and about the crowd he ran with back then. Her
told her all of it one night as they lay in bed together, after
they made love. She listened patiently and silently, then told
him if anyone from that crowd ever stepped foot in their
house she'd remove their balls with a hatchet. DB had

smiled when he heard this. He pulled her close, kissed her on the top of the head, and told her not to worry—they were on the other side of the country and probably forgot all about him.

"Shit, DB, the last thing I worry about is alarm systems," Fletcher said. He appraised the living room, with its high ceilings and sparse wrought-iron furniture. "This is one nice place."

"Thanks."

"So how's it been going for you?"

"It's been going pretty good."

"I can see that. Game room in the cellar, little movie theater, big TV in the bedroom . . ."

Bailey laughed. "Thanks for taking the grand tour by yourself. Did you see the two Magritte paintings?"

"Is that what they are? Weird shit, man. You like that stuff?"

"Nah . . . they're investments. Bernadette takes care of all that. She's pretty good with money. I can make it, but she's better than me at managing it."

Fletcher was nodding. "You're a lucky guy."

"Yeah, I know."

Fletcher appraised the entire room one more time with a sweeping look and then said, "So, to what do I owe this pleasure? I assume this isn't a social call."

Bailey's smile faded. "No, no. Cory, I need some stuff."

"Some coke? Meth? I thought you'd—?"

Bailey shook his head. "No, nothing like that. Cortisone. I need some small dosages. About twenty. And needles, too."

"Cortisone? For what?"

"My right foot," Bailey pointed, as if Cory Fletcher had no idea where the right foot was. "I was working out about two weeks ago and I pulled it. I'm not sure what happened, but it's killing me." He sat down on a huge ottoman and began massaging the ankle. "I don't want it to get worse. It's gotta be back to normal when minicamps start."

Fletcher sat on the couch across from him. "Does it hurt now?"

"Yeah, a little bit." He sounded like he was struggling for breath, and his face was twisted with pain. "This is the last year of my contract, too. If I don't play this year, no one'll sign me after that. I'll be finished. And I know I still have some good games left in me."

Fletcher watched his old friend in bewilderment. "Shouldn't you, y'know, go to your trainer or the team doctor or someone?"

"Our team physician is an asshole. He'd tell me I got what I deserved for taking part in an unauthorized workout program. What's worse, there's a clause in my contract about keeping myself in peak condition at all times." He winced again. "So look, can you get me the stuff? I'll pay top dollar for it. And I'll pay for your trip out here, too."

"Uh, sure. No problem, man."

Bailey nodded. "Good, thanks. Hey, do you have any on you right now?"

"No, but I know where I can get some pretty quick."

"Cool. Please . . . I've got cash on me." Bailey smiled— that endearing grin that made him look like a little boy in spite of his size. "Unless you already found it when you went through the house."

Fletcher laughed, and in that moment Bailey knew everything would be fine. He'd found his source.

"No, I would've taken it all and bolted." He rose from the couch and headed toward the door. "I'll be right back."

"Thanks, man."

And hurry . . .

FLETCHER WAS BACK IN JUST OVER AN HOUR. HE HAD the stuff in a brown paper bag and offered no information as to where he'd acquired it. There were five doses of 250mg each, along with five small syringes.

"You know, DB, you really shouldn't administer this shit by yourself. You want some help?"

Bailey was up again and holding a drink. He had changed into a fresh jogging suit and white sneakers that appeared to be brand new. There was another basketball game on the enormous flat-panel TV screen hanging on the wall across the room.

"No, I'll be all right. The pain subsided a bit while you were gone, so I'll have Bernadette help me with it later. Here . . ."

He took a baseball-size wad of crisp bills from his front pocket and, with enormous fingers that were covered in gold, counted out twenty hundred-dollar bills. "This should cover the stuff plus your trip. If you need more, let me know."

Fletcher looked at the bills in his hand in astonishment. "Thanks, man. DB, this is really—"

"I'll need about twenty more doses, remember?"

"Yeah, sure, no problem."

"Cool." Bailey looked at his watch, purposely making the gesture obvious. "Look, you'd better get going. If Bernadette comes in and sees one of my old dogs in here, she'll freak. You wanna have dinner tomorrow night? I'll take care of that, too."

"Sure."

"Good." He led his guest to the door. Fletcher couldn't help but notice the change in mood. Before, he was being treated like royalty. But from the moment DB got the stuff in his hands, he was a very different man. He'd seen this behavior in his other customers, but those were users of recreational drugs. Cortisone was a painkiller. What was the rush?

"I'll give you a call in a little bit," Bailey said from the doorway. Fletcher nodded as he got back into his rented Mercedes.

Bailey shut the door and locked it. Bernadette wouldn't be here until nightfall, he knew. He went back to the living room, passed through it, down the hallway, through their bedroom, and into the small adjoining bathroom. He locked that door as well. He was now safe in a small womb. He turned on the ceiling fan and ran the hot water, but didn't turn on the overhead light. Instead, he flicked on the little nightlight.

He sat down on the toilet and pulled up his pants leg. The ankle he'd been massaging when Fletcher was here looked fine. He reached down and scratched it a few times, then let the pants fall over it again. He would give it no more attention.

He set the brown bag on the sink and removed one cortisone dosage and one needle. He handled everything expertly, filling the latter with the former and flicking the bubbles away. Then he set the needle back down.

Gingerly, he pulled his shirt over his head and dropped it on the floor. The pain from this relatively simply action was almost unbearable. He managed to keep from crying out, but a tear broke free and streamed down his cheek. He wiped it away quickly. Then he looked at himself briefly in the mirror. There was no visible sign of the injury. That was the one small blessing.

He lifted the syringe from the sink, checked it one last time, then, with a tightened jaw, plunged it into the sharp curve between his neck and left shoulder. This time the pain exploded into every corner of his body, and he dropped onto the floor as if forced there by an invisible hand. He curled into a fetal position, screaming like a torture victim. Through the haze of agony he managed to thumb the plunger down, driven by the desire to get this over with as quickly as possible. The screaming and the writhing lasted for maybe thirty more seconds, but it felt endless.

When the needle chamber was empty, the pain began losing intensity. It mellowed first into a dull throb, and then to nothing. Bailey remained on the floor for a few minutes, sweating profusely as he tried to catch his breath. More tears had streamed out, but he didn't attempt to wipe them away this time. He just wanted to regain his sanity. He got up on all fours, then fell into a sitting position and leaned against the wall. The exhaust fan was still rumbling away, and steam was rising from the marble basin. Eventually his breathing returned to normal, and the pain was but a memory. He wouldn't be able to lift the arm for a while, but that was okay. As long as it was better by the start of minicamps. As long as that happened, everything would be fine. *It'll be as if the injury never happened . . .*

At least that's what he believed.

6

GEORGE WASHINGTON HIGH SCHOOL WAS BUILT IN 1965, during the rise of Lyndon Johnson's "Great Society," in an impoverished suburb of Philadelphia. Thanks to funds from the federal government, it had many features that a lot of the older area high schools did not, including a science lab, a drama theatre, and a football field with a scoreboard, bleachers, and an announcer's booth. From all appearances, G. W. High was well on its way.

Then in 1992 a male student was knifed to death in one of the upstairs bathrooms. He was a member of a local gang, so it was generally believed his death was the result of a drug deal gone wrong. But, in spite of concerted efforts by the local police and the FBI, his murderer was never found, and the subsequent avalanche of lawsuits by the boy's family forced the school to close. A chainlink fence went up around the property, and the windows were covered over with plywood. The state wanted to sell the land, but, due to a series of legal snafus, they never could. So the building and the surrounding grounds just sat, year after year, neglected and rotting. Weeds grew waist high and graffiti appeared. A rumor would occasionally surface about someone venturing inside via one of the basement windows, and the inevitable folktale arose about the ghost of the murdered boy roaming the halls, seeking vengeance.

The football field had not been enclosed by the fence and was soon adopted as an unofficial public lot; the school looming like a sentinel in the distance. Maintaining it became a community affair, the unwritten rule being if you played on it you helped take care of it. On any given Sunday you could hear the groan of a lawn mower, and each spring some mystery person generously applied new lines of limestone. Local leagues were loosely formed, and one year they even managed their own version of the Super Bowl. Nearly fifty "fans" showed up to watch the Wildcats beat the Playboys, 35–21.

During the week the field was usually empty; this was when Raymond Coolidge used it. He brought a bunch of balls in a net bag and was usually accompanied by a friend named Mark Dalton. They had played together at La Salle, Mark as a wide receiver and Raymond as the quarterback. Most notable, however, was the fact that together they had broken twenty-nine school records. Raymond was personally responsible for twenty of them.

On this particular sunny spring afternoon a third person came with them. He was an older man with the weary, troubled face of a blues guitarist. He wore jeans and a flannel shirt, and walked with a slight limp from a machine-shop accident he'd had in 1992. Since the accident, Raymond's Uncle Joe had survived on meager disability payments and the charity of friends and relatives.

He stood with his arms folded over his sizable belly and watched his nephew run the drills. Dalton was doing his best to throw his quarterback out of rhythm, but Raymond was more than equal to the challenge.

After a while Joe asked, "How's your mama doing with her back?"

"Okay."

"Yeah? That's not what I heard. I heard she's having a lot of trouble over there, getting around, doing housework.

Some of the simple stuff is becoming not-so-simple any-more."

Raymond didn't respond.

"Have you thought any more about what you're gonna do now that you're out of school?"

"I don't know."

"You don't know? Well, are you gonna get a job?"

"Probably."

Joe shook his head. " 'Probably.' Your mama isn't gonna be able to work forever. You'll need to take care of her. A year from now she'll have trouble just driving over there. In five years she won't be able to work at all."

Again no response. Joe wasn't surprised. Raymond had always been stoic, even as a child. He had a chip on his shoulder almost from the day he was born. And he knew who put it there, too.

"It ain't easy out in the world, Ray. In fact it's damned hard. Working all day just to get by. Not many opportunities to make any real money."

Dalton ran a slant pattern about sixty yards out, and Raymond laid the ball right in his lap.

"If you tried out for a pro team, though, you could have enough money to take care of your mama forever. You'd have enough money to do whatever you wanted. You'd be a king."

Raymond waited for Dalton to run the next route, seemingly unaware that he was being spoken to.

"I heard the new backup quarterback for the Colts got over a million bucks as a signing bonus. A million bucks as a *backup*. You'd never make that kind of money anywhere else. Never. So how about it? How about giving it a shot? Or at least the Arena League or NFL Europe or something?"

Raymond picked up the last ball and waited. Dalton ran down the right side, cut toward the center, then switched back. Raymond released the ball with a grunt and it sailed over the head of its target. Dalton never knew what Raymond and his uncle talked about, but it clearly wasn't anything good.

"No," he said simply, and Joe knew that was all the response he'd get.

THAT NIGHT, HANDS TUCKED BEHIND HIS HEAD, Raymond lay awake and watched the clouds pass by his bedroom window. He knew his Uncle Joe would bring up the NFL again. And again he would say no. Nothing more than that, for anything more would be disrespectful. He didn't want to be disrespectful to his Uncle Joe—also known as Uncle "Pearly" because of his perfect teeth. He loved Pearly, and he knew Pearly loved him. He'd been a part of Raymond's life for as long as Raymond could remember.

He turned over and found the trading card on the nightstand. It was encased in hard plastic to arrest the aging process. Football cards had never been regarded with the same reverence as their baseball equivalents, and this one in particular probably had a market value of about a buck. But to Raymond it was priceless. The man in the photo was wearing a smile almost identical to Pearly's. In fact, many of their features bore a haunting similarity, which made sense since they were brothers. Quincy Pressner was standing on a sunny field with a ball tucked into his left arm. He was proudly wearing his Rams jersey and looked so young and happy that Raymond often couldn't believe it was the same man he knew now. This Quincy Pressner looked as though he was ready to conquer the universe. He looked healthy, strong, and supremely confident. Another person in another time, so far removed from the present that it was almost impossible to believe it ever existed at all. This was the father Raymond never really knew.

He loved this photo in part because he was about twenty feet out of the frame when it was taken. He was only a small child at the time, but he remembered several details. His dad had taken him to a local field so the card company could do the shoot. There were three guys—the photographer, his assistant, and some other guy in a suit and tie; a liaison or something. Raymond remembers him being particularly friendly to his dad, shaking his hand a lot and asking him to sign several things. Quincy obliged without complaint, and Raymond could sense, even then, that his dad was somebody important. Quincy also remembered telling the men that Raymond was his nephew. When Raymond asked why he did this, his father said, "To protect you." Raymond found this puzzling, but his father told him he'd understand someday. And he was right.

After the three men left, father and son played tag football. The sun was shining, the sky was blue, the air was warm and sweet, and it was just the two of them. It was a day that would live vividly in Raymond's memory. He remembered giggling uncontrollably, and his dad rolling with him in the grass. He remembered the indescribable joy of knowing that his father, whatever else his concerns, was focused solely on *him* that afternoon. Just the two of them in their own universe. They played for what seemed like hours, and Raymond wished it would never end. In years to come, he would think back to that singular occasion and say to himself, *That's the one I wanted all the others to be like. If I had my choice, that would've been the blueprint for every other day.*

But it wasn't; not even close. As time rolled ruthlessly forward, a new reality emerged. Slowly and painfully, it adopted a form that bore absolutely no resemblance to the one from that golden afternoon. He was still a child when the change began, and like a line on a stockbroker's chart, it kept heading downward, year after year. And Raymond knew when the those changes had started. He knew when, he knew who, and he knew why.

Because of this, he had no interest in playing in the National Football League.

RAYMOND WASN'T THE ONLY ONE IN A CONTEMPLATIVE mood that evening.

Pearly Pressner was not one of nature's writers. Unlike his father and grandfather, he did earn a high school diploma. He even did reasonably well in math and history. But he nearly flunked out of English and hated it with a passion. He couldn't remember the last time he wrote more than three sentences. Nevertheless, he spent nearly an hour under the singular light of his tiny kitchen poring over every word of a letter that he hoped would change the course of his nephew's life.

The intended recipient was a Mr. Freddie Friedman, agent and ally to nearly four dozen professional athletes. Most of them were in the NFL, but a handful were in the NBA, and two played professional baseball. Pearly had never met Friedman, but he knew him by reputation, mostly through several extensive and well-researched feature articles he found at the library. Friedman was a small, fast-talking individual who came from a poor Jewish home in Brooklyn. He'd put himself through business school while working various menial jobs and running numbers on the weekends.

What Pearly liked most about him was the fact that he apparently never screwed any of his clients. No embezzlement, no fraudulent investments, no shady contracts. In a business where watching your back had to become second nature if you had any hope of survival, he was apparently a straight shooter. A rare breed, to be sure.

In spite of the letter's relatively brief content, Pearly had been thinking about writing it for years. He knew Raymond would go berserk if he found out. That was one of the main reasons it took him this long to get it together. He'd hoped Raymond might write it himself one day, but the boy's hatred of the NFL had gotten worse instead of better. Pearly knew there were times when a young mind needed an older, wiser one to guide it. This, he decided, was one of those times. He knew Raymond considered him a father figure, and that was okay with him. He never had any children of his own, and Raymond really never had a full-time dad, so there was a certain inevitability to the symbiosis. Most of the time he stayed in the background and let Raymond do his own thing, but every now and then he'd step forward and tap the boy in one direction or another to keep him on course.

Writing this letter and sending the package that lay open on his kitchen table was the most aggressive thing he'd ever done in this capacity, and a certain guilt came with it. But he believed in his heart that it ultimately was the right thing to do. He just hoped the boy would understand someday.

Dear Mr. Friedman,

These are videotapes of my nephew, Raymond Coolidge, who played QB for La Salle College and graduated last year. Please look at them and see if you'd be interested in being his agent. I think he is good enough to have a shot at the NFL, but he doesn't want to because of what he believes the league did to his father, Quincy Pressner. He doesn't know what really happened, though, and I don't want him to waste a chance to make it in the league without at least trying. If you think you'd like to help him, please call me. I can have him come and meet with you.

Joe Pressner

He read the letter over a few times, judged it professional sounding enough, then tri-folded it. It went into the box with the videotapes, which had been given to him by Raymond's coach, Hal Arden. Arden and Pearly were on the same wavelength concerning Raymond's future. They had discussed it a few times without Raymond's knowledge. And Arden was one of the very few people who knew Quincy Pressner was Raymond's dad. Pearly and Raymond's mom had gone to great pains to hide this fact. Raising the boy with his mom's maiden name had been surprisingly effective, and Raymond had a much stronger resemblance to her than to his father. Through the years the legend of Quincy Pressner grew following his mysterious "disappearance," and the rumor that he had a son became a point of certain intrigue among the fans and the media. But Raymond's true identity was never exposed. Hal Arden had done his part to keep the family secret. Nevertheless, he didn't want to see Raymond waste his considerable talents any more than Pearly did.

The game tapes were labeled in neat black print by opponent and date. Pearly put the letter on top, then set down another layer of bubble wrap. He taped the box shut and carefully scrawled Friedman's address. He would mail the package in the morning, after he stopped at the local convenience store for his daily cup of coffee.

He got up and pulled the chain on the overhead light, transforming the room into a nondescript world of shapes and shadows, and shuffled wearily to bed.

As he drifted into sleep, he thought more about Freddie Friedman. He wondered if the guy would give a damn about his nephew at all. Surely he got packages like this all the time—desperate pleas from desperate athletes hoping for a shot at the ultimate gridiron dream. Would Raymond be written off as just another face in that crowd? Would Freddie's final summary be that he was just another nobody looking to be a somebody? There was always that chance. But the boy had done remarkably well at La Salle, with tremendous stats. Regardless, he never declared for the draft afterward; Pearly knew this would be one the first questions someone would ask. And he made no attempt to get noticed by pro scouts. La Salle wasn't Division 1-A, but that didn't mean pro teams wouldn't have at least glanced in his direction. When you were trying to hide your abilities, however, it raised questions. Now Pearly wanted nothing more for his nephew than a fair opportunity. He hoped Friedman would at least be curious.

There was no way he could have foreseen the effect his innocent and good-natured effort would have on the usually unshakable world of the NFL.

7

SITTING IN HIS COMFORTABLE CHAIR WITH BRONCOS memorabilia hanging from every wall around him, Brendan Cavanaugh felt like bleary eyes might fall out of his head. He couldn't stand to look at the Ravens roster for another minute.

He dropped the damn thing onto the glass top of his desk and fell back into his chair. He'd studied it so many times he could quote every bit of data from memory. He knew Terry Butler went to Virginia, Lawrence Dixon was six feet one inch, and that Scott Montgomery was in his eleventh year. He also knew, with a little help from some friends, about injuries past and present, a wealth of contract details, and who Blanchard's favorites were. What he didn't know was how Jon Sabino was going to work his deal with that bastard Skip Henderson.

He studied the roster in the hopes of thinking like Sabino, getting behind his eyes and seeing what he saw. He'd tried this before, even in situations that had nothing to do with him, and the results were always frustrating. It was like a high-stakes poker game—the key was to think like you're opponent. If you could get inside his head, the battle was won. And he'd done this with every other GM in the league.

He watched them, he listened, he took notes. He knew how to get information, knew how to massage and schmooze others. Everything was important—every little detail had meaning. He knew which GMs were conservative and which were gamblers. He knew which were given carte blanche by their organization, and which were kept on a short leash. He could predict damn near everything everyone one of them did.

Except Sabino.

This was going to be regarded as a seminal moment in his career. He thought again that he *had* to come out on top. He had to best Sabino on this thing. He'd shoved virtually all other work aside and focused on this like the crazed fan of a Hollywood starlet, gripped by obsession. He hadn't left the office—hadn't been home, hadn't seen his wife or his kids. They called a few times, but he barely heard to a word they'd said. His wife was a patient and understanding woman, and even she had never seen him so intense.

In his slumped-back position he closed his eyes and went over his ideas again. Sabino could trade this guy for that, or he could offer these draft picks to this team in exchange for this defensive player. . . . The possibilities were endless; there was just no way to predict with any certainty. And Sabino had proven himself able to think in unconventional ways—to come up with ideas no one else had even considered. Cavanaugh had the same ability, but, he admitted bitterly only to himself, he began exercising that part of his mental discipline only as a result of wanting to keep up with his archrival. Enemies, they say, often bring out the best in each other.

He picked up a copy of his own team's roster and scanned it briefly, then let it fall alongside Baltimore's. The only real advantage he had in the situation was the simple fact that he'd already been vying for the "McKinley pick" when Sabino entered the picture. He'd been working on possible trades and other deals with other teams. *We could send Mason to the Colts for that second-string linebacker they have . . . maybe our second- and third-round draft picks, which are pretty high, to the Browns, who aren't looking to draft a quarterback this year. . . .* He'd already had preliminary discussions with several teams. They knew he was in the race, and they had some sense of what he had to offer. So at least he had an edge on Sabino in that respect.

The door to his office flew back and a fresh-faced kid in a navy blue suit flew in, his tie waving back and forth like a metronome.

"What's up, Cav? Are we ready to rock, or what?"

Carlson Whittaker had been with the organization for just over a year now. He was the second son of Adam Whittaker III, multimillionaire and close friend of the Broncos ownership. Carlson had an MBA from Fordham, a boyish face, and more drive and aggression than actual talent. He was one of several white-collar gofers the team employed.

"Getting there," Cavanaugh said, his eyes still shut.

"How's it looking?"

"Hard to say, Whit, hard to say. I've got a pretty good idea of what Henderson wants and what Sabino has to give."

Whittaker was moving from place to place around the office, checking out Cavanaugh's considerable collection of memorabilia, most of which would command a hefty price on eBay. He didn't appear to be listening.

"Yeah? So why don't we get Hendrickson on the phone and get the deal done right now?"

"Henderson."

"Whatever. Let's get to it." He spun around, clapping his hands. "Come on, chief, I smell blood!"

Cavanaugh looked at him and laughed. "Patience, Junior, patience. I'll call when the time is right."

"But shouldn't we—"

"And when the time is right, I'll make sure you're the first to know," Cavanaugh said, cutting him off. He leaned forward again and grabbed a random sheaf of papers from his desk. "In the meantime, print and collate two copies of this, and stick each one in a binder for me, would you?"

Whittaker stared at the papers as if he had no idea what they were, or what it meant to copy and collate something.

He smiled and shook his head. "Sure, whatever," he said, taking them.

"Good. Now out."

The kid left without another word and Cavanaugh returned to his thoughts. *Always important to appear in control in front of the hired help*, he thought. But the truth was that he had no idea when he should jump back into the race for McKinley. There was no way to define that kind of thing—it would come down to instinct. And on that score he was supremely confident. The "little voice" that dwelled inside his mind had rarely misled him. It was the one that ignored statistics and tradition and the advice of others, and usually hit the board squarely on the bull's-eye. And right now it was telling him to lay back and wait. *Patience, Junior, patience.* That's what he'd said, and that's what he believed. It was indeed a virtue, and it had paid off handsomely many times in the past.

You just never knew what might happen.

THE VOICES WERE FAINT, DISTANT. THERE WERE A LOT of them—maybe hundreds—jumbled together in one crazy cacophony. There were sobs and cries, people trying to catch their breath. Someone was shouting. It was an older man, and there was authority in his voice, but Michael Bell couldn't make out what he was saying. Funny, that—he'd stood on every football field in every major stadium in the country, amid the roar of thousands of spectators, and zeroed in on the smallest sounds. Yet he couldn't focus on any one of these voices now. They were just too far away.

A siren began growing in volume. The pastiche of voices grew along with it. Everything reached a natural peak, filling every crack and corner of his mind. Then, as quickly as it had come, it faded again and there was only silence.

He had a sense that he was on his back, so he tried to get up. Impossible. He wiggled his fingers and clenched his hands into fists. At least that's what he *thought* he was doing, but he couldn't be sure. He couldn't even lift his head to look. He seemed to be glued down.

A realization struck him—wherever he was, he'd been here for a while. He didn't know how long, but a while. He believed his eyes were open, but there was nothing to see. He was enveloped by darkness, stretching to infinity in every direction. A hollow, echoed place, like something out of a dream. It wasn't frightening, but it wasn't pleasant, either. It was nothing. Nothing in a place of utter nothingness. *Yes, I've been here for some time, but I'm only becoming aware of it now.* Somehow he knew this. He would bet a game check on it.

The darkness began to recede, triggering a peculiar kind of excitement. It was akin to the anticipation one felt when the lights went down just before a movie started. At this point three shapes appeared. They jutted out on either side of his periphery—one of the left, two on the right. *People*, Bell thought. *People checking me out.*

Then a new voice, much clearer than any of those he'd heard before—"Mr. Bell? Mr. Bell, can you hear me?"

He turned his head to the shape on the left. He was pretty sure that person was the speaker. His voice was soft, soothing, and patient.

"Mr. Bell? Michael? Can you hear me? Nod once if you can."

He did as instructed, or at least believed he did.

"Excellent."

The figures were becoming clearer now, but when he tried to blink his eyes felt like they were on fire. He went to rub them but still couldn't move his arms. When he tried to speak, bolts of pain shot up through the bones in his jaw. The joints felt ancient; mummy joints. He was sure they'd crumble if he tried them again.

"It might be best if you don't speak," the same person suggested. "At least not until you get something to drink."

Soon he could see his audience in detail. The guy on the left was without a doubt a doctor, with his white lab coat and his steel-rimmed glasses. Bell thought he looked like an accountant.

On the right were a pair of nurses. The one closest to him, he couldn't help noticing, wore one of those acrylic nurse's uniforms with the long zipper that ran up the front, and it was hitched down far enough to reveal the rounded tops of her considerable cleavage. As soon as Bell saw this, he felt a little better.

The second nurse didn't have quite the same effect. She was much older and heavier, with gray hair and a stern, almost grim face. Bell immediately thought of Nurse Ratched from *One Flew Over the Cuckoo's Nest*. It was one of the only novels he'd ever read. *She probably hasn't been laid since Eisenhower was in office.*

In spite of the doctor's orders, he tried his voice again. "Where am I?" came out in a dry croak. It was the voice of an old man.

"You're in St. Caroline's Memorial Hospital," Dr. Blackman told him. He made a conscious decision not to add, ". . . in intensive care" because he didn't want to alarm the patient.

A series of images flashed through Bell's mind—sitting in his car, leaning slightly to the right as he went through his CD collection, then being violently pushed forward. From his left the grill of a large truck filled the window, and then . . . nothing.

"I was in an accident," he said matter-of-factly.

"Yes, that's correct."

He looked at the younger nurse again, taking note of her face this time. She was a natural beauty, although in a purposely understated way. She was probably a suburban housewife; a soccer mom. The kind of girl who had inspired equal amounts of resentment and envy among the other girls in high school and college. Could've been a model, chose something more sensible and ordinary instead.

"I guess I survived it," he managed to say, studying her eyes, "although from here it looks like I'm in heaven."

The object of his current affections put on a tolerant

smile and busied herself with his pillows. The other nurse's expression didn't change a whit. The doctor laughed politely.

"Yes, you survived it. And you were very lucky, too. As I told your general manager, Mr. Sabino, if you weren't used to getting hit by all those linebackers, you might not have survived."

"What happened?"

"An elderly woman who was on medication struck you from behind, pushing you into a busy intersection. Then you were struck again, by a truck filled with railroad ties."

"Whoa."

The doctor laughed again. In that instant, somehow, Bell knew he was a fan.

" 'Whoa' is right. You're lucky you weren't killed. Your car wasn't so lucky, I regret to inform you. It's headed for the junkyard."

"How long have I been out of it? I haven't been gone for like ten years or anything, right?"

"No, just a few days. Frankly we were expecting you to come back any time. There doesn't appear to be any permanent damage to your brain, I'm very glad to say."

Bell managed a smile. "Other than the damage I already had, right?"

"Right."

He took a deep breath and closed his eyes. The burning came back with a vengeance. He tried to rub them again, and again his hand refused to obey. This time the motory disobedience filled Bell with a fear like none he'd ever known before.

"I can't move my hand!"

"I know." The doctor's voice had changed. The gentleness was still there, but the carefree aspect had vanished. It was more businesslike.

"Why not?"

"Because we've got your arms and legs restrained. We didn't want you moving around too much, which some people do even when they're comatose."

"And why would that be?"

Blackman and the nurses looked to each other.

"Michael, you suffered some spinal damage."

A cold finger touched the pit of Bell's stomach.

"I *what*?"

"Your spine suffered severe trauma during the accident."

"Do you mean I can't walk?"

"No, no, I don't mean that. It's too early to tell what the long-term effects will be."

"But my legs . . . I can feel them just fine."

The doctor motioned to the twin sister of Nurse Ratched, and together they removed the sheet from Bell's feet.

"Can you move your toes?"

Bell tried, but it was more difficult than he expected. All of a sudden this simple action required the supreme effort of his life. He strained like he was on the last mile of the Boston Marathon.

"Did they move?"

Doctor and nurse threw the sheet back to its original position. "Yes, there was some movement." Bell was relieved to see the doctor's smile return. "That's very good, especially at this stage."

"So I'll be able to walk again?"

Blackman said to the younger nurse, "Jennifer? Please tell Margie that Mr. Bell is back with us."

"Yes, doctor," she said before heading out. Bell did not follow her with his eyes. She didn't exist now.

"I can't predict the future, Michael, but as far as I can tell, yes, you'll be back to your normal self eventually."

"Full recovery?"

"I believe so."

"And I'll be able to play again?"

"I don't see why not."

Now it was his turn to smile. "Well that's great, doc. Fantastic. Just tell me what I have to do, and I'll do it."

"Good. Nurse Moreland here will oversee most of your physical therapy."

Bell shot her a quick look. Her eyes were already going over him. Probably searching for signs of weakness, he thought.

"How's it going, sweet thing?"

The doctor said quickly, "Uh, Michael, I'm going to check on some other patients now. But I'll be back in an hour or two to see how you're coming along."

"Okay, thanks, doc, I really appreciate it. I appreciate everything you've done so far."

Blackman put a comforting hand on his patient's shoulder. "It's been my pleasure. This is something of an honor for me—I'm a big fan of yours. Haven't missed a home game in three seasons."

"Thanks."

Just before he got to the door, Bell said, "Oh, one more thing, doc."

"Yes?"

"Minicamps start late next month. Will I be ready for them?"

Doctor and nurse looked to each other again. In that instant Bell knew the answer.

"No, I'm afraid not. I'm sorry, Michael, but you won't be able to play at all this season."

The numbness returned. Bell searched the ceiling for something to say, but no words were there. Then came with yet another concrete certainty—the team would try to replace him with Christian McKinley. And with that, to Bell's complete surprise, followed an almost drug-like feeling of relaxation. *Of course they would.* McKinley was the only other QB available that could get the job done. Bell knew it. He'd watched the kid, knew he had the right stuff. He even once thought, *Damn, he's as good as I am.* And that's how it went in this business—one day your were The Man, the next you were The Memory. He wanted to be upset, wanted to be frightened and angry, but he just couldn't muster it. He reached down, and it wasn't there. Just a sense of ease and, also to his surprise, a feeling of tremendous relief.

A smile broke across his face. "Well, it was great while it lasted," he told his two-person audience. They responded only with expressions of confusion.

"YOU'VE GOT THAT KID FROM FRESNO STATE," JON said into the phone. "Marcus Draper. He's a tremendous linebacker, and I'd be interested in acquiring him if you'd like to make a deal."

There was a pause, and then, "Well, let me think about it," Anderson said. Greg Anderson had been the GM of the Carolina Panthers for three years, and many theorized this would be his last. He was a competent man, but nothing more. No imagination, no willingness to take a risk. He'd built a team with mediocre talent, and thus the Panthers were just that—mediocre. Draper was a fourth-round draft acquisition from the previous management who'd turned out better than anyone expected, and he had a bright future to be sure.

Jon already knew Anderson didn't care for him very much. He knew about some of the snide remarks he'd made to the media. Sometimes Susan Schiff, in her unswerving loyalty, would Google Jon's name in search of interesting items, and if she found anything negative, no matter how small, she'd print it and leave it on his desk. Not to taunt him, but to make sure he knew who his enemies were. The latest Anderson comment came from the online version of *The Charlotte Observer*. When asked if he thought he would still have his job next season, Anderson replied, "We can't all have the security enjoyed by guys like Jon Sabino, who seems to have made a pact with the devil. Luck follows that guy around like cats follow garbage trucks." Jon was long used to this kind of petty jealousy; it was to be expected when one was successful. But was it so severe with Anderson that it would actually get in the way?

"Okay, how long? I'm sorry to push, Greg, but I'm running on a tight deadline with this one." Another pause, no response, and he added, "And I can make it a pretty good deal for you. I'm familiar with the details of Draper's contract, and I know your cap hit won't be that much if you give him up. But if you keep him, it could cost you. Give him to me for two less-expensive players and save yourself more cap stress next year. I'll give you two decent players that'll end up costing you less."

"Um. . . ." Jon could hear the sound of papers being shuffled. "Yeah, let me toss it around here a bit and see what happens."

Jon shook his head. *He's stalling on purpose. He's just busting my balls.*

"Okay, but can I ask when you'll get back to me?"

"I don't know. I'm just not sure."

More silence. Anderson was waiting; Jon could feel it.

"How about later today?"

"I can't, I won't be around."

"First thing tomorrow?"

"No, Mr. Burke won't be in all day."

"Okay, when?"

Anderson let out a long sigh. In that one gesture, the message was clear—*I'm trying to give you the runaround here, and you're not letting me get away with it.*

"I'll . . . I'll have to call you back." Jon was just about to reply to this when Anderson continued with, "You know, other teams are interested in Draper, too."

This was his idea of negotiation. About as awkward and clumsy as it got.

With thinly controlled anger, Jon said, "Like the Chiefs and the Seahawks? Yeah, I know."

"It'd be unfair of me to reneg on the deal I've been negotiating already."

If Jon could've reached through the phone and choked the bastard to death, he would've done so without hesitation. Having to come begging to this poster boy for the Peter Principle made him sick to his stomach. The guy knew it and was twisting the knife just for the fun of it.

"Well, perhaps we can do a *better* deal, Greg."

"I'm sorry, I don't think that's possible."

"You have no intention of helping me out here, do you?"

Another pause, and then, very quietly, "No, I don't."

JON WAS STILL BEHIND HIS DESK TWO HOURS AND four more fruitless phone calls later when he found Robert Macintosh leaning into his doorway, an eager look on his face.

Macintosh was invisible unless he wanted something. There were times when Jon didn't see him for weeks. He knew what Macintosh did, technically—he was an assistant in their marketing department. But whether he actually *did* anything related to marketing was another issue. He was almost ghostlike, a leftover from the previous regime who was harmless enough and, Jon believed, functional enough to be kept around. Whether he had any value beyond that, however, was still up for debate.

"Robert, what can I do for you?"

"Do you have a minute? Can I talk to you about something?"

"Sure, come on in and have a seat."

"Thanks."

Macintosh stepped in and, avoiding direct eye contact, made a beeline for one of the chairs. He was slim and good-looking, with dark hair and a fresh, boyish face. He wore plastic-rimmed glasses that made him look more like someone sitting outside a Paris café or wandering through an art museum than the front office of a football team. Otherwise he fit the image pretty well—the cotton trousers, the Polo button-down, the conservative haircut. Neat as a pin, as if he mother still dressed him every morning. In fact he dressed and groomed himself as he had done for the last thirty odd years, and he took great pains to make sure he always looked perfect.

Jon stood and stretched. "So what's up?"

"I, um . . . I heard Keith Armstrong got that communications position."

"Yes, I gave it to him today."

Macintosh nodded, looked around the room. He was hunched forward, his elbows on the armrests and his hands laced together.

"Why do you ask?"

"Oh, no reason." Macintosh laughed quietly. "I was kind of hoping for that spot myself, but that's how it goes. Keith's a good guy."

"Yes," Jon said, suddenly hoping there was a larger, more meaningful reason for this interruption than to praise the promotion of Keith Armstrong. "He's a very good guy."

Macintosh kept nodding. "There's one other position still open, I believe—that management spot in personnel. If it's okay with you, I'd like to be considered for that, too. I've been here eight years now and—"

"I'm sorry, Robert, but we're going to find someone outside for that job."

Macintosh turned, locking his eyes onto Jon's. "Outside?"

"Yeah. We want someone fresh, maybe even a little naive. Someone with new ideas, not someone stale. Someone who *hasn't* been here before."

"But I—"

"In fact I think we've already found someone. We'll be bringing him in one more time next week," Jon added quickly to avoid a bickering match about it.

Macintosh opened his mouth to say something more, then closed it again and went back to his affable, patronizing nods.

"I see, I see," Macintosh said. Then, abruptly, he stood and said, "Well, thanks very much for sparing me a few moments. I appreciate it."

"Sure. I'm sorry I couldn't give you better news. If something else opens up in the future and you're interested, let me know well ahead of time."

"I will, I definitely will. Thanks."

Macintosh turned and went out.

HE WAITED UNTIL JON WENT OUT FOR LUNCH, THEN ventured back to the top floor and found the sign he was hoping for—Peter Connally's door was open just a few inches. It was common knowledge around the Raven offices that this meant he was inside and available. Macintosh pushed it back gently and stuck his head in. Connally was behind his desk, turned sideways, reviewing some papers.

As always, Macintosh was surprised by what a *dump* Connally's office was. The furniture was worn, almost ratty, like stuff you'd find at a yard sale. The blinds hung crookedly. There were piles of papers on the desk, on the filing cabinets . . . everywhere. And the carpet looked as though it hadn't been vacuumed in months. Interestingly, however, there were no unpleasant odors. Connally appeared to be a clutterbug, but a hygienic clutterbug.

"Mr. Connally?"

"Yes?" He said it crisply, as if he'd known someone was there all along. He did not, however, stop reading.

"Can I talk to you for a minute?"

"Mm-hmm."

Macintosh slipped inside and came forward, unsure if he should invite himself into a chair. There were three of them, but two were occupied by more papers and folders.

Connally solved the problem by saying, "Have a seat."

Then he muttered, "Christ, these fucking assholes," and turned back, tossing the papers onto the desk in disgust. "All right, Macintosh, what can I do for you?"

The fact that Connally was the only one in the organization who never called him by his first name bothered Macintosh. He believed the formality was calculated to keep a distance between them, and this made him nervous. He'd had an easy, almost friendly relationship with the previous owner. This was by design. Schmoozing, he firmly believed, was integral to getting ahead in business. If you couldn't sidle up to the person who pulled the purse strings, you'd never go anywhere. And up to this point he did not feel he'd developed any warmth between himself and Peter Connally.

He leaned back and propped one leg on the knee of the other. He wanted to appear casual and chummy.

"I understand Jon Sabino gave Keith Armstrong that promotion in communications."

"Yes, I believe that's correct."

"Well, I'd like to be considered for the other position—the management job in personnel that Karen Dobler has now but will be vacating after she gets married next month."

Macintosh was proud of the confident delivery. It was the voice of a man worthy of such a request.

But Connally wasn't buying it. He shook his head, smiled, and reached for another pile of papers. "No, no . . . I don't think that would work out."

The quick dismissal was irritating. "You don't? Why not?"

"Because you're not a worker." Connally said. He made it sound as though everyone in the organization already knew this. "Karen comes in early and leaves late. She works on Saturdays, sometimes Sundays. That's not your style."

Macintosh didn't know how to respond. What rattled him the most was how accurately Connally had summed him up—and Connally barely noticed him most of the time! Between the Ravens and his numerous other business interests, he probably had between five hundred and a thousand employees. Yet he cut through the bullshit and squarely evaluated one tiny cog in the machine as if he'd been studying him for years.

The simple fact that Macintosh knew he wasn't deserving of the promotion, however, didn't stop him from arguing the point further.

"I work harder than you might think."

"Okay, maybe you do, but you're still not on Karen's level. In fact, I'm not sure what level you're on at all."

Macintosh didn't know what that meant, but he didn't like the sound of it.

"Every time I walk down the halls," Connally continued, sifting through a sea of papers to figure out what to read next, "I see you leaning against someone's doorway, talking to them. That not only means you're not getting anything done, it means *they're* not getting anything done, either. So you're wasting two people's time. And you don't even talk about Ravens' issues. You talk about books, movies, music, that kind of shit."

Macintosh's stomach tightened. How in the world did this guy who rarely saw him during the course of a day know all this? Did he have spies? Hidden cameras?

"I'll be honest with you. I've had moments where I thought about letting you go."

Connally made eye contact—direct and unflinching—for the first time. Macintosh was as stiff as a cigar-store Indian. That famous Connally bluntness. Was this the lead-in to an employee termination? By coming in here today, did he inadvertently give Connally an opportunity he'd been waiting for?

Macintosh was too punch drunk at this point to offer even a feeble response.

"Now, if you'd kindly get back to your office and go do something of productive value, I'd appreciate it. I've got a lot to do."

Macintosh would not remember rising from the chair and leaving. It was too dreamlike, too surreal. In fact he would not remember walking through the hallway and closing and locking his office door, either. His basic senses didn't really return until some hours later, by which time the humiliation had mellowed into something else.

MACINTOSH HAD NEVER ASKED HER WHERE SHE learned to cook. They'd been together almost eight months now, and never once had he asked her.

It was an amazing meal—rolled breast of veal with roasted potatoes, a warm goat cheese salad, and a bottle of Vernaccia di San Gimignano, one of the finest of all Tuscan white wines. She ate like this every night, he knew. She was an attorney, and not just any attorney—a corporate hawk in her fourth year at Henderson, Landers, and Flynn. Not a place for the faint of heart.

She hadn't said a word since they sat down. He watched her from his end of the long lacquered table; watched her without trying to *appear* as though he was watching her, as the city of Baltimore twinkled through the giant windows to his left. He didn't want to gawk, but it wasn't easy. She wasn't just beautiful, she was a goddamn knockout. Long black hair that hung straight down either side of her delicate face, small mouth, and the almond eyes of an A-list fashion model. He wondered again how he'd gotten so lucky. He wondered, but in truth he knew—he'd lied. When the key moments came, he'd lied. He'd lied about his importance to the team, about how much money he made, about the college he'd attended, everything. He was a good liar, and he wasn't afraid to make use of this talent.

She took another sip of the wine, carefully wiped her mouth, and replaced the linen napkin in her lap. Without looking up, she said, "So what happened with that promotion today? Did you get it?"

With the fork in midair, Macintosh froze. He'd hoped this subject wouldn't come up.

"They haven't ruled on it yet."

She continued eating as if she hadn't heard him.

"What are you going to do if you don't get it?" she asked eventually.

"I'll get it," he said.

"What if you don't?"

"Then I'll get something else."

She went silent again, and he went back to watching her. She had the greatest poker face of anyone he'd ever seen. If there was anything going on behind those eyes, he couldn't sense it.

Abruptly she said, "I won't be around this weekend. We've got to go to the West Coast to see a client."

Macintosh's stomach tightened. He knew what this meant—her boss, J. Ellis Northrup, had to see a client on the West Coast and wanted her to come with him. He'd been after her for ages. He was patient and calculating; he knew how to extract a woman from another man's grasp. He was richer, taller, leaner, better looking, and better educated than Macintosh could ever be; could ever even *lie* about being. They'd met once, at the firm's New Year's party just a few months ago. Northrup smiled, delivered a bone-crushing handshake, and studied his competition all night. As they were leaving, Macintosh caught one last glimpse of him from the corner of his eye. Northrup's expression seemed to indicate that he wasn't the least bit worried about whether or not he could pull Jenny Chandler away. This guy was ruthless, Macintosh thought. Made him feel like an amateur.

What unnerved Macintosh most was the realization that Jenny might not *mind* the idea of being taken by Northrup. It wasn't exactly a secret that she admired men of wealth, success, and power. Macintosh had to fake those things—Northrup actually had them. She never came out and said as much, but Macintosh was pretty certain she wasn't going to commit the rest of her life to a guy who trolled the lower ranks of life with the rest of the bottom feeders. She planned to move steadily upward, and if you couldn't help her, you wouldn't be allowed to stick around.

How much longer could he hold out? How much longer until the scales tipped in Northrup's favor? Was it already happening? Was the fact that he clearly wasn't going anywhere with the Ravens the deciding factor? He'd been with the team six years, and in that time he'd been given just one promotion—and that from Art Modell, the previous owner. Modell had promised him great things, and he had no doubt the old man would've kept those promises. But now. . . .

"Will you be gone long?" he asked. It sounded feeble and pathetic. The voice of a man who knows his wife is cheating on him but doesn't have the guts to confront her about it. He had a pretty good idea of what Jenny thought about people like that.

"About a week."

Macintosh nodded, straightened up, tried to appear unconcerned. He wanted to be sentimental, wanted to say something nakedly human like, "Think about me while you're out there," or "Try to miss me a little bit, because I'll be missing you," but there wasn't room in their relationship for this kind of talk.

"Well, have a good time."

She nodded, again without looking up.

The knot in Macintosh's stomach tightened even more.

Something in his professional life had to change, and fast.

DARRYL BAILEY BUILT HIS PERSONAL GYM IN THE basement of his Baltimore home. He wanted it there because it provided the kind of privacy he required during workouts. Other players he knew had theirs on the first floor, with French doors leading to sunny decks overlooking forested mountains or Olympic-size swimming pools. He would've found this distracting. There were two small windows in the foundation that could be opened inward to let in fresh air, but he'd had them covered with plywood and locked tight long ago.

The gym contained a variety of equipment, including full sets of freeweights and dumbbells, a squat rack, flat and incline benches, and a multifunction workout center. He also had a treadmill and a stationary bike. There were two TV sets hanging high in the corners, which he used to keep up with sports and world news via ESPN and CNN, respectively. Three of the four walls were bare cement painted white, the other covered with giant mirrors. There was a medicine ball on a cushioned mat, plus a set of jump ropes hanging from a hook. A tall cabinet contained neatly folded workout clothes—shorts, tank tops, jogging suits, lifting gloves, socks, sneakers, etc.—and was kept in order by the housekeeper. There was also a stereo with four speakers, through which he would, when in the right mood, pump rap music at an earsplitting volume.

His longtime offseason workout regimen had been two sessions per day—three hours in the morning, and three more in the afternoon. It wasn't as much as some other players', but he was consistent, and it was the continuity that provided the desired results. These workouts plus a good diet and a relatively clean lifestyle had kept him in peak shape and at his ideal weight, as dictated by his coaches, for so long. He had, in fact, found it surprisingly easy, because once you got into the routine it was no trouble to keep it going. Getting started was the hard part, but he'd passed that step many years ago. Now it was a normal part of his life.

Or at least it had been until three months ago, during the last few minutes of the championship game.

He'd gone over the play a thousands times in his mind, trying to figure out what went wrong. On the surface, it all seemed so ordinary. But then he'd heard that that was exactly how some of the worst injuries occurred—with no drama or fanfare.

There'd less than three minutes left, and they were beating the Panthers by the ridiculous score of 42–7. Blanchard wanted to take out his remaining starters—most of them were already on the bench, congratulating each other and mugging for the TV cameras—but DB felt particularly good that day and begged to stay in. Since Carolina's defense was exhausted and dispirited, Blanchard figured there was little harm. It was the last game of the year, and Carolina knew there was nothing left to fight for. Also, Carolina coach John Fox was a decent man and a personal friend of Blanchard's.

He wouldn't tolerate his players taking cheap shots out of bitterness.

With 2:34 remaining and the Ravens on their own 44, Bell, who at this point was calling the plays himself, decided on a relatively simple rollout that they hadn't used in a while. Bailey was thrilled—the last time they'd used it, he'd taken it in for a touchdown against the Colts, in Indianapolis. He already had one touchdown in this Super Bowl and had otherwise played flawlessly, including two key blocks that led to two of their three running touchdowns. Another score and he'd have a great shot at MVP.

From the snap, everything went perfectly. When the throw came from Bell it was a little high, so DB had to go up to get it. This wasn't a problem, as he'd had to do this on many occasions. He had also anticipated it, as he knew Bell's arm was growing tired. Michael had a habit of throwing harder than necessary toward the end of a game to compensate for fatigue. Bailey went up about three feet and caught the ball close to his right shoulder. A sixth sense that had evolved from experience told him that he'd be coming down around Carolina's 43 yard line, and that he had a clear field ahead of him. If he could land flat on his feet and take off quickly, he might be able to reach the end zone.

He also knew Sheldon Bishop, Carolina's strong safety, was speeding toward him. But he badly miscalculated Bishop's distance and was hit in the legs before he reached the turf. It wasn't a particularly hard hit, as Bishop's only goal was to kill the play and erase the possibility of another score and further humiliation.

Bailey's body spun like a propeller, becoming perfectly horizontal at one point. If he'd landed this way, he thought afterward, he would've been fine. Instead he continued to rotate, and when the grass finally came up to meet him, he landed on the side of his head, which caused his neck to twist sharply before the rest of him came crashing down.

From a fan's point of view—both at the game and at home—there was nothing unusual about the hit or the landing. Yes, it looked painful. Yes, Bishop had scored a few bragging points off his opponent. But hits like this were the norm. By the time the next snap was in Michael Bell's hands, it would be forgotten about. Probably wouldn't even make a highlight reel.

Bailey, lying there on the turf, felt the same way. His first thought was, *So much for the touchdown. Maybe I can still get it before the game's over.* He shook off the initial shock, as always, then let go of the ball, rolled onto his stomach, and pushed himself off the ground.

As he was about halfway up, however, his left arm gave way. It folded into a little less-than sign, and he tumbled over. He managed to get his left knee down before hitting the ground again, and he jumped quickly to his feet. *Get up, millions are watching you.* He jogged off the field with the rest of his team, doing his best to act as though nothing un-usual had happened. Just a little clumsy, that's all. The end of a long and exhausting season.

Steve Salem, the wide receivers coach, didn't say a word, so he hadn't noticed. Neither had any of the trainers or physicians. He was thankful for that. But he knew something wasn't right. By the time he got back to the bench, he was unable to lift his left arm higher than halfway without tremendous pain. If he kept it at his side, it felt both numb and tingly. The shoulder ached, and there was a burning in his neck. As it grew in intensity, he was able to form an ac-curate self-diagnosis—he had just acquired a stinger.

All players knew about stingers. DB got his details, anonymously, from a site he found on the Internet—*"A stinger occurs when the bundle of woven nerves that runs from the neck to the arm is stretched or compressed to the extreme. An electrical discharge follows, shooting down to the fingers. Afterwards, the athlete often will have trouble using the arm, and severe pain will appear in the neck and shoulder . . ."*

Most stingers lasted for just a few hours, sometimes a few days. But they could also be tricky. For an unlucky few, un-treated stingers became the beginning of the end of their ca-reers.

By contract, by league rule, and by rule of common sense, DB should have immediately reported the symptoms to Mendel. Instead, he made the fateful decision on that otherwise magnificent afternoon to keep them to himself. Next year would be the last of his contract with the team, and he would most likely have to think about finding a new home somewhere. No one wanted an injured player. While it was true most stingers went away, it was also true that, psychologically, many coaches and GMs were unable to overlook the fact that a player had had one in the first place. There was always concern about arm strength, about quickness, and about dexterity. If word got out, regardless of how well DB recovered, there would always be doubt. Each time he dropped a pass, each time he didn't quite reach high enough for a pass, someone would wonder if it was because of that stinger he got during the Super Bowl. So he decided to keep quiet about it and gamble that the condition would fade in time.

It did not.

By the third week he was able to lift his arm about three-quarters up and no more. By six weeks he could lift it over his head, but not without pain. And his ability to grip a ball had diminished. The tingling was still there, and some mornings after he'd slept on his left side the burning was unbearable. He didn't tell Bernadette about it; she would've been in his face and had him to a hospital in a flash. And he didn't dare tell Mendel or anyone else on the team. One of the stupidest mistakes a player could make was hiding an injury, but it wasn't as if he'd meant to hide it this long. He simply figured it would heal. He didn't figure the injury would get so bad so fast—if he didn't tell anyone about it the day it happened, he couldn't tell them at all.

He learned more about stingers by calling friends who'd had them, being careful to make it sound as though he wasn't calling solely for this reason. He put together what he believed to be an effective recovery program, one that he could follow at home, in private, without anyone else getting wise. The goal, of course, was to return to full health in time for minicamps. They were months away, after all. He could do it.

Now those camps were drawing so close that he could hear a clock ticking in his head, and the stinger was worse, not better. Some days the slightest movement made him wince. Once, in an absentminded moment, he'd reached up on a high shelf to remove a flower vase for Bernadette and ended up dropping it on her head. The accident turned out to be advantageous because it explained why he cried out. She never suspected a thing.

But he knew he was in trouble—deep, serious trouble. If word got out, the team would not only cut him, they'd have legal right to deny him another penny. He stood to earn more than three million next year, plus another two on his pro-rated signing bonus. And then his next contract would come—The Big One. Unless you were drafted high in the first round, your first pro contract was rarely The Big One. You signed your first one, made some decent money, and then played your ass off in the hopes of scoring *huge* on the second. That was the model the most ambitious players followed—including him. His first contract had been terrific, thanks to the generosity and faith of Jon Sabino. But the next one was to be the deal that changed not only his life, but the lives of those he loved. It would be the one that provided for his eventual children, and his grandchildren. It would be the one that carried his very lineage to the next level *and kept it there*. No more struggles, no more wanting, for generations. The first deal gave a player the nice house, the nice car, the nice vacations. But it was the fabled follow-up deal that had the *lasting* effect. A vision of grandeur, perhaps, but it was within reach. This was the dream, the only objective. It was everything he'd worked for, everything he'd prayed for. And now, because of one mistake—*one goddamn mistake*—all would be lost. His career would be over, and he'd leave the league in disgrace. Sometimes, when Bernadette wasn't around, he'd sit and worry about it for hours, turning it over and over in his mind. But there was no way to turn back, so he moved forward and hoped for a miracle.

Bernadette walked into the gym with her jacket on and her bag slung over her shoulder. At twenty-six she was, technically, still a student. As both her parents were university professors, she, too, had contemplated a career in the academic community. But after receiving her masters in psychology, she took a few years off to make a final decision. She met Darryl during this period, at a banquet dinner honoring wealthy donors to a children's hospital. Now she was making a final run toward her psych Ph. D., with the hopes of opening a private practice soon thereafter. Aside from her remarkable mental talents, she also had the body of a fashion model and the presence of a movie star.

"Hey, I'm leaving," she said, taking a pair of leather gloves out of her pockets and wriggling her fingers into them.

Darryl turned, surprised, as he hadn't heard her come in. He was massaging his shoulder and occasionally grimacing in pain, but, fortunately, was not facing the doorway. *Lucky this time*, he thought. *In the future, I keep the door closed.* If she'd seen him agonizing, she'd make inquiries. The problem with being in a relationship with a shrink was that you couldn't hide much.

He smiled, of course. "Okay, sweetheart." He walked over to her. "Where to?"

"I'm going to meet Francesca at McNally's."

"Tell her I said hello."

"I will."

A brief kiss, and when they parted she did a quick study of his face. *Taking my mental temperature,* he thought, using a phrase he'd learned from her. *Habit.* She always did it, wasn't able *not* to do it. He knew it was because she loved him, cared about him. But it was still unsettling at times.

"See you later."

"See ya."

After she was gone, he sat on the edge of his flat bench and curled a fifty-pound dumbbell with the arm. It always hurt at the beginning, but it got a little better after the first ten or twenty lifts. That was all, though—only a *little* better, and a little wasn't enough. More importantly, however, was the fact that, over time, the arm wasn't improving. Under normal circumstances it should have.

After the curls, he held the dumbbell loose at his side and brought the arm up straight, very slowly. The higher it got, the greater the pain. By the time his arm was at a ninety-degree angle, he was puffing and sweating, his teeth clenched in agony. When he couldn't stand it any longer he brought the weight back down, but the moment the burning subsided he started again.

After ten such lifts, he was hurting so bad that he could barely lift the arm at all. He knew this was a bad sign. No, it was worse than bad—*The arm is growing useless,* he thought for the very first time, and it terrified him. It was beyond the point where he could hide it now. He was being forced to confront it. He *had* to tell someone. His plan to do this in secret was failing.

As all the frustration finally exploded inside, he screamed out *"Goddammit!!!"* and, in enraged defiance, forced the arm up, dumbbell still in hand, as high as it would go.

The overloaded bolt of heat and energy that flashed through his body was, he was certain, worse than a gunshot. The dumbbell dropped from his hand and hit the floor with a dull thud. He dropped along with it, clutching his shoulder tight in an attempt to cut off any feeling. Bernadette could've still been upstairs, for all he knew. In spite of this, he was unable to hold back a scream that would've chilled a murderer's heart.

After a prolonged period of moaning and writhing, Bailey managed to crawl to the door leading to a smaller adjoining room. It was their utility room, complete with washer and dryer, slop sink, and water heater. Wrapping his good hand around the edge of the sink, he pulled himself to his feet, then used the same good arm to push aside one of the tiles in the hung ceiling. The paper bag was exactly where he'd hidden it. As the throbbing continued merciless and unabated, he went to bury the needle into his shoulder. This, he knew, was likely to be the worst injection ever. He found an ankle sock in a basket full of dirty laundry and, without the slightest hesitation, stuffed it into his mouth. He was faintly aware of the gross taste but had his mind on much bigger things and couldn't have cared less.

He stuck the needle in and pushed the plunger down at the same time. The pain nearly blinded him, and his screams were so powerful that it took only seconds for his throat to turn raw. He crumbled to the cement floor.

When he finally began to feel normal again, some fifteen minutes later, he got to his feet again and put the spent bottle and needle, along with the remaining dosages and their companion needles, back into the brown paper bag. Then, his chest still heaving, he replaced the bag in the ceiling and slid the panel over. He leaned against the washing machine for what felt like a long time, eyes closed, waiting for his heart rate to drop. Then he walked out of the room on weakened legs and continued through the gym and back upstairs.

The problem wasn't getting any better.

9

JON FELT LIKE HE'D NEVER LEFT HIS OFFICE. IT HAD
all been a blur.

He walked out the previous night just after eleven and got
home just before midnight. His brain was numb to the core.
He couldn't feel anything, couldn't hear anything, could
barely see anything. His eyes were red and puffy, and they
stung like hell.

He came into the house as quietly as he could, laying his
bag and his jacket on a big chair in the living room. Everything was dark and quiet, a world of shadows and night-lights.
He stripped to his boxers and crawled gently into bed next to
Kelley, hoping he wouldn't wake her. The baby monitor
hissed with white noise on the nightstand. He let out a long,
weary breath and set his head on the pillow. No sooner had he
done so than the alarm went off, beeping with the urgency of
an intruder-alert system in a government installation.

He slapped the snooze bar and cursed, wondering if the
damn thing was defective. *I just laid down, for Christ's sake!*
Then he saw that it was exactly four-fifteen in the morning.
The last four hours had passed as though they were mere
seconds.

He didn't feel any more rested, but there was little he

could do about it. He shook his head and reminded himself again of how much he loved his job and that he wanted to continue doing it. He threw the covers back and hustled into the adjoining bathroom, where he showered and shaved. Then into a new pair of khaki trousers and a Ravens polo, and he was downstairs stuffing a banana into his mouth. As he stalked back out the door, he realized he hadn't actually *seen* Kelley at any point. Lately she was just a shape under the sheets.

He didn't listen to the radio on the way in. He wanted to maintain the silence so he could continue going over deal possibilities. He'd done this so many times in the last few days he felt like one of those stats wizards who could quote every significant number pertaining to every player in the league since the merger. He swore he knew every bit of data about defensive guy on every team. He could write a god-damn book about them.

Susan Schiff, much to his gratitude, was already in the office, ready to roll. She had his paperwork organized on his desk and a mug of steaming coffee on its coaster. She wasn't anywhere in sight when he came in, but he realized she'd already been there a while.

He got into his chair and took a long sip of the coffee. She always made it just right. When the mug was half empty, he set it aside and dove right into the day's torture. He turned on his computer, launched Microsoft Excel, and first went to his own roster, into which he'd been keeping notes—

RAVENS ROSTER W/NOTES FROM CARY BLANCHARD

#	NAME	POS.	HT.	WT.	YRS.	COLLEGE	NOTES
11	Scott Clark	QB	6-4	208	2	Brigham Young	CAN TRADE (not to Henderson—no offensive players)
~~20~~	~~Milton Love~~	~~S~~	~~6-2~~	~~211~~	~~3~~	~~Troy State~~	~~Include in deal with Skip~~

(continued on next page)

RAVENS ROSTER W/NOTES FROM CARY BLANCHARD *(continued)*

#	NAME	POS.	HT.	WT.	YRS.	COLLEGE	NOTES
23	Greg Buckley	CB	6-1	199	9	Western Illinois	CAN TRADE (not to Henderson—he already said he doesn't want him)
30	Buster McDaniels	RB	5-11	201	7	Mississippi	To Steelers for Willie Gunther
32	Aaron Holloway	RB	6-1	205	2	Florida State	CAN TRADE (not to Henderson—no offensive players)
33	Nick Wakefield	CB	6-0	201	R	Auburn	CAN TRADE (not to Henderson—no rookies)
34	Andre Jenkins	S	6-1	214	R	Temple	CAN TRADE (not to Henderson—no rookies)
51	Brian Northbrook	LB	6-2	240	4	Arkansas State	CAN TRADE (not to Henderson—he already said he doesn't want him)
53	Brett Savage	LB	6-4	250	11	Washington State	CAN TRADE (not to Henderson—he already said he doesn't want him)
61	Jared Cope	G	6-2	310	8	Georgia Tech	To Steelers for Willie Gunther
66	Barrett Blake	G	6-3	305	R	Stanford	To Patriots for Lyle Jameson
67	Jason Freemont	LC	6-6	277	7	Texas Tech	CAN TRADE (not to Henderson—no offensive players)
69	Scott Montgomery	G	6-3	324	11	Illinois	CAN TRADE (not to Henderson—no offensive players)
71	Keith Kubat	T	6-5	277	8	Hofstra	To Patriots for Lyle Jameson

(continued on next page)

RAVENS ROSTER W/NOTES FROM GARY BLANCHARD *(continued)*

#	NAME	POS.	HT.	WT.	YRS.	COLLEGE	NOTES
82	Jordan Patterson	WR	6-1	203	R	Kentucky	CAN TRADE (not to Henderson—no offensive players)
84	Sam Sargent	TE	6-6	261	3	West Virginia	CAN TRADE (not to Henderson—no offensive players)
89	Kevin Curtis	DT	6-3	274	R	Rutgers	CAN TRADE (not to Henderson—no rookies)
90	Corey Holbrook	DE	6-4	277	9	Syracuse	CAN TRADE (not to Henderson—he already said he doesn't want him)
92	Donald Harper	DT	6-3	277	8	Florida State	CAN TRADE (not to Henderson—he already said he doesn't want him)
96	Alan Hill	DE	6-3	274	R	Temple	CAN TRADE (not to Henderson—he already said he doesn't want him)
12	Nate Brown	QB	6-4	207	10	Penn State	PREFER TO KEEP
26	Pete Wolverton	S	6-2	220	4	Iowa	PREFER TO KEEP
28	TJ Matthews	RB	6-0	200	5	Wisconsin	PREFER TO KEEP
31	~~Walter Bartlett~~	~~CB~~	~~6-3~~	~~201~~	~~2~~	~~Kansas State~~	~~included in deal with Skip~~
57	Ryan Mason	LB	6-5	242	2	Baylor	PREFER TO KEEP
85	Raymont Carter	WR	6-1	198	2	Troy State	PREFER TO KEEP
91	George Kontoleon	DT	6-2	275	2	Purdue	PREFER TO KEEP
98	Ted Forrest	DE	6-2	276	4	Texas A&M	PREFER TO KEEP
3	Terry Butler	K	5-11	205	6	Virginia	STARTER—DO NOT TRADE
8	Michael Bell	QB	6-5	210	5	LSU	STARTER—DO NOT TRADE
13	Steve Russell	P	6-1	205	5	Kansas State	STARTER—DO NOT TRADE
21	Paul Ellis	FB	6-1	235	4	Tennessee	STARTER—DO NOT TRADE
22	Chris Redmond	S	6-0	209	8	Illinois	STARTER—DO NOT TRADE
24	Harold Rowling	CB	6-1	203	3	Michigan	STARTER—DO NOT TRADE

(continued on next page)

RAVENS ROSTER W/NOTES FROM GARY BLANCHARD *(continued)*

#	NAME	POS.	HT.	WT.	YRS.	COLLEGE	NOTES
25	Thomas Rhodes	CB	6-0	205	7	UCLA	STARTER—DO NOT TRADE
27	Lawrence Dixon	RB	6-1	202	3	Virginia	STARTER—DO NOT TRADE
29	Herb Axelrod	S	6-1	217	6	Northern Arizona	STARTER—DO NOT TRADE
52	Elliot Easton	LB	6-3	243	6	Wake Forest	STARTER—DO NOT TRADE
54	Earle Webster	LB	6-4	244	2	Purdue	STARTER—DO NOT TRADE
56	Larry Townsend	LB	6-6	247	5	Alabama	STARTER—DO NOT TRADE
60	Derrick Gorden	C	6-4	312	4	Penn State	STARTER—DO NOT TRADE
63	Matt Israel	G	6-1	312	4	Miami	STARTER—DO NOT TRADE
68	Shaun Erickson	G	6-1	320	7	Michigan	STARTER—DO NOT TRADE
70	Frank James	T	6-4	263	5	Rutgers	STARTER—DO NOT TRADE
74	Craig Little	T	6-6	278	9	Maryland	STARTER—DO NOT TRADE
80	Ryan Hart	TE	6-4	250	7	Kentucky	STARTER—DO NOT TRADE
81	Anthony Jennings	WR	6-4	209	6	Mississippi	STARTER—DO NOT TRADE
87	Darryl Bailey	WR	6-0	200	5	North Carolina St	STARTER—DO NOT TRADE
88	Tony Kramer	WR	6-3	211	3	Notre Dame	STARTER—DO NOT TRADE
93	Jon Harris	DE	6-6	281	3	Virginia	STARTER—DO NOT TRADE
94	Dexter Simmons	DE	6-3	280	7	Wisconsin	STARTER—DO NOT TRADE
95	Tony Seidl	DT	6-5	280	5	Miami	STARTER—DO NOT TRADE
97	Howard Sawyer	DT	6-4	277	6	Iowa	STARTER—DO NOT TRADE

Then he turned to his updated list of draft picks—

RAVENS DRAFT PICKS

YEAR	PICK	NOTES
Current	1st round/32nd overall	
	~~2nd round/44th overall~~	~~To Bengals for Martin Brynmoor~~
	~~2nd round/64th overall~~	~~To Patriots for Lyle Jameson~~
	~~3rd round/96th overall~~	~~To Patriots for Lyle Jameson~~
	~~6th round/182nd overall~~	~~To Broncos for Willie Gunther~~
	~~7th round/224th overall~~	~~To Broncos for Willie Gunther~~

(continued on next page)

RAVENS DRAFT PICKS *(continued)*

YEAR	PICK	NOTES
2007	1st round	
	2nd round	~~To Steelers for Willie Gunther~~
	~~3rd round~~	~~To Bengals for Martin Brynmoor~~
	~~4th round~~	~~To Bengals for Martin Brynmoor~~
	5th round	
	6th round	
	7th round	
2008	1st round	
	~~2nd round~~	~~To Bengals for Martin Brynmoor~~
	3rd round	
	4th round	
	5th round	
	6th round	
	7th round	

And finally to the new, and certainly most important, list he had created in the last few days—

DEFENSIVE PACKAGE FOR SKIP HENDERSON

POS.	NAME	HT.	WT.	YRS.	COLLEGE	NOTES
CB	Walter Bartlett	6-3	201	2	Kansas State	From our own roster
CB						
DE	Willie Gunther	6-3	291	2	Purdue	To be rec'd from Steelers in exchange for Buster McDaniels, Jared Cope, and 6th- and 7th-round picks this year, and 2nd-round pick next year.

(continued on next page)

DEFENSIVE PACKAGE FOR SKIP HENDERSON *(continued)*

POS.	NAME	HT.	WT.	YRS.	COLLEGE	NOTES
DE DT DT	Lyle Jameson	6-4	303	4	Georgia	To be rec'd from Patriots in exchange for Barrett Blake, Keith Kubat, and 2nd-round pick (96th overall) and 3rd-round pick this year.
LB LB S S	Milton Love	6-2	211	3	Troy State	From our own roster

The first one was the most depressing. What a mess. The draft picks he didn't mind so much. But the players—the *guys*. He was throwing them out there like poker chips. And all for the sake of one man.

If McKinley doesn't pan out, they're going to come to my house and hang me from the nearest phone pole.

He was still six defensive players away from a solid package. The two he'd received from other teams so far had been expensive. How would it go from here? Part of him didn't want to know. He wanted this to be nothing more than a bad dream. He wanted to wake up and find himself lying in bed at home, with Kelley and Lauren next to him, Michael Bell still in perfect health . . .

With a deep sigh he turned back to the list of talent that might be available around the league. The first five names were crossed off. Two of them were now part of the package for Henderson. Technically they didn't represent final deals but instead tender offers; little more than a gentleman's agreement. So, in a sense, they were hypothetical at best. But all parties had given their word. No one would back out. They'd be crazy considering what Jon had given up.

The seventh name on the list was that of Martin Brynmoor. A second-string, third-year defensive tackle on the Bengals. Very talented, showed great promise when their starter went down with a broken leg the previous season. People were watching him now. His contract was ending this year, and it was no secret that he wanted to move on from Cincinnati. He and the head coach didn't get along, so he was seeing minimal playing time. Brynmoor was a difference maker, and he wanted out.

The problem was that getting him meant going through the team's GM, Tommy Greer. Jon groaned. Greer was sharp—too sharp. Dealing with him was like dealing with a mind reader. Jon admired and respected his business skills, but secretly wished he could turned them off like a light when *he* had to deal with the guy.

The phone rang twice and an assistant answered. She put Jon on hold for a moment, then Greer came on—

"Jon Sabino!"

"Good morning, Tommy."

"How's it going?"

"Could be better."

"So I've heard. What can I do for you?"

"I'm interested in making a deal for one of your guys, if you're interested."

"Which one?"

"Martin Brynmoor."

"Brynmoor?" Jon could hear papers being shuffled. He shook his head.

"The defensive tackle, Tommy. From Loyola."

"Our defensive tackle from Loyola."

"That's him. Six-five, three hundred and seven pounds. Going into the third year of his contract."

"Correct. Third and final."

"Right. . . . He's been a real contributor to this club," Greer said, beginning the sales pitch Jon knew was coming.

"He hasn't played much, but when he has, he's been pretty good. He averaged three solo tackles and three assists per game when he filled in for Jenkins last year. Not bad for someone who came off the bench."

"Yeah, he's decent," Jon replied, ready with his counter-pitch. "But he's also a second-stringer, and frankly, Tommy, he knows he's good. He's had a chance to show his stuff. Others are sniffing him out now. Good DTs are hard to come by. It's not a glamour position, but he's a natural. He's big and strong, and he's quick as hell. He's coming into the prime of his career, and he'll want a good contract next time. Trust me, Tommy, he'll be looking to move up. He's going to cost you."

This was the phrase that would get him, Jon knew. If there was one thing Tommy Greer was not allowed to do in that organization, it was spend money.

There was a pause, and Jon smiled. He had a pretty good idea what was going on in Greer's mind at the moment.

"You think so, huh?"

"Definitely," Jon said. "He's in the perfect position to ask for a raise, so to speak."

"We got him cheap the first time. He was a fifth-round pick."

"That was then, this is now. His value has gone up. And with other teams looking his way, he knows he's in a good position to make a deal."

"I don't think we could really help him with that," Greer said quietly, almost to himself.

"Then let me take him off your hands. I promise to give you some guys who won't be pawing at you for every dime. You can have some draft picks, too." Jon laughed. "They almost always come cheap, right?"

Greer laughed, too. They were suddenly good buddies. "Right, sure. Okay, what do you have in mind?"

"How about Kevin Curtis, the defensive tackle we picked up in the draft last year? He's a rookie and he hasn't played a down yet. He's not costing us much, so he should be a good replacement for Brynmoor."

"Okay, I'm writing him down."

"And I see your running game's a little thin," Jon said. *Last in the league in yards per run and yards overall*, he thought. *Calling their running game "a little thin" is being saintly.* "How about Aaron Holloway? He's in his second year and looking pretty good. We simply don't need another guy in that position."

"Okay . . ."

"Finally, I can give you three draft picks—our second from this year, and our third for next year. That's a total of four players, none of whom should put a strain on your wallet."

He could hear Greer mumbling, going over everything in his mind.

"Yeah, that's pretty good," he said finally. "That'd sure help us out."

"Great. So we have a deal?"

"Uh, no."

It was said with such decisiveness that Jon found himself dumbstruck.

"No?"

"That's right."

Jon tapped the point of his pencil on his legal pad. "Not enough?"

"Not nearly enough."

"Not *nearly* enough? Four players for *one guy*? A guy who has only played in *eight games*?"

"That's right. I know it doesn't sound nice, but I know what you're trying to do, what package you're trying to put together. You want McKinley. Even better—at least from my perspective, is the fact that you *need* him. Am I right?"

Now Jon paused. And every moment of silence that passed, Jon knew, put him in a shittier position.

"Well, I don't know about *nee*—"

"More, Jon," Greer said in a tone that was absolutely chilling. "If you want me to give this guy to you instead of the Chiefs, I want more."

There was another long silence, until Jon finally said, "Okay, let me take a look at what I have."

BRENDAN CAVANAUGH RETURNED TO HIS OFFICE WITH mug of fresh coffee. The mug, of course, bore the Broncos' logo. His secretary walked in with a pile of mail bound by a rubber band.

"Here's today's," she said, dropping it into his wire basket.

He pulled off the rubber band and began sifting. A few magazines, a catalog, a letter from an agent, a letter from the league . . . and then a nice-looking envelope with a name on the return address that had a familiar ring—Robert Macintosh.

He took a brass opener from the drawer and slit the top. Inside were three items—a cover letter, a business card, and a résumé.

The business card caught his attention simply because it had the Ravens' logo on it. Setting it aside, he read through the cover letter. Macintosh was wondering if the Broncos had any positions available now or in the near future. His tone was polite and professional, but between the lines was the voice of someone who was looking to escape. He gave no official reason as to *why* he sought employment elsewhere; no "I'm getting married and moving up there," or "The company has announced a series of layoffs starting in two weeks." No explanation at all.

More clues could be found in the résumé itself—Macintosh had been with the Ravens a while. Too long, in fact, to not have reached the next rung on the ladder. For whatever reason, he felt his time in Baltimore had run its course. The future lay elsewhere. Maybe someone had taken a disliking to him. It happened all the time in the league. If one of your superiors didn't like you, you were finished. Cavanaugh knew this all too well—he'd held more people down than he could remember.

But this was more than that. This was opportunity knocking. In a matter of seconds, Brendan Cavanaugh had a fully formed plan in his mind. Every nuance, every detail—and if it played out correctly, it would pay huge dividends. If it didn't . . . well, he knew how to protect himself in that event. But it would. He was going to make sure of that.

He replaced the contents of the letter and, smiling, slipped the envelope into his briefcase.

GARRICK HART WAS UNHAPPY. NOTHING NEW THERE, Freddie Friedman thought. But when a player of Hart's caliber was unhappy, you had to deal with it. As much as you wanted to tell him to grow up and shut up, you couldn't. Not when he was making just over four million dollars a year and 15 percent of it was yours. When a client like that had a problem, you went from agent to parent, best friend, and/or therapist. Freddie didn't like it, but he didn't hate it, either. It simply went with the job.

"I realize they haven't finalized the lease yet, but trust me, they will. In the meantime, loan your girlfriend one of your other cars. It shouldn't be for more than a week or two. Just make sure your wife doesn't find out. The last thing you need right now is marital problems."

He moved freely around the office with the aid of a telephone headset. It had become a permanent part of his anatomy. He had three power packs for it—one main, one spare, and one for emergencies. Few things made him more nervous than the prospect of a dead battery. The mere thought of using an "old-style" telephone with a cord, or even a cordless phone that had to be supported with your shoulder, made him cringe. He liked to have both hands free to do other things. If he couldn't do more than one thing at a time he got restless.

"Yes, yes . . . I understand she wants that model, but it isn't available in America. The team is having one shipped from Germany this week. I saw a copy of the flight manifest. It should be here in a day or two. . . ."

His office was spacious and tastefully decorated, but not overly so. The centerpiece was a kidney-shaped desk buried under piles of paperwork. Behind it, through a gigantic single pane of glass, lay the misty Adirondack Mountains. The view was breathtaking by anyone's standards, like a postcard come to life. Freddie admired it from time to time but suspected he didn't appreciate it as much as others would. Visitors always commented on it, though.

"If the car isn't delivered by the beginning of next week, give me a call back and I'll rattle some cages. . . ."

He liked to keep a casual atmosphere around the office. There were only twelve other people in the company—Good Sports, Ltd.—so there was no need for a tight-ass corporate mentality. On most days he wore a dress shirt (pastels with a white collar) but no tie, and suspenders but no blazer. He removed his shoes the moment he came in, as he secretly loved the feeling of the freshly vacuumed carpet under his silk socks.

While Hart continued to whine (but was losing steam, thank goodness), Freddie's secretary came in. She was hunched over as she struggled to keep the day's mail—a pile of letters and a few packages, one of which was Pearly Pressner's—against her chest. She hurried to nearest corner of the desk and dropped the load just in time.

As she turned to leave, Freddie expertly pressed the mute button on the transmitter and said, "Janey, could you please dig up the files for Grant Cole, Michael Harris, and Todd Blakely? I'm especially interested in Todd's contract. There's a conditional clause I'd like to review before I call him this afternoon. Thanks." Just before he disengaged the mute button, he added, "Oh, and please wish Tommy a happy birthday for me, would you? Give him a copy of that new Tom Clancy book and put it on my account."

In all of her thirty-two years, Janey Davidson had never known anyone with Friedman's power of retention. The Blakely contract was a prime example—it'd been finalized almost three years ago, and Freddie hadn't glanced at it once since then. Yet he had just recalled a tiny facet of it as if it'd been drafted yesterday. And he always remembered her husband's birthday every year, without fail, no matter how much other stuff was going on.

She went out, and Freddie reluctantly returned to his babysitting.

"Right, uh-huh . . . I understand. Yes, I know. I know they are. Well, don't worry about it, I'll take care of it. Okay. And don't forget that you have a photo shoot with Adidas on the twenty-ninth. You missed the last one and they were pretty pissed. What's that? No, I don't think she'd be interested . . . right, okay. Have a great time in St. Croix. Have a few on me. Talk to you later."

He terminated the connection, called Hart a douchebag, and began digging through the pile of new mail, all the while placing another call.

"Janey! Are you having trouble finding those files?"

"No," came her muted reply from the next room. The door was open, but just a crack. "Just give me a minute!"

He got behind his desk while the call went through, grumbling something about minutes being money, and went through the letters. All junk, he decided, and tossed them aside.

The first two packages weren't much better. One of them, he could tell by the return address, was a signed jersey from one of his clients who played for the Rams. Freddie asked for it as a get-well gift for the twelve-year-old son of one of his employees. The other package came from the NBA and looked semiofficial, but not official enough to warrant immediate attention. It, too, was relegated to a secondary sector of the desk.

The final item was a cardboard box that shined from all the clear tape that'd been wrapped around it. The handwriting was nearly illegible; the sender was lucky it got here, Friedman thought. He glanced at the name on the return address—Joe Pressner.

Pressner? Why is that name familiar?

He took a folding knife from his pocket and began slicing.

Pressner . . . Pressner . . .

His heart sank when he saw the videotapes. He got unsolicited "showcase" material all the time. His first impulse in these instances was to have Janey send them back with a polite rejection note. But he rarely followed that impulse—and he didn't follow it now, either. Not because of the familiarity of the name Pressner, but because you just never knew. There was a lot of talent out there, and Freddie had been around long enough to know the age-old adage about the cream always rising to the top was a load of bullshit. The ugly truth was sometimes it got stuck on the way up, and other times it never got off the bottom to begin with.

He unfolded Pearly's letter and sat down. At the same moment he heard a young female voice say, "Hello?"

"Hi, this is Freddie. Is Tory around?"

"Hold on, I'll get him."

He read through the letter as he waited, thinking how familiar the sentiments were—*I feel my boy has the potential to play in the NFL . . . he's good but no one has noticed him yet . . .* There didn't seem to be anything new here. There were a lot of tapes in the box. Maybe—just maybe—if he had time at the end of the day he'd check one out.

Then his eyes landed on the name of Quincy Pressner and stuck there.

No . . .

"Yeah, hello?" said a deep, gruff voice, but Freddie barely heard it. "Hey, Freddie, are you there, man?"

"Huh? Oh . . . sorry, Tory. What's up?"

"What's up?! You called *me.*"

"I what? Oh, right. I'm sorry. Hey, can I call you back?" Whatever he'd wanted Tory Trask, Kansas City's perennial Pro Bowl tackle, for, it could wait.

"What? Look, Freddie, I'm kind of busy right n—"

"Thanks, Tory," he said. His voice was distant, dreamy. "I'll talk to you in a few."

He terminated the connection before Trask had a chance to object and pulled the headset down around his neck. Then he read the letter again . . . and again and again. He consid-

ered the possibility that it was a practical joke; a little something from one of his clients or that one peckerhead VP from
the league offices in NYC who considered himself something of a comedian.

No . . . this is no joke.

Within five minutes the Adirondacks were hidden behind
an electronic sliding curtain and the lights were dimmed. By
the time he finished watching the first tape, he was reaching
for the phone.

ERIC ROSS WAS A CONGENIAL MAN OF SIXTY-TWO. HE
first met Freddie Friedman back in 1988. At that time Freddie wasn't much more than a greasy-haired kid who spoke
too fast and knew too little. But the more reserved Ross had
a gut feeling the youngster might just make something of
himself in the agenting business.

The fact that Ross turned out to be right came as a surprise to no one—he'd been the top scout of his day, as close
to a legend as one could get in that discipline. He'd predicted
the ascent of many greats—Dan Marino, Jerry Rice, Joe
Montana. Every time he got "that feeling" about someone,
that someone turned into a superstar.

He spent the bulk of his career with the Buffalo Bills,
toward the end of the era when there was still a modicum of
job security in the league. He began as a ball boy and
worked his way up, and by his tenth year he was their head
scout.

He stayed in touch with his friends after retiring in 1997,
and that included Freddie Friedman. He did freelance con-
sultation for him from time to time, helping Freddie avoid
various disasters. One time he talked him out of signing a
running back who would eventually be drafted with the first
overall pick. Freddie was furious, but Ross told him in his
normally relaxed way to sit tight and see what happened.
Sure enough the kid broke his leg in only his second game.
The fracture didn't heal properly, and he never played an-

other down. Freddie could never figure out how Eric foresaw that one, but he never doubted him again.

Now he sat on the other side of Freddie's desk, Scotch in hand, dressed in the standard uniform of the comfortably retired—loafers, cotton slacks, and a polo shirt. The latter bore a Bills logo. He was still a company man at heart.

"Do you still talk with any of the boys?" Friedman asked.

"Sometimes." He sipped his Scotch. "But it's tough, you know, with my busy schedule." He grinned broadly.

"Oh yeah, I can imagine. Golf every morning, dinner out every night. Sounds like torture."

"It is, believe me."

"Who have you seen on the field lately that you like?"

Ross gave the question some thought. "Are you looking for more clients?"

"Always, but that's not why I'm asking. I'm just kinda curious."

"Mmm. Well . . . Christian McKinley is the real thing, no doubt about it."

Freddie nodded. "He's all you hear about. You'd think no one else was being drafted this year."

"Gary Goldman's already got him," Ross teased.

"Yeah, yeah . . . Goldman gets all of them. Tell me something I don't know."

"McKinley's got amazing potential. If he stays healthy and has good coaches to guide and develop him, he'll be a Hall of Famer. I guarantee it."

"I don't doubt it. Who else?"

"Well, there's Franklin from Florida, and Darby from Virginia Tech. And you know who looks like a sweet lower-round pick is that receiver from Boston College, Aldrich Dawson. He was out most of his senior year with an injury, so a lot of the scouts didn't see him. But he was phenomenal before that."

Freddie nodded and scribbled a quick note to check into Dawson when he got a moment.

"Remember," Ross went on, "Curtis Martin didn't really

play in his senior year, either, so Parcells and Mo Carthon got him for a song and a dance. Now he's on his way to Canton, too." Ross downed the rest of the Scotch. "There are so many good players the scouts miss these days. So many."

It was a commonly accepted fact of life around the league that many gifted athletes got overlooked. That was the greatest irony. People like Kurt Warner and Tom Brady were considered "amazing discoveries," great talents who somehow got lost in the shuffle and were given opportunities only because a coach's first choice for their position went down with an injury. But insiders knew there were a fair number of kids who were fully able to function at the highest levels of the game and simply never got noticed. More than six thousand players are eligible for the draft each year, but only three hundred received invitations to the NFL combines. Many were never considered simply because they didn't go to a Division 1-A school. In some cases that didn't automatically mean league scouts felt they had no ability, but rather that they weren't truly being tested because they were playing against second-rate teams. Players in low-profile schools who compiled good stats were often suspect for just this reason. For those who were never chosen in the draft to begin with, they would soon learn that the "undrafted free agent" tag was often given the same regard as a leper's bell. In the big-money world of the NFL, where it was all about perception, many coaches and GMs didn't want to risk their own credibility by recommending someone no one else had ever heard of. The only advantage to being missed the first time around was that the salary cap provided opportunities for organizations to acquire talent for very little money. Teams that had virtually nothing left to spend could find decent stopgap guys for little or no signing bonuses, league-minimum salaries, and no commitment for the future on their end. Jets receiver Wayne Chrebet, for example, received a signing bonus of just $1,500 after being invited to a tryout simply because he attended the same college where the team held their training camps. From a business perspective, these kinds of contracts were magnificent. In the unusual event that an undrafted free agent turned out to be considerably more talented than previously realized, they could simply offer a better deal later on. Rod Smith, of the Broncos, was never drafted and signed to the team for a pittance. Then, after five consecutive seasons with one thousand receiving yards, he inked a deal with more than seven million in guaranteed bonus money.

When Ross turned back to Freddie and saw him smiling he said, "What's so funny?"

"Kind of convenient that you should mention overlooked players."

"Oh yeah? Why?"

Freddie leaned back and put hands behind his head. "I got something in the mail the other day. Something that might interest you. It sure as hell interested me. That's why I asked you over today."

"Insisted is more like it. Asked me to cancel my golf and everything. I was beginning to wonder. I didn't think you wanted to just chat."

"No, I wanted you to see something. And I'll give you your normal fee."

"Sure, okay."

Freddie pressed the intercom and said, "Okay, Janey, hold down the fort for a while. No calls."

"Wow," Eric said. "This *must* be something big."

"I'm not sure yet," Freddie replied, "but we'll see. I got this package in the mail the other day. It's from this guy in Philly, and it's loaded with videotapes of his nephew, who played quarterback for La Salle University."

"Raymond Coolidge," Eric says.

"Right, Raym—shit, you know about him, too?"

"I've heard a few things. He was supposed to be pretty good, but he was stuck in a school where no one ever saw him." Eric shrugged. "Like I said, the scouts miss a lot of real talent these days. I just figured Coolidge would be another casualty."

Freddie's smiled returned. "Maybe not."

"Oh no? Why not?"

"Like I said, I got a package from his uncle, and my first instinct was to send it back. I try to look at stuff like that once in a while, but I've been busy as hell lately and don't have a lot of time. But then I noticed an interesting name on the return address—Joe Pressner."

Ross let out a small laugh. "Oh yeah . . . just like Quincy Pressner. That's funny. I can see where that would get your attention."

"It sure did, because you're right—it's a lot like Quincy Pressner. *Exactly* like it, in fact."

"Huh? I don't understand."

Freddie smiled. "Raymond Coolidge is Quincy Pressner's son."

Ross froze with the glass halfway to his mouth.

"Raymond Coolidge is the son of Quincy Pressner? *The* Quincy Pressner?"

"That's right."

"The same Quincy Pressner who was drafted with the first overall pick in 1982 by the Los Angeles Rams?"

"That's him."

"The Quincy Pressner who could toss a football from end zone to end zone without so much as a grunt?"

"You got it."

"And then disappeared, without a trace, as if he'd never been more than a ghost to begin with?"

"Yep."

Ross sat back. "You're full of shit."

Freddie's eyebrows rose. "I am?"

"Yeah. Quincy Pressner didn't have a son. That was just a rumor."

"Was it ever proven that he did?"

"No."

"Was it ever proven that he *didn't*?"

"Well, no . . . but a couple of writers I know looked into it. Sam Mitchell was one of them. Sam could find a virgin in a strip club."

"That doesn't mean a thing. Raymond doesn't have the same last name, and he doesn't look anything like his father on the tapes. It would be hard as hell to make a connection."

"Then how do you know he's really Pressner's kid? How does anyone even know where Quincy Pressner *is*? Has anyone seen the guy in twenty years? No interviews, no appearances. How do you know this whole thing isn't a hoax? The guy who sent the tapes could've made it up to get your attention."

Freddie nodded. "I considered all that, but then I decided it was impossible."

"Why's that?"

"Because I *watched* the tapes," he said.

Friedman's calm confidence—the kind that could only come from someone who was right—was unnerving.

"Is he that good?"

"Well, but I'm not an expert. I mean, I can see he's got potential. The question is *how much* potential. That's why I asked you to stop by." Friedman took the remote from desk. "Have a look . . ."

WHEN THE LAST TAPE   NALLY ROLLED TO A CLOSE some nine hours later, the mountains were cloaked in darkness and all of Friedman's employees had gone home.

"Well, what do you think?"

Ross, still staring, eyes wide, at the darkened screen, said, "I think this is your lucky day, Freddie. That's what I think."

10

JERRY WAHLBERG—WHO WAS EASILY ONE OF THE most hated men in professional football—got his start in the sports-agenting game with a chance meeting with a former college classmate named Dale Williams. Williams planned to stay in the sports business for only a year or two and then move into real estate. But he got lucky and signed a kid from Nebraska who ended up being drafted high in the second round by the Dolphins. He made the starting team his rookie year, and after his third season he signed a new contract for $14 million with a $3.2 million signing bonus, the latter being guaranteed money. By that time, Williams had become the kid's exclusive agent, and his share of the profits in the end was 15 percent—which instantly made him a millionaire.

Wahlberg was hypnotized as he listened to this story, and others. Armed with Williams's advice and a crash course on the fundamentals, Wahlberg haunted all the local colleges in the hopes of making his big find. Just like Williams, he struggled at first and began to grow discouraged. Then came Michael Bell.

Initially Bell was represented by a firm called Today's Athletes, Inc. Because Bell was a backup, he was regarded as a second-class citizen. Everyone from the firm's owner to the high school girl who answered the phones treated him like he was more of a burden than anything else, and that they were doing him a huge favor by representing him. Wahlberg, on the other hand, gambled that Bell was considerably more talented than Jacksonville would ever allow anyone to see, and moved in for the kill. He told him the goal was a much bigger and much better contract, and to get it he needed to reinvent himself. Bell loved the idea and listened to Jerry Wahlberg like he was an Indian guru. The key to the plan, Wahlberg told him, was to become a much better quarterback. Bell agreed, and together they designed a punishing off-season program with the help of one of Bell's old coaches from high school. No one else knew about it, not even Bell's closest friends. If word got out, he'd lose the element of surprise when he returned to minicamps the following spring.

When he did, he not only secured the starting job but was offered a generous new contract toward the end of the season, the only stipulation being that the Jags wanted to tag him a franchise player. Wahlberg said no, his client wanted to try his luck elsewhere. He knew the plan had worked—in the quarterback-poor NFL, Michael Bell was a hot commodity. Wahlberg announced that he was a free agent interested in reviewing offers.

They came fast and furious, and the best by far was from Brendan Cavanaugh, of the Denver Broncos. He fantasized about taking the team into a new era of dizzying success and being called the "new Elway." It was a dream he wouldn't have thought possible the year before.

Then the Ravens called. At first Wahlberg balked, trying to terminate the conversation with Jon Sabino before it got started. He told Jon they had already made their decision and that the contract they'd been offered was unbelievable, etc. But Jon persisted, and when he presented the terms of his own contract, Wahlberg was stunned. The signing bonus alone was almost $2 million higher. It was also longer and had fewer incentive clauses. From a playing angle, Baltimore had a slightly better team; certainly a better offensive line. That meant more protection for his client, which meant fewer injuries, which meant less time spent in traction.

And there was part of Michael Bell, of course, that wanted a Super Bowl ring. The media devoted a great deal of time and energy programming the fans into believing modern athletes cared nothing for trophies and ribbons; only money. In reality nearly every athlete, regardless of their tax bracket, still wanted to win a championship. The money would run out sooner or later, but to be part of a championship team was to be part of history. History lasted a lot longer than cash.

It was this element that motivated Bell to change his mind. In the hotel room in Denver, as he and Wahlberg sat at the small round table playing cards, smoking cigars, and drinking Jack Daniels, they made the decision to go with the Ravens on the basis that they had a better chance of winning a Super Bowl. They called Jon Sabino back just after nine thirty, and by the next morning the deal was done.

Wahlberg signed other clients through the years, some of them moderately successful. But Bell was the goose laying the golden eggs. And he wasn't troublesome, either. He had a moral streak that Wahlberg could barely relate to but was nevertheless thankful for. Bell provided him with more money and status than he ever dreamed of.

When he opened the door to Bell's hospital room, he found his number one client being tended to by an attractive young nurse. *Typical,* he thought. *They probably made sure he only got the good-looking ones.* He had no idea about Ratched, the lunatic woman who had made a hobby out of bullying Bell during his painful physical therapy sessions.

The nurse was attaching a new line to Bell's drip bag when Wahlberg entered. The squeal of the door caught her attention and she turned.

"Hi," Wahlberg said with a quick wave. He kept his voice low. "Is he awake?"

"Yes, I'm awake, Jerry," came a deep, groggy voice. "Do you think I'd stay asleep while this beautiful young thing leaned over me like this? I'm only about eight inches from paradise."

Wahlberg chuckled, but the nurse didn't. In fact, she didn't react at all. *She's used to it by now,* Wahlberg thought.

He went to the other side of the bed and found Bell wrapped from the waist down in a rugged white blanket, the knitted kind common to hospitals all over the world. PROPERTY OF JOHNS HOPKINS was stamped on it in some type of super ink that could withstand a thousand washings. Bell was dressed in a short-sleeved gown and still decorated with a variety of tubes and wires. It was a fairly gruesome image, but one Wahlberg had seen before. Athletes were frequent hospital guests.

"Jerry, Allison Blake. Ally, this is my agent, Jerry Wahlberg."

Allison Blake smiled at last.

"Nice to meet you," she said. They shook hands over the patient.

"You, too."

"Okay, Mr. Bell, you're all set until tonight. I'm sure you two will want to be alone. I'll come back in a little while."

"Thanks."

"Nice to meet you, Mr. Wahlberg."

"Same here." After she was gone he said, "Pretty formal place."

"Yeah, too formal."

"So how are you feeling, all things considered?"

"All things considered I feel all right. My back is killing me, but they keep me doped up so it doesn't get too bad. I'd like more, but they've already said no twice."

"Yeah? And how's everything else?"

"Everything else is fine."

"That's good. You've got more tubes and wires than a jet engine." He motioned toward the small population of medical equipment behind the bed. "What is all this stuff?"

"I have no idea. One's for blood pressure, another's for heart rate. One of them is for my brain. They brought it in yesterday." *After I started having dizzy spells,* he thought. "I think they're searching for signs of intelligence, but I keep telling them they're wasting their time."

Wahlberg laughed but kept his eyes on the machines. They made him nervous. He had come here as a businessman worried about his central investment. His value in the agenting community would sink like a brick if his best client couldn't take the field anymore.

"When do you think you'll be up and about again?"

"By next season, as long as I do everything right," Bell told him. "That's what they're telling me."

"Will you do everything right?"

"You think I wanna be here?"

"No, of course not."

There was a pause, and then Bell said, "You know the Ravens will try to get Christian McKinley in order to replace me, right?"

"Why do you say that?"

"Look at it from their side. Wouldn't you? The first question Peter Connally will ask is, 'Why do I need two expensive quarterbacks?' You know how it goes in this business."

Wahlberg *had* considered this but hoped it was nothing more than typical worrying on his part. It was part of his job to review all possiblities, even if most of them never arose.

"They want that third trophy, and I don't blame them," Bell went on. "I would, too."

Wahlberg didn't appear to be listening now. He was staring into space, lost in thought.

Finally he patted his star client on the arm. "I'll take care of it, Mike."

"You'll what? What do you mean?"

"Don't worry." Wahlberg headed for the door.

"Jerry, don't do anything nasty," Bell said. "The Ravens have been good to me."

"I know that. I won't do anything you won't like," Wahlberg said over his shoulder, lying through his teeth. If Bell only knew half of what had gone on behind closed doors. He wasn't one of the wealthiest players in NFL history simply because he had a nice smile and an engaging personality. . . .

In his car on the way back to the hotel, Wahlberg began exploring the situation further in his mind. If he didn't do something fast, everything he'd worked for would be gone. And he knew no one else would sign with him; not with his reputation. He'd made plenty of enemies, all of whom would be outwardly delighted to see him crash and burn.

Not this time, fellas, he thought with a nasty smile. *I've still got a good trick or two up my sleeve.*

11

UNAWARE THAT ONE OF THE TURNING POINTS IN HIS life was only moments away, Rob Macintosh sat on the couch watching television and eating Chinese food with chopsticks. He flipped from channel to channel, coming to rest every now and then on ESPN in the hopes of seeing himself. He'd had a brief interaction with the press today as he was leaving the offices. One of his great pleasures was making appearances on television, talking team business. He was neither handsome nor beastly, but he had natural presence on screen and knew how to use it. Unfortunately, the media generally ignored him, opting for the bigger fish—Connally, Sabino, Blanchard. But every now and then fate would toss him a bone and send the cameras his way.

The phone rang. He jumped as if he'd been poked with a stick. He wasn't expecting any calls. In fact the phone rarely rang here. The number was unlisted, and less than a dozen people knew it. He had almost no friends and liked it that way. Friends were a burden he didn't need. It couldn't be anyone in his family, either. His parents, brother, and sister were all still alive and well, but they only had his office number; it was easier to cut a conversation short using work as an excuse. It might be Jennifer calling from California, but that was doubtful.

Curious, he strolled across the carpet in his bare feet and lifted the cordless phone from its base on the glass table. He placed his thumb over the off button, ready to press at the first sign of solicitation.

"Hello?"

"Robert?"

"Yes?"

"It's Brendan Cavanaugh, of the Denver Broncos."

Macintosh's heart began thumping. *He received the résumé . . .*

"Oh . . . hi."

"Hi. I'm sorry to be calling out of the blue like this." He kept his voice calm, friendly. Always charm them at the start. You catch more flies with honey than vinegar. . . .

"That's okay, no problem."

They'd met once before—at a league meeting in Tampa two years earlier. Cavanaugh remembered getting along with him well despite the lingering tension between the Broncos and the Ravens over the whole Bell debacle.

"Do you have a moment? Did I catch you in the middle of something?"

"Huh? Oh no, no. Just watching some basketball."

He went back to the couch and muted the TV, silencing the first game in the NCAA's Sweet Sixteen tournament.

"What's up?"

"Well, I received this résumé from you, and frankly it looks pretty good."

Macintosh paused. It couldn't be this easy, could it?

"Really?"

"Mm-hmm. You've got plenty of experience. I'm surprised, though, that you're leaving a team you've been with for so long."

Silence from the other end.

"Are you having problems there?" Cavanaugh asked,

goading him. He didn't think it would take much.

"I'm . . . concerned about the future," Macintosh said.

"Your future?"

"Yeah."

"Let me guess—nowhere to go, right?"

Another pause, and then, "Not for me, it seems." The bitterness was unmistakable, so Cavanaugh went in for the kill.

"Is it Sabino?"

"Oh no, he's okay. I mean, I know you two aren't crazy about each other, but he's not the problem."

"Higher up, then?" Cavanaugh continued. He knew there was only one person in that area. "Right?" It was no secret Peter Connally wasn't the most personable individual in the world, particularly if he took a disliking to you.

Macintosh replayed the humiliating encounter in Connally's office in his mind. "Yeah, higher up."

"I'm sorry to hear that," Cavanaugh said in a gentle, almost fatherly manner. He wanted Macintosh to feel comfortable with him, trusting.

It worked. Unable to hold himself back, Macintosh launched into a long-simmering tirade about how he'd had such a bright future with the club during the previous regime and thought he would end up either the general manager someday or maybe even go into the pure business side of it and become one of the financial officers. Real power, real influence. But then Peter Connally came along and left him drying on the vine.

Cavanaugh couldn't have cared less, but he listened patiently and delivered the appropriate sympathies at the appropriate moments. He could feel the hook sinking in.

"So now I've got to start over," Macintosh said in conclusion.

"That's awful," Cavanaugh said, managing to sound just disgusted enough. "Ridiculously unfair. By the way, have you sent this résumé to anyone else?"

"No, I thought I'd try you first. I have some friends in Denver, so I can move up there pretty easily." This was a lie, but he wasn't about to give the impression getting to work every day would be a hassle.

Cavanaugh drew a deep breath. This was the big moment. His instincts told him he was on the right side of the odds and the victim had been adequately primed.

"Okay, look, I've got something in mind for you. Technically you could consider it work for the Broncos, but you're going to have to stay in Baltimore to do it."

"Huh?"

"I need some information, Robert. I need a pair of eyes and ears on the inside."

Macintosh smiled.

"Spying?"

"You could call it that," Cavanaugh said.

"Whoa." The game required that he sound at least mildly shocked.

"It would all have to be kept fully confidential, of course. No paper trail, no e-mails, that kind of stuff."

"Sure, sure."

"It happens more often than you think, Robert. Remember that rumor about a Falcons' special-teams coach spying on a Giants' practice from atop the Meadowlands Sheraton? Everyone said it was nonsense, but later that week the Falcons crushed the Giants as if they'd known every offensive play ahead of time."

"Yeah, I remember that."

"It really does happen."

"Okay, look, do you mind if I ask you something?"

"What's that?"

"For the sake of argument, let's say I accept this, uh, 'job' and everything works out great. Once that's done, can I have a position on the team?"

"Absolutely."

"Something decent?"

"Yes."

"I won't be washing the goddamn towels or anything, right?"

"No." Cavanaugh laughed. "No towel washing."

"Can I ask what, specifically, you'd have in mind for me?"

There was a pause. Macintosh wondered if perhaps he'd pushed too hard. In reality, Cavanaugh was simply thinking of who he'd been hoping to get rid of.

"How about operations manager?"

Now it was Macintosh's turn to pause.

"You're kidding, right?"

"Not at all. You've been there for eight years—eight years of solid experience. That's more than enough to run operations, at least as far as I'm concerned."

"Really?"

"Yes."

"We can consider this an official part of the deal?"

"Yes, we can. You help me with what I need, and I promise I'll take care of you. It'll be worth it, believe me."

Macintosh paused again, thought about the obvious dangers—and tremendous consequences—of spying in the NFL. Cavanaugh was right—people had done it before, and some got caught. Those who did weren't around anymore. It wasn't so much the sin that got them blackballed, but the fact that they weren't good enough to succeed.

Macintosh believed he was good enough, more than good enough. The rewards far outweighed the risks. He allowed himself a momentary fantasy, one that involved his new position, his greatly enhanced salary, and stealing the girl of his dreams away from that two-bit asshole.

The words seem to come out on their own—"I'll do it," he said firmly.

Cavanaugh smiled.

Bingo.

RAVENS ROSTER W/NOTES FROM CARY BLANCHARD

#	NAME	POS.	RT.	WT.	YRS.	COLLEGE	NOTES
11	Scott Clark	QB	6-4	208	2	Brigham Young	CAN TRADE (no to Henderson—no offensive players)
20	Milton Love	S	6-2	211	3	Troy State	Included in deal with Skip
23	Greg Buckley	CB	6-1	199	9	Western Illinois	CAN TRADE (not Henderson—he already said he doesn't want him)
30	Buster McDaniels	RB	5-11	201	7	Mississippi	To Steelers for Willie Gunther
32	Aaron Holloway	RB	6-1	205	2	Florida State	To Bengals for Martin Brynmoor
33	Nick Wakefield	CB	6-0	201	R	Auburn	CAN TRADE (not to Henderson—no rookies)
34	Andre Jenkins	S	6-1	214	R	Temple	To Bengals for Martin Brynmoor
51	Brian Northbrook	LB	6-2	240	4	Arkansas State	CAN TRADE (not to Henderson—he already said he doesn't want him)
53	Brett Savage	LB	6-4	250	11	Washington State	CAN TRADE (not to Henderson—he already said he doesn't want him)
61	Jared Cope	G	6-2	310	8	Georgia Tech	To Steelers for Willie Gunther
66	Barrett Blake	G	6-3	305	R	Stanford	To Patriots for Lyle Jameson
67	Jason Freemont	LC	6-6	277	7	Texas Tech	CAN TRADE (not to Henderson—no offensive players)

(continued on next page)

RAVENS ROSTER W/NOTES FROM CARY BLANCHARD *(continued)*

#	NAME	POS.	HT.	WT.	YRS.	COLLEGE	NOTES
69	Scott Montgomery	G	6-3	324	11	Illinois	CAN TRADE (not to Henderson—no offensive players)
71	Keith Kubat	T	6-5	277	3	Hofstra	To Patriots for Lyle Jameson
82	Jordan Patterson	WR	6-1	203	R	Kentucky	To Bengals for Martin Brynmoor
84	Sam Sargent	TE	6-6	261	3	West Virginia	CAN TRADE (not to Henderson—no offensive players)
88	Kevin Curtis	DT	6-3	274	R	Rutgers	To Bengals for Martin Brynmoor
90	Corey Holbrook	DE	6-4	277	9	Syracuse	CAN TRADE (not to Henderson—he already said he doesn't want him)
92	Donald Harper	DT	6-3	277	8	Florida State	CAN TRADE (not to Henderson—he already said he doesn't want him)
96	Alan Hill	DE	6-3	274	R	Temple	CAN TRADE (not to Henderson—he already said he doesn't want him)
12	Nate Brown	QB	6-4	207	10	Penn State	PREFER TO KEEP
26	Pete Wolverton	S	6-2	220	4	Iowa	PREFER TO KEEP
28	TJ Matthews	RB	6-0	200	5	Wisconsin	PREFER TO KEEP
31	Walter Bartlett	CB	6-3	201	2	Kansas State	Included in deal with Skip
57	Ryan Mason	LB	6-5	242	2	Baylor	PREFER TO KEEP
85	Raymont Carter	WR	6-1	198	2	Troy State	PREFER TO KEEP
91	George Kontoleon	DT	6-2	275	2	Purdue	PREFER TO KEEP
98	Ted Forrest	DE	6-2	276	4	Texas A&M	PREFER TO KEEP
3	Terry Butler	K	5-11	205	6	Virginia	STARTER—DO NOT TRADE
8	Michael Bell	QB	6-5	210	5	LSU	STARTER—DO NOT TRADE
13	Steve Russell	P	6-1	205	5	Kansas State	STARTER—DO NOT TRADE

(continued on next page)

RAVENS ROSTER W/NOTES FROM CARY BLANCHARD *(continued)*

#	NAME	POS.	RT.	WT.	YRS.	COLLEGE	NOTES
21	Paul Ellis	FB	6-1	235	4	Tennessee	STARTER—DO NOT TRADE
22	Chris Redmond	S	6-0	209	8	Illinois	STARTER—DO NOT TRADE
24	Harold Rowling	CB	6-1	203	3	Michigan	STARTER—DO NOT TRADE
25	Thomas Rhodes	CB	6-0	205	7	UCLA	STARTER—DO NOT TRADE
27	Lawrence Dixon	RB	6-1	202	3	Virginia	STARTER—DO NOT TRADE
29	Herb Axelrod	S	6-1	217	6	Northern Arizona	STARTER—DO NOT TRADE
52	Elliot Easton	LB	6-3	243	6	Wake Forest	STARTER—DO NOT TRADE
54	Earle Webster	LB	6-4	244	2	Purdue	STARTER—DO NOT TRADE
56	Larry Townsend	LB	6-6	247	5	Alabama	STARTER—DO NOT TRADE
60	Derrick Gorden	C	6-4	312	4	Penn State	STARTER—DO NOT TRADE
63	Matt Israel	G	6-1	312	4	Miami	STARTER—DO NOT TRADE
68	Shaun Erickson	G	6-1	320	7	Michigan	STARTER—DO NOT TRADE
70	Frank James	T	6-4	263	5	Rutgers	STARTER—DO NOT TRADE
74	Craig Little	T	6-6	278	9	Maryland	STARTER—DO NOT TRADE
80	Ryan Hart	TE	6-4	250	7	Kentucky	STARTER—DO NOT TRADE
81	Anthony Jennings	WR	6-4	209	6	Mississippi	STARTER—DO NOT TRADE
87	Darryl Bailey	WR	6-0	200	5	North Carolina St	STARTER—DO NOT TRADE
88	Tony Kramer	WR	6-3	211	3	Notre Dame	STARTER—DO NOT TRADE
93	Jon Harris	DE	6-6	281	3	Virginia	STARTER—DO NOT TRADE
94	Dexter Simmons	DE	6-3	280	7	Wisconsin	STARTER—DO NOT TRADE
95	Tony Seidl	DT	6-5	280	5	Miami	STARTER—DO NOT TRADE
97	Howard Sawyer	DT	6-4	277	6	Iowa	STARTER—DO NOT TRADE

RAVENS DRAFT PICKS

YEAR	PICK	NOTES
Current	1st round/32nd overall	
	~~2nd round/44th overall~~	~~To Bengals for Martin Brynmoor~~
	~~2nd round/64th overall~~	~~To Patriots for Lyle Jameson~~
	~~3rd round/96th overall~~	~~To Patriots for Lyle Jameson~~
	~~6th round/192nd overall~~	~~To Steelers for Willie Gunther~~
	~~7th round/224th overall~~	~~To Steelers for Willie Gunther~~
2007	~~1st round~~	~~To Bucs for Clarence Doll~~
	~~2nd round~~	~~To Steelers for Willie Gunther~~
	~~3rd round~~	~~To Bengals for Martin Brynmoor~~
	~~4th round~~	~~To Bengals for Martin Brynmoor~~
	~~5th round~~	~~To Jags for Bobby Kellerman~~
	~~6th round~~	~~To Jags for Bobby Kellerman~~
	~~7th round~~	~~To Bucs for Clarence Doll~~
2008	1st round	
	~~2nd round~~	~~To Bengals for Martin Brynmoor~~
	~~3rd round~~	~~To Cowboys for Dustin McHenry~~
	~~4th round~~	~~To Cowboys for Dustin McHenry~~
	5th round	
	6th round	
	7th round	

DEFENSIVE PACKAGE FOR SKIP HENDERSON

#	NAME	HT.	WT.	YRS.	COLLEGE	NOTES
CB	Walter Bartlett	6-3	201	2	Kansas State	From our own roster
CB DE	Willie Gunther	6-3	291	2	Purdue	To be rec'd from Steelers in exchange for Buster McDaniels, Jared Cope, and 6th- and 7th-round picks this year, and 2nd-round pick next year.
DE DT	Martin Brynmoor	6-5	307	3	Loyola	To be rec'd from Bengals in exchange for Aaron Holloway, Jordan Patterson, Kevin Curtis, 2nd-round pick this year, 3rd- and 4th-round picks next year, and 2nd-round pick in '08.
DT	Lyle Jameson	6-4	303	4	Georgia	To be rec'd from Patriots in exchange for Barrett Blake, Keith Kubat, and 2nd-round pick (96th overall) and 3rd-round pick this year.
LB LB S S	Milton Love	6-2	211	3	Troy State	From our own roster

"He's going to fire my ass," Jon said into the phone. "I should send you my résumé right now. If Connally doesn't fire me, Blanchard will shoot me dead in my office. You know he hunts, right? And he's pretty good, I hear. Two quick ones—*pop! pop!*—and it'll be over. And no one will care, either."

Gayle Markham was laughing uncontrollably at the other end.

"Take it easy, Jon."

"Were you listening to what I just said? Did you hear what I'm giving up to get this guy?"

"Deadwood, Jon. Think of it as cleaning house. And when most guys clean house, they don't get a Christian McKinley in return."

Jon wasn't listening. He was staring into his computer monitor and shaking his head. His loafers had been removed and were lying under the desk.

"We'll have no draft this year, no draft next year."

"You've managed to hold on to your first-round picks, right?"

"Only for this year and for '08. Not '07."

"That went to the . . . Bucs?"

"Yeah."

"Okay, well, that's not such a bad thing. A first-round guy will cost you plenty, and you'll have cap problems anyway. By '08 you should be coming out of it."

Jon groaned. He knew Markham was right, but it didn't make him feel any better.

Gayle Markham was as close to a best friend as Jon Sabino had in the league. They met during the 1989 owners' meeting, when they were grinding it out as low men on the totem pole for other teams. Both had been brought along to get a little experience under their belts. They hit it off immediately, amazed by the similarities in both their personal and professional philosophies, not to mention the parallel course their lives seemed to have taken. Both were from broken homes and found an solace and fulfillment in the high-energy environment of the NFL. They'd played football in high school and college, but neither had the skills or the talent to make it to the pros. They went on to earn business degrees and, immediately upon graduation, sought positions with any team that would take them. They were even the same age, Jon being older by just over three months.

A symbiosis naturally developed that worked out nicely through the years. They compared notes, shared hot tips, and recommended each other when a choice position opened up. It was Gayle who helped Jon get back to his hometown of Baltimore when the Browns moved down from Cleveland, and it was on Jon's powerful urging that Tom Johnson, the Saints' owner, promoted Gayle to the position of president of player personnel. This gave Gayle complete control over player acquisition. Their general manager at the time, who did not have a personnel pedigree, focused more on the business side of things.

"What a mess," Jon murmured, navigating through the spreadsheets. "What a damn mess. What I'm doing to this team . . ."

"But you're taking a shot at history," Markham reminded him.

"And in turn, everyone's having a grand old time taking shots at me," Jon told him. "Do you know what that little bastard Cochran said to me?"

Markham was already laughing. Neither of them cared much for the general manager of the 49ers. He was a cantankerous old grump who resented everyone under the age of fifty.

"No, what?"

"He told me teams like mine were a disease, and he was going to be the cure."

Markham's hyena-like cackle elevated a full octave, forcing Jon into a smile he didn't want.

"And Northfield told me he wouldn't give me a player if I offered him the cure for cancer."

There was nothing but silence on the other end as Markham tried to catch his breath.

"Well," he said finally, "you've certainly made some friends, haven't you?"

"I had no idea the animosity was *this* bad."

"Maybe if you'd been a little less smug after that second championship."

"Smug?" Jon said. "Me?"

"Oh, right," Markham replied. "Innocent as a choirboy. Anyway, look, you didn't call just to blow off steam, did you? I've got my own messes to deal with. We're still working on the new stadium, courtesy of that bitch Katrina. That alone is gobbling up huge chunks of my time. So let's get to it—I'm guessing you've got something else in mind."

Jon switched to another screen, one that had full details of the Saints' roster.

"Yeah, I'm calling because I'm interested in one of your guys."

"I had a feeling. It's Bramledge, right?"

"How'd you know?"

"The Seahawks and the Chiefs have also called about him. It didn't take me too long to figure out what Henderson wants."

"Is he still available?"

"Yeah, he is. But I have to tell you, pal, your competitors have made some nice offers for him. And I'm not just saying that to put the squeeze on you."

Jon nodded. He knew he could trust Gayle beyond any doubt. Credibility was not an issue here.

"Well, I have enough left to make an offer, too. But tell me about him. Tell me what I don't know."

"What do you know now?"

"I know he's a monster of a linebacker. Six-three, two hundred and sixty pounds. Third year in the league. He's only played sixteen games and he's already compiled nearly twenty sacks. That's incredible."

"It sure is."

"And yet, he's on the bench. I know Fellows and Ramos are your starters, but I'm surprised you don't use this guy somewhere else. Anywhere. What am I not seeing on the screen here?"

"He's a troublemaker," Markham said simply. "He gets

into fights, he's moody and sullen, and we're not sure, but we think he may have some drugs in his past."

As Gayle was talking, Jon did a quick Google search, keywords "Austin," "Bramledge," and "drugs." Nothing.

"You guys didn't look into it before you drafted him? A TAP report, at least?" TAP stood for "Troutwine Athletic Profile," a seventy-five-question multiple-choice test designed primarily to evaluate an athlete's mental capacity for competition. It came into vogue in the league in the early '80s and was designed by respected sports psychologist Dr. Robert Troutwine.

"We did, and we didn't find anything. But a lot of rumors were floating around. We're pretty thorough about that stuff. Like everyone else, we sometimes consult the feds about certain guys. The FBI didn't come up with anything, but they said they same thing—they thought they'd heard rumors."

"What about random drug tests?"

"He's had four, clean on all of them."

"Huh. Well, I don't know what more you can do. I'd consider him clean."

"Yeah," Gayle said, "except for the other stuff. He's trouble around the locker room and on the practice field. That's why the coach doesn't like him. He'd be happy to get rid of him."

Jon nodded. He was at a moral crossroad. Bramledge's skills were certainly on par, and he fit the profile Henderson was looking for. But problem players never did well in San Diego. The ownership were all straight shooters, and Henderson was no different. Bramledge looked good on paper, so Jon was pretty sure he could get him under Henderson's radar. But what about afterward? What about the first time the kid gave somebody a broken nose for looking at him the wrong way? It wouldn't take long for his past to catch up with him, and then Henderson would know Jon had sold him a lemon.

"Does he have any redeeming qualities at all?"

"Well, he does charity work. Not just money, but time.

Works in the kitchens, works with kids. Keeps real quiet about it, too."

"That's good. That's a good sign."

"Yeah, he's complicated." Markham sighed. "I don't know, Jon. I'm not sure I want to stick you with him."

"You told the Chiefs and the 'Hawks all this, too, right?"

"Yes."

Jon took a deep breath, closed his eyes, and checked his gut. Whenever the call was fifty-fifty, he always went there.

The sound of the clock ticking on the wall provided a certain measure of motivation as well.

"All right, let me tell you what I can give you for him. . . ."

PEARLY PRESSNER'S FINGERS WEREN'T WHAT THEY used to be. He couldn't even hold onto the tiny screws, much less get them into the holes. Nevertheless, under the bright light of the kitchen table—the same table upon which he'd written the letter to Freddie Friedman—he kept trying. Damn cheap eyeglasses were always falling apart. But a new pair was out of the question. The state wouldn't pay for them, and he certainly didn't have the money. Such was the burden of an elderly man on a fixed income.

He was just about to give up when someone knocked on the screen door.

"Who is it?"

Raymond's voice drifted in from the porch. "It's me, Uncle Pearly."

"Come on in, it's open."

The rusty hinges sang out a note that rose until it vanished, and Raymond appeared in the doorway. He wore a hooded sweatsuit and a windbreaker, his hands thrust deep in the pockets.

"Hi."

"Hi," Pearly replied, not bothering to conceal his frustration. "Have a seat."

Raymond pulled out a chair and sat down. He watched his uncle struggle with the glasses for a few moments.

"Here, let me give it a try."

Pearly, looking thoroughly exasperated, didn't resist. Raymond's hands, although larger than his uncle's, were swift and nimble, expertly manipulating the tiny screwdriver.

"That should do it," he said, handing everything back.

"Thanks." Pearly fit them carefully over his broad face. "I appreciate it. Ah, that's better."

"Sure. Uh . . . that's not why you asked me here, is it?"

"What? Oh no, no."

"So what's up?" Raymond asked.

"Umm . . ." The old man stroked the back of his head a few times.

"Uncle Pearly, is something wrong?"

"Well . . ." Pearly began, "that depends."

"On what?"

"On you."

"On me? I don't understand."

"I know, I know." He ran his fingers around his mouth as if to wipe it clean.

"Ray, I received a phone call this afternoon. It was from a man named Freddie Friedman. Have you ever heard of him?"

Raymond shook his head. "No. Should I have?"

"No, no. I just thought . . ."

"Who is he?"

Pearly sighed. Only direction to go is forward.

"He's a sports agent from upstate New York."

Raymond stiffened visibly but said nothing.

"He called me because . . . well, because I sent him a bunch of your game tapes." Pearly pointed to Raymond to emphasize the word *your,* hoping in some distant way it would instill a sense of pride.

It didn't. Raymond's mouth fell open. "You *what*?" Only his natural respect for his uncle kept him from exploding.

"I sent him some game tapes from your last two years at school and—"

"I can't believe you'd do that. You know how I feel about the pros."

"He thinks you may have a real shot, son."

Raymond stood up, hands on his hips, and walked around the room like an animal in a cage. "Uncle Pearly, how could you go behind my back like that?"

"You're not thinking with your head! Do you know how many people even get an opportunity like this? Do you?" Raymond didn't reply. "Maybe one in a million, if that. And do you know what happens to the rest of them? They either end up in some shit job for the rest of their life, or they get killed in the streets before they're twenty-five."

Pearly got up and came toward him, his dime store shoes scraping on the filthy linoleum. "Don't you see, Raymond? This could be your chance to get out of this place, to beat the odds and make a good life for yourself. To have all the things most of us never will. You've got a gift, a gift that can get you things most people only dream about. You should use it. I don't know how far it'll take you, but you've got to *try*. Friedman thinks you might be able to sign somewhere as a free agent. Do you know what the NFL's minimum player salary is these days?"

Raymond turned to face him but said nothing.

"It's more than two hundred grand for the rookies, and more then three hundred grand for the veterans. *More than three hundred thousand dollars*, Raymond. I never made a tenth of that in any one year of my life!"

Raymond shook his head in a slow, measured motion, like he was following the movement of a ping-pong ball.

"I can't do it, Uncle Pearly. Not after what happened to Daddy. I just can't."

Pearly studied him for a moment, the typical angry young man. He burned with loyalty and pride. What an amazing kid. What strength of will. Pearly could not help but admire him.

"Raymond, look, I don't know if there's a right way to tell you this, so I'm just going to say it." He prayed he wasn't making a mistake. "Son, a lot of what your daddy told you about what happened to him isn't . . . well, it isn't completely true."

The boy's eyes thinned. "What?"

"I don't know everything he told you over the years, but I know he didn't tell you the whole story, or the real story, because he couldn't have. You wouldn't feel the way you do if he had."

"I don't understand."

"Ray . . . your daddy had some problems when he started in the league. He ran with a bad crowd and got caught up with drugs and alcohol. He—"

Raymond was shaking his head. "No, I know what you're trying to do. Don't say things like that."

"Raymond, you can't go on thinking—"

"No, Uncle Pearly . . ."

"Raymond, you need to know the truth."

"I already know the truth."

"No, Ray. Listen to me. You need to know wh—"

Trembling, Raymond said, "I'm not going to let you betray him!"

"Ray . . ."

"No!"

He turned and stalked from the house, banging the screen door on the way out. Pearly went after him, but his old bowed legs made the effort futile. By the time he got to the front step Raymond was halfway down the sidewalk, visible only when he passed under a streetlamp.

"Raymond!"

Pearly lingered for a moment in the faint hope his nephew might come back. But of course he didn't.

"Damn."

QUINCY PRESSNER BROUGHT THE BOTTLE TO HIS LIPS, tossed it back, and emptied it. Then he set it down on the bar with a sharp thud, although no one paid any attention. Bottles were slammed down all the time in the Blue Rose, one of Philadelphia's less-admired establishments.

"One more!" he called out, drumming the bottle on the tired copper surface.

The bartender, an enormous black man with thick glasses, ambled over and set his hands down, flat and well apart.

"Quince, you know I can't do that. I told you before, the bill you owe now is enormous. That was your last one."

"Come on, Connie. I'll get the money."

"Sorry, Quince. This time it's too much." He took a small piece of paper from a metal spike on top of the cash register. "Over three hundred this month," he said, holding it up.

Pressner dropped his head as if he'd suddenly fell asleep. "Oh, man. Okay."

Connie put a hand on his shoulder. "I hate seeing you like this, y'know."

The former NFL star looked up again. "Yeah, me too." He laughed.

That famous face, one that Connie somehow never tired of seeing. How many journalists would love to get just one photo of it, would love to talk to him for just one minute, snag one quote? For someone who had been drinking all morning, he appeared to be remarkably clear-eyed and alert.

Connie Duellman had known Quincy Pressner for nearly ten years now. He didn't recognize him that first day he came in, but something about him was familiar. It wasn't until a woman sportswriter named Patti something-or-other followed him in one autumn afternoon to try to interview him that Duellman realized he was a Somebody. With a little help from others he knew in the neighborhood, he put the pieces together—big star in the league, then apparently dropped out of it for reasons unknown. Tried to make a go at a "normal" living, first in construction, then some kind of retail position selling boats or something. Then the depression set in. Drugs, booze, and the fade began. Quincy poured out the whole confession one long afternoon when business was slow. He was only half-drunk that day, but he knew what he was doing. Connie was deeply touched by Quincy's confidence in him. And, like any good bartender, he decided he to keep his customer's secrets locked up tight. Through the years, several people had come around sniffing for information. Connie didn't know a thing. Neither did anyone else in the community, such was their affection for their most famous resident. It was like Pressner had a personal army.

"How's that boy of yours doing?" Connie asked.

This produced a smile. "He's doing fine. Haven't seen him in a while."

"You should. Give him a call."

"Oh hell, I call him all the time. I just don't . . . you know."

Connie nodded. "Yeah, I know. But you should go see him anyway. Don't worry about the reasons why you shouldn't."

Pressner seemed to consider the idea, then nodded. "Yeah . . . yeah."

He checked his watch, which wasn't exactly a piece of junk but was still a far cry from the gold Rolex he used to see down there. That one ended up on eBay in the late '90s.

"Well, I'm gonna get going."

"Okay, Quince. Have a good day." Connie gave him one last pat on the back.

Pressner nodded and slid off the stool. Across the smoky room, two kids were playing pool. Quincy could tell they were watching him. They stood together at the far end of the table, one holding his cue straight up, the other at an angle as he chalked the tip. They were in the shadows, enveloped by a smoky haze, but Pressner could feel their eyes upon him. There was a time, he remembered, when youngsters looked at him like a god. *What do they think of me now?* he wondered.

He shuffled to the door and pulled it back, momentarily bathing the cavernous club in a blaze of afternoon sunlight. It staggered him for a moment, burning his weary eyes. He had to shield them as he went out.

His apartment complex was two blocks away. On one side of it was a condemned building sometimes used by drug dealers and loan sharks. On the other was a mountain of rubble that served as an elementary school about a million years ago.

Pressner walked listlessly up the front steps and to the door, which was being held open with rope. The fluorescent light in the foyer buzzed and stuttered. After climbing a long flight of steps, he went to the end of the second-floor hallway, found number seventeen, and turned the knob. Beyond lay four small rooms with ancient fixtures and uneven floorboards. It was reasonably clean, but he'd lived in better. Much better.

He went into the kitchen to search for more beer. Nothing in the fridge, nothing in the cabinets. There was a round table near the window, freckled with burn holes from Pressner's cigarettes. He sat down and had one, watching some kids play basketball in a public lot across the street. They were all pretty good, but one was much better than the rest.

Keep practicing, son, Pressner couldn't help thinking. *Give it all you've got and get the hell out of here. And remember that sometimes, even if you escape, you end up coming back. Take it from one who knows.*

When the cigarette was finished he doused it in the sink and tossed it into the garbage can. Then he went into the bedroom. A load of *Sports Illustrated* issues were piled in the corner. It was the one indulgence he allowed himself, using a false name on the mailing address. He grabbed the latest one and lay down on the bed. The springs squeaked rhythmically beneath. He made it halfway through one article before he was out cold and snoring softly.

LESS THAN AN HOUR LATER, A BROWN GRAN TORINO pulled up in front of the building, and Quincy's brother Pearly stepped out. He locked the vehicle, not because it was worth anything but because he had no other way of getting home if it was stolen.

Pearly spoke to his brother occasionally, and it was more contact than Quincy had with his other brother or his sister. The brother was a software architect living on the outskirts of Silicon Valley. He had money to burn but was tighter with it than a clam's ass. He kept Quincy at a distance simply because he was afraid his brother might ask for a loan. The sister wasn't much better. She lived in a well-to-do Chicago suburb with her husband and two children and had no idea "what to do" with Quincy, so she did nothing. What little information these extant siblings received about their infamous brother came unsolicited through Pearly. As far as they were concerned, he was Quincy's keeper.

The joints in Pearly's knees screamed as he made his way up the stairs. He paused at the top catch his breath and patted his forehead with a handkerchief.

He knocked on Quincy's door and called his name but received no response. He knew this meant nothing. He pressed his ear against the door, and when he detected the snoring he turned the knob and went in.

"Quincy, get up! It's me, Pearly!"

He heard his brother roll over and mumble.

"Quince, come on!"

Pearly took a chair from the kitchen and set it next to the bed. He eased himself down but had to drop last few inches due to the stress on his knees. Then he gave his brother a shake, triggering another symphony of metallic squeaks and squeals.

"Quince, come on . . ."

"Hmm? Huh?"

"It's me, get up." He checked his watch. "Not even one o'clock yet. Christ."

"Pearly?"

"Yeah, that's right. Come on, up."

Quincy slid up onto his elbows. The magazine dropped to the floor.

"I can't believe I fell asleep."

"Me neither. You usually make it until at least five."

"Yeah, that's funny. Say, do you have two hundred and eighty bucks I could borrow? I'll pay you back."

"No. I don't even have eight bucks."

"Damn. Okay."

"Look, we need to talk about something."

"Like what?"

"Like Raymond."

"My Raymond?" His eyes flashed to the collection of photos that decorated the perimeter of the dresser mirror, each one stuck between the glass and the frame. They were arranged chronologically and ran clockwise, starting in the upper lefthand corner; a photographic history of his son's life. They were Quincy's most cherished possessions.

"Yeah."

At the mention of his son's name, Quincy entire demeanor changed. The transformation was so abrupt and severe that it was almost frightening.

Very awake now, he said, "What about him?"

12

THE VERY LAST GUY ON JON'S LIST WAS A SAFETY WITH the Cleveland Browns named Otis Vancleave. He was Skip Henderson's type of guy—tall and lithe, with great speed and ferocity. He'd put good stats together in his four years in the league, but Cleveland's two starters were both occasional Pro Bowlers, and one of them—the one Vancleave was supposed to replace—instead became the NFL's Comeback Player of the Year after missing two seasons with a back injury. Now Vancleave was all but disposable. He gave the team great depth, but they, too, were heading toward cap problems, so they couldn't afford extraneous guys who weren't ready to take the next step.

Jon didn't know the Browns' director of player personnel, Drew Saks, all that well. Saks had been promoted to the position just two months before, after their previous personnel director retired.

He turned out to be pleasant and affable, and notably more diplomatic than most others Jon had dealt with over the last few days. He seemed to understand Jon's predicament and asked for no more than a fair deal. In the end he received two players and one pick—the Ravens' first overall in 2008. Jon was grateful for small mercies and faxed over the paperwork for the tender offer with his signature. Saks signed it and sent it right back, and Jon decided he'd made a new friend.

And with that last piece of paper, his package for Skip Henderson was complete. He read the rundown several times, and he was blown away by it—there was simply no way that old bastard could turn his nose up this time. It was just *too good*. Hell, it was almost a better defense than the Ravens already had. Whether or not they gelled as a unit was Skip's problem. It wouldn't be the first time a bunch of talented guys got together and nothing happened in the chemistry department. That was the unfortunate variable. You put egos and big money in the same place, there's always a chance the shit is going to start hitting the fan. Jon couldn't care less. None of the guys on that list would ever don a Ravens' uniform.

He went to navigate back to the spreadsheet illustrating his own team's roster, but he stopped himself. He simply couldn't look. His stomach had been in knots for days. It reminded him of his college years, when money was so tight that a Big Gulp at the local 7-Eleven brought a certain guilt. He'd simply spent too much. But this was what Connally wanted—that third championship, at any cost. McKinley could give it to him. If he couldn't, no one could. And if they didn't make it, it wouldn't be from a lack of trying on his part.

He took a deep breath, then reached for the phone.

AS IT TURNED OUT, SPYING CAME NATURALLY TO Robert Macintosh. True, he was jittery at the beginning and his paranoia ran wild. But that passed quickly enough. Soon the procedure was almost casual.

A number of sportswriters had called today, asking for information on a rumored deal in principle between the Ravens and the Chargers. The media was going crazy over it. Would Baltimore really land Christian McKinley? Would they once again emerge victorious from the heat of battle? It was all they talked about.

Macintosh waited until dark. Jon had left for the day but could still return unannounced. Sometimes he went home, other times he went out for dinner and came back. The man was a machine.

As he settled into Jon's chair, he thought about the final details of the deal he'd made with Cavanaugh—not just the job in Denver after this first "project" was finished, but the cash bonus for getting it done cleanly. His heart had been thumping; it was like something out of a James Bond movie. He'd heard about stuff like this happening in the league. It wasn't surprising, really—the NFL was, in essence, a war between factions competing for the same prize. And the stakes were enormous—millions of dollars and the futures of thousands of people. One moment you were making six or seven figures, the next you were updating your résumé and wondering if your kids would have to pay for their own college education. The league was a lot like a big corporation that way. Secrets were sacred and the right information was priceless. He'd been warned about the possibility of being contacted by the competition. The procedure, of course, was to reject such offers and report them immediately.

"What kind of money are we talking about here?" Macintosh had asked.

"We're talking about twenty thousand dollars, cash."

Macintosh was sure his heart had skipped a beat.

Twenty thousand in cash. That's more money than I've ever had in my life.

His first instinct was to jump on it, reel it in before it got away like that once-in-a-lifetime tuna. Then a second instinct overpowered it—an instinct evolved from watching hustlers like Peter Connally work their magic day in and day out. What was it Connally always said? The first offer should be rejected no matter how generous?

"Twenty thousand?!" he said, hoping the laugh didn't sound too snotty. He wanted to seem genuinely offended, but not dismissive. Then a semicomforting thought struck him—he pretty much had Cavanaugh by the balls already because Cavanaugh had no one else to turn to. It was him or no one. Macintosh already *knew* his intentions. He was the only game in town. That put him in a sweet position indeed.

"Okay, okay," Cavanaugh replied, sounding like someone who'd been caught in a lie. "Forty thousand. But that's it."

"Fifty," Macintosh said coolly.

"Done," Cavanaugh snapped, and Macintosh realize too late he could have gotten more. When you were talking about a player who'd be worth millions, fifty thousand bucks was negligible.

Macintosh smiled anyway. "Great. So, uh, how is payment made? I assume I won't receive a check?"

"No, the money will be delivered to your door. Don't worry about how. It'll get there. In fact, to show my good faith, I'll get the first half to you later this week."

And he did—a few days later Macintosh came home to find a small brown package, the size and shape of a brick, lying outside the door of his apartment. His name and address were on it, but there were no stamps, postmarks, or other evidence it had been delivered through any of the conventional delivery systems. He thought about asking one of his neighbors if they'd seen anybody, then thought better of it.

He unwrapped the box on the kitchen counter, amid a shaft of spring sunlight that, ironically, gave him the look of a holy figure, and found a condensed stack of hundred-dollar bills in a small cardboard box with a lid. He was now an official mole. He felt a faint sensation of self-loathing, but ignored it until it went away. That was to be expected. Nothing a few nights on the town couldn't cure.

Cavanaugh wanted regular calls every time something happened involving the package Jon was building for Skip Henderson. Good, bad, or otherwise, he wanted the details. He suggested—and Macintosh had already figured this out on his own—that he should only use his personal cell phone. Using one of the office phones was flat-out stupid. Teams sometimes randomly tapped their lines during security sweeps. And it was easy to trace where outgoing calls went; you simply had to review the monthly bill. There was a very good chance a series of regular phone calls from Robert Macintosh to the general manager of a division rival would arouse suspicion.

He knew exactly where to search for the information Cavanaugh wanted. Jon kept updated printouts of the spreadsheets in the top left drawer of his desk. And the desk was rarely locked—one of Jon's many moronic "open-door policies" that was meant to create an atmosphere of fuzzy warmth throughout the organization. *See?* Macintosh thought. *The nice guys really do finish last.*

He opened the drawer, and the sheaf of printouts was sitting on top, held together by a small binder clip. He read through everything until the details were burned into memory. Then he replaced the pages and left. No one saw him because no one was around.

It was a clean getaway.

BILLIE JO RYDELL WOULD BE TWENTY-FOUR IN JUNE and she already had three children, all from different men. The youngest of the three, a little boy she named LaVelle, was the spitting image of his father. Unfortunately, that man, a part-time auto mechanic and full-time drunk, had packed his bags and left three weeks earlier.

Billie Jo had worked as a domestic cleaning woman since she was eighteen. She had no college education and no high school diploma. She had taken her GED test once and failed, and was planning on trying it again, sooner or later. The last seven months of her professional life were spent with the White Glove Service, an ultra-exclusive East Coast franchise that catered only to the wealthy. They told their clients they ran background checks on all their employees, but they only really did this if a potential hire was a complete stranger. Billie Jo knew one of their other maids, so they didn't bother with her. She was willing to work cheap, too, and the owner of White Glove cherished people who worked cheap.

In her company uniform—light pink with a white apron front—she went about her weekly chores in the house of Darryl Bailey, star wide receiver for the Baltimore Ravens, dusting and polishing thousands of dollars' worth of furniture. It occurred to her many times that she would never own furniture like this, never even come within a thousand light years of owning such a home. The art that hung on the walls, the jewelry that lay on the dressers; the only way she would ever intermingle with this standard of living was to do exactly what she was doing now—be a servant. The bitterness of this harsh reality always lay just under the surface. She had learned through the years to conceal it, but was unable to erase it.

Her routine had always been the same—start at the top and work your way down. She would do an attic on special request (White Glove rarely said no to anything—it wasn't good for business), but on an ordinary day she began on the second floor. In Bailey's house the second floor constituted an office, a living room, two spare bedrooms, and a full bath. It was the easiest part of the job because Bailey never went up there, and that bitch girlfriend of his, Bernadette, only used the office.

Nevertheless, she dusted and polished everything, opened the windows to circulate fresh air, changed all the sheets, and emptied all the wastebaskets. She straightened everything that was on the desk in the office but rearranged nothing. She had learned long ago that offices were minefields. You had to straighten up but not rearrange. If a customer couldn't find something because you moved it, you'd get heat for it. One young and overzealous girl a few years back had ignored this cardinal rule and reorganized the home office of a Smith Barney VP. White Glove's owner, a millionaire in her own right, spent half an hour apologizing over the phone, then invested another sixty seconds in the girl's termination. Reputation was everything.

The first floor was a little harder than the second. This was where the couple spent most of their time. They weren't slobs—unlike some of her customers—but they had their quirks. Bailey worked out every morning and usually left his sweat-soaked clothes in a separate hamper in the bedroom closet. It was air-sealed so the odor wouldn't drift through the house, but Billie Jo had to open it sooner or later, and when she did a stench drifted out that was so raunchy it made her eyes water. Discreet or not, she always held her breath as she dumped the load into the washing machine. Sometimes even that didn't help.

When she was done there she went into the basement. There were five rooms, all with carpeting and sheet rock, and all painted and decorated. The main attraction was the game room, featuring a marble pool table, a bank of vintage video games, a poker table, and a bar, which was always fully stocked.

She lugged a bag of laundry into the utility room and dropped it in front of the washing machine, then paused to catch her breath. A bead of perspiration ran from her forehead into her eye, stinging like mad. She lifted the washer lid, took a deep breath and held it, then dumped the clothes in.

As she turned to leave, something caught her attention. She looked up and saw that one of the ceiling tiles was slightly out of place. She noticed things like this—whether something was a little crooked or had been moved from a spot where it usually was.

Her first instinct was to simply move it back. A folding stepladder was stored nearby, in the narrow gap between the supply cabinet and the wall. As soon as she touched the tile, she heard something roll off it.

Something's up there.

Neither of her clients was home right now, and yet she took a moment to peer out the doorway and make sure no one was there. She listened hard but didn't hear anything. She went back up the stepladder and carefully moved the tile aside. She wasn't tall enough to actually see what was there, but she could feel around. Her fingers came across a small, cylindrical object. When she brought the empty cortisone bottle down, she let out a tiny gasp. Further exploration garnered the brown bag containing the rest of the injections.

She didn't know much about much, but she knew one thing—professional athletes weren't supposed to use drugs. They got in trouble. Sometimes she heard stories about guys getting fined. She also remembered something about baseball players testifying before some government committee about using steroids. She wasn't sure if cortisone was a steroid, but she was pretty sure it was illegal one way or the other. If it wasn't, Bailey wouldn't be hiding it.

She knew she was on to something.

WHEN RAYMOND COOLIDGE WAS UPSET, HE THREW balls around the field at Washington High by himself. The workout helped diminish his anger and give him time to think.

He would emulate a game situation, starting in a crouched position and calling signals. Then he'd try to lay the ball into the hands of an imaginary receiver. He had a good imagination—clear and sharp—and sometimes lost himself in the dream. He could hear the crowd, the band, the slap of the pads.

His old playbook lay nearby. He would run the common designs from memory, then try some of the other schemes just to keep up on them. He found the memorization easy and rarely needed the book. He'd created a few plays of his own but never showed them to anyone. All part of the secrecy he had developed, the same as the endless hours of game tape he watched—studying himself, studying his opponents, studying pros—and the books he read. He was eternally preparing for a career that a big part of him didn't want.

The imaginary receiver started on the left and ran fifteen yards, then cut inside to receive a pass over the middle. A dangerous play, Raymond knew. He'd have to get the ball to him quickly. No tossing or lobbing—it had to be a laser beam or the cornerbacks would catch up to him and slam him like a doll. Raymond took two steps and raised the ball. Then, back in reality, he spotted someone sitting on the warped and rotting bleachers and turned. The dream game dissipated.

At first he thought it was Pearly. Then he recognized his father's slim figure. The two men stared at each other, the April wind bending the grass between them. Then Raymond started toward the rusting fence, the ball still in hand.

"Dad?"

"Hiya, son."

Raymond managed a tiny smile. "What are you doing here?"

"I'm watching you. You know you hold it too high when you throw the long ones? That makes it harder to get good distance. Hold it back a little farther instead. You'll have to work on your control afterward, but it'll be worth it."

"Oh, okay." *That's the first time in years he's given me playing advice.*

"I had the same trouble early on."

"You did?"

"That's right. Actually, I wasn't even that good in college. I sat on the bench for the first two years. I never thought I'd have a chance. I had to work on my mechanics like crazy. It took most of those two years just to *un*learn the bad habits I picked up in high school."

"Wow, I didn't know that."

"It's all true. Anyway, you got a minute?"

"Sure."

Quincy patted the wood. "Come on up here. I want to talk to you about something."

Ray hurdled the fence and sat down. The waning afternoon sunlight complemented the poignant father-and-son picture.

"Someone came to see me the other day."

"Who?"

"Your Uncle Pearly."

Raymond began spinning the ball. "Oh yeah? What'd he want?"

"He wanted to talk to me about you."

"Me?"

"Yeah. He told me he contacted an agent."

Raymond's smile faded. "Yes, he did."

"He said this agent thinks you might be good enough to play in the pros."

"That's what he said."

"But you don't want to play in the pros."

The young man shook his head defiantly. "No."

"Why not?" Quincy waited only a few seconds before adding, "Is it because of what happened to me?"

"Well . . . yeah. Of course"

Quincy studied his son's face—the tight jaw, the impassive eyes—then turned back to the field.

"Pearly said you walked out on him, too."

"Well . . . yeah, I did. But—"

Quincy put his hand up. "I didn't ask for an explanation, did I?"

"No, sir." It was almost a whisper.

"You're not in trouble, son. I'm not mad at you."

"Dad, how can I play for a league that—"

"Raymond, Pearly was right—you don't know everything. You only know the parts of the story. The parts that . . . well, that I wanted you to know about."

"What?"

"Look, I was young and stupid back then. I wanted someone to be mad with me. Everyone else knew the whole story—Pearly, your mama, some people in the league. A lot of people knew." He turned away and added, "It's a miracle the press never found out."

"So . . . all this time . . ."

"No, I never lied to you. What I told you was the truth," Quincy said, then broke away from his beloved son's adoring eyes and, with all the courage he could muster, added, "It just wasn't the whole truth."

Raymond stared at his father for what seemed like a long time. In that brief span he decided he already forgave him.

"Well, can you tell me the whole truth now?"

Pressner took a deep breath. "Yeah, I think it's about time."

HE LIT A CIGARETTE. WHEN IT HAD BURNED ABOUT halfway down, he said, "I had the opportunity to make history and I blew it. When I first came into the league there were no black quarterbacks. None." He emphasized the word by slicing his hand through the air horizontally. The cigarette drew a line of smoke above it. "But I was good, really good, and I knew it. I also knew a lot of people would have a problem with that. Not everyone was ready for a black quarterback back even in the '80s—coaches, owners, players. Some were okay with it, attitudes were changing. But not everyone's. I knew I was still facing an uphill battle. But I kept at it, working hard and doing everything right. I took my team to the Rose Bowl, and we won it thirty-four to ten." Quincy smiled at this bright spot in his personal history. "I had a hell of a game that day. Threw for three hundred twenty-two yards and four touchdowns against the best defense in college that year. We tore through them like tissue paper."

"It sounds great."

"It *was* great. The guys carried me off the field like I was the hometown hero." He ground the cigarette into the wood and went for another, pulling a deck of Pall Malls from his shirt pocket. "Anyway, in spite of a great senior year, the writers were saying I wouldn't be drafted until late in the first round, maybe not even until the second. Those bastards sure as hell didn't like the idea of a black quarterback being a starter in the pros. A big white boys' club is what they were, make no mistake. And I believed what they were saying. I thought for sure I'd go in the second round, maybe even the third.

"Then I get a call from Herb Schummer, the Rams' president, about a half hour before the draft begins. He tells me Artie Newhouse, one of the owners, wants to take me with the first pick." Quincy looked to his son. "I thought it was a prank call, but it wasn't. Artie and Herb drafted me less than thirty minutes later. Next thing I knew I was being handed a Rams' uniform and a Rams' playbook, and carrying all their hopes into the future."

"Wow."

Quincy nodded. "It was a lot for a kid to handle. But Art and Herb believed in me. That was the key. They took a lot of heat from people who didn't want to see me succeed. They figured it was bad enough that I was drafted before all those white players, but to have me be the starter and maybe turn the team around, too? No way."

"But that's exactly what happened, right?"

"At first. Artie and Herb wanted to win and decided to look past the fact that I was black. I was never sure if it bothered Herb anyway, but I know it didn't bother Artie. He was a rare breed—a multimillionaire conservative who didn't give a damn about race. All he wanted to do was win, and if you could help him do that, he wanted you. He and Herb treated me as good as they treated the white players. They knew I had a chip on my shoulder but they never made an issue out of it. I had all the same privileges, all the same perks." He paused, blowing a lungful of smoke into the air. "They also gave me the same kind of fat contract any other number one pick would get . . . and that's where my problems started."

"I don't understand."

Quincy surveyed the field. "It was too much money for a kid to handle," he said softly. "They didn't have money managers and personal advisors and all that stuff in those days. They just handed you a pile of cash. I didn't know what to do with it. I was a poor kid from the streets of Philly. My old man disappeared when I was nine, and my mama died three years later. I was raised by my Aunt Jean. You knew that, right?"

"I know a little bit about it."

"I never had more than twenty bucks in my pocket in my life, and all of a sudden I've got four hundred thousand. That ain't a mouse turd compared to what they're paying out now, but back then it was a fortune. I had no idea what to do with a fortune. I put some of it in the bank for you, some of it in the bank for your mama so she'd have some spending money—she was just as poor as me when she was a kid—and the rest . . ." He shook his head in disgust. "The rest went to whores, booze, and dope." He looked back at his son. "That's right. Your old man was a philanderer. Oh, I had it all—a big black Cadillac, fine threads, gold rings, sideburns. I even had a wide-brimmed hat with a damn feather sticking out of it. Shit, I looked more like a pimp than a quarterback.

"Your mama kept quiet about it at first. I think she was hoping it was just a phase I was going through. But then pictures started showing up in the papers and on TV. Pictures of me with other women, coming out of bars, a bottle in my hand. . . ." He held up his cigarette. "One of these hanging out of my mouth. That's when your mama decided she'd had enough. We had a lot of fights over it, and I was in denial the whole time. I was telling her the reporters were making more out of it than it really was, but they weren't. You get sucked into that world. You never control it—it controls you. And your mama didn't want any part of it. Not long after you were born, she left, dropped my last name and everything. She didn't want you growing up in that world. I pretended I was angry at first, but all I was really interested in was the next joint or the next drink. I couldn't help it—I was hooked."

"Didn't Art Newhouse or Herb Schummer say anything?"

Quincy laughed. "Herb didn't say much, but Artie did. Maybe he didn't give a damn what color you were, which is why I loved him, but he sure as hell didn't like you boozin' and dopin'. He'd had a strict Catholic upbringing, all fire and brimstone. He wasn't a Bible-thumping lunatic, but he was close. He tried to warn me away from what I was doing, and I knew he was speaking from the heart. But I didn't listen. I was too cocky. I was creating magic on the field, breaking all sorts of records and turning the team around. By my second year we won fourteen regular season games. *Sports Illustrated* ran that long article on me, and I was being interviewed on TV every week. I was the hottest dude around, and I knew it. I figured I could get away with anything because I was getting results.

"But like I said, there were still a lot of people in the league who didn't like the idea of a black hotshot quarterback, and those people got together and decided to take me down. I know that sounds paranoid, but you got to remember the world was a different place back then. There was still a lot of that white supremacy shit around. And to be honest with you, I wasn't helping my cause very much. People were saying blacks were only interested in drinkin' and dopin' and gettin' laid, and that was exactly what I was doing. The NFL tried to maintain a clean public image, and here I was stumbling around drunk in the streets with a woman under each arm, neither of whom was my wife." He shook his head again and flicked the dead cigarette over the rusted fence. "I was a real piece of work."

"You were young. You didn't know any better," Raymond said.

Quincy shook his head. "Yeah, and I paid a big price for it. Guys started roughing me up on the field, taking the penalties for late hits and stuff like that. I think they figured if I got hurt, I wouldn't be quite so valuable any more, and then I wouldn't be able to get away with everything else. Man, the hits I took back then. . . ." He rotated his right arm and grimaced. "I took a shot from a Chiefs' linebacker that dislocated my shoulder. They popped it back into place on the sidelines, and I screamed like a little girl. I never knew such pain."

"Is that why you stopped playing?"

"No, I hung in there. All they did by pushing me around was make me more determined than ever. I got tougher and played better. And that made me even cockier. I partied more, and I caused more trouble. I started speaking out to the press, criticizing people, which they definitely did not appreciate. They still don't tolerate it, but they were really against it back then. But I figured I was indestructible. Nothing could touch me. And then came Judgment Day—December twenty-fourth, 1988. A date I'll remember it if I live to be a million years old. . . ."

He shook a third cigarette from the pack and positioned it between his lips. "We were playing the Redskins in the first round of the playoffs. They were damn good. But I knew we could beat them, so I went out the night before, prowling around like a tomcat in spite of Coach Jessel's orders to stay in and rest up. I was hung over and feeling like crap.

"I came to the stadium early because this kid who worked for the league, Bobby Cartwright, called and asked me to. I didn't know him, but I knew he was part of the inner circle, so I wasn't about to say no.

"I get there before anyone else and go down to the locker rooms. Newley wasn't there, but three other guys were. I'd never seen them before. One was small and fat, dressed in a gray suit. He was, as it turns out, one of the silent partners in the Rams' ownership. The other two wore dark suits. One of the dark suits was older than the fat dude, the other looked like he was fresh out of college. They were all white and they all looked pissed. The moment I saw them I knew I was in trouble . . ."

The heavyset man motions for Quincy to come toward him. "Mr. Pressner, can we have a word with you?"

"What's this about?"

"Come on in here. We want to talk to you for a moment."

He puts his arm around the big black man—around his waist because he can't reach his shoulders—and leads him into the showers. One of the heads is dripping, the drops ticking off the minutes on the tiled floor. When they stop, each man takes a different position, surrounding Pressner. The two dark suits fold their hands together at the crotch and bear down on him with their eyes. The other man puts one hand in his pocket and the other to his lips in a pose of deep reflection.

"Mr. Pressner, I'll get right to the point—we've received some complaints about you."

"What kind of complaints?"

"Complaints about drugs, alcohol, and prostitutes."

Pressner's eyes go from man to man. "Who are you guys? Who sent you?"

"Don't worry about who we are," *the same man replies. Quincy realizes he's the head of this little nest of serpents and thus the one who will do most of the talking.* "That's not important. What's important is the league. There are a lot of people working very hard to keep its image clean, and frankly you're not helping with your behavior."

"My behavior? What I do off the field is my business, understand?"

The dark suits suddenly look uncomfortable, but the gray suit is unfazed. He tilts his head back and evaluates Pressner carefully, as if trying to guess his age or exact height. Then one of the other men sweeps back the flaps of his jacket and puts his hands on his hips. As he does, a Browning 9mm handgun is revealed. Pressner realizes the gesture was intentional.

"No, Mr. Pressner, what you do off the field isn't just your business," *the heavyset man continues.* "What you do off the field is everyone's business, because it affects everyone in this business. Do you understand?"

Pressner doesn't answer, and in spite of the gun he has no intention to.

"A lot of people have tried to be reasonable with you. You've been asked to keep your drinking under control. You've been asked to keep your womanizing quiet. And you've been asked to lay off the dope. But you don't listen. You seem to think you can do anything you want, anytime you want, just because you're a star."

"Other guys dope and drink. I've seen them. But you don't bother them because they're white."

"Take it easy," the older of the dark suits says, nudging Pressner with a long, bony finger. He's much older than Pressner originally thought.

"Mr. Pressner," the fat one continues, "we don't want any trouble. We're just here to deliver a message, that's all."

"Yeah? What message?"

"It's time for you to step down."

"Step down?"

"That's right. Walk away, hang it up. Call it whatever you want. It's time for you to go away, Mr. Pressner. You won't play along, so you've become too much of a risk."

"To who?"

"Mr. Pressner . . ."

"If you think I'm going to throw away my career, you're out of your fucking mind."

"Mr. Pressner?"

"You can kiss my ass if you think—"

The man with the gun reaches into his jacket, and Pressner stops. The man doesn't pull out the weapon, however. Instead he retrieves a small envelope.

"Have a look at these."

Inside, Pressner finds a collection of photographs. They were taken at different times and in different places. Some are of him alone, others are with friends or prostitutes. In all of them he's either snorting coke or using a needle.

"Those would be very hard to explain to your wife, Mr. Pressner. Or the media." Then the fat man smiles. "Or a prosecutor."

Pressner looks at the other dark suits. They're smiling, too.

"You're a bunch of fucking parasites."

"No, we're doing our job." The man takes the photos back and replaces them in his jacket pocket. "Try to remember, Mr. Pressner—the good of the league. So what's it going to be? You can go to jail for a long time, or you can walk away at the end of this season by declining to sign a new contract, and keep your money and the warm memories of your brief but spectacular career. . . ."

The last cigarette lay dead between his fingers. He never took a single puff. "I played a great game that day. One of my best ever. We went on to win the next game, but lost in the conference championship."

"And then you quit," Raymond said.

Quincy nodded. "And then I quit. I didn't sign for the following season. I didn't do anything. I just went underground, as the saying goes. I didn't want to talk to anyone, didn't want to be seen by anyone, so I vanished. And it made those guys very happy."

"Sons of bitches."

"Yeah, they were."

"And Uncle Pearly wants me to play for them?"

"No, Ray, not them. Those guys didn't represent every person in the league. They were a dying breed, on their way out. Maybe they really thought they were protecting the league; I don't know. But other people were more open minded, more forgiving. I should've realized that then, but I was too young. I didn't know enough about things. They knew how to scare me, and let's face it—I *was* way out of line. If the wrong people found out about the drugs, I could've gone to jail for a long time. Twenty years at least. My life would've been over. I was big and strong, but I never could've survived prison. I had a big mouth and I didn't know when to shut it. I would've ended up face down in a pool of my own blood somewhere, and no one would've cared."

He paused and took a deep breath. Then he reached over and took the football in hand.

"Not a day goes by that I don't think about playing. I can't watch it on television because it makes me think about what might have been. Those bastards stole my career, but I helped them. I wanted to blame it on racism, but there were other black guys in the league who went on to greatness. O. J. Simpson, Walter Payton. Being a black quarterback wouldn't have been such a big deal. Look at how well Doug Williams and Warren Moon did. Moon had an amazing career. And plenty of new ones, too, like that McKinley kid. It's no big deal."

He threw the ball in the air a few times, then gripped it tight. His long fingers still had some power.

"My chance has come and gone." He looked over at his son. "But yours hasn't. It's just starting. And you could make it, Ray. You've got what it takes. I know. I can spot it a mile away. I've watched you play."

"You have?"

"Yep. No one knows that, not even Pearly. It's easy to walk around unnoticed when you don't look the same anymore, especially with the help of a pair of sunglasses and a cap. I came to a few of the games. Your best was against St. John's. They had a good defense, but you figured it out real quick. You got that from me. I could always dissect a defensive scheme. There are a few smart defensive coordinators in the pros, but most of them are hacks. No originality at all." He shook his head and laughed. "What I wouldn't give to be back out there, running them around in circles."

Raymond chose his next words carefully. "I'm sorry, Dad. I'm sorry about what happened to you. I wish there was something I could do."

Quincy smiled. "There is." He tossed the ball back. "You can go out there and do all the things that I didn't. You can play your best and try to become a pro and carry on the family name. And you can stay out of trouble so you don't blow it like I did. Be everything I was, and be everything I wasn't."

"Are you serious?"

"You bet. Pearly's right—you're not going to get another chance like this. Take it for all it's worth. Don't end up a loser like me. Be a winner. Climb as high as you can, then climb a little higher. Make me proud."

Raymond was smiling; smiling and nodding. He gripped the ball the same way Quincy had only moments before.

"Will you help me?"

"You're damn right I will."

A great ball of warmth exploded inside the handsome young man, starting in his belly and slowly expanding to the rest of him. He never thought he would know such happiness.

"Okay, Dad, I'll give it a shot."

"Good."

"But . . . first I have to talk to somebody."

"Who's that?"

With one eyebrow raised, Raymond said, "I think you can guess."

"Ah, right. Of course."

13

UNABLE TO REPRESS HIS SMILE, JON SABINO SET THE
phone back into its cradle and got up.

"How's it going today?" he asked an intern as he breezed
past her. She gave some small reply, but he didn't hear it. He
cruised down the hallway, which also served as a gallery of
large, framed photos featuring great moments in the Ravens'
brief but mostly happy history. There were shots of the last
two Super Bowl victories, and one of the first regular-season
game they ever won—a 19–14 home-field victory over the
Raiders on September 1, 1996. There was a formal portrait
of Art Modell, the team's first owner, and of the stadium
during construction. Each frame had a little brass plaque
along the bottom with a caption, as if anyone in the building
dared be so ignorant.

He passed a little alcove that served as the office's copy-
ing and mailing station. There was a massive Xerox machine
that had been bought outright rather than leased (and was
decorated with various Ravens' stickers), plus a long white
table with a variety of FedEx and UPS boxes. In spite of the
obscene amounts of money the team harvested, they had no
full-time mail or copy clerks; there was always someone
around to take care of those chores. Half the time the higher-

ups were in such a hurry to get something copied or mailed that they did it themselves. Taped to the walls were a variety of clipped cartoons, including a few old *Far Side*s, and one inspirational note—"If you fail to plan, plan to fail." These little motivational, corporate-type messages were common to NFL clubs, targeting not just the players but anyone who drew a team paycheck. They were posted everywhere, even the bathrooms. The one painted above the locker room door-way (visible on the way *out*) read, "What you do today determines what you do tomorrow." Jon, notably, did not keep any in his office. He preferred to follow a collection of accumulated personal ideologies, and those only in his mind.

He passed the other offices, each bearing the occupant's name. There were no titles, however—NFL clubs were relatively small organizations, so every knew who every else was. In keeping with the Ravens' casual style, most doors were left open. The offensive line coach, an enormous black man who had played for the Browns in the late '70s, was reviewing a game tape with his feet on his desk. Two other assistant coaches were having a hallway conversation about conditioning drills. They nodded and smiled to Jon Sabino as he passed.

The office at the far end of the hallway was Peter Connally's. Jon Sabino knocked before entering and found the owner behind his desk, Cary Blanchard in the chair on the other side.

"Am I interrupting?"

"No, no," Connally said, "come on in."

"Good morning, Cary."

"'Morning, Jon."

"I have some news that may interest both of you."

Connally held his hands up. "Let's hear it."

The smile came back automatically.

"I just got off the phone with Skip Henderson. The number one pick is all ours."

Connally clapped once. "Fantastic!" He rose and shook Jon Sabino's hand. "Good work, Jon. Really excellent. A done deal!"

"Well . . . I don't want to celebrate just yet. The draft isn't for a few more days. Someone else could still try to get it."

"Oh, but who could? We gave up half the team, right?"

"It feels that way. I was just about out of ammunition."

In total, he'd given up twenty-one members of the team—three of which were on Blanchard's "Prefer to Keep" list—in order to secure ten quality defensive players for Skip Henderson. He'd also parted with every draft pick for the present year and the year following, and those for the first four rounds in 2008. Susan Schiff told him he'd made a total of seventy-four phone calls to fifty-one different people, covering more than fifty solid hours. Since Michael Bell's accident, he had come to the office no later than seven, and stayed for a minimum of thirteen hours each day. Susan also claimed he drank five cases of Coca-Cola and ate nineteen tacos.

Jon let out a long, weary sigh. "Thank God that's over."

"I agree. Let's celebrate!" Connally went to his desk and pulled a bottle of malt whiskey out of the drawer. "Cary?"

"Sure."

He poured three glasses and handed them out.

"Here's to Jon Sabino, our resident miracle worker."

They clinked the glasses together and drank.

"So, Cary, how do you feel about coaching the next Hall of Fame quarterback?"

"Pretty good."

"I think we should tell the media."

Jon paled. "No, Peter, not yet. Just wait until Saturday. If anything changes . . ."

"What's going to change? Who's going to offer more than you did?"

"Well, probably no one. But anything can happen."

Connally studied his water cooler for a moment, then turned back. "All right, we won't say anything yet. But I want to get a momentum going over this as soon as McKinley is ours."

"We will, Peter," Jon assured him. "I'll see to it myself."

"Good. Nice work," he said one more time. "Really."

"Thanks."

He couldn't help feeling a little cocky as he walked back to his office. He'd done it—he'd taken his team from the bottom of the draft's first round to the top. An unbelievable feat; some would've said impossible. But he'd done it. Another astonishing achievement on a list of dozens. His status in the fans' eyes would go from exalted to godlike. More writers would use the word *genius* now. That also meant more jealousy and resentment among his peers, but that was to be expected. And if the team claimed a third straight championship . . . *the first general manager to reach the Hall of Fame?*

He could hear the fans cheering when the commissioner stepped up to that podium at noon on Saturday and made the announcement. He could feel the rumble under his feet as the football world was rocked to its core. What a moment that would be.

And Peter was right—who could match his offer? Nobody. Nobody had the picks *and* the players to spare like the Ravens did. He shouldn't have been so paranoid about telling the media. Skip Henderson was blown off his feet, and he should have been. This one was in the bag. Take it easy, Jon told himself.

Like Peter said, it's a done deal.

MACINTOSH JIGGLED THE TINY, FOAM-COVERED BUD into his ear until it snug, then tapped in the number on his cell phone. Traffic was relatively light in I-795 at the moment. A trailer rattled past him in the left lane.

Cavanaugh answered on the second ring.

"Hello?"

"It's Rob."

"What's up?"

Macintosh gave him the details of the final offer. Much to his surprise, Cavanaugh laughed.

"Christ, he's cleaning house all right."

"Yeah, and I don't think there's too much left to clean."

Cavanaugh paused. "Really? Do you mean that?"

"Yeah. We're running out of picks and players. Even Connally, the asshole of the world, doesn't want to mortgage *everything*. He wants this third championship, and he's willing to mortgage the future to get it. But as for the immediate season, he has to be careful. There's really nothing left."

"Well, that's good to know. Very good."

"You gonna put in your own offer now?"

"I might," Cavanaugh replied.

"Oh come on, don't deny me this. Let me savor the knowledge of what's coming."

Cavanaugh laughed again. "You're having fun with this, aren't you?"

"You're damn right I am."

"Okay—yes, I'm going to be submitting something soon."

Macintosh came up to an elderly woman puttering along well under the speed limit. He checked his mirrors quickly, then roared around her.

"Why not wait until the last moment, make it impossible for him to respond?"

"Because Skip Henderson's a goddamn Boy Scout. He'll never go for that. Besides, it'll be fun knowing Sabino and Connally are squirming for a while. Shit, you'll get to see it in person."

"Mmm, true. Okay, I'm outta here. If anything else happens, I'll let you know."

"Thanks."

Macintosh terminated the call and set the phone on the passenger seat. Then he inserted an Eric Clapton CD and started singing along.

ALTHEA COOLIDGE PULLED IN FRONT OF THE SMALL suburban home she shared with her son Raymond, parked, and got out. She retrieved a maroon leather case from the back seat—a gift from her boss last Christmas—and headed to the front door. On the way she exchanged small talk with

Ms. Parker, a neighbor, who was out front assessing her flower beds.

Althea had been a corporate assistant at Smith Barney since the early '90s, when the last of the money from Quincy's playing days dried up and she was forced to find a job. In truth there *was* some other cash left, but it had been tucked away in various places. That was back in the days when she, the daughter of an alcoholic father and a chronically depressed and unreliable mother, allowed herself to believe she might actually have a shot at the American dream. Her husband was the toast of the town, money was pouring in from all directions, and the possibilities seemed limitless.

The short trip up the three concrete steps was becoming more difficult every day. She wasn't exactly "fat," but she was a bit over the ideal weight for a woman of forty-eight who stood five foot five. She didn't complain, however, for that wasn't her way. Life could be harsh, and you either dealt with it or it dealt with you.

Through the enclosed porch and into the living room, she set the briefcase on top of a small bookcase and slipped out of her jacket, which she then hung in the front closet with her characteristic orderliness. Still out of breath, she went back to the porch and leaned down to collect the day's mail. Two bills, the new *TV Guide,* and the rest junk. An example of the latter, an invitation to have her chimney swept, was addressed to "A. Pressner." She shook her head and tossed it into the garbage can in the hallway. She had reverted back to her maiden name the day the divorce was finalized. That same week she had Raymond's surname changed as well. It wasn't that she hated Quincy and would feel somehow soiled if she kept his name, but she had come to understand that the life of a relative of a professional athlete had more downs than ups. She didn't want any part of that, and she certainly didn't want it for her son. Better to stay as close to anonymous as possible.

She removed her shoes, propped up the pillows on her

bed, and read quietly for a while. The book was a collection of poems and short stories by Dorothy Parker, which she'd borrowed from the local library. It was worn almost to the point of dysfunctionality; even the clear plastic protector was cracked and cloudy.

When the thirty minutes were up, she went into the kitchen, filled a large steel pot with water, and set it on the stove. They'd have pasta tonight. Raymond never complained about her cooking even though it wasn't exactly cordon bleu. Her son had a healthy appetite and few quirks. Put something in front of him and he'd eat it.

She poured a can of sauce into another pot and was stirring it when Raymond came in. His white sweatshirt and gray sweatpants were decorated with grass stains and dirt smears.

"Hi, Ma."

"Hi. Spaghetti okay?"

"Huh? Oh, yeah. That's fine."

He watched her for a long moment—the quiet, sturdy woman whom he loved with every ounce of his heart. He was by no means a wizened and worldly adult, fluent in the language of life and nimble in his understanding of things cosmic and ethereal, yet he knew on some primal level that his mother had sacrificed for him, starved whatever dreams and ambitions she may have had to make sure he was raised properly, given as good a chance as anyone else, and without asking for anything in return. Each day brought him a greater sense of awe.

"Ma, can I talk to you for a minute?"

"Sure."

He shuffled his feet. "Um, I was at the field today, throwing the ball around . . . and Dad showed up."

He watched her carefully. Her reaction was minor, almost imperceptible—she stopped stirring for just a moment.

"Really? And how's he doing?"

Raymond wanted to be careful here. Unlike some divorced mothers he knew, his mom had never discouraged him from talking about his father. She knew how important Quincy was to him, and she didn't want him sharing in any bitterness or resentment she might harbor over the failed relationship. Raymond also understood there was a part of her that had always loved him and still did, and it was this part that concerned him. He was afraid the mere mention of his father would irritate old wounds.

"He seemed okay. Ma . . . he told me what happened."

" 'What happened?' What do you mean?"

"With him . . . in the NFL."

She stopped stirring and turned.

"He told you about that?"

"Yeah."

"Everything?"

"Everything."

She drifted into some far-off place for a few seconds, then returned to her duties.

"How do you feel about it?"

Raymond laughed a little. "I was surprised at first. I mean, I thought. . . ."

"I know what you thought. That's what your father wanted everyone to think."

"What those guys did to him was wrong, but he did some things, too."

His mother nodded slowly. "Yes, he did."

"I don't know what to think about it, Ma. That was a long time ago. It didn't have anything to do with me. I'm sorry he hurt you, though. I'm really sorry about that."

"It's okay," she said softly. "Like you said, that was a long time ago."

"Yeah, well . . . did you hear what Uncle Pearly did? He sent some of my game tapes to this guy, this agent." Again he watched her carefully.

"Really?"

"Yeah. I was mad at first, but . . . now I don't know."

"Did this agent respond?"

"Yeah. He thought I was pretty good."

Althea nodded. "You are good. I thought you should've

tried to get into the draft last June, after you graduated."

Raymond smiled. "Well, this guy said he thought I had a shot at making an NFL team anyway. A real shot."

"I see."

There was another pause, and then Raymond said with excruciating delicacy, "I want to go for it."

At first his mother didn't speak, move, or show any other reaction. In fact it almost seemed as though she hadn't heard him at all. Then she said, "What about graduate school?"

"If I don't get signed, I'll go," he said quickly. He had already anticipated this question. "Or, I'll use my bachelor's degree to get a job."

"Is that what you want? To get a job?"

"Well . . . not really."

"What do you really want?"

He paused, then spilled it out—"I want to play."

It felt good to say after so many years—*I want to play.* Deep down, that had always been the truth. He loved football, loved everything about it. He loved the feel of the ball in his hands, loved connecting with a receiver, loved the pressure and the intensity, loved being out there in the midst of chaos. And most of all, without a doubt, he loved *winning.* Finally being able to admit all of this was perhaps the most cathartic moment of his life. But would his mother approve? If she didn't, he knew, this great love would remain confined to a public field in suburban Philly for the rest of its life. So he held his breath and waited for the verdict.

When it came, it was in a form he never expected—the saintly woman who had raised him almost singlehandedly and was the strongest, most resilient soul he had ever known, turned to him with a rare smile and a gleam in her eye.

"Then get to it," she said simply.

Raymond realized this was a catharsis for her, too. And never in his life had he felt so motivated.

THE BALTIMORE SHERATON DIDN'T HAVE ANY SMOK-ing rooms available, but that didn't stop Jerry Wahlberg from lighting up. He sat at the little round table by the heavy curtains (which were closed) and read through Bell's contract one line at a time. He didn't recall it being so dense, but then he wasn't looking at it the same way this time. He wasn't even sure what he was looking for *exactly,* but he was sure he'd know when he found it. He was well aware that player contracts varied tremendously in certain areas, such as pay—signing bonuses, performance incentives, licensing fees, etc.—and status within an organization—whether a player would be restricted or unrestricted as a free agent when the term of his contract was up. But in other areas they were standardized, fashioned after the template contract in the Collective Bargaining Agreement. There were boilerplate sections on injuries, pay deductions, conduct, grievance procedures, and so on, i.e., points that were almost never negotiable. The average contract was rarely more than ten pages long, with six copies being distributed among the player, his agent, the league office, the team, the National Football League Players' Association (NFLPA), and the management council.

When the print began to blur and the content became meaningless, Wahlberg rose and stretched. He hadn't found the weak spot he was searching for. He pressed every inch of the ice, but no cracks appeared. He shuffled across the carpet and grabbed the complimentary newspaper the hotel had left on the dresser. It was lying next to a room-service tray full of empty plates and glasses (he never, *ever* left food uneaten). Then he went into the bathroom and switched on the ceiling fan.

He had just sat down when the answer came to him. He froze, then a tiny smile appeared. He threw the paper on the tile floor, yanked up his pants, and dashed outside.

The flaw he was looking for didn't exist in the words that were in the contract—it was in the words that *weren't* in the contract. The idea was a stretch, of course, but it was *possible.* His gut told him it was the right approach. He laughed out loud—a horrible cackle that sounded like a small animal caught in a trap.

He reconnected the phone and dialed his office.

• • •

THE NEXT MORNING, SITTING BEHIND HIS DESK, JON reviewed a request from one of the trainers for a new piece of equipment. It had been designed in California a few months ago and was supposed to improve agility. The trainer was bright and ambitious, just the kind of person who would know all about the latest technologies. Sabino liked him, admired his drive and youthful enthusiasm. But the kid had a tendency to be long-winded in his writing. The description of the device was so detailed that Jon felt like he could build one from scratch.

The phone rang. Susan wouldn't be in for another hour. Reluctantly he reached over and grabbed it. An already bad day was about to get ten times worse.

"Hello?"

"Jon Sabino?"

The voice was vaguely familiar. He couldn't place the name through his sleep-deprived haze, but his stomach tightened automatically. Whoever it was, his instincts told him it wasn't someone he liked.

"Yes?"

"Jerry Wahlberg."

Oh shit, not him . . . not now . . .

"Little early for you, isn't it?"

"Actually I've been up for a while. Already been to the hospital to see my boy."

He sounded chipper, and that always meant trouble.

"I thought visiting hours didn't start until eight."

"They don't, unless you know how to get around it."

Jon didn't really want to hear Jerry Wahlberg's handy tips for superseding the rules of the average hospital.

"How's he doing?"

"Great, just great," Wahlberg replied. Then, gravely, he added, "But he's very concerned."

"About what?"

"About his future with the Ravens."

"What exactly are his concerns?" Jon had learned long ago that the best way to handle Jerry Wahlberg was to answer his questions with questions of your own. Direct answers—especially those that had any legal implications, no matter how seemingly abstract—would be stored away for future use. Wahlberg had very few real talents, but a lockbox memory was one of them.

"Well, he's worried about this rumor that's been going around about you guys replacing him with Christian McKinley."

"You know I can't discuss our draft plans one way or the other."

"I think I—er, we, have a right to know."

"Yes you do—*after* the draft."

"I'd like to know right now."

"I'm sure you would."

"I've heard rumors, and I'd like them confirmed."

"Good for you."

"I'd like to remind you that my client has a contract with you."

"I'm aware of that."

"I'd also like to remind you that *we* are well aware of your salary cap situation. It would be impossible for you to sign Christian McKinley and keep Michael Bell at the same time."

"I agree," Jon said. It would be pointless to argue this obvious detail.

"So I'm assuming you're going to release Michael if you get McKinley?"

"You can assume whatever you like."

"If that happens because of his accident, will he be compensated?"

"If that happened, he'd get whatever the rules called for him to get. We wouldn't try to deny him anything that wasn't rightfully his."

"I see." Wahlberg paused, cleared his throat. "According to the Collective Bargaining Agreement, I believe that would call for his full salary for the remainder of this year."

Jon's headache began to expand. "Yes, that's correct."

"And what about the rest of it?"

"What about it?"

"We'd be interested in receiving it, or, at the very least, a portion of it."

Headache notwithstanding, Jon sat up again. At last they'd reached the real reason for this call.

"You're kidding, right?"

"Not in the least."

"If the situation you describe was to come about, there's no way in hell we'd strap ourselves that badly. Why would we?"

"He deserves every penny."

"Oh really? And who decided that? You?"

"Are you placing him on the PUP or the NFI?"

It was clear Wahlberg had prepared thoroughly for this phone call. A player placed on the physically unable to perform list, or PUP, was entitled to his full salary while he was recuperating, whereas an NFI player was not entitled to any compensation. And as Bell's agent, it was well within Wahlberg's right to discuss this.

"For now he'll be placed on the NFI. His injury was, after all, unrelated to the game."

"And then?"

Jon sighed. "And then we'll see."

"I'm afraid that's not good enough."

"It'll have to be, for the moment."

"You can't just cut him."

"Excuse me?"

"You can't release him, because you have no grounds. He kept himself in perfect physical condition, so you can't cut him because he wasn't in good shape. He's the best quarterback on the team—maybe the best in the league—so you can't cut him for competitive reasons. He's done nothing to embarrass the organization, either. And, perhaps most importantly, there's nothing in his contract that specifically deals with termination in conjunction with a non-football–related injury."

"There doesn't need to be," Jon shot back. "The guidelines in the Collective Bargaining Agreement are very clear."

"We want more than one year."

"You're not entitled to more than one year."

"That will be for an arbitrator to decide."

Jon froze as the words—and the meaning behind them—sunk in.

"Are you serious?"

"Completely."

"You'd have no chance of winning."

"Perhaps," Wahlberg said, and it was his casual, carefree tone that made everything clear—Wahlberg wasn't interested in winning in arbitration. That wasn't his strategy at all. The ugly fact of the matter was that a grievance could take weeks to settle, and a lawsuit, if it came to that, could drag on for years. Even if the team managed to draft McKinley, they'd never be able to sign him. Bell's contract would be valid until the dispute was settled. If McKinley wasn't signed, he couldn't play. If he couldn't play, the Ravens could forget about reaching a third Super Bowl.

And Wahlberg knew it.

"You're the biggest sonofabitch I've ever known," Jon said.

"You'd be, too, if you were in my position."

"Don't try to justify what you're doing, you f—"

"But maybe we can work something out," Wahlberg inserted.

"What?"

"Maybe we can work out a deal."

"You mean a blackmail arrangement?"

"Call it whatever you like."

Jon got up and began pacing. If Wahlberg was in the room instead on the phone, he'd be lying unconscious by now.

"I'm sure you've already got some idea about the terms?"

"In fact I do. I was thinking of, aside from the remainder of his salary for this season, a lump sum of twenty-two million."

Jon chuckled as he stared out the window. "Forget it.

That's more than three-quarters of his remaining contract. I'm not paying that to anyone who isn't contributing."

"Okay, twenty million."

"Not a chance."

"Jon," Wahlberg said in the type of singsong voice one normally reserves for children and pets, "this can be easy, or it can be hard."

"That much money would devastate our cap for the next three seasons."

"Not if it's deferred correctly."

"No," Jon said sharply. "I'm not strapping us like that for a player who isn't playing. Forget about it. You'd have to be insane."

A silence stretched into eternity between them.

"Okay, look," Wahlberg said finally. "You obviously need some time to think this through. I'll call you back tomorrow and get your final offer."

"Don't make it too early," Jon snapped.

"I won't, don't worry."

"You're a fucking leech, you know that? Nothing more than a common parasite."

"Have a nice day," Wahlberg said, then the line went dead.

14

BILLIE JO RECOGNIZED THE EAGER LITTLE REPORTER as he came through the door—midtwenties, lean, and wearing a Ravens' cap. He was kind of cute, she couldn't help thinking. But he also appeared to be a brainy type, and she didn't like brainy types.

He surveyed the restaurant until he spotted her, sitting alone at one of the small, elevated tables. He was fresh off a Delta flight from Los Angeles but didn't feel the least bit tired. He was too jazzed up for that. Kenny Meehan had landed some big stories before, but never one as big as this. If this girl lived up to everything she'd claimed on the phone the day before, his name would be bouncing all over the world of sports journalism for months.

He worked for a monthly full-color rag called *Pro Football Today*, one of dozens of substandard periodicals desperately trying to gain share in a market dominated by *Sports Illustrated* and *ESPN: The Magazine*. It was printed on cheap paper, used cheap labor, and ran poorly written feature articles from questionable sources. Meehan, who'd been on the masthead from the beginning, was tired of toiling in obscurity and had been secretly planning to catapult it—and, in turn, himself—to the next level by breaking something big. Just one story, one that made waves and got people talking, and he'd be on the map.

And this just might just be it.

With a small knapsack slung over his shoulder, he weaved through a sea of other tables and customers. When he reached Billie Jo, he smiled and said, "Ms. Forrest?" There was no way he could have known it was a pseudonym, and that was fine with her.

"That's right," she replied, taking a long, purposeful drag from her cigarette. She didn't bother asking if he minded the smoke. This, too, was purposeful. She wanted to establish that she had the alpha position in the relationship. That meant she didn't ask for permission for anything; etiquette and courtesy were *his* burden. She also kept a blank face, although a touch of arrogance and assurance didn't hurt. "You're Kenny Meehan, I take it?"

"Yes, I am. Do you mind if I sit?"

"No."

He transferred the knapsack from his shoulder to the back of the chair and took out a small notebook.

"I'm going to take some notes, too, if that's okay."

"Fine with me. Do you have the money on you?"

Meehan hesitated for just a moment and diverted his eyes. She sensed she had committed some type of error with her bluntness. But when he looked back at her and said, "Yeah, sure," with a little laugh, she somehow knew he was desperate. This would be easy.

They spoke for a little under an hour, and she told him everything except her real name and the fact that she worked in Bailey's home; he didn't need those details. When Meehan insisted on some kind of proof that her story was true, she produced the empty cortisone bottle and needle. She'd put them first in a clear plastic bag, then in a yellow Giant supermarket bag.

"I guarantee you'll find his fingerprints on there," she told him. "I know he's been in trouble before, so you should be able to get them."

Meehan stared at her, astonished by the remorseless fashion in which she was selling this man down the river. Then he realized he was an accomplice to the act—she gave him the story, but it was his choice to run it or not to run it. He knew what he was; he had always known. Here they were, two bottom-feeders trying to pull another person off the ladder and down to their level so they could feel better about themselves. It really was that simple.

"Now, I believe we had an agreement," she said after he'd had time to drool over the evidence.

"Huh? Oh, yeah. . . ."

He reached around for his knapsack and took out a small Whitman Sampler box. She controlled the urge to leap across the table and grab it. Once it was in her hands, she lifted the lid and found a roll of hundreds held tight by a rubber band that had been wound around it several times and looked ready to snap.

"Is it all here?" she asked, unable to keep her voice from breaking.

"Yep. Five thousand," he said in a whisper.

She wrapped her hand around the wad and stuffed it quickly into her purse, dropping the sampler box on the table.

"Thanks," she said, then took a final sip of her soda and slid off the stool.

"You're welcome," Meehan said. "If I have any questions, I can reach you at that cell phone number you gave me?"

"Sure can," she said. *But you better hurry, because I'm canceling the service tomorrow.*

She was gone in seconds, and Meehan figured he would never see her again. He also guessed correctly that she hadn't provided her real name, and that she'd been wearing a wig and probably didn't really need those glasses. He didn't give a damn. He was all but certain her story was true. Why else the disguise and the phony name, and the secret meeting? And the bottle and the syringe . . . she was right— he could easily find out if Bailey's prints were on them. He'd already done some background checking to see if he was currently taking the medication legally. There was no recent reports of Bailey having sustained an injury. So, odds were her claim was true—Bailey was hiding one. It looked like he really caught the break he'd been praying for.

He returned to the airport and caught the first flight back to the West Coast.

JON SNAPPED AT SUSAN SCHIFF, WHICH HE'D NEVER done before.

He'd asked to be left in peace for a while and shut the door. He paced and thought about Wahlberg. *Only that sleazy little bastard could dream up such a reprehensible scheme.*

Then Susan stuck her head in ten minutes later, holding a manila folder.

"I thought I asked not to be disturbed?" he said sharply.

For the briefest moment, Susan looked as though she'd been slapped. Then her eyes darkened in that way they always did when she got pissed.

"You wanted to see this folder, so I'm bringing it to you, Jon."

He looked at the folder like it was some kind of alien object. Then he realized she was right. And her willingness to stand up for herself had a secondary benefit here—it pulled him out of his bad mood and into a more focused frame of mind.

"Yeah, you're right. I'm sorry. Just . . . just some bad stuff going on."

"Wahlberg, right?"

He took the folder from her. "Yeah. Who else?"

"Anything I can do to help?"

"No, I have to work it out on my own."

"Okay."

"Thanks."

"Sure." She turned to go back out. Just before she closed the door, however, she said, "By the way, you already *are* disturbed."

He smiled. "Funny."

"Yes, it is."

He hadn't told anyone else about the Wahlberg mess yet. Connally would go berserk. He wasn't just hoping for McKinley anymore—he was *expecting* him. He didn't take disappointment well. It had been a mistake to go in there and get his hopes up.

Jon consulted the wall calendar—three days left. *Shit— three days.* There was no way this matter could be resolved in three days. Wahlberg was approaching a landmark contractual crisis, one that would add new pages to the legal books. The commissioner would have to get involved; maybe a review committee. This wasn't someone paying a parking ticket. This was full-scale litigation. *Could things get any worse?* he asked himself, about ready to scream. *The draft mess, Michael's injury, and now this . . . my God.*

The phone rang. Jon was reluctant to pick it up. It had to be someone with a problem of some kind—general managers were the problem solvers, after all. Then he decided he could use the distraction. A ten-minute discussion about ordering more athletic supporters would be refreshing right now.

"Yes?"

"Jon? Freddie Friedman!"

His shoulders sagged. *An agent.* Life could be so cruel. The funny thing was, he and Friedman had a pleasant repartee. Freddie had a sterling reputation in the front office community, secretly admired for his ethics. Yes, he usually acted like a hyperactive child, and yes, he could wear you down in negotiations while trying to squeeze every last dime out of you for his clients. But he was basically an honest guy. If he had a client who wasn't worth big money, he wouldn't try to get it. If he had a client who had covered up a past injury, he'd tell you about it. He was a pain in the ass, but everyone liked him.

Nevertheless, all agents were demons in Jon's book right now.

"What can I help you with, Freddie?"

"I'm calling because I understand you might be interested in acquiring a quarterback."

"The thought's crossed my mind, yes."

"See why it's good to read the papers? Look, I have someone you should at least take a look at."

"Oh yeah? Null gonna give it another shot?"

Jon managed to smile at his own joke, cheap shot though it was. Barry Nuller had been Friedman's "Great Discovery" twelve years ago—a kid from Kentucky who was nearly seven feet tall and could throw a ball through a tire at fifty yards. Friedman noticed him on a practice field while driving around lost one day. He signed Nuller to a free-agent contract and bragged that he would be the next Joe Montana. In spite of his physical skills, however, Nuller had the mind of a child. Friedman never bothered to check his school records, for if he had he would've known Nuller had been kept back three times and only made it to college because he could throw a ball a country mile and couldn't be knocked down with a steam shovel. In the NFL, however, he would be required to memorize playbooks as thick as phone books, and he could barely remember where his locker was.

"Yeah, you're *so* funny. No, I got someone here a little better than that."

"And who would that be?"

"His name is Raymond Coolidge."

"Coolidge? I think I've heard of him."

"From a small school near Philly. But there's a lot more to him than you might think."

Friedman was notorious for this kind if hype. Jon thought his true calling was sales or advertising. He could sell a pile of cow crap as a dinner table centerpiece.

"I'd like to bring him there and have you meet him in person."

"I'm sorry, Freddie, not now. I'm up to my ears in a crisis."

"Oh . . . how about tonight? We could meet at Hops, your favorite joint. I'll buy."

Jon stopped pacing. "You're in Baltimore?"

"Uh-huh. At the Hilton, about ten minutes away."

"And this kid is with you?"

"Of course he is. What did you think, I was going to fax him to you?"

Jon had to admit he was intrigued. Freddie Friedman had interrupted his own work day—which happened once every century or so—to come down here and present this kid. In spite of his high-spiritedness and appalling fashion sense, he was very serious about his business. And he had never been one to waste other people's time—if he called you about something, he believed it was something worth calling about.

"Well . . . all right, I'll join you around seven."

"Great. You won't regret it. I promise."

"Okay, Freddie. See you then."

He replaced the phone and tried to return to his paperwork, but the name kept echoing in his mind—*Coolidge . . . Raymond Coolidge . . . from Philly.*

He couldn't quite place the memory, but he knew someone who would probably know more.

Patti Sheridan picked up on the second ring.

"Hello?"

"Patti, it's Jon Sabino." He was turned away from the speakerphone and facing his computer, running yet another Google search on Coolidge. He wasn't finding much, and it was as puzzling as it was frustrating.

"Oh hi, Jon. I wasn't expecting a call from you. Is anything wrong?"

"No, no. Well, yeah, the normal stuff. But you already know about all that. I'm calling about something else. I've got a quick question for you."

"Sure, what's up?"

Sabino paused when he thought he'd found a site with some information. Turned out to be nothing.

"Uh . . . what can you tell me about a kid named Raymond Coolidge?"

Now Patti paused; nothing but dead air from the little speaker.

"Patti? Did I lose y—?"

"Did you say Raymond Coolidge?"

"Yes."

She laughed. "Boy, you can pick 'em. I know a little bit about him, but not much. He's quite an enigma."

"You lived in the same area for a while, right? Weren't you writing for the Philly *Daily News* when he was in school?"

"Yes, and I covered a lot of his games. But I never had much luck covering *him*."

Sabino looked towards the phone, as if Patti could see this. "No? Why not?"

"Because he didn't seem to like the media. He never came out and said so, but that's the impression I got. Truth is, he never said much to anyone. He was definitely in his own little world."

"Huh . . ." Sabino turned back to the screen and navigated to the one site that had some stuff on him—La Salle University's alumnus page. "I'm looking at his college stats here, and I have to say they don't look too bad, especially considering he went up against some fairly tough opponents in his later years. In fact, it seems to me that their entire football program accelerated in the time that he played. It's as if he singlehandedly made the difference."

"He was very good," Patti said. "You should have seen him—smart, quick, and able to make great defensive reads. He knew what they were going to do before they did. And he had a nice touch, too. Tightest spiral I ever saw outside the pros."

"So what happened? No one drafted him?"

"He never declared," she said. "After college, he disappeared. No one ever heard from him again. If I'm not mistaken, he was invited to the combines. That was last year. Three teams were scouting him, or at least sniffing him out—the Chiefs, the Bears, and the Bengals."

"But he told them no?"

"He never even returned their calls."

Jon turned back to the computer and stared hard at Raymond's photo, trying to get a read on him. He appeared to be ordinary enough, which only made the mystery more tantalizing.

"I wonder why," Sabino said quietly, mostly to himself.

"I could never find out," Patti answered. "I remember once, when he was in his senior year and doing really well, my editor wanted me to get an exclusive on him. We figured he was headed for a second- or third-round pick, and we wanted to be the ones who broke the story on him. But I was stonewalled in every direction. Nothing nasty, just . . . it's hard to explain. It's like he was being protected or something. His coaches wouldn't talk, his uncle wouldn't talk, his mom wouldn't talk . . ."

"What about his dad?"

"Couldn't find him. Couldn't even get any information on him."

Jon shook his head. "Okay, thanks, Patti. Thanks very much."

"Sure. Hey, why do you want to know about him?" Jon was expecting this question. Sheridan was, after all, a reporter. "Are you trying to get him out of hiding, maybe to replace Bell?"

He laughed. "Patti, I really can't tell you anything right now because, honestly, nothing has happened yet. But how about this—if something does, I'll give you the first word."

"Is that a promise?"

"Yes."

"Okay, you got a deal."

Jon closed the line and went back to his computer. Then he dug into a few other trusted sources, none of which revealed anything he didn't already know.

This dinner was suddenly looking a lot more interesting.

JON LIKED HOPS FOR THE SAME REASON MANY OF THE Ravens' players did not—it was low key. It was nestled on an obscure side street in a quiet suburban grid, almost as if the original owners had wanted it to go unnoticed. But it wasn't—it was more of a meticulously guarded local secret, a haven for those who cherished peace and quiet. Jon liked it because the sportswriters never went there. Neither did the fans, it appeared, for no one had ever recognized him.

He stepped into the foyer and was immediately greeted by an Asian woman named Kim. She and her husband had been the owners for as long as he could remember. She was small and demure and had retained much of her natural beauty in that enviable way Asian women often do in their later years.

"Good evening, Jon."

"Hello, Kim," he said with a smile, removing his coat. She put it on a wooden hanger in the coat room. "How's David?"

"He's fine, thank you. He's in the back. I'll tell him you're here."

"Okay."

"Will you be alone this evening?"

"No, I'm meeting some—"

"Jon!"

Friedman emerged from the dining room. He looked quite respectable in his navy suit, starched white shirt, and maroon tie. He had a drink in hand—a clear fluid with ice and a slice of lime. Probably a vodka tonic. A red stirring straw was sticking out of it.

He put out his free hand and Jon shook it.

"Hi, Freddie."

"How are you? Thanks so much for coming."

"No problem."

"I really appreciate your taking the time." Freddie lowered his voice as they entered the dining room. A few people turned to see who the new guests were. Jon recognized some faces and knew a few names. There were a lot of couples, lost in their private worlds. Every table had a linen table-cloth and a china setting. Candles flickered in crystal globes. The pervading sounds were the steady din of hushed conversation and the clinking of glasses and silverware. Piano music leaked quietly from invisible speakers.

Freddie steered them toward the second and larger dining area. "Take a deep breath," he said, "you might need it." Jon laughed. What a huckster.

He came through the archway, and the four other men at Freddie's table rose. Jon recognized Eric Ross immediately, as they had known each other for years. Of the other three, it was easy to guess which one was Freddie's hot new client. He was the only one young enough. Jon appraised Pearly Pressner long enough to be sure he didn't know him. Then his eyes fell upon Quincy and stuck there. It took him a moment to dig up the name, not because he didn't know it but because he was distracted by disbelief. Memories began rushing forward. Quincy Pressner on television, Quincy Pressner on the field, Quincy Pressner on the cover of *Sports Illustrated.* Jon looked closer to make sure he wasn't delusional. Quincy smiled, as if he was used to this by now. No, Jon decided, he wasn't delusional. The Howard Hughes of pro football was really standing right there.

Eric laughed and put his hand out. "Hi, Jon. Nice to see you again."

"You too, Eric. How've you been?"

"Pretty good, pretty good."

"Jon, let me introduce you around," Freddie said. "This is Joe Pressner, from Philadelphia."

A brother? Jon wondered. He didn't know a thing about Quincy's family; who did? They shook hands.

"Nice to meet you, Joe."

"You too."

"And this is his brother, Quincy. He played for the Rams for a time in the eighties."

"Sure, I remember." Jon studied the eyes again, then tried to absorb everything else. The guy appeared human, almost ordinary. But there was also an indefinable quality—that certain *something* that made him stand out. The last time Jon sensed it in someone was three weeks ago, when he met Joe Namath at a banquet dinner.

"I was a big fan of yours when I was a kid," Jon told him. "I remember seeing you play once, in fact, at a game my dad took me to. He kept saying how amazing you were."

"Thank you," Quincy said. "Thanks a lot."

"And this," Freddie continued, setting a hand on his client's shoulder, "is Raymond Coolidge, the next great quarterback in the NFL. He's Joe's nephew, and Quincy's son."

There was no way Jon could have been prepared for this little nuclear bomb of information. He felt as if every function in his body had been zapped to a halt. He was proud of the way he handled moments that would shock other people, but this was too much even for him.

"His *son?*" he heard himself say. It came out awkward, almost rude, but no one seemed surprised.

"That's correct," Freddie said.

Jon extended his hand, "Nice to meet you, Raymond," he managed to say after a pause that was mercifully brief but still impossible to miss. From the corner of his eye, Jon saw Freddie chuckle.

"Same here," Raymond replied.

They settled into their seats and ordered another round of drinks.

"You went to La Salle, right?" Jon asked.

"Yes."

"I had heard you were making waves over there, but you never declared for the draft. Do you mind if I ask why?"

Uncomfortable glances went around the table. Jon sensed a faux pas.

"I'm sorry, I don't mean to pry. If it's something personal, forget it. I was just wond—"

"It was because of me," Quincy said. "Me and my anger toward something that happened a long time ago." He looked at his boy with a mixture of admiration and regret.

Jon nodded. "I see." He would've loved to hear the details

on the "something that happened a long time ago." Like anyone else who followed the game back then, he was stunned
by the news of Quincy Pressner deciding to suddenly leave
the game behind rather than sign a new contract with the
Rams or any other team. But he had a feeling those coveted
details weren't forthcoming.

"We're presenting him as a free agent," Freddie said.
"And we think he might even be able to make a second
squad."

"Really?" Jon didn't want to seem presumptuous, but it
was hard not to express a certain degree of disbelief. The
odds of someone coming out of the blue and backing up a
starter in the most difficult position in all of sports were so
tiny they were almost nonexistent.

"He's pretty darn good, Jon," Eric said. "You should see
the game tapes."

"He's doing stuff I couldn't do at his age," Quincy added.
"He's faster at reading defenses, and he's a better scram-
bler."

"But the NFL is a whole other world," Jon said, shifting
back into the role of a general manager. In spite of the shock
of walking into his favorite local restaurant and finding the
mythical Quincy Pressner waiting for him, he knew his primary function tonight, in the most basic terms, was to decide
whether or not he wanted to give Freddie Friedman's newest
client a shot. That had to be handled objectively. "A lot of
college phenoms couldn't make the transition. It would take
hours just to list all their names."

"He can do it, Jon," Eric said. Jon knew him well enough
to know he was being serious. "Give him a tryout. You'll
see."

The others watched and waited. Freddie chose to contact
Jon Sabino before anyone else because he knew he would be
the fairest and most open-minded.

Jon remained silent for a long time, staring into space.
He'd never seen Raymond play, knew nothing about his
habits, style, strengths, or weaknesses. Okay, so he was the

long-lost son of Quincy Pressner. That was a novelty. It would garner a great deal of media attention and sell some tickets. But did that mean he'd be able to get the job done on the field? Of course not. A good general manager examined a situation from all angles, and from the angle of Raymond's playing abilities, he was a nobody from nowhere. Yes, Eric gave him an endorsement, and that certainly carried some weight. But could Raymond work in the Ravens' system? Could he really be a reliable backup for Christian McKinley, if McKinley went down? They needed someone who could help them get to a third straight Super Bowl. And what if McKinley suffered a season-ending injury? Could this kid with no pro experience carry the whole load? It was a pretty tall order to say the least. That meant getting it done *now,* not three or four years down the line. It was an absurd stretch of the imagination—they needed someone very special. Was Raymond that person, clear out of the blue? Stranger things had happened in the league over the years, but the odds were still against it. Tremendously against it.

"I'll tell you what," he said, reaching around to retrieve his glass. "I'll make you a short-term deal. Raymond is essentially an untried and unproven talent. I have no doubt that he's got ability," he told Eric Ross, "and I've no doubt that he has the potential to play in the pros. But the Ravens are looking to win the big one again. That's why we all play the game."

"And to make history," Freddie commented.

"Yes, we'd like very much to be the first team to win three straight Super Bowls. Who wouldn't? So here's what I propose—let's give Raymond a tryout. That said, I'd like to retain his rights for a short time."

Freddie looked puzzled. "How short?"

Jon put up a finger. "One week."

The others seemed confused, but Freddie smiled. "Until the draft is over."

Jon smiled back. "That's right."

"So you *are* after Christian McKinley."

"I can't comment on that. Maybe we are, maybe we're not. Maybe we have an entirely different deal in the works that doesn't involve McKinley at all. I really can't say at this time."

Freddie's smile didn't fade. He nodded and wiped his mouth. "His way of saying skip the questions and get down to business," he told the others. "Okay, I'll play along. What kind of a deal are we talking about here, numbers-wise?"

Jon looked around the group. "I was thinking ten thousand?"

"Too low," Freddie said before anyone else had a chance to react. This was standard procedure rather than the product of quick reflection—always reject the first offer.

"Okay, twelve."

"Still too low."

"Now wait a minute," Quincy said, putting up a hand. "Doesn't Raymond have anything to say about it?"

"Freddie, I'm not going to ask Raymond to do anything for the next seven days other than come to the facility to the coaches can have a look at him," Jon pointed out. "I just want to retain his rights until after the draft. Then, if the situation calls for it, we'll talk about his future with the team. If he's good enough to make the cut, I promise you I'll sign him. And if he makes it to the second QB spot on the depth chart, I'll give him a bonus. A good one."

Friedman thought it over.

"Fifteen," he said, "is our final offer. If that's okay with you, Raymond?"

The boy who had never carried more than fifty bucks in his pocket, was wide-eyed with disbelief and managed a nod. Quincy, watching his son's reaction, smiled with amusement.

"Then we've got a temporary deal?" Jon asked.

Freddie nodded. "We've got a temporary deal." He reached over and shook Jon's hand. Papers would be drawn up and faxed around tomorrow, but Jon knew from experience that Freddie's handshake was his bond. He was a real pill, but he was good on his word.

"And I'll even pay for dinner tonight," Friedman added.

"You're a prince," Jon told him.

"I know that."

Now please tell me I didn't just blow fifteen grand, Jon thought.

15

SKIP HENDERSON READ THE REPORT FOR THE THIRD time. Typical due diligence stuff, documenting players' backgrounds for signs of trouble—arrests, convictions, etc. Time was when a kid's skills on the field were all that mattered, but nowadays character was a big issue. Troublemakers spawned bad press, and bad press often led to reduced sales in merchandising. On the field, they caused distractions. A coach could squelch most of them, but not all. Just like everywhere else in life, these types were more trouble than they were worth. Conversely, kids of good character were regarded as pure gold. Football skills were easier to teach than integrity. Good kids came with extras, bonuses. They provided the little niceties that often made all the difference. This was one of life's greatest secrets, and Henderson had discovered it early on. Others were still scratching their heads trying to figure out why certain players looked so good on paper and performed so well in the combines yet never did much for their team.

Reading through the two-page report on Isaac Bardwell as the morning sun peeked through his office blinds, he thought again about the importance of character. And on that scale, Bardwell, a guard from the Auburn, wasn't looking good. The bulk of the report discussed his two arrests for marijuana possession. In both cases the police could not prove Bardwell had actually used the stuff, but "the odor was strong on his person, as if he'd just smoked a joint."

What bothered Henderson most, though, was the time between the arrests—three years. Not three weeks or three months, which would've suggested a phase in which Bardwell was experimenting. Three *years*. For all Henderson knew, Bardwell could've been smoking pot the whole time and just didn't get caught. Or maybe he had been caught but somehow squirmed his way out of it. Charm or outright bribery, perhaps. It was even possible the officers in question didn't want to damage the reputation of a local sports hero. That certainly wasn't beyond the realm of possibility.

Whatever the case, the Ventnor report didn't illustrate a complete picture, so Henderson was left with intuition and gut instinct. At the moment Bardwell was a third-rounder on their draft chart, and a low one at that. The skills were there, but they wouldn't be worth a dime if the team had to deal with a pothead. All they needed was to sign this kid to a big contract and then lose him to the feds on his third substance-abuse arrest. Three strikes and you were definitely gone in their eyes. On the other hand, maybe Bardwell really had done it only a few times and just had a bad run of luck. It seemed like damn near everyone tried the stuff at least *once* these days. Would concern over character cause them to lose out on a great opportunity?

Henderson scanned the report one more time, hoping maybe he'd see something he'd missed before, when the phone rang. He reached over and grabbed it without taking his eyes off the paper.

"Hello?"

"Skip?"

"Yes?"

"Brendan Cavanaugh."

"Hey, Brendan, how's it going over there in Colorado?"

"Not too bad, Skip. Same old."

"Yeah, ain't that the truth. What can I do for you?"

"I'm calling about your pick."

"Which one?" Henderson asked, genuinely unsure.

"The first one. The first overall."

Henderson paused out of surprise. He set Bardwell's report down. "Oh . . . what about it?"

"I'd like to submit an offer for it."

"You're interested in it again?"

"Yes. You said you'd be taking them right up until tomorrow. Is that still the case?"

"Well, yes, but . . . I've got to tell you the current offer for it is pretty big. To be honest, I'd be amazed if anyone topped it."

"I understand. I'd like to submit one anyway, if that's okay."

"Sure," he replied. "What have you got in mind?"

Thousands of miles away, Cavanaugh leaned back, put his feet up on his desk, and smiled. *I've got the end of Jon Sabino's career in mind, that's what.*

"Are you ready?"

"I am."

"Okay, here goes . . ."

PHYSICALLY, THE RAVENS' DRAFT-DAY WAR ROOM WAS a lot less intriguing than its dramatic name implied. Like the team's other conference room, its centerpiece was a large rectangular table surrounded by comfortable leather chairs. There was another markerboard, a few cabinets, and a framed Ravens' logo hanging by itself on one of the long walls. This could be a meeting room in the office building of any American corporation.

A man in a khaki uniform was down on one knee in a corner, wearing a toolbelt and a pair of headphones. Stitched onto his shirt was an emblem that read "Hoffer Security." The headphones were connected to a small handheld device that then connected to one of the phone jacks. As he listened carefully for any signs of weakness in the line, Jon stood by and watched with his hands on his hips. The Ravens had been using Hoffer for all such security matters for years. They were professional and highly discreet, and run by an ex-FBI agent.

Today the man from Hoffer would check the integrity of the phone lines, for there would be nothing more embarrassing, not to mention devastating, than missing an opportunity on draft day simply because your phone didn't work. Jon wasn't so much concerned with making calls as he was in receiving them. A problem with an outgoing call on one of these phones could be solved just by using another phone. But to most people in the outside world, the Ravens had only two or three phone numbers. League officials didn't want long lists of every damn phone in the building. They didn't want every cell number. They wanted one main number and one for emergencies, so these phones had to work.

"Everything seem okay so far?"

The man nodded. "So far," he said without looking up.

Jon was fascinated, not because he possessed some deep desire to work in the securities industry but because it was something he knew nothing about. He was a curious and inquisitive type by nature and would love nothing more than to bombard this guy with questions until he felt he had at least a fundamental understanding of what he was doing.

Again he considered asking the guy to sweep for bugs, then decided not to. He'd had this argument with himself several times over the last week. Some teams did run such tests as part of their normal preparation for draft day, and Jon had done it in the past. In the fans' minds, he thought, it must sound ridiculously paranoid. He always imagined someone shaking their head and saying, "Gimme a break, it's only a *game.*" But the truth was professional football was a high-stakes business like any other, involving millions and dollars and the futures of hundreds of people. Planting tiny electronic ears in the offices of your rivals really wasn't such a bad idea. Besides, it had happened before; more than once, in fact.

Ultimately, however, Jon decided it wouldn't be necessary. At least not this year. As far as anyone knew, the

Ravens still hadn't made any deal with the Chargers. There was a lot of speculation in the media, plenty of rumors floating around, but no facts and no confirmations. Both Jon and Skip Henderson had done a marvelous job of holding their tongues. As usual, the press didn't find out anything a team didn't really want them to know. As far as the rest of the world was concerned, what would happen on draft day was still a mystery.

The Hoffer man unplugged his line from the first jack and rose. "That one's okay," he said and moved to the next.

Jon nodded and glanced at the huge white sheet that covered the markerboard. Underneath were hundreds of little placecards, each bearing the name of an eligible player plus the name of his college, his position, height, weight, and his speed in the 40-yard dash. This draft board had been set up weeks ago, long before Bell's accident, and Jon really hadn't given it much thought since then. It was more or less irrelevant now, but he was still glad it was there. It had been covered solely for the benefit of the security guy. If it was exposed and he got a look at who the team had originally been considering in the first round, he might mention it to someone. Then again maybe he wouldn't, but it wasn't worth the risk. Jon frankly didn't care if the guy's feelings were hurt by this mild display of mistrust. Besides, the guy worked in security, so surely he understood. He didn't seem the least bit interested in it anyway.

There was some other sensitive material around the room—unkempt piles of paper, files with rubber bands around them. In one corner ESPN had set up a camera the day before, although there were no wires or cables connected to it yet. To an outsider this, too, might seem like a security gamble, but in reality it wasn't. ESPN had a solid reputation in the sports world, which was logical since sports reporting was their bread and butter. Regardless, many NFL teams refused them access to their war rooms. Jon thought this was ridiculous. He understood they had a job to do, and that many fans would be intrigued by what was happening on the inside. The only condition he imposed was that no sound be transmitted until the second day, and that the cameras be turned off upon request. Otherwise, ESPN was free to do as they wished.

Connally had enthusiastically agreed to indulge the ESPN people, too, although Jon suspected it was for different reasons. Peter was eager to get in front of the cameras the moment the announcement came down that the Ravens had secured McKinley. He would want to stand in the spotlight and gloat—in as dignified a manner as possible—about this team's amazing acquisition. He'd give the normal speech about being happy that such a talented young player would be coming to Baltimore and that he was glad for the fans, etc., but what he'd really be waiting for was the opportunity to bring up the subject of a third Super Bowl victory. Any opportunity to talk about that was seized. It seemed to be his singular obsession these days.

Jon was not as comfortable in the limelight, but he had to admit he kind of looked forward to it this time. As he stood there watching the security guy tinker with his equipment, he got a strong sense that this was the beginning of the end of something, so he figured hell, why not live it up a little? Maybe he'd get in front of that camera, too. Perhaps he'd even comb his hair and put on a jacket for a change. The McKinley acquisition was his baby, after all; another success in a fairly long line of them. Once the announcement was made, surely they'd want to talk to him and get the juicy details. In years to come he'd probably look back and think it was an asinine, self-indulgent thing to do. But hell, it might never be this good again, so why not, just this once, have a little fun with it?

He was smiling to himself, imagining the things he might say, when the door opened and Susan Schiff stuck her head in. She looked pale, almost sick, and Jon's whimsical fantasy evaporated.

"Susan?"

"There's a call for you."

She made a motion toward the Hoffer guy that said, *I don't want to say more in front of him.* Jon got the translation with no problem and came forward.

"I'll be right back," he told the guy, who nodded.

As they hurried down the hallway, Jon's first thought was of his daughter—Kelley was calling to say Lauren had tumbled down the stairs and broken her neck. Funny, he thought, how clear and detailed mental images were when you imagined horrible things happening to the people you loved.

"Who is it?" he asked, more to distract himself than anything else.

"Skip Henderson."

He stopped, and then she stopped.

"Really?" That can't be good.

He got behind his desk and plucked the phone from its cradle. Outside, Susan tried her best not to eavesdrop.

Jon went to press the blinking hold button, then paused to make sure this wasn't just a bad dream. No such luck. He cleared his throat and brought the phone to his ear.

"Skip? Hey, it's Jon," he said casually, hoping his cheerful tone would somehow sway the odds in his favor. "What's up?"

"Jon, I can't believe I'm saying this, but I have some bad news for you."

16

TEN MINUTES LATER, JON SET THE PHONE DOWN gently, put his hands together, and stared into space. He was numb and cold. A million thoughts swirled together.

The first thing he had to do, he knew, was tell Connally. He closed his eyes and shook his head at the prospect. The old bastard had been stomping around like a monster in a Japanese horror film all morning. One of the people in marketing and promotions had been given the responsibility of ordering a thousand T-shirts; cheapos that the team could give away at various PR functions to keep the fans happy. But she sent the printer the wrong logo—the old one from the Ravens' first two seasons that they eventually had to discard after a lawsuit filed by one of their former security people who claimed, apparently rightfully so, that he in fact created the design and was never compensated for it—and all the shirts had to be destroyed. Over two thousand dollars down the drain. And since the girl who made the mistake was new, it really wouldn't be fair to fire her. It was just one of those instances when you had to bite the bullet. But Connally was absolutely livid. It wasn't the dollar amount that bothered him but the idea that it had been wasted. If there was one thing Peter Connally abhorred, it was waste.

And what of the new offer Skip had received? It must've been unbelievable. Jon thought *he* was out of his mind when he tendered his last proposal. Somewhere out there was a team about to lose a lot of talent. Whoever had made the final decision, Jon was happy he wasn't in his shoes. The fans would kill the guy. Who even had that much to spare? When this was all over, he would be very curious to find out who was behind the deal and what they gave up. It never occurred to him that it might be Brendan Cavanaugh. He figured it was one of the other three teams that had been most aggressively after McKinley—the Chiefs, the Seahawks, or the Texans.

Regardless, the objective now, impossible though it may be, was to forge a superior counteroffer. And this needed to be done—he checked his watch—within twenty-four hours. What were the choices? The first one was to throw more chips into the pot—add more players. But who did they have left?

He scanned the roster again and again, and could no longer avoid the name of Darryl Bailey. If he didn't make a difference, then Jon might as well wave the white flag right now, because they had nothing else that Skip wanted, and there weren't any other decent defensive leftovers around to trade for. Bailey was a playmaker. Skip said repeatedly he didn't want offensive guys, but he had expressed an admiration for Bailey many times. Maybe that was all it would take. Jon had never mentioned the possibility of including Bailey to anyone. It had always been more theoretical than anything else. He desperately wanted to find some other name on their roster that Skip would jump at. But there wasn't one.

Jon thought briefly about Raymond Coolidge. He did own the kid's rights for the moment. Would he be able to use him as trading fodder? Could he be a factor? It was an interesting idea. Skip would need a quarterback, after all. Of course he wouldn't take McKinley and give up the chance to obtain so many other players. But what if he got all those others *and* a promising young quarterback?

He realized he was drifting out of reality now. First of all, there was very little chance brokering such a deal would be legal. The commissioner would never sanction it. The paper he'd faxed to Freddie yesterday was very clear; Friedman had taken a number of prelaw classes at night and, although he never earned a law degree, knew legalese as well as anyone. Distilled into a language anyone could understand, the agreement stated that the Ravens retained Raymond's rights until the Monday after draft weekend because they wanted the first chance to try him out in the event they didn't acquire another quarterback. All Jon had requested was the chance to bring him in and have the coaches look him over before anyone else, nothing more.

Then a horrible thought occurred to him—he might simply be out of ammunition. This was sickening. Like everyone else in the NFL, both on the field and off, Jon *hated* losing. There were *always* ways to win. In the past he had wondered if this was one of the trademarks of true genius—believing there was always a way, and that the only real challenge was finding it.

All the traditional routes were exhausted—trimming the roster, offering more draft picks, making trades. Darryl Bailey was a panic-button choice, and even that wasn't a guarantee. Raymond Coolidge was a no-way.

What else was there?

HE PACED FURIOUSLY, CORDLESS PHONE PRESSED against his ear, waiting for Gayle to pick up. He almost wished he had one of those hands-free headsets Friedman had. Holding the damn thing against his face was painful after a while. And if you supported it with your shoulder long enough you got a kink in your back. Still, the headsets made you look like you worked the drive-through at McDonald's.

"Come on . . . come on . . ."

He glanced at the clock for the tenth time in so many minutes. His heart was racing, his hands trembling slightly. He was on a high like no other. This was what he loved most about the NFL—that razor's-edge competition that delineated the winners from the losers. It was what made the job worthwhile.

He froze when he heard a click on the other end. "Hello?"

"Gayle? It's Jon. I've got—"

"I'm sorry, Jon, this is Melissa."

He recognized Gayle's secretary right away. "Oh, hi, Melissa. Is Gayle around? It's sort of an emergency."

He dropped down on the leather couch and set his feet on the glass coffee table, wrinkling the cover of the latest issue of *NFL Insider*. His co-workers would've been amazed—he had a standing rule against putting feet up on this table.

"Sorry, Jon, he's in a meeting with the coaches." Jon's stomach sank. "If you'd like, I can give him a mes—oh, wait, here he is."

Jon jumped back up. "Thank God."

The line went dead again, and Jon straightened some papers on his desk while he waited. When he was done with that, he grabbed a large paper clip, set it with one finger, and "kicked" it across the room with the another. It landed in a small wastepaper basket.

"Score!" he said quietly.

"Jon?"

"Gayle?"

"Hey, what's up?"

Jon sighed. "You're not going to believe this. . . ."

"What? Don't tell me someone outbid you."

"Yeah."

"My *God.*"

"I know, un-goddamn-believable."

"Who had that much to give up?"

Jon threw up his hands. "Who knows? Skip wouldn't tell me. If I had to guess, I'd say it was the Chiefs. They have some depth, plenty of cap room, and some picks to spare. Gostranich is a pretty wily guy. I'm sure he's been doing all the same things I've been doing for the last week. Then again it could've been anyone. There are plenty of teams that could use McKinley."

"Jeez, I'm sorry," Gayle said. "So I assume you're looking to sweeten your own offer now?"

"You got it."

"Is there anything I can do to help?"

"Actually, yes, there is."

"Okay, shoot."

Jon took a deep breath. "Any chance I can get Aaron Timmerman back?"

At first there was only silence. Jon expected as much, so he waited.

"Who?" Gayle said finally.

"Aaron Timmerman. Remember, three years ago?"

"Yeah, I remember. Are you crazy? He's the best linebacker we've got. Are you on drugs? Have you been getting help? Does Kelley know?"

"I'm not on drugs, asshole, I'm serious. I'll give you. . . ." He scanned the spreadsheets on screen, although he'd seen so many times he really didn't need to look at all. "Oh hell, I'll give you whatever you want."

"If I let Timmerman go, they'll feed me to the alligators. You know they have alligators down here, right? They say the Mafia loves them because they eat the—"

"I thought you were having contract problems with him. The rumor is he wants to renegotiate a year early. If you dealt him back to us, you'd save yourself a lot of heartache."

"No, we need him. We've got plenty of salary cap problems coming up, yes, but that's because the last moron who had this job was under the impression money grew on trees." He groaned. "That's next year's headache. Timmerman won't make it any easier by asking to renegotiate, but at least he's worth it. It would be stupid to give up a good player when we're stuck with so many average ones."

He knew it was a longshot, but he had to try. "You sure?"

"Yeah. Sorry, buddy."

Jon glanced at the clock again.

"All right. I gotta go. I'm running out of time."

"Who's next?"

Jon chuckled. "You wouldn't believe me if I told you."

"Not Cavanaugh."

"Obviously."

"Then who?"

"Like I said, you wouldn't believe me. . . ."

There was a pause, and then Gayle said, "Wow, you *are* desperate."

"Desperate times call for desperate measures, right?"

Gayle was laughing. "Clearly. Well, good luck with *that,* my friend."

"Yeah, thanks."

WITH THE SUPREME EFFORT OF HIS LIFE, JON LIFTED the phone and dialed the number Susan had given him for Tom Wright. The face she made when he asked for it was priceless. Her first thought, clearly, was that he was kidding. Then she dug through her Rolodex to find the dustiest card she had.

It was no secret around the league that Jon wasn't a member of the Tom Wright fan club. Wright was cold and impersonal, insensitive and unapproachable, and he had a streak of megalomania that would've kept a team of psychoanalysts busy for years. Worst of all, though, was the simple fact that he wasn't very good at his job. Unlike Jon, Gayle, Skip, and most other GMs, he had virtually no experience with personnel acquisition, yet he insisted on maintaining total control over that side of the Cardinal organization. Consequently, most of the players he'd drafted and acquired through free agency were washouts. Rumor had it he once based a pick on the fact that he liked the guy's name.

True or not, it was hard to defend his incompetence—the Cards never had a winning season under his direction. He was generally disliked not only on the outside but also by his own people. The assistants complained that he was too detached, the trainers and coaches complained he was too cheap, and the marketing people complained that his ideas were idiotic and impractical. The only person in the club who seemed to like him was Frank Merriweather, the owner.

And Wright seemed to like him, too. They shared a love of sailing and golfing, and together with their wives they often took trips together in the offseason.

Jon had managed to keep his distaste to himself until a party in Baltimore a few days after they'd won their first Super Bowl. He had a little too much to drink and, when asked if he thought his job was secure now that he'd put together a championship squad, replied, "Look, if Tom Wright still has a job, no one else has anything to worry about." The comment was heard by more people than he intended, and it eventually got back to its victim. It made a small splash in the press, but Wright refused to respond to it, and it was soon forgotten. In fact the only response it received was from the Arizona fans who, ironically, seemed to agree.

As Jon tapped in the number, he wondered if Wright still harbored a grudge after more than a year. Surely not, for they were all professionals and could remain objective, right?

A female voice answered. "Hello, Tom Wright's office."

"Hi, may I speak with Tom, please?"

"Who's calling?"

Damn.

"It's Jon Sabino."

A pause, and then, "Who?"

He smiled in spite of himself. No surprise there, he thought. Whenever they needed to take care of any business with Arizona, which was rare, he let Kevin Tanner do it. They probably thought there was a better chance of Knute Rockne calling.

"Jon Sabino. Of the Baltimore Ravens."

"Um . . . okay. Hold on."

The line went quiet, and for a moment he thought he might be left hanging there. Then a voice appeared—"Hello, Tom Wright."

It was that same flat, almost robotic tone Jon disliked so much. This guy had the most dispiriting personality Jon ever encountered. Who on earth would hire someone like that to run a football club? He was a walking corpse.

"Tom? Jon Sabino."

"Yes, how can I help you?"

With that one line, and the tone in which it was delivered, Jon knew beyond any doubt that Wright still had a chip on his shoulder. And a fairly large one at that. *This guy wouldn't piss on me if I was on fire.*

"I'm calling to inquire about your first round pick in the draft tomorrow. The second overall."

The idea was sheer genius—to include the second overall pick in the package to Skip. Regardless of who got the first pick, McKinley would be gone. But McKinley, in spite of all the hype, wasn't the only gem in the draft. There was a defensive lineman from Southern Mississippi named Gavin Hamble who had shown a devastating ability to squelch running games. He wasn't as visible as McKinley largely because defensive players weren't as showy as those on offense; fans could more easily grasp and appreciate the value of scoring points than tackling or blocking. But Hamble was one of the best hole pluggers to come along in years. Following the law that good defenses won championships, a lot of defensively weak teams would want him. It was generally agreed that he would be taken after McKinley. Most believed Arizona, who had weaknesses to spare, would grab him. But with a wild card like Wright at the helm, you never knew. If that pick could be offered to Skip, Jon reasoned, he could trade it for even more players. There was still time.

"What about it?" Wright asked.

"I'd like to know if you'd be interested in dealing it to us."

Wright did not answer immediately. When he did, it was a frosty, "For what?"

"I can offer you several quality players, and a scattering of draft picks." He ran down the list, picking out players at random. He had no idea what the Cardinals needed, nor did he frankly give a damn.

Wright's response was quick this time—"Nope."

It wasn't so much the rejection of the offer that started Jon's blood boiling, but the obvious enjoyment in it. Wright was having fun with the knowledge that he had something Jon wanted.

"Just like that? 'Nope?' "

"Uh-huh."

Jon offered another player, and then another.

"Sorry," was Wright's quick response.

"Well, what would you want, then?"

"Everything," Wright said simply.

"Everything?"

"Everything you've got left to spare."

Jon paused, temporarily paralyzed by disbelief.

"Are you kidding?"

"No. And throw in Matt Israel, too."

Israel was one of the Ravens' guards, a perennial Pro Bowler and generally considered the best at his position in the league. Of all Wright's flaws, perhaps his most severe was his inability to acquire effective offensive lineman. The five he had drafted during his tenure were no longer with the team; three of them were out of football altogether. Wright had made the mistake in 1998 of publicly criticizing Israel, calling him an "overrated overachiever." The press crucified him for the remark after Israel began to shine with the Ravens, and it soon became another bone of contention between him and Jon.

"You're out of your fuh—you're crazy, you know that?"

"Maybe, but those are my terms."

"Well, here's what you can do with them!"

He slammed the phone down with such force that a silver cup on the edge of the desk tipped over, spilling pens and pencils everywhere.

Susan Schiff appeared, holding a folder against her chest. She wore the scowling expression of a disapproving wife.

"That didn't help."

Jon looked out the window at nothing in particular. "I know."

• • •

BY THREE THIRTY HE WAS BACK BEHIND HIS DESK, staring at the phone, reluctant to pick it up but fully aware that he had no choice. The draft was less than twenty-four hours away; time was running out. The task before him loomed like a death sentence.

He had explored other options, lifted other stones to see what was underneath. But, eventually, he was forced to call a meeting and break the bad news. Connally had calmed down from the T-shirt blunder but blew his top again when he heard this. Clearly he regarded the McKinley issue as yesterday's crisis and already settled. If there was one thing he hated, it was a recurring problem. In the end, however, he gave his blessing to parting with Darryl Bailey. So did Cary Blanchard, although he was clearly pissed. They reasoned that keeping him and not having a quarterback was worse than dealing him and having Christian McKinley. The loss would be tremendous, but not debilitating—they did have two other receivers. One was a five-year veteran easily as talented and capable as DB. The other was a kid entering his second year, having been drafted in the third round the previous April, and was starting to show signs of maturity and reliability. He'd just have to develop a little faster. Maybe they'd rely a little more on the running game and on short passes, too, Blanchard said. Either way, they'd make it work. They had no choice.

Regardless, Jon couldn't be happy about letting DB go, whom he considered something of an adopted son. That was the nature of the business, he reminded himself as he picked up the phone and tapped in Henderson's number. Thinking this usually made him feel better, but not today.

Skip picked up on the first ring. "Hello?"

"Skip? Jon Sabino."

"Well, I didn't expect to hear from you again so soon. Calling about the first overall pick again?"

"Yes I am."

"With a new offer?"

"Yes."

Skip laughed. Jon could picture him shaking his head. "This is getting ridiculous. No one's going to believe it."

"I'm not sure I believe it myself."

"Okay, what have you got?"

"Not much different from last time, except . . . you can have Darryl Bailey."

"Really?"

"Yeah, if that'll do it. I know you said you didn't want offensive guys, but we simply have nothing left on defense to give, here or elsewhere. And I'm gambling that you still like the guy. If not, I think we're going to have to let it go. This really is our final offer. Will it do the trick?"

Skip didn't hesitate—"You bet it will. The pick is yours."

Jon closed his eyes and took a deep breath. "Thank God." The wave of satisfaction that followed was considerably smaller than it had been in the past. This was about as bitter a victory as he'd ever experienced. *McKinley, you better turn out to be the best damn quarterback in history. . . .*

"I'll have Susie fax over the terms to make it official."

"Sounds good."

"If anything changes, will you let me know?"

"Of course, but I wouldn't worry too much."

"That's what you said last time."

"True, but this is a pretty big deal."

"Okay, I'll talk to you later."

"You got it. And hey—don't worry, we'll take good care of him."

Jon allowed himself a tiny smile. "I know you will."

He hung up the phone and summoned his secretary.

"Susie, we've cut another deal with Skip for that pick. It's ours again."

She glanced at the clock—a habit she seemed to have acquired in the last few hours—and said, "That's great."

"I guess. Please fax the details."

"Let me get my pad." She turned to leave.

"You won't need it," Jon said, stopping her. "All you have to do is add one name to the last offer."

"Okay."

Jon sighed and looked at her helplessly. "Darryl Bailey."

Her small mouth fell open.

"Yeah, I know." He wanted to explain his reasoning, like a man who knew he'd committed a crime but felt it would be looked upon differently if everyone *understood* why he did it. But the truth was he wasn't sure *he* understood. He thought about the galling number of picks and players they were giving up to get one guy—*one damn guy*—and realized it would be impossible to explain it in such a way that it made sense to her or anyone else.

He shook his head and waved her away. "Just do it before I change my mind."

He waited a little while before picking up the phone again. Breaking the news to DB was going to be, he suddenly realized, a lot more difficult than making the offer to Skip. He hated—*hated*—the idea of doing it over the phone. It was about as impersonal as dumping a girlfriend over e-mail. In the past Jon gave players the bad news in person; it was his policy. When a player was cut after training camp during the league's mandatory paring down of the roster, the coaches took care of it. When it was a business decision, Jon did it.

Some days this job really sucks. . . .

17

DARRYL BAILEY HAD JUST COME OUT OF THE SHOWER, wearing only a towel and a pair of Adidas flip-flops, when the call came.

He was in a great mood. He and Ryan Hart, the Ravens' tight end, had a dinner reservation at the Havana Club, one of Baltimore's hottest new hangouts. Ryan was bringing his latest girlfriend, whom he said he loved with all his heart. He asked Darryl if she should bring along a friend for him; Darryl declined. Afterwards they were going to a party being held by another teammate. He laid out a new $1,200 suit that he was looking forward to seeing himself in. Bernadette was in DC visiting an old college friend and wouldn't be back for a few days. He missed her, but he enjoyed his time alone, too. This was going to be a fun night.

He sat down on the bed and plucked the phone from its cradle.

"Hello?"

"Darryl? It's Jon Sabino."

DB smiled. "Hey, what's happening, big daddy?" He took his gold bracelet from the nightstand and hung it over his wrist, half paying attention to the call while trying to get the damn thing hooked together with his oversized fingers.

"Not a whole lot. How about you?"

"Oh, nothing much. Just getting ready to go out with Ryan." He didn't need to add the surname—Jon knew who was friends with who on his team.

"Oh, very good."

Jon's voice was flat, weary, Darryl noticed. Then he realized how unusual this call was—the draft was less than twenty-four hours away. Why would he be contacting one of his players now?

"What's up? Is something wrong?"

"Um . . ." Jon paused, sighed. "Well, I don't know. That depends, I guess."

Darryl's smile faded. Something hard and cold formed in his stomach.

"On what?"

"God, I wish there was time to handle this properly. Look, Darryl, I think I have to trade you tomorrow. You're going to go to the Chargers so we can get the first overall pick and take Christian McKinley."

Darryl, hunched over with his elbows on his thighs, froze.

"What . . . ?" It was barely a whisper.

"If there was some other way to get the deal done, I'd do it, I swear. I held out as long as I could." He paused, then added, "I just ran out of options. I'm sorry."

"I don't understand . . ."

"I'm sorry, Darryl," Jon repeated. "If there's anything I can do to make it easier for you, just let me know. I know how much you love it here."

"No . . . no, that's all right. I understand. It's a business."

"It is a business," Jon replied, "and sometimes I have to make unpleasant decisions. Believe me, if there was any other way I could've made this deal, I would've done so. I waited until there were no other options. Do you believe that?"

"Yeah, sure I do."

"Good, because it's true."

There was a longish pause, during which Jon was waiting for Darryl to say something; anything.

"Hey, are you there?"

"Yeah, I'm here."

"Again, I'm sorry. If you need anything, just let me know. And please, don't say anything to the media, okay? They'll know tomorrow."

"Okay, sure."

"Thanks."

Bailey pressed the off button and tossed the phone on the bed. His eyes were wide with disbelief, his movements slow and dreamlike.

And just like that, his long and glorious ride through the football heavens was over. He wouldn't see another Super Bowl, that was for sure. The Ravens would acquire McKinley and get there instead, and he would miss his chance to be a part of one of the biggest moments in football history.

He folded his hands together and rested them against his mouth in a posture of deep contemplation. He wished Bernadette was here. He feared going back to the West Coast, where his old friends would no doubt be waiting. The temptation would be too great. There wouldn't be a throng of adoring fans to compensate like there was here. Everyone loved you when you were a winner. Simply being a winner was enough of a high, so artificial highs were unnecessary. But being on a struggling team was a different story. You sought solace wherever you could find it. Going back to California was more than a professional death sentence. It would be personally devastating, too.

He picked up the phone and entered the number Bernadette had left. They talked for over an hour, and she was wonderfully supportive. He still didn't tell her about the injury, but he came close several times and knew he would eventually; and probably sooner rather than later.

He also thought about calling his agent, but what would be the point? The Ravens had the right to do what they did. Trying to fight it would only make him look childish. Besides, why fight to stay on a team that decided it doesn't want you?

He left the phone off the hook and buried it under a pillow. The hardness in his stomach was now roughly the size of a bowling ball. He felt close to vomiting. How could he go out with Ryan now? He didn't want to see anyone, but he didn't want to sit around here, either. He wasn't sure what he wanted to do.

Then, like waking from a dream, reality rushed back in and he remembered—You've got a stinger. You're damaged goods. No one knows that. Not Jon, not Skip Henderson.

What's going to happen when they find out?

THEY ASSEMBLED ON THE FIELD AT LA SALLE UNIVER-sity just as the sun was rising behind the bleachers.

At first it was just Raymond and Quincy, beginning one the most important days in Raymond's football career with what seemed to the young quarterback like an endless litany of stretches and calisthenics. Then a two-mile jog around the track, followed by a series of wind sprints. Quincy was merciless when it came to warm-up exercises, but Raymond gritted his teeth and forged ahead. He was dressed in light shorts and a hooded nylon jacket. Quincy, for the first time in nearly twenty years, put on a sweatsuit and sneakers. He had no intention of running alongside his beloved son, for he knew he would've collapsed, gasping for breath, after the first hundred yards. But the process of getting into the outfit was a near-religious experience for him, carrying his spirit to euphoric heights. The suit, along with new socks, sneakers, and cap, had been purchased by Raymond with some of the money from Jon Sabino's temporary rights deal. Quincy felt an old excitement—one that he thought was long gone from his emotional menu—when he stepped onto that field, opened the canvas bag full of equipment they'd brought along, and caught the scent of the freshly mown grass beneath him. It was as if time had stood still, the years had vanished, and he was a young man again. And he decided in that moment that he would bury the last of the bitterness, slough the bad memories, and, at last, move ahead. He would share in his son's journey, guide him around traps and pitfalls, and

lead him to whatever greatness awaited. This wasn't just a
chance for the boy, he realized—it was a chance for *him* as
well.

Raymond's college coach, Hal Arden—one of the few
people outside Raymond's family who knew Quincy was his
father and had done an admirable job of keeping this pre-
cious information to himself—arrived next. A former college star himself, he missed out on his own NFL opportunity
when he went down the wrong way during a sack in his senior year and permanently damaged his left knee. It took
three reconstructive surgeries and sixteen months of agonizing rehabilitation to get him walking again, and even now
one could detect a slight limp. He brought more equipment
from the school and ran Raymond through a series of position drills; anything that he thought the Ravens might throw
at him during the next day's tryout. Several times he wanted
to say something about Raymond's follow-through, a slight
problem he'd had in his school years. After throwing the
ball, Raymond would often continue moving forward rather
than discipline himself to resist the momentum and instead
learn to fade either left or right. The forward movement
would eventually, Arden knew, lead him into some monster
linebacker in the pros coming forward, and the resulting impact would cause some kind of nasty injury. But each time
Raymond threw today, Arden noticed, he would then drift
laterally and automatically relax his body to accept whatever
shock was coming—he had corrected the problem on his
own. When he noted this to Quincy, his father shrugged and
said he hadn't worked on it with him. That's when Arden realized Raymond had been practicing and improving himself,
basically in secret, for the bulk of the last year. He thought
Raymond was a tremendous player when he graduated; he
was utterly blown away by what he was seeing now.

Pearly arrived by midmorning, moving slowly down the
track with his cane and taking a seat in the bleachers. Then,
to Raymond and Quincy's surprise, La Salle's entire starting
squad, both offense and defense, appeared, all smiles. Included in the group was Mark Dalton, the receiver Raymond

had befriended and who used to go with him to the field at
Washington High to run pattern drills. Most of the kids had
played with Raymond the year before and were thrilled to
see him again. They knew about his tryout the following day
and were happy to give up an afternoon to help him prepare.
Raymond was genuinely moved by their friendship. When
two of the boys recognized Quincy from some bar in the
city, word quickly spread that he was Raymond's father.
Quincy and Raymond laughed about it but decided to do
nothing more. It was a turning point for them, the first time
they made no attempt to maintain the secret any longer. People would find out anyway, so their friends may as well find
out first. Quincy ended up signing autographs while the heir
to his throne continued his workout.

After lunch they scrimmaged, and Raymond told the defense not to "redshirt" him. He would have none of this.
Against the advice of his father and coach, he insisted on being put under what he called "real game pressure." Arden
called obscure and complicated plays from last year's book,
testing Raymond's memory and pushing what he perceived
to be the limits of the boy's physical and mental abilities. He
threw different defensive schemes at him, forcing him to
pass on the run, into traffic, multiple coverage, and so on.
Honoring Raymond's wishes, he made things difficult. The
players were pumped, excited by the prospect that one of
their own might make a pro team. Two fights even broke out,
both of which sent Quincy into laughing fits.

By the end of the afternoon, Raymond was exhausted, but
he refused to show it. His performance had been nothing
short of brilliant in Hal Arden's eyes. Every one of his bad
habits was gone. He'd effectively eradicated them to the
point where no evidence remained. Arden had thrown everything at him that his boys could muster. At one point it even
occurred to him that Raymond might just be toying with
them; he might just be that good now. Arden laughed and
shook his head.

As they walked off the field, he reminded Raymond again
that the pros were a different story entirely. A different uni-

verse. Everyone was bigger, and they moved faster. They were vicious and ruthless. He would become scared, and he *should* be, because they could hurt him badly. A lot of players were unable to take that step, to successfully carry their skills to the next level. But Raymond was certain he would not fall into this trap. He was suddenly aware of a confidence that he had never known before. And when Arden sensed this—saw that twinkle of near-magical assuredness in his eyes—he smiled and put an arm around his former pupil's shoulder.

"You're ready, kiddo," he said simply.

WHILE RAYMOND WAS PREPARING FOR THE TRYOUT OF his life, Brendan Cavanaugh was trying to hold onto his sanity. His day had gone from good to bad in one phone call.

He'd been having a grand time contacting the players he'd traded, particularly enjoying that moment of stunned silence after the bomb was dropped. Grown men engaged in a cold war, more subtle than a battle between children but ten times as vicious. He was about to zero in on his next victim when the phone rang. He was grinning when he reached for it, figuring it was one of the others calling back, mad as a hornet and ready for a screaming match.

When he heard Skip Henderson's voice instead, his stomach dropped. He knew the message before it was delivered. He didn't ask if it was Sabino; he didn't have to. Henderson would tell him, and he knew it anyway. He ended the conversation quickly, promised to call back when—not if, but *when*—he got a new deal together.

He lifted the phone again. It was going on four thirty, and the clock seemed to be moving faster than usual. First he tried Macintosh's cell phone, but all he got was an answering service. He had to try the team offices. It was a huge risk, but what choice did he have now?

Macintosh picked up on the second ring. "I can't believe it," he said.

"What did Sabino give up?"

"Darryl Bailey."

"You're kidding."

"No. Henderson's been in love with him forever."

"What about no offensive players? That's what Henderson told me. He told everyone that."

"What do you want me to say? Jon knew that, too. I have no idea what happened."

Cavanaugh shook his head. *Sabino and his goddamned creative thinking.* His hatred for the man grew a little more, fueled by the ugly realization that, as capable as he was, Sabino had access to a level of thinking that would probably always be out of his own reach.

He sighed. "So he gave up one of his best receivers to get that pick?"

"Uh-huh."

"Well, I'm going to dig around and see what else I can find. Meanwhile, try to dig up some more information I can use."

"Like what?"

"Anything that might help. Anything. I didn't give you fifty grand for nothing."

"Okay, okay . . ."

"Get back to me as soon as you can. And put your cell phone on. I don't want to call this number again."

MACINTOSH HAD LITTLE CHOICE BUT TO WAIT UNTIL jon was gone. That didn't happen until nearly seven o'clock. And since this was the night before the draft, he'd be back, so he figured the window of opportunity was a tiny one. He probably went out to get something to eat. Cavanaugh, undoubtedly waiting by the phone for the last few hours, had to be climbing the walls by now.

He started with the papers on the desk. They were arranged in reasonably orderly piles. He didn't find anything useful, but he did pause when he discovered a set of due diligence reports on players' backgrounds. He loved these and could read them all day long. But there wasn't time for that right now.

He went to the drawers next. Jon didn't keep them locked as a matter of policy. He felt doing so conveyed a message of mistrust to his coworkers. He wanted his office to be free and open to all. If he had any truly top secret issues, he simply kept them on his computer or in his head. Macintosh considered this open-door policy absurd. The hell with the message it sent to the underlings. They would know only what they needed to know. They had no business going through someone else's stuff. It was a security risk, plain and simple. He couldn't help thinking of what he was doing right now as a perfect example. If Jon had been more careful, he wouldn't be able to play the part of the mole in the first place. As a result, Jon's cutesy idealism would be his downfall. What a chump.

Macintosh found it nearly impossible to concentrate on all the notes and papers and watch the door at the same time. He had to keep his ears open, too. He was about to give up when he came across a new spiral-bound notebook. On the first page he found a set of notes from a meeting earlier in the day. At first it didn't look as though Jon had written anything useful, but then he came across the line, "We agree that offering Bailey will be it—if we are outbid again, we will withdraw and take our chances with Birch."

Macintosh smiled. This was the kind of information Cavanaugh wanted. Whether or not he would increase his own offer one more time was *his* problem. At least he would know where Jon had drawn the line. That was very useful indeed.

He put the notebook back exactly as he found it and hurried out of the office. He hit the stairs running and went down to the parking lot, pulling his cell phone from his pocket. One more call, he thought, and he was done with this little project. He'd already made plans to take Jennifer to Hawaii for a week, impressing her with fine wine, expensive dinners, and—best of all—tales of his bright future in the

NFL. He'd tell her the fifty grand was the bonus he received along with his promotion. He'd tell her he was just a few years away from becoming the assistant general manager of the Denver Broncos. He'd tell her they were on their way to an almost certain Super Bowl victory now that they had Christian McKinley. He'd tell her a lot of things.

It was all within reach now.

AN ACHING RAYMOND CLOSED THE REFRIGERATOR door sat back down. The only sounds in the small, brightly lit kitchen came from the bubbling pot his mother hovered over. Pearly sat across from his nephew and fiddled with a fork.

The door leading to the side porch opened unexpectedly, and Quincy appeared wearing jeans and a white dress shirt that had passed its prime a few years back. The cuffs were unbuttoned, and a pack of cigarettes could be seen hazily through the breast pocket.

"Sorry for dropping in like this. Raymond, I forgot to bring these today. They might help."

He handed his son a brown paper bag, which Raymond emptied onto the table. Four Rams playbooks, yellowing and scented with age, slid out.

"I thought you'd like to look through them, to get some idea of what a pro playbook looks like."

Raymond handled them with the reverence of a theological scholar examining the Dead Sea Scrolls. They were each as thick as a small phone book, with two plays per page, crudely drawn by hand and photocopied decades ago. X's and O's, with little notes at the bottom.

"You still had these?"

"Yeah, they were in a closet where I kept some old stuff. They're no good to me anymore."

It occurred to Raymond, for just an instant, that these would be considered priceless relics by some—the personal playbooks of Quincy Pressner. Probably worth a fortune.

And now they're mine. The changing of the guard, a largely symbolic moment that was not lost on the young man.

"Wow. Thanks, Dad."

"Sure. If you don't need them, you can just throw them out."

Raymond laughed. "No, I think I'll keep them."

"Good."

Raymond stopped paging through the first book and looked up. "Dad, I was thinking about something after my workout today. Just *being* in the league isn't easy, is it? No matter how good you are on the field, there's a lot more to it than just playing, isn't there?"

Quincy paused to consider his answer. Pearly watched him intently.

"I'm not going to lie to you. It's tough, and maybe tougher than ever now."

"It's like it just chews people up. If I make the Ravens' roster, I don't want anything like that happen to me. Some guys get injured and can't play anymore. Others go down like you did. And it wasn't even your fault, dad. You got caught up. It's like a wave—it just grabs you, and you can't do anything but go along. It's like you have no control over it."

Quincy studied the boy for a moment, then walked over and crouched down in front of him. "That's where you're wrong, son," he said. For what is was worth, the word Althea was thinking when she heard him was *fatherly*. "You have more control over it than you think. That stuff about getting caught up and having it take you away is nonsense. It's just an excuse. I should know. I used to say the same thing— 'You can't control it, it controls you.' That's the biggest load of crap going. People who make mistakes don't want to think anything is their fault. But the truth is, it's largely about *choices*. I chose to do what I did. There's always a moment, Raymond—maybe it's a small one, but it's *yours*—the one instant when you, all by yourself, make the decision to do it or not to do it. If you say no, you might get some heat, might lose some friends, maybe even lose some opportunities. But at least you get the keep your dignity and your self-respect."

He pinched and then held up the shoulders of his Salvation Army shirt. "Look at this, you see this? You see what I've become? It was because I had choices and I made the wrong ones. I could've said no to so many things, but I didn't."

"But—"

"No, no 'buts.'" Quincy got back up. "You might get the chance to do something very few people can—play quarterback in the NFL. You can climb as far or fall as hard as you like, but it's more up to you than you realize. I made mistakes, Raymond. So have a lot of other guys. But you won't. You're tough and you're determined. You've got that streak of righteousness in you that I never had. You know right from wrong, and that will be what keeps your head above water."

Raymond managed a tiny smile. "Okay, Dad."

"That's my boy. So I'll see you tomorrow then, bright and early."

"Absolutely."

"And remember—choices."

"I'll remember."

"Good."

As Quincy was walking out, Althea said, "Quince?"

The tall man froze—he could not recall the last time he'd heard her address him in this way.

He leaned back, his head appearing around the open door. "Yes?"

"Would you like to stay for dinner?"

No one moved, no one breathed, for what seemed like a long time but was probably no more than five seconds.

"I'd like that," Quincy replied with a surprised smile, turning back and, almost without realizing it, tucking his shirt in and buttoning the cuffs.

WHEN CONNALLY HEARD ABOUT THE SETTLEMENT JON had to make with Wahlberg, he took it particularly hard. He wanted to "sue that little bastard into oblivion." He even went so far as to suggest hiring someone to find a few skeletons in Wahlberg's closet. He must have a few, Connally reasoned. People of that ilk always did. Find them and use them. It was a very effective technique, he said with an air of experience that Jon found particularly unsettling.

In the end, however, Jon convinced him to just let it go. Drafting McKinley was the priority now, and in order to do that they simply had to get Wahlberg out of their hair. If it cost them a little, so be it. They couldn't win every battle. You could lose a few battles and still win the war, he pointed out. But Connally would never completely let go of his bitterness toward Wahlberg. Jon knew simply by his body language that it was something he'd think about. The downside was that Wahlberg probably didn't plan on agenting another athlete in his life, and he wouldn't have to, either. He'd have enough money to live in comfort until he was a hundred and fifty.

Back in his office, Jon called him on his cell phone.

"Okay, this is the offer—*if* we draft and decide to sign McKinley, we'll give you nine-point-six million over three years." The only aspect of the deal that didn't make his stomach churn was the fact that at least most of the money would be going to Bell. After he healed he would still have some good years left on the field.

"That will be fine," Wahlberg replied. He was all peaches and cream now, Jon's good buddy and just another upstanding member of the football community.

"The smallest payment will come in the first year, and the other two progressively larger. But we can't afford to take a big hit in the first year because McKinley will no doubt ask for a big signing bonus."

"Right, I understand," Wahlberg said, open-minded fellow that he was. "No problem."

"In return, your client will be released from the team and all ties severed." Just the idea of it was heartbreaking. *So long, Mike. Don't forget all the good times we had. . . .*

"Correct. And the paperwork?"

"I'll fax the proposal to you as soon as we're finished writing it up. Remember, it's just a proposal at this stage, not a deal. It's all academic until after the draft."

"Got it."

"Is there anything else?"

"No, that's about it."

"Fine."

"Thanks for everything, Jon. I really appreciate it."

Jon hung up without responding. No sooner had he hung up the phone than it rang again.

Without the formality of a hello, Kevin Tanner said, "Jon, have you heard?"

"Heard what?"

"I think you'd better turn on ESPN right now."

18

BRENDAN CAVANAUGH WAS SITTING BEHIND HIS DESK when the news hit.

The information Macintosh had given him an hour earlier was useful, but only to a degree. It was good to know the Ravens had reached their limit, but he still had to top it. If there was more room to trim, he sure as hell couldn't find it. He went up and down the roster looking for a name.

He thought about the deal Sabino tried to make with the Cardinals—Macintosh had told him all about it. Not a bad idea, really. Maybe he would give it a shot, too. He didn't like Tom Wright much either, but he had never been stupid enough to say so publicly. Maybe Wright would cut him a break. Maybe he'd be more amenable to a deal once he knew he'd be helping to wrestle McKinley away from Jon Sabino.

Cavanaugh was mildly annoyed when the phone rang— he'd asked Jodi to hold all calls for the time being.

"Me again," Macintosh said.

"Yeah, what's up?"

"Have you heard?"

"Heard what?"

"About Darryl Ba—oh wait, turn on ESPN, quick. Trust me, you're gonna wanna to see this."

Cavanaugh spun around and snatched up the remote that he kept on his desk. A large, recessed screen came to life. One of the station's fresh-faced young broadcasters was behind the desk, holding some papers and looking rather serious. In the upper right-hand corner was an inset picture of Darryl Bailey.

"What the hell is this?"

"Just watch."

". . . has reported in their latest issue that Baltimore Ravens wide receiver Darryl Bailey has been taking unauthorized cortisone shots to hide an injury suffered during the last Super Bowl. The article goes on to say that Bailey would neither deny nor confirm the report, and calls to both Bailey and his agent, Derrick Bayliss, have gone unanswered."

Cavanaugh, smiling and unable to take his eyes off the screen, said softly, "I can't believe it."

"Believe it. The deal's off with the Chargers. Sabino just got through talking with Skip Henderson." Macintosh laughed.

"What a loser."

"Yeah. Anyway, I thought you should know. I have a feeling you'll be getting a call from the West Coast any time."

"Thanks, thanks a lot."

"My pleasure."

Cavanaugh felt the stress drain from his system. Leaning back in his chair to enjoy the rest of the report, he began humming "Happy Days Are Here Again."

JON SABINO HAD NEVER BEEN TO DARRYL BAILEY'S house before. He wished his first visit could've been under better circumstances. Bernadette showed him into the living room and gave him a Coke. They chatted for a few minutes, and Jon realized Bernadette knew about the stinger, and that she, too, hadn't been told about it right away, because she was clearly pretty pissed off. He also sensed she wasn't going to discuss it to any degree; she was leaving that for the two of them.

Then the door to the master bedroom opened and DB appeared. He was dressed in a black tracksuit and sneakers. The top was unzipped most of the way, revealing a plain white T-shirt.

He did not, Jon noted, make immediate eye contact. His head was hung low; a posture of defeat. Amazing, how no trace of that winner's swagger could be found. *Miserable*, Jon thought. That's how he looked. The very embodiment of the word *miserable*.

He slumped into the love seat and Bernadette withdrew, giving DB a fairly frosty look at the way out.

Jon sighed. "So it's true? You're taking cortisone and hiding an injury? I came to get it straight from you."

DB closed his eyes and nodded. "Yeah, it's all true."

"What's the injury?"

"A stinger." He motioned towards the affected area. "Right up here, where they always are."

"You got it at the Super Bowl?"

"Yeah."

"That last catch, right?"

"Uh-huh."

Jon shook his head. "I *knew* you shouldn't have been playing. Why didn't Cary—"

"Coach had nothing to do with it," Bailey said quickly. "I wanted to play. I wanted to be in there. I kept bugging him."

"Why? The game was already won. You didn't need—"

"The normal stupid reasons—more stats, more exposure. You know how it goes. Can't get enough. There's a feeling at the big one, Jon, like no other. I wanted to be out there, living it. You never know if you're gonna get back. I didn't want to let it go. One more minute, one more play. . . ." He buried his head in his hands. "You have to be out there to understand."

"Why didn't you say anything?"

Bailey managed a laugh. "Because I would've been gone. I know how it is with stingers. Everybody thinks you're damaged goods. I would've been gone."

Jon didn't respond, but he knew DB was right. If he'd

come clean about it, Blanchard may very well have placed him in the can trade category on the roster last week.

Finally, Bailey said, "I'm so sorry, man."

Jon sighed. "Yeah, me too. Have you spoken to your attorney yet?"

"On the phone once. He'll be here in a little while."

"Good."

"Has anyone else come to see you or called?"

"My mom."

Sabino surprised himself with a little smile. "That was nice," he said.

"Yeah."

An awkward moment crept in. Maybe it was time to go, Jon thought.

Then DB said, "So I guess that's it for me, huh?"

"What do you mean?"

"In the game. I guess I'm finished."

"Why do you say that?"

He shrugged. "How many chances do you get? The Chargers won't want me now."

"You aren't part of the Chargers' organization. You're part of ours."

For the first time in a while, some light shone in DB's eyes. "You're going to keep me around? After this?"

"Well, let's see what happens with the injury. Let's get you some real medical attention and see how things turn out."

"What about your deal for McKinley?"

"Oh hell, that's history."

"Because of this?"

"Yeah, because of this."

Bailey closed his eyes and dropped his head again. "I'm sorry."

"It's okay. We'll figure out something else," Sabino said, although he had no idea what that something might be.

"I'm gonna be suspended."

"Maybe, maybe not. Let's see what happens. Let's see if

we can find a way to make it all work out, for us, for you . . . everyone."

Bailey looked up and smiled.

"Thanks, man." He put his hand out and Jon took it.

"You're welcome."

On the way back to the offices, Jon pondered the situation further. *We'll figure out something else*, he'd said. But with so little time and so few options left, all he felt he could do was pray for a miracle.

So he prayed.

19

RAYMOND ARRIVED AT THE RAVENS' TRAINING FACIL-
ity in his aging Ford Explorer just before one thirty. Quincy
was in the passenger seat, Pearly in the back. Pearly had
barely said a word during the two-hour journey down I-95.
Mostly it was Quincy trying to get his son into the optimal
frame of mind for the situation. He offered his best guesses
as to what Blanchard would be looking at most closely, what
his highest priorities might be.

Raymond pulled into a parking space near the front and
got out. He took one look at the facade of the main building—
with its handsome archways and stately stonework—and felt
the first pangs of nervousness. He managed to get a full
night's sleep and wake up with no jitters. And even his father's constant chatter on the ride down hadn't let loose the
butterflies. But now, standing in this sunny visitors' lot, a
very small figure shadowed by of one of the most beautiful
buildings he'd ever seen—like something from an Ivy
League college campus—he suddenly realized the magnitude of the situation.

This is really happening.

Quincy helped extract Pearly from the back seat. He was
stiff from the long ride and stepped to the pavement with a

groan. Raymond watched this and could not help but be moved. There he was, making the trip to see his nephew, as faithfully supportive as always. *This wouldn't even be happening if it wasn't for him*, Raymond thought. *I wouldn't even be here.*

Another vehicle pulled in—a stone grey BMW with New York plates. It turned into the spot two over from Raymond's, and Freddie Friedman got out, twirling his keys around his finger and smiling. From the other side, Eric Ross also appeared, wearing mirror sunglasses and a grin of his own.

"So, whaddaya think?" he asked, motioning towards the magnificent architecture. "Pretty impressive, huh?"

"It's amazing," Raymond said. "La Salle had nothing like this."

Friedman and Ross both laughed. "No other team in the *NFL* has anything like this," Freddie told him. "This is as state of the art as it gets. It cost more than thirty million bucks. It has swimming pools, lounges, a full-service kitchen, and several practice fields, including one that's indoors."

"My God," Quincy said.

The front door to the complex opened, and Jon Sabino emerged.

"Welcome to our headquarters," he said. "Did you have a good trip?"

"It was fine," Raymond said, staring past him, still in awe.

Jon laughed. "It's quite a place, isn't it? Come on in and I'll give you the tour."

They moved across the road in a herd and filed inside. Over the next thirty minutes they were taken past a game room (where linebacker Earle Webster was playing a Ravens pinball machine while defensive end Dexter Simmons shot pool with wide receiver Anthony Jennings), two racquetball courts, a suite of executive offices, several corporate meeting rooms, a media area, a dining hall, a fully equipped digital film center, and a locker room that was immaculately clean. Raymond noted in particular the large number of plasma TV screens; they seemed to be everywhere. He must've seen thirty of them already.

Finally, Jon took them into the weight room, which seemed to stretch on forever. More widescreen plasma TVs everywhere, so the players would have something to watch while they sweat.

"I come down here and work out most mornings," Jon said. "Gives me the energy and stamina I need to get through the day. If you make the team," he said to Raymond, "you'll be allowed to use this any time you like."

Raymond took a long look around and nodded. He had no idea what to say. It was a football player's paradise; a fantasy world. This far surpassed any dreams he had conjured. He felt numb, apart from himself.

"Okay," Jon said, rubbing his hands together, "so let's get started. This is James Carr, one of our trainers."

Carr, in his midfifties and smallish with silver hair that he kept perfectly combed, seemed to have appeared from nowhere. Dressed in khaki pants and a white polo shirt with the omnipresent Ravens' logo on the left breast, he smiled quietly and put out his hand. As Raymond took it, he noticed Carr had a clipboard in the other, and a pencil behind his ear.

"Nice to meet you, son."

"You, too, Mr. Carr."

"If you follow me, I need to take some measurements."

He led Raymond into a small cement-walled room where there was a scale, an examination table, and, to Raymond's puzzlement, a camera on a tripod. There was also a cabinet with glass-fronted doors, through which he could see a variety of medical equipment.

Carr asked Raymond to strip down to his underwear, then had him stand on the scale so he could weigh him—212 pounds—and get his height to the nearest eighth—six feet, five and one-half inches. Next he measured the span of Raymond's throwing hand from the tip of his thumb to that of his pinkie, and then his arm length—the distance from the shoulder blade to the tip of the middle finger. Carr jotted down all these measurements on his clipboard without any indication as to whether they were good, bad, or otherwise. In fact, he was so impassive and clinical during the whole procedure that Raymond felt like a cow being readied for a meat auction.

When Carr was done, he took Raymond back out to his entourage. Jon was telling the others how proud he was that most of the new facility had been built using local companies and local labor. After a quick *good luck,* Carr withdrew, and Raymond did not see him again.

They next went to the indoor field. It was like nothing Raymond had ever seen—as spacious as an airplane hangar, with immaculately maintained turf and a towering white canvas ceiling. Industrial fans kept the air circulating, and in each corner was a revolving door. All sounds, he realized very quickly, echoed like crazy in here. He wondered just how noisy it was during a formal practice, with pads striking pads, coaches barking orders, and whistles blowing.

One of the revolving doors began turning, and two men emerged. Raymond recognized the first one instantly—Cary Blanchard. He was dressed in a Ravens' windbreaker and matching hat, plus khaki shorts and new white sneakers. It seemed almost strange to see a man of his age in athletic garb, but Raymond suspected he dressed this way all the time.

Like Carr, Blanchard carried a clipboard. When he got close enough, he put on a big smile.

"You're Raymond Coolidge?" the future Hall of Famer asked, putting his hand out.

"Yes, sir," Raymond replied.

"Very nice to meet you." Blanchard turned towards the rest of the group and zeroed in on Quincy.

"And you're Quincy Pressner, his father?"

"Yes, that's right."

Blanchard laughed as they shook hands. "I'm going to bet you don't remember, but we met once before."

"We did?"

"In 1984, in Chicago. I was a defensive assistant with the Bears. We stopped and chatted at midfield just before the game."

"Hmm . . . I'm sorry, coach, I don't remember that."

"That's okay, that's okay. I was sizing you up, trying to get a feel for you," Blanchard said.

"Did it work?"

"Nah—you beat the hell out of us."

Jon introduced the rest of the group, then Blanchard turned back to Raymond.

"Son, this is my quarterbacks coach, Glenn Hallworth."

Raymond nodded and said hello but received only a slight nod in return. Hallworth, who looked to be in his midtwenties at the most, seemed almost indifferent. This made Ray more nervous.

"All right," Blanchard said, "so let's get moving. Raymond, I took a look at your game tapes this morning. Not bad, really, but they don't tell me what I need to know the most—can you play on this level? La Salle is a fine school, and you had some tough opponents. Your numbers were very good, and you no doubt brought your team to a higher plane. But college isn't the pros. This is a different universe. Guys are bigger, meaner, and faster. *Much* faster. They play for keeps here. Linebackers don't care if they hurt you. They *want* to hurt you. I'm sure you father has told you a lot of this already."

"Yes, he has."

"There is very little room for error. Most guys can't make the change. If I had a dollar for every college star I saw that failed miserably in professional ball, I could probably buy a Rolls-Royce. Understand?"

"Yes, sir."

"You can call me coach."

"Yes, Coach."

"Good. Like I said, we're here to answer just one question—can you play in this league? That's what we're going to try to determine. Got it?"

"Got it."

"Okay, then." Blanchard motioned toward Hallworth, who stepped forward. At the same time, a few Ravens players in full pads and uniforms began streaming in.

Jon shepherded the rest of Raymond's support staff to the sidelines, conveying the message that the tryout was beginning, and only those directly involved would be allowed on the field.

A chair was brought out for Pearly, who accepted it gratefully. He eased into it, then set his cane between his legs and took a deep breath. And as he watched his nephew, taking direction from the Raven coaches and looking more ready and eager than he ever had, Pearly realized *This is really it*—the opportunity for the boy that he had worked for, hoped for, prayed for time and time again. For years, all he wanted was for Raymond to have a chance. *Just give him a shot. Let him prove himself, that's all I ask.* But now that dream had transformed; evolved for the very first time. Initially it was pure hope, nothing more. He felt Raymond could blow them away if they just took the time to look him over. Now he was *certain* Raymond would blow them away. Maybe that was why the chance hadn't arrived until now. Maybe it was one of the laws of life—that you didn't get an opportunity, no matter how badly you wanted it, until you were ready for it. All the hours of hard work, all the sacrifice, and all the emotional strain was time and effort well spent based solely on the events that were unfolding in front of him now. This was becoming one of the proudest and most satisfying days of his life.

"Raymond," Hallworth said, "let's start by getting you warmed up. Do some stretches and that stuff. You've got fifteen minutes, then report back to me."

Raymond ran the perimeter of the field twice, then hit the ground and vigorously stretched, making sure all key muscles were suitably loosened up—groin, hamstring, thigh, calf, and Achilles. Quincy stood nearby, making sure his son didn't overdo it. Then Hallworth blew the whistled that dangled around his neck, and Raymond jogged over.

Raymond began the tryout of his life with the forty-yard

dash. The forty was the gold standard for determining a prospect's speed and explosiveness, and Raymond had practiced it repeatedly over the years. He set himself into the perfect stance—left hand on the white line with thumb and forefinger well apart, other arm up at his side with the elbow bent at roughly a 45° angle, right foot—often called the "plant foot"—about four inches behind the line, the other— the "drive foot"—set six inches behind the first. He kept his head lowered and waited for the whistle. When it blew, he lunged forward with might and determination, knowing the first ten yards often set the pattern for the remaining thirty. He held his breath for those ten, leaning slightly forward, head down, and hands open and relaxed. The open hands were crucial because, closed, they would tighten the arms and shoulders, thus reducing the range of motion. In the next ten yards he exhaled mightily and imaged that there was a pack of wolves—which terrified him—just inches behind, hoping to drag him down. This kind of illusionary motivation, he discovered a few months ago, really helped. The first time he tried it, he bested his previous forty time by two-tenths of a second. In the pros, that could be the difference between contract and cut.

He inhaled deeply as he passed the thirty-yard mark. He was tempted to look up, to gauge the reaction of the others by getting a glimpse of their faces. But he held back, knowing unnecessary movement would add time to the run. In the last ten yards he exhaled normally and felt his body give an extra push as soon as the finish line came into view. Raymond often had this kind of "bonus" burst of energy; especially, it seemed, when he needed it most. He had no idea where it came from but was thankful for it. He also suspected it would be one of the first traits to go when age finally settled in.

As he crossed the line, he glanced over at Hallworth. The coach was staring at his digital stopwatch, and Raymond detected a look of surprise on his face. It was there for just a flicker of an instant.

"How was that?" he asked.

"Not bad," Hallworth said, "but it could be better. Let's go again. We always do it twice, then take the best of the two."

"Yeah, there's room for improvement," Quincy said, creating motivation.

Raymond nodded and began walking back to the starting line. He wanted to ask what the exact time had been, but he had a feeling Hallworth wouldn't tell him. And he was right. What he didn't know was that Hallworth was so impressed that he didn't want Raymond slacking off on the second run by knowing that the time of the first was 4.4 seconds. That was good for a *wide receiver*, almost unheard of for a quarterback. On the second try, Raymond again hit 4.4, and Hallworth shook his head in disbelief.

He was no less impressed by the results of Raymond's next three tests. The first was the twenty-yard short shuttle, which determines quickness and agility. Raymond began by straddling the five-yard line in a three-point stance. He was required to run left and touch the ten with his hand, then run right and touch the goal line, then go back to the five. A normal time for a quarterback hopeful was about 4.8. With Quincy barking at him ("Hustle! Hustle! Let's *go*!"), he nailed a 4.4 on the first try, and a stunning 4.2 on the second.

On his vertical-jump test, which measured lower-body strength, he reached thirty-four inches the first time, thirty-five on the second. Average for a quarterback was in the twenty-four- to twenty-eight-inch range. And when Hallworth took him back to the weight room for his 225-pound bench press, Raymond blew him away with twenty-four reps, the first fifteen seemingly without effort. For a quarterback to manage twenty was unusual.

After a short break, Raymond was brought back to the field, where he was introduced to Ravens wide receiver Anthony Jennings, who had been in one of the player lounges earlier. From the waist down he was dressed in a full game uniform. On top, only a white microthermic shirt. The tight fabric shaped itself around his torso so perfectly that every abdominal ripple was clearly outlined.

"You're Raymond?" Jennings asked.

"Yes," Raymond replied. He wasn't sure if he should say "sir" or "Anthony" or "Mr. Jennings," so he decided to play it safe.

Jennings put out a hand and smiled. "I hear you're pretty good."

Raymond shook his hand and smiled back. "Thanks. I guess we'll find out."

Jennings leaned in close. "Don't let these ladies intimidate you—the defense *or* the coaches. They're just trying to rattle your head."

"Don't worry, I won't."

Jennings was caught off guard by the young man's confidence. Then his smile grew. "Good answer, my friend. Very good answer. Most guys are peeing in their pants at this point."

"The day's not over yet," Raymond replied, causing Jennings to laugh out loud.

Hallworth wanted Jennings's help in the position drills. He gave Raymond a set of basic play designs, allowed him only ten minutes to study and memorize them, then stood behind him and barked out both the patterns and the number of steps he wanted Raymond to take in each drop before firing to Jennings. This went on for nearly thirty minutes, and in that time Raymond missed only twice. In truth, he found the whole thing ridiculously easy. Hallworth got a sense of this and upped the stakes by getting some coverage men involved; first single, then dual. Raymond handled it beautifully, mailing the ball to the receiver with a perfect spiral and just enough finesse to make it easy to handle. Even when Jennings tried to throw him a curve by breaking a pattern at the last moment or overshooting his targeted catch site, Raymond adjusted. Although the veteran receiver didn't say so, he thought at the end of the drills that this kid was the kind of quarterback every receiver dreamed of—someone who seemed to know, just *know*, what the receiver was thinking. It was as if Raymond could actually see into his mind. Aside from enjoying that relationship with Michael Bell, Jennings had never experienced it with any other QB.

As he walked back past Raymond, he tossed the ball to him and said quietly, "So when you can start?" Then winked and slapped him on the shoulder. Raymond sensed he'd made his first friend on the team.

Blanchard got involved again when it was time for a full scrimmage—the starting offense versus the starting defense. Raymond hadn't expected this, and neither had anyone else. Freddie Friedman wanted to say something, then thought better of it. And as Blanchard passed Hallworth walking off the field, Hallworth smiled and winked at his head coach. Hallworth's bad-cop facade could be set aside now, and the evaluation delivered—*this kid's got it*. But Blanchard still showed no reaction; not yet.

As the two-time Super Bowl champion team came moseying over, Raymond looked to his father. He needed reassurance, and he got it—Quincy did not seem the least bit concerned about this unexpected turn of events. If anything, he looked more confident than ever. Instinctively, Raymond realized why—*if they didn't think I was good, they wouldn't bother with a scrimmage. They would've already made up their minds.*

Blanchard gave Raymond a helmet instead of a red shirt and, in front of the boy, instructed the defense to show no mercy. They stuck to plays that Raymond knew from La Salle. They ran everything from play action to shotgun, reverses and flea flickers, slants and fades; anything that might expose a weakness. There were isolated moments of uncertainty, but they were clearly the exception rather than the rule. It didn't take more than an hour for every observer to reach the same stark realization—Raymond Coolidge was the Real Thing. He could scramble with the agility of a spider, wasn't afraid to take a hit, and, perhaps most impressively, had a savantlike instinct for defensive schemes. Time and time again he left linebackers and safeties humiliated as his receivers fled downfield towards the end zone. And if he ever felt any fear, he didn't show it. After trying unsuccessfully to sack Raymond three times, Earle Webster, the Ravens' second-year linebacker, thought he was one of the most evasive quarterbacks he'd ever seen, almost on par with speed demon Michael Vick. Tight end Ryan Hart, a stoic "student-of-the-game" type who had maintained a 3.8 average while earning a degree in mathematics at Kentucky, was impressed by his natural leadership presence—he felt Raymond had that certain "it" that made other men fall in line, unquestioningly, behind him. And after being smoked on four different pass plays thanks largely to Raymond's remarkably convincing pump fakes, cornerback Harold Rowling jogged over to his counterpart on the other side of the field, Tom Rhodes, and quipped, "Shit, I'm glad he won't be playing for anyone else. Son of a *bitch*."

As the tryout was winding down, Jon went over to Cary Blanchard and said, "So, impressed?"

Blanchard was unable to take his eyes off this newest discovery. When he finally turned, the look of excitement and delight was unmistakable.

"Huh?"

"He looks good, doesn't he?"

Blanchard laughed. "Good? Are you watching the same kid I am?"

Jon laughed. "Yeah, I think I am. I just wanted to be sure I wasn't dreaming."

"You're not."

"I didn't think so. In my opinion, Cary, he's genuine starter material. He's got the tools and the talent, and he's certainly got the drive. But when does the moment come that he's ready to go?" Jon had been wondering about this for some time. Getting a feel for a player's developmental timeline would be figured into numerous contractual issues.

Blanchard paused again, his eyes shifting away as he considered his next words carefully.

"I'll tell you something, Jon. With a some work—and I can definitely work with this young man—he could start *now*."

It was Jon's turn to pause. "You're kidding."

"Am I? Have you ever known me to kid about stuff like this?"

"No."

"He's got the goods, no question. I know we've only seen him this one time and watched some of his college tapes, but I've been doing this long enough. He could start in this league immediately, as in this coming season."

"What about our system? Could he fit into it?"

"His system at La Salle was largely derivative. It wouldn't take much adjustment. He already knows the basics. I'm telling you, Jon, barring some unfortunate disaster, he could easily be our starter this season."

Jon smiled and shook his head. "Wow, incredi—"

And in that instant—that exact moment—the plan fell together in Jon's mind. Every detail, every nuance. It all came together, like pieces of a broken bottle zooming back into shape in a reverse-action video. It was the most magnificent vision Jon ever had, striking in its simplicity, devastating in its genius. And for the first time in many days—maybe since he got word of Bell's accident—he felt overwhelmed with confidence.

His team was going to win a third consecutive Super Bowl—and now he saw precisely how they were going to do it.

JON WAS SITTING IN HIS OFFICE AN HOUR AFTER Raymond left when Cary Blanchard came in.

"Howdy," he said simply.

Jon looked up. "Oh, hi. Great stuff, huh?"

Blanchard came forward, hands in his pockets, and sat down. "Sure was. That kid's really something."

"I thought you'd like him. I'm pleased."

Blanchard was nodding. "Yeah, yeah. But that's not what I'm here to talk to you about."

Jon quickly forgot about the report he'd been reading. "Oh?"

"There's someone else I'm interested in. *Very* interested in."

Jon felt his heart drop. *And just like that, Raymond's future with this team is shot?*

"Another QB?"

Blanchard laughed. "No, no. Raymond's my new boy, no doubt about that. No, I'm talking about a different position entirely. I'm talking about coaching."

Nothing could have prepared Jon for this admission. "Coaching? What are you talking about?"

"I'm talking about Quincy."

This second shock jolted him into momentary silence. "I don't understand."

"He's a natural, Jon. Did you hear him out there? Did you see him?"

"No . . . not really. I was paying attention to Raymond."

"You should've heard him, talking about stance and poise, giving Raymond advice on mechanics and downfield vision. And the other boys were listening to him, too. The way they were standing there, eyes glued to him, you'd think they were watching a stripper or something. The guy's a natural. I've never seen anything quite like it."

"For real?"

"Yeah. I've seen it all—good coaches, mediocre coaches, bad coaches. I may not know *everything* about the game, but I know natural talent when I see it. The guy's got it in his blood. And he doesn't even realize it—that's how I know. He doesn't think about it, he just *does* it. If he hadn't been such a great quarterback, I would say this was his true calling. He'd already as good as guys I know who've been doing it for twenty years."

Jon issued a small, astonished chuckle. "Amazing."

"You're damn right it is."

"So, what are you saying?"

Blanchard smiled. "I'm saying I have an idea. . . ."

JON ARRIVED HOME LATE THAT EVENING, EXHAUSTED in every way possible. What an amazing day it had been; what an amazing turn of events. He had these flirtations with luck on many occasions, and he usually came out on the winning side. His life had always been that way—things just fell into place when he needed them to.

He flicked the switch on the wall of his den. A green banker's lamp went on, illuminating little else than his desk and everything on it. Invisible in the rest of the room were the dozens of framed photos, glass-encased balls, and shelves of books. Behind the desk and through a pair of French doors, the backyard was dark and quiet. The motion sensors would activate the floodlights when a squirrel or raccoon ambled through the grass, which happened fairly frequently.

He slumped into the chair and blew out a long, tired breath, running his fingers through his hair. There was a pile of mail waiting for him. It was stacked in that special way his wife always stacked it—everything running either north–south or east–west depending on when it arrived. If Monday's was east–west, Tuesday's would be on top of it, north–south. The current day's haul was always on the very top. This made it easy for Jon to gauge how long it'd been since he last went through it. Easy, but in this case depressing—he had five days' worth. He hadn't been home long enough to go through his mail in *five days*. He sighed again. And here was the greatest irony—he didn't feel like going through it now, either. He started, then gave up. Too tired, too disinterested.

He sat alone in the half-dark for a while, listening only to the wind and the steady wooden tick of a pendulum clock he couldn't see. Then the phone rang. He had no choice but to answer it. It was the night before the draft, and no one would call unless it was important.

"Hello?"

"Jon? Gary Stone. I'm sorry to call you at home."

"That's okay. Is there a problem?"

"You could say that."

"What? What's wrong?"

"I think you'd better come back."

"Can you give me any details over the phone?"

"I'd rather not."

He glanced at his watch—nine thirty.

"Okay, I'll be right there."

Reluctantly, he slipped into his jacket and went out.

WHEN HE ENTERED HIS OFFICE HE FOUND NOT ONE
but two people waiting—Stone, and, to his astonishment,
Susan Schiff. She was standing in front of his desk between
the two guest chairs, with her arms crossed and her pocketbook over her shoulder. She turned when he came in, and although she wasn't crying, she was clearly miserable. Gary,
sitting on the couch, immediately rose.

Jon hoped to lighten the situation with a smile. "What's
up, guys?"

Stone began with, "Okay, Susie, tell him."

"I saw someone in here today," she said.

"Someone in here? You mean in this office?" She nodded.
"Well, lots of people come in here."

"But he was going through your things, your desk."

"Who?"

She paused, then said, "Robert Macintosh."

"Rob Macintosh? Really?"

He pulled open some of the drawers and made a cursory
inspection.

"Nothing seems to be missing or otherwise disrupted.
Maybe he was trying to find something he needed, like a pen
or some—"

Susan shook her head. "No, I watched him, although he
didn't know I was there. I'd forgotten my keys and came
back. When I went to my desk, I heard him. I thought that

was strange because you'd already gone home. I peeked in and found him reading one of your notebooks. The red one."

He opened the top left drawer and held out a cheap spiral-bound. It had a fire engine red cover. Three for a buck at any Staples. Jon had bought red, blue, and green, each for a different purpose.

"This one?" he asked. She nodded. "This contains my draft notes. Why would he care about those?" It was more of a question to himself, but when he looked back at Susan she was biting her bottom lip.

She knows why.

"What did he do next?"

"He put the notebook back and went straight to his car."

Jon felt the first rumblings of anger.

"Don't tell me—he made a call on his cell phone?"

She nodded. "Yes."

"Any idea who he called?" he asked, but he already had a pretty good idea.

She nodded again. "I found out."

"For sure?"

"Yes."

"How?"

"You'll like this, Jon," Stone interjected quickly. "Smart girl."

"I called his service provider," Susan said, "and told them I was his wife, wanting to know why the bill was so high. They told me a lot of calls had been placed outside the normal calling area. . . ."

Jon's face darkened.

"Don't tell me . . . to Denver?"

"Uh-huh."

"To a number that just happens to belong to Brendan Cavanaugh?"

She nodded. "Yeah."

He slammed his fist down. "Sonofa*bitch*!" He got back up and began pacing. Susan sank into one of the chairs and watched him. "That's why I—god*dammit*!"

"Are you sure of all this? Absolutely certain?"

"Yes."

"Positive?"

"Positive."

He stopped in his tracks. Then, to Susan's amazement, his smile came back. The transformation, so quick and seamless, was somehow eerie.

He rubbed his hands together and got back behind his desk. "Okay, look, I know it's late, but could you do me a small favor?"

"What?"

"Could you stay for a little while? There's a lot to do, and I'll need your help."

"Well, sure," she replied, setting her pocketbook on the other chair as Jon quietly gave Stone a set of instructions. Stone nodded and left without another word.

ROBERT MACINTOSH WAS SITTING ON HIS COUCH, watching ESPN's pre-draft coverage with the sound off.

"That's right, sweetheart, Hawaii," he said into the cordless phone, smiling. He'd savored this moment all the way home. "Five days and five nights in Maui. Or we can go to Honolulu if you prefer. Whatever you want." *Whatever you want*, he thought delightedly. *There is perhaps no phrase more beloved by a girl like her than "Whatever you want."*

"What's that? No, it's no problem. But we won't be able to go until after we get all our draft picks signed." Boy, did that sound important. He was a lynchpin in the Ravens' organization, a key player, a mover and a shaker. Indeed, the two of them wouldn't be able to take any trips until *he* was done getting the rookie contracts settled. Without him, after all, the team would drift like a rudderless vessel.

"I'll call the airline tomorrow and make the reservation for the first week in May. Don't worry, I'll take care of everything. Just make sure you bring one of those string bikinis I like. You know, the one w—"

He jumped at the sound of the doorbell. *Who in God's name could that be?* He wasn't expecting anyone.

"Hang on a second, babe, someone's at the damn door."

He left the phone on the couch and got up. A second shock came when he found Gary Stone standing in the hallway.

"Hey, Gary. What are you doing here?"

Stone, who was normally a friendly and cheerful sort, looked downright pissed. Macintosh found this distinctly unsettling.

"You need to come with me."

"Why? What's wrong?"

"Come on, you'll find out shortly."

In that instant, Macintosh had a pretty good idea he'd been caught. His stomach lurched. *They found out. But how . . . ?*

"I . . . I'd like to call someone fir—"

Stone shook his head. "No, Robert. *Now.*"

"Can I at least get dressed?"

Stone paused, then said, "Sure, but if you so much as go near the telephone, I'll tear you a new asshole and stuff your head into it. Are we clear on this point?"

Macintosh looked into his eyes, saw the hate and the revulsion, and nodded resignedly.

Jennifer was still waiting on the phone when they went out.

20

NFL COMMISSIONER GEORGE J. MORAN SAT IN A COM-
fortable chair in the living room of his Manhattan town-
house reading a book. It was nearly ten o'clock, and after a
long and busy day he wanted to relax and clear his mind. On
the couch across from him, his wife, Patricia, sifted through
paperwork from an open briefcase. She was a marketing executive by trade and liked to keep a full schedule. Their children were both grown and had moved on to their own lives.

Along with his regular duties, Moran spent part of the
day with the handful of the college players who were expected to go in the first round of tomorrow's draft and would
be making an onstage appearance, including Christian
McKinley. The meetings were brief and cordial, more tradition than anything else. Moran also finalized last-minute
preparations for his role in the proceedings, at least the public part of it, and found himself leaving the league offices, as
he did so often, long after the sun had set and most people
were home watching television.

As he turned another page, the phone rang. The commissioner, deep in his reading, didn't appear to notice. His wife
reached over and picked it up. After a brief exchange with
the caller, she said, "It's for you, George."

Moran marked his placed with a playing card and closed the book, setting it on his lap. He didn't sigh, but he looked as though he wanted to. His wife got up and handed him the phone.

"Hello?"

"Mr. Commissioner? It's Jon Sabino, of the Baltimore Ravens. I'm sorry to bother you at home, sir."

Moran glanced at his watch. "It's getting very late, Jon," he said with the tiniest hint of irritation. "Is this an emergency?"

"Yes, Mr. Moran, I believe it is. Let me explain . . ."

Which Jon did, in detail. Fifteen minutes later he finished with, "So we were hoping you would make a ruling on this before the draft begins, for obvious reasons."

Moran shifted in his chair. "I can't rule on this without Alderman present. Any decision would deeply affect them as much as it would affect you and your club."

Jon paused purely for effect, then said, "I understand." He wanted to sound displeased, too, which he believed he did. *So far so good.*

"I suggest we have a conference call early in the morning. I will be in my office at seven thirty and will speak to all of you then."

"Okay, seven thirty. Thank you, Mr. Moran."

"Uh-huh. Good night."

The commissioner went back to his book

MICHAEL BELL LAY STILL IN HIS BED, SHEETS PULLED up to his chest, arms lying on the blanket. The hospital machinery blinked and beeped softly around him. It was just after four thirty in the morning.

The door opened, bathing the room in a bright fluorescent glow. The nurse who stuck her head in was young, blond, and pretty. The nameplate on her tight-fitting nylon uniform read "K. Hailey." She was new to this floor but a veteran to the night shift. She was a serious woman of thirty-eight, patiently ambitious and without a sense of humor.

She had two small boys at home, Dennis and Kyle, and they were huge fans of Michael Bell. They wanted to be NFL quarterbacks, too. They had little Bell jerseys and Bell posters in their room. There were Ravens sheets on their bunk beds, and the lamp on their dresser featured a little Ravens helmet. Dennis was the older of the two and had once been given a thumbs-up by Bell while he and his father watched the players arrive at the stadium before a game against the Bengals. Kyle had been green with envy and cried for hours.

When they heard their mom would be one of Bell's nurses, they begged for autographs—one for each of them. She decided to issue the parents' standard "maybe with no promises" edict. Personally she had no such fascination with sports stars, or any other stars for that matter, and had never asked for an autograph in her life. Bell seemed nice enough in spite of his swashbuckling reputation.

His eyes blinked several times before opening fully. He was disoriented for a moment, then smiled as he recognized her.

"Hi there," he said.

"Hello, Michael. How are you feeling?"

"A little groggy, but then you guys are still pumping all sorts of pharmaceuticals into me, right?"

"Only those that you need," she said, straightening his pillows and blankets.

"What time is it?"

"About six thirty A.M."

Dr. Blackman came in a moment later, looking fresh and ready for another day.

"Good morning, Michael."

"Hi, doc. How are things?"

"Good, good."

He looked at the nurse in a way that caught Bell's attention—as if he wanted to tell her something but was holding back. As soon as the nurse noticed this, she nodded and left. *Something's wrong,* Bell told himself, and suddenly he felt real fear coursing through him.

When the door clicked shut, Blackman pulled a rolling stool to Bell's bedside and sat down. His grin was still there, but it was accompanied by genuine concern. It was a fatherly smile, a "son-I-have-some-bad-news" kind of look.

"What's wrong, doc?" Bell began, trying to take control of a conversation he knew he wasn't going to like. "Is there a problem?"

Blackman looked away for just a second, then back.

"Yes, I'm afraid there is."

Bell felt every muscle go cold. They say when you receive devastating news, you first become chilly and tingly, like you've been hit by a blast of arctic air. Bell noted, somewhere far in the back of his mind, that this is exactly what happened.

"Go ahead," he said, trying to be brave but barely able to steady his voice. "Tell me."

Blackman took a deep breath and released it before continuing.

"As you know, we've continued to run tests on you. Taken more blood, more X-rays, everything."

"Uh-huh."

"And I'm afraid we've found something. Several tiny fractures . . . in your spine."

"Oh, good God."

Blackman quickly put a hand to his patient's shoulder.

"Oh no—no, don't take that the wrong way. It doesn't mean you won't be able to walk or anything like that." He managed a little laugh. "No, no paralysis."

Bell looked down and saw the shape of his two feet moving under the blankets.

"See?"

"So then what's the problem? I don't really *feel* any pain when I do that. Shouldn't I?"

"Well, we've got some heavy medication in you right now. Without it, you'd feel plenty of pain, believe me."

"Then what's the bad news?"

Blackman looked away again—a gesture of brief procrastination that Bell considered a sign of weakness.

Blackman straightened his glasses. "Well, I'm afraid you're not going to be able to go back," he said gently.

"Go back? Where? To my house?"

"No—to football. I'm afraid your career ends with this injury, Michael."

Bell suddenly realized the doctor had wrapped a hand around his wrist. In any other circumstance it would've been considered a questionable action between men, but Bell immediately realized this was simply Joshua Blackman's way of being comforting.

"My career?" he heard himself reply. The voice seemed tiny, almost frail. "Over? Th-that's it?"

Blackman nodded once. "I'm afraid so, Michael. I could give you the detailed medical explanation, but I don't think it would help. Put simply, if you continue playing and take one good hit back there—*just one*—you would indeed run a tremendous risk of paralysis. Better than fifty-fifty, I'd say."

"Even with rehab now? And plenty of time to—"

Blackman was already nodding. "No matter what we do. Your spine has suffered tremendous trauma. We knew that when you came in, but we didn't know the full extent of it. Now we do."

Bell pulled his gaze away from Blackman's and stared up at the ceiling.

"My God . . . it's over."

Blackman stood and tightened his grip on Bell's wrist.

"Listen, Michael, you've got to focus on the other side of it. You're *lucky,* son. It's a miracle you survived that crash in the first place, let alone without permanent brain or spinal damage. Like I told your friend, Jon Sabino, it was all those years of taking hits on the field and all that training that allowed you to get through the accident in one piece."

Still staring at the ceiling, Bell nodded.

"I know."

Blackman studied him closely for a few seconds, searching for any further indication of what was going on behind those famous eyes. He had limited training in human psychology, but he'd learned enough to know that a person who has just received harsh news can always use a friend.

"Michael, is there anything I can do for you right now?"

"No," Bell replied. It came out as a hoarse whisper. "Thank you, though."

Blackman lingered another moment, then patted him on the shoulder. "Look, I have to check on two other patients and then I'll be right back. Okay?"

"Sure, doc."

"If you need anything at all, please ring us and we'll come right in."

"Thanks."

Michael Bell continued staring hard into the nothingness above him. Seconds turned into minutes, and those turned into hours. He sometimes wondered what the end of his career would be like. Would it happen with a flourish of drama, like one final Hail Mary caught in the end zone to win a big game? Or with a fizzle, like a handoff to some lukewarm running back during the meaningless last match of a 4–12 season after he was traded to one of the crappier teams? He often thought about this, and in all those fantasies—good, bad, or indifferent—he never once envisioned his days in the NFL terminating with an impassioned announcement from a man he barely knew, in a quiet and lonely hospital room.

He wanted to feel sorry for himself, and he tried for a time. But instead, a different emotion came up from the depths—to his utter surprise, he sensed the tiniest hint of relief.

BRENDAN CAVANAUGH PULLED HIS SHINY BLACK BMW into its assigned spot at the Broncos' administrative offices and got out. He slung a leather bag over his shoulder, and from it he pulled a plump apple; a McIntosh, ironically enough. It would be his breakfast this morning, for he was unable to sit still long enough to eat anything at home—he wanted to get here and get this day moving. He took the first bite as he headed for the door.

Sleeping hadn't been any easier—he couldn't suppress his excitement about that supercharged moment, less than twelve hours away now, when George Moran would step up to the podium and announce that the Chargers had given him the first overall pick. The crowd would gasp. *No—the entire football world would gasp.* And then, just seconds later, Moran would confirm that Christian McKinley was headed to Denver. Cavanaugh had given up a mint for him; everyone was screaming about it. But it would be worth it in the end. McKinley would usher in a new era in Denver history, and Cavanaugh would finally have his final, definitive victory over that SOB in Baltimore.

The rest of the story would break slowly—how Jon had swiped Michael Bell from the Broncos all those years ago, making him look like a fool, but he hung in there, patiently, and got his revenge. Somehow he had beaten the mighty Jon Sabino and the world champion Ravens. Maybe there was more to him than everyone believed. That was the best part, Cavanaugh had thought as his wife slept soundlessly beside him—the perception of him would be forever altered. *Let Sabino be the loser now.* It was time for someone else to wear that crown. Yes, the fans would be as appreciative, but in the NFL's cloistered subcommunity, it would be big news for years to come. A lot of his peers would be secretly jealous, and he'd love every minute of it.

He went through the glass doors and smiled at Holly Preston, the pretty girl at the front desk. Munching on a power bar, she smiled back and waved; a little wiggle of the fingers. He gave a half-hearted smile in return, then hit the stairs. He was too busy thinking about how he was going to handle McKinley's contract. McKinley's agent was a tough sonofabitch. He'd want big numbers; probably the biggest ever for a rookie. He'd want to make a statement with it, push the bar a little higher. It wasn't going to be an easy negotiation. But he'd get it done, somehow. That was his new reputation, he decided—he was a man who Got Things Done.

Once in his office, he tossed the apple core into the wastebasket and set his bag on his desk. And he suddenly realized how quiet everything was—almost like an ordinary day rather than draft day. Usually there were staffers running around, phones ringing. What the hell was going on?

He was about to step into the hallway to find out when Phillip Alderman appeared.

Cavanaugh smiled. "Good morning, Phil." He never really felt comfortable calling the boss by his first name, but now that he was just hours away from being a hero in this organization, surely it was okay.

Alderman did not return the greeting or, for that matter, even the smile. He closed the door quietly and turned to face his general manager. The disgusted expression said it all—in that one look Cavanaugh knew he'd been caught. Somehow, some way, his connection to Macintosh and the dirty little deeds they'd been doing were now public knowledge.

Figuring he had nothing to lose now, he decided to go down fighting.

Adopting an expression of puzzlement and a tone of genuine concern, he said, "Phil, what's wrong?"

JON CLOSED HIS OFFICE DOOR AND RETURNED TO HIS chair. He tapped the speaker and microphone buttons on the multiline telephone and said, "Can you hear me, Mr. Commissioner?"

"Yes, I can hear you."

"And you, Phil?"

"I can hear you, Jon."

"How about you, Skip?"

"Loud and clear."

Jon folded his hands and set them flat on the desk. "Good. First let me very briefly say I appreciate you all taking the time for this. I know what a busy day this will be. With that in mind, let me get right to the point—knowing all that has transpired, it is my considered opinion that the last offer made between the Broncos and the Chargers, in light of how Brendan Cavanaugh acquired the information, be voided."

"I would agree with that," the Commissioner replied quickly, and Jon smiled. "Would you also agree, Mr. Alderman?"

A pause, and then, "Yes, that seems reasonable."

"And you, Mr. Henderson?"

"Obviously I can't say I'm happy about it, but yes, I understand what's happening here."

"Good," Jon said.

Then Alderman followed with, "However, regardless of the manner in which Brendan Cavanaugh obtained his information, I still think my organization should be able to bid for the Chargers' pick." Jon's smile widened. *Perfect.* "Would you say this is fair, Mr. Commissioner?" Alderman asked.

"I would certainly think so," Moran replied. Then he added, "Mr. Henderson, is there still time for other teams to place offers for your pick?"

"Sure," Skip said. "It's not even eight o'clock on the East Coast yet. The draft doesn't start for another four hours."

Four hours was more than enough time for another team to tender an offer, as they all knew. Some of the most historic deals in draft history had been finalized with only minutes to go before a pick was declared.

"Wait a second," Jon said, knowing he was expected to put up a fight. "I'm not debating whether Skip has a right to continue making deals for any of his picks. The issue here is whether or not the Broncos, with all due respect to you, Mr. Alderman, should have a shot at the first overall pick in light of their general manager's behavior during his pursuit of it."

Alderman spoke first—"Jon, Brendan Cavanaugh has been released from our organization. Considering the intimate nature of this business, I'm sure his career in professional football is finished. Furthermore, we may receive a fine from the league for his actions. Isn't that punishment enough? Do you really think denying us a chance to compete for a pick in the draft is also necessary?"

"I find myself in agreement with Mr. Alderman," the commissioner inserted. "The whole point of the draft is to compete for the right to obtain new players. I fail to see the value in denying the Broncos this basic right."

"But now they know my threshold for it," Jon pleaded. "That makes things considerably easier for them. I know my drafting duties would be a lot easier if I knew the limits of all the other teams.

"I agree with you, Jon," Alderman said. "But whether we had that information or not, we could still continue offering players and picks to the Chargers until ours was the superior package."

"Exactly my point," Moran continued. "If Denver still wanted the pick, it is reasonable to assume they would have continued bidding for it regardless."

Jon sighed heavily. "All right, that's fine," he said. "So, will you be offering the Chargers another deal, then?"

"We still have to discuss that," Alderman said casually, tightening the screws a little more. There was no support from the others, no one willing to play devil's advocate in his defense. This was how the business side of professional football went sometimes.

"Skip, if the Broncos tender another offer and there's still some time left, would you please let me know?" In that moment he realized Alderman could, if he so desired, simply resubmit Cavanaugh's last package, and he could wait as long as he liked to do so.

"Yes, I will."

And this is exactly what the bastard will do, Jon thought with a truly sinister grin.

I'm counting on it.

21

THE NFL MADE THE DECISION TO BRING THE NFL draft to the Theater at Madison Square Garden, and into public view, in 1971. The idea was the brainchild of first commissioner Pete Rozelle who, while taking his early morning stroll through Central Park one day, overhead three fans engaged in a heated discussion over who the Giants should recruit that season. Gambling that this small group was a microcosm of pro football's entire fan base, he decided to treat the draft as any other full-scale event. Before that fateful day, it was little more than a corporate huddle held in the top floor of the Sheraton Hotel on West 52nd Street. Then, in 2005, the league held the draft at New York's Jacob Javits Center. Beyond that, they were open to the idea of "bringing it on the road" in the future, perhaps to a different locale each year.

Regardless of who plays host, the league goes to great pains to dress up the venue accordingly. The stage becomes a slice of NFL history, featuring a selection of gridiron memorabilia that would have any collector's tongue wagging. This memorabilia—which includes helmets, jerseys, game balls, plaques, and trophies—is arranged on a set of hodgepodge shelves and is in fact taken from the Hall of

Fame displays in Canton, Ohio. It is meticulously guarded and, mere moments after the draft concludes and the cameras switch off, is returned to its shipping containers and whisked away.

At the front of the stage is a simple podium bearing the league's shield-like logo. Directly above and behind the podium is a huge viewing screen. There are sympathetic screens high on each wall that face the audience as well. These will display any announcements made from the podium, plus highlight clips and stats of drafted players. Team flags hang dramatically from the ceiling and over the balconies.

The area immediately in front of the stage is populated by rows of long tables; thirty-two to be exact. This is where the representatives from each team sit. The league provides them with two telephones, two sets of headphones with mikes, and a small black box with a light that stutters each time the phone rings; a necessity due to the occasionally high noise levels. Other amenities include a jug of ice water and several glasses, a dish or globe filled with candy, and a helmet, placecard, and set of coffee mugs bearing their team's logo.

The first section of seats beyond this is occupied by the media. The elite corps sit at the front and, in symbolic deference to the general pecking order, those of less importance or lower profile sit further back. The front rows are where one is likely to find ESPN's John Clayton or WFAN's Chris "Mad Dog" Russo. In the back rows you might find a stringer for some local newspaper in Jersey or a guy who has managed to churn out a newsletter for the last six months.

Beyond the media section are the fans. These are the diehards, the league's ever faithful, people who think nothing of sacrificing one of the first warm weekends of the year to sit and watch what amounts to little more than a glorified business meeting. It is not unusual for all the Giants fans to flock together, as well as Redskins fans, Jets fans, and so on. When their team makes a pick, they will boo or cheer depending on their collective opinion of the player. More often than not every crowd has a few people who take meticulous notes of the proceedings.

Other entities include a full cordon of security personnel, a small crew from NFL Films, a slew of league staffers and execs, and a team of familiar faces from ESPN, e.g., Chris Berman and Mike Terico, who will broadcast all seven rounds of the draft; a particularly exhausting task toward the end when there's very little left to say and the players being taken have, at best, only a microscopic chance of making a starting squad.

During the weeks and months leading up to the present draft, the only person anyone seemed interested in discussing was McKinley. But the buzz that filled the room as noon slowly approached had switched to the man he might be replacing—Michael Bell. The fact that Bell's career appeared to be over seemed to stun the crowd. Again they were reminded just how delicate and fleeting life could be in the NFL. With proper care, Bell would heal well enough to live a normal life, but never again would he don a uniform and march a team downfield to another score and on to another glorious victory. In a matter of seconds, his dream had ended. And now, it was generally accepted as fact, his former job would be filled by the phenomenal Christian McKinley.

Two people sat at the Ravens' table—an oversized black man with thick-framed glasses and a stubbly beard, and a skinny white kid with a crew cut and a tie who looked like he'd just stepped out of an Ivy League yearbook. They were neither at the top nor the bottom of the Baltimore organization—the black man handled ticket sales, the white kid was a marketing assistant. Contrary to popular belief, teams never sent their top people to the draft, preferring to keep them at headquarters where they could discuss last-minute decisions and other sensitive issues in private and without distraction. They sent people who otherwise had little or nothing to do with the draft and thus could be trusted by virtue of the simple fact that they knew very little and therefore couldn't give anything away.

At exactly twenty minutes before noon, the black man reached for the telephone, began tapping in a number, then set the receiver back down. His young colleague glanced at him uncomfortably.

"Do you think we should we call?"

The man wiped his face with his hand in a gesture of frustration. "I don't know." He checked his watch again. "I can't believe they haven't called *us.*" Willie Pace was a four-time veteran of the draft, yet he had never felt so unprepared. Usually he was given instructions upon arriving at the hotel the night before. Jon Sabino would give him a list of names, categorized by the round in which they would most likely be taken, then call again when it was time to make their pick. But he had received no list of names this time; only a cryptic, "Just stay by the phone," and hadn't heard from anyone since. He couldn't help but wonder if maybe there was something wrong with the phones. Everyone else's was ringing off the hook, but the two at their table sat in defiant silence. He was afraid to pick them up, though, for fear of blocking a call that might be incoming.

"I mean, shouldn't we just go ahead and take McKinley? That's the only guy they've been talking about. Maybe there was a miscommunication, and that's what we're supposed to do."

"Let's try my cell phone, just to be sure," the kid suggested, taking it from its hip case and holding it out. This was Paul Petralia's first draft, so a crisis only doubled his inherent nervousness. "I don't want to be wrong. My God, can you imagine?"

Pace looked at the phone skeptically. From the corner of his eye he spotted Commissioner Moran, who appeared briefly in the entranceway of his antechamber just off the stage. The show was about to begin.

"Okay, give it here."

He took the phone, which looked comically small in his gigantic hand, and began entering a number. Then, as if prompted by his impatience, one of the two telephones on the table rang at last.

"Willie!" Petralia screeched, pointing to the stuttering light.

He sighed. "Finally!"

He brought the receiver to his ear as Petralia watched and waited. He nodded a few times and grunted a few generic responses, all the while watching the stage and the clock. Then his eyes widened and his jaw dropped. Petralia's nerves went into overdrive.

"Yes, yes, I understand. Okay, talk to you later."

He hung up and turned to his young colleague.

"You're not going to believe this. . . ."

AT PRECISELY TWELVE NOON, GEORGE MORAN emerged from the antechamber to the left of the stage where he customarily waited for each team to decide their next pick. Moran would announce the picks for the first and second rounds, then relinquish the chore to one of his lieutenants. After that he would mingle briefly with the audience, albeit accompanied by a sizable security team, then disappear for good.

As he began making his way to the podium, he was handed a small white card by an anonymous figure who stood just outside the anteroom archway. At the top of the card was whatever logo the NFL's designers had come up with for that year's draft. At the bottom was the logo of team that possessed the current pick. In between were blank spaces for the number of the current draft round, the name of the player about to be taken, his position, school, and the number of his overall pick.

The crowd exploded when the commissioner appeared, and he smiled in response.

"Good morning, and welcome to the NFL draft." Another round of deafening applause, and then he continued simply with, "The San Diego Chargers have the first pick and are now on the clock."

Moran lingered for a moment—even he wasn't sure what

would happen next. Then he strolled casually back to his little waiting room. At the ESPN desk—a semicircle set on a
riser in the middle of the media section—Chris Berman,
Mel Kiper, Chris Mortensen, and Mike Terico began their
analysis in front of a bank of live cameras.

"Well," Berman began, "this breaking news about Brendan Cavanaugh being fired is certainly the second big story
of the day. Almost on par with whether or not the Baltimore
Ravens will in fact be receiving the first pick from San
Diego, as was previously expected."

The camera switched to a serious-looking Chris
Mortensen, who addressed viewers directly. "That's right,
Boomer. If you don't already know, it has now been confirmed that Brendan Cavanaugh, general manager of the
Denver Broncos, has been fired for allegedly having contact
with someone in the Ravens' organization concerning the
deal the Ravens were trying to work out with the Chargers
for the first overall pick. Now I've tried to get further details
on the story, but thus far everyone in the Chargers, Broncos,
and Ravens organizations are being tight-lipped."

"It was rumored that the Broncos and the Ravens were
the only two teams left competing for that pick, is that correct?"

"Yes, that's right. But I've also been told by a league
source that a private phone conference took place early this
morning between the three teams and Commissioner Moran
concerning the matter. However, I can't get any confirmation
on what was discussed."

"Is it possible the Ravens have lost the chance to—?"

Berman stopped when Moran reappeared. He was handed
another card and approached the podium. Again the room
fell silent. Three enormous images of the man appeared on
the overhead screens.

"With the first overall pick of the draft, the San Diego
Chargers have elected to make a trade. The pick now be-
longs to the Denver Broncos." A collective gasp came from
the audience.

• • •

JON SAT BEHIND THE VAST, PAPER-LITTERED TABLE IN
the ravens' war room, watching events unfold on the two
flat-screen television monitors that hung from the corners.
He chewed on a pen without realizing it. Cary Blanchard
and his coaching staff sat in a row behind him. Kevin Tanner
was at his left. Connally paced furiously and kept raking his
fingers through his hair.

Finally, Connally turned to Jon and said, "Are you sure
this is the right thing to do?"

Jon looked to Blanchard, who nodded. Then he turned
back to his boss.

"Yes, I'm positive."

KEYBOARDS CHATTERED AND VOICES BLENDED INTO A
feverish cacophony as word of this stunning development
raced through the MSG theater and out to the waiting football world.

Back on the ESPN riser, Berman turned to Kiper, who up
to this point had remained silent. "Mel, what's your take on
this?"

Kiper went to speak, then laughed and threw his hands
up. "I have no idea. This is just . . . beyond imagination.
Like all of you, and in fact most everyone else, I was under
the impression the Ravens had the pick pretty much in the
bag."

Back in the pit, two league representatives stood in front
of the Broncos table and waited. One of the Bronco reps was
on the phone. After he hung up, he hurriedly filled in a new
draft card and handed it to the officials. They in turn brought
it to a group of league execs seated in a row at the front of
the stage. They distributed the information among their
record keepers and among ESPN personnel, the latter so
they would have it ready for instant broadcasting. Then, finally, the card was given to the anonymous figure standing
just outside the commissioner's lair. The commissioner was
alerted that another pick was ready.

* * *

JON STOPPED SWIVELING IN HIS CHAIR AND LEANED forward. Connally stopped pacing.

"Here it comes," he said softly.

MORAN TOOK THE CARD IN STRIDE, THE INK ON IT barely dry, and came to the podium. He glanced at the card once, registering the information, then looked back up. As usual, his expression conveyed nothing.

"With the first overall pick of the draft . . . the Denver Broncos have selected, from Michigan, quarterback Christian—"

The rest of his speech was dampened by gasps and a smattering of applause. A respectable-sized cadre of Broncos faithful, who had made the pilgrimage in support of their beloved championship team, exploded in a symphony of screams and howls. Ravens fans, seated on the other side of the theater, stood motionless, thoroughly confused. In this sense, they truly represented the rest of their base back home.

Their bewilderment would not last long.

22

A SMUG PHILLIP ALDERMAN THOUGHT HE WAS STAND-
ing in the midst of history as it was being made.

They were all in the press room at the Broncos' facility. It
was small and unspectacular, to say the least. A giant sheet
decorated with the team logo hung from one wall, a lectern
stood in front of it. There were two rows of cubbyholes, and
each station had a light and a phone line so the writers could
connect their laptops to the Internet. A local catering service
provided platters of food and giant plastic tubs filled with ice
and bottled beverages.

McKinley handled the press remarkably well. He was
calm, smooth, and dynamic. He knew when to be serious
and when to be playful. He seemed to enjoy the experience,
and the reporters clearly enjoyed him. Alderman, standing
just out of view of the cameras along with McKinley's
mother and his agent, thought the kid had either studied the
mannerisms and techniques of a thousand other press conference veterans, or he was really just that good by nature.
Alderman joined him for the standard shot of him holding
up his new Broncos jersey, a repeat of what McKinley had
done with Commissioner Moran in New York City just a few
hours earlier. He wanted to make sure his face was con-

nected to this turning point moment in Broncos history. McKinley would lead them into a new and glorious era. The organization had been suffering from a long line of mediocre QBs since Elway. Now that would change. Yes, Brendan Cavanaugh had started the deal, but Alderman had finished it. He didn't like Cavanaugh's methods, but he knew the guy had been right about the team's greatest need.

What still troubled Phil Alderman, however, was why the Ravens, in the end, gave up the pick so easily. One moment there was Jon Sabino on the phone, almost whining like a child to the commissioner after weeks of intense negotiation and dealmaking. And then, with just minutes left, Skip Henderson called to say the Ravens decided to give up their pursuit of the pick. At first Alderman figured he had simply outbid them, that he and the Denver organization had, in the end, offered a more attractive package. That had certainly given up plenty, so it was a believable explanation on the surface.

But something about it didn't sit right. Alderman knew Sabino too well, knew the guy's reputation for cunning and brilliance. It just didn't make sense that he was simply *beaten*. This nagged at him from the edges of his mind for a while.

Then, four days after the draft, the answer came with sickening clarity—while Alderman was sitting in his office reviewing a list of potential candidates to officially replace Cavanaugh, an e-mail landed in his inbox, following by a chime. He usually only tended to e-mails twice a day—once in the morning, and once at lunch. But when he glanced over at the screen and saw that this one was sent by a longtime friend who had retired from the league years ago and sent e-mails only when the matter was important—and that the subject line read, YOU MIGHT WANT TO LOOK AT THIS—he immediately opened it. The message contained nothing more than a live Web link. Clicking on it, Alderman was taken to an article posted by sportswriter Patti Sheridan less than an hour before. The headline—"A Father's Pride: Baltimore Signs the Talented Son of Legendary Quincy Pressner."

It took Alderman less than two minutes to read and fully absorb the piece. In that brief span, his greatest fears—plus a few he hadn't even considered—were realized. He saw how Sabino had screwed him. He understood the damage that had been done. And he knew that, once again, his organization had been beaten.

Then he did something he hadn't done since his college days—rushing into his private bathroom, he vomited.

WHEN JON ENTERED THE HOSPITAL ROOM, BELL WAS sitting up, reading the latest *Sports Illustrated*.

"Hey," he said.

"Hey, thanks for coming over so fast. I know you're busy today. It could've waited until the draft was over, y'know."

Jon smiled and waved away the comment. "No problem. The worst is over." He sat on the same rolling stool Blackman had used.

"How'd it go? Did you get your boy?"

"No, I think we might've done a little better."

Bell, like every other Ravens fan, was stunned. "No shit? Who'd you get?"

Jon gave him all the details, finishing with Raymond's incredible tryout.

"Wow, the son of Quincy Pressner."

"I know. Incredible, isn't it?"

"It sure is."

They were silent for a moment, each looking at the other with tiny smiles and thousands of unspoken sentiments between them. It was a conversation neither of them wanted to have.

"So," Jon said quietly. "You're calling it a day."

Bell nodded. "Yeah, I am."

"I had a feeling. When you told me on the phone before, the first thing that went through my mind was, 'There's more to his injury than we first thought.'"

"You got it."

"Will you be all right?"

"Yeah, I'll be fine. Josh is going to be taking care of me for a while. He's the man."

Jon laughed. "You're calling him 'Josh' already?"

"Shit, yeah."

"Amazing. You could charm a dying man out of his last heartbeat."

"It's not the men I'm interested in charming, Jon."

"Right, right. So . . . what happens now?"

"You tell me."

Jon thought it over for a moment. "Well, we'll give you some kind of ceremony."

Bell rolled his eyes. "Please don't."

"I don't think the fans will let you off that easy. You'll have ceremonies, parades, free food, free booze, lots of gifts. The press might even write something nice about you."

"The hell you say." They broke into uproarious laughter at this line. It was one of their favorites from a movie they both loved—*The Shawshank Redemption*. Over the years, they'd used it on each other on many occasions.

"You'd be surprised."

"Yeah, well, I guess I can deal with all that." Bell looked his old friend squarely in the eyes. "Y'know, I'm not bitter. I mean, I wanted to go a few more years, but . . . damn, I've been doing a lot of thinking as I've been lying here; there's not much else *to* do. I've been lucky, Jon, damn lucky. I've had some great games, I've got two Super Bowl rings on my hand, laid lots of beautiful women, traveled all over the world. What do I have to be bitter about?"

"I agree."

"Everything's gone my way for so long that I guess I got used to it. Maybe this is the way the numbers balance themselves out in life."

"Yeah, maybe."

"I don't know. I'm not smart enough to know that kind of stuff. But I know I'm happy. And I'll be able to leave the league in one piece."

"That's right," Jon said, nodding. "Which is more than some guys can say. You'll be leaving happy, healthy, and rich as hell."

"Yeah, that too. I've made lots of money."

"And you'll make plenty more before you leave."

Michael was staring straight ahead, thinking about something else, when Jon said this, so his reaction was delayed. He turned with a look of utter bewilderment and said, "What are you talking about?"

"The multimillion-dollar settlement for the remainder of your contract. The one I made with that agent of yours."

Bell pushed himself up further, the copy of *SI* slid off his lap.

"What the hell are you talking about, Jon? I didn't make any—"

"Wahlberg, your agent. He called me the other d—" Two men couldn't have looked more perplexed with each other. "You don't know anything about this?"

"No, I don't. What the hell's going on?"

The anger that alighted in Michael Bell's brain when Jon began the story developed into full-blown rage in a matter of minutes. It reached a crescendo when Bell whipped the magazine across the room and screamed out several choice obscenities, which brought two nurses running.

Over the next hour, the following three things happened in following order—Bell apologized personally to Jon Sabino. Then he apologized over the phone to Peter Connally. And then he called Jerry Wahlberg to inform him, with the help of some more colorful words and phrases, that his services would no longer be required.

BACK IN HIS OFFICE ON SUNDAY EVENING, JON BUS-ied himself with some last minute cleaning up now that the draft was over. His desk was finally getting neat again, papers in their relative piles, pens and pencils in the cup, no loose clips lying around. He liked to have his desk cleared and "reset" at the end of each day. It was a philosophy he had picked up while reading a biography of Ronald Reagan years earlier, and he found it surprisingly effective.

Finally, he got up and took his jacket from the back of the chair. As he slipped it on, Kevin Tanner appeared.

"Oh, hi, Kev. What's up?"

Tanner was grinning from ear to ear.

"Don't give me that 'what's up' crap, you sly devil."

Jon grinned back. "Devil? Me?"

"While most of our fans are ready to tar and feather you, the most astute ones are talking about canonizing you as the Patron Saint of Ingenuity. They're starting to figure it all out. So's the media. You should read the articles that are being posted on the Net."

Jon laughed and diverted his eyes downward in a gesture of self-deprecation.

"I can't imagine what you're talking about."

Tanner just stood there, staring, until Jon felt like a zoo specimen.

"Okay, look," he said, sitting down again, "it's a huge gamble, nothing more. There's no guarantee this is going to work. Cary thinks Raymond Coolidge is the real thing, so I'm taking a chance he's right. The fans may very well still tar and feather me and then hang my corpse upside from a lamppost like the Italians did to Mussolini in World War II."

Tanner also sat. "Yeah, but there are no guarantees one way or the other. Getting McKinley wouldn't have *guaranteed* a third championship, either."

Jon nodded. "I know. That's why I made the choice that I did. McKinley's amazing, no doubt, but one man doesn't make a whole team in this sport. Everyone knows that."

"But everything else you did. . . ." Tanner continued, pausing to marvel over the details for a few more seconds. "The way Cavanaugh went down, and the fact that we don't have to sell off half our roster, and . . . all of it. We came up on the winning side of this in *such . . . a . . . big . . . way.*" He emphasized the last four words a hand gesture that looked like he was trying the judge the weight of a bowling ball.

"Well, that's the idea, isn't it? Winning isn't just for the players, you know."

Tanner laughed and shook his head. "It took me a while to figure out why, when you had that phone conference with Moran, that you acted as though you still really wanted the pick. Then I realized—and correct me if I'm wrong here—all you were really doing was making sure *Denver* took it."

Jon was nodding. "Yep. I know I have no fans over there. Alderman dislikes me almost as much as Cavanaugh. I knew if I whined a little bit, it would make them want the pick all the more. It increased their motivation—the thrill of getting it and being able to brag about it. It's like in poker, where you get someone to call a bet by enticing them into it. There are several ways to accomplish this. In this case, by making it seem like my pride would be hurt, I made irresistible for them."

Tanner's heavyset body shook with laughter. "I love it, I just love it."

"So in the end," Jon went on, "we maintain our depth, Brendan Cavanaugh will be pumping gas somewhere in the Midwest, and we've got a great new quarterback at the helm." He waved his hand. "Raymond will be fine. He just needs to be solid and sensible. Cary will make sure that happens. Remember when Trent Dilfer won it for us back in 2000? Everyone said he was average this, average that. But go take a look at the films and see how *steady* he was. He wasn't a highlight-clip kind of guy, but he made very few mistakes. Like I said, *solid.* That's what Raymond Coolidge is. And he's got so much support around him it's ridiculous. The guys already love him. He's going to be terrific."

"The contract you offered him was nice," Tanner said. "Very generous. And easy on the cap, too, because of the relatively small bonus."

"Manageable for us," Jon replied, "but a huge shot in the arm for him and his family. His mom can retire now, and his uncle will get some proper medical attention. . . . It's all good." Then Jon said, "By the way, have you figured out the *very* best part of the whole deal yet?"

"The best part? Haven't we already covered the best parts?"

"Well, most of them. But no, not the best part of all, at least from *my* perspective." Jon rose and rolled the chair back into a neat position again. His workspace now looked as though it was ready to be photographed for an article about beautiful offices.

"Uh . . . no. I have no idea."

"Well, think for a moment. What have I said, many times, was my one unfulfilled ambition in this business? What is the one football thing I always wanted to do but never did?"

Tanner's eyes shifted from spot to spot. Then he snapped his fingers and pointed. "Play. You always wanted to play on a pro team."

"That's right. I never did because I simply wasn't good enough. I did okay back in school, but I sure as hell was never going to reach the next level."

"All right, yeah. So . . . I don't get how this ties in with—"

"Tell me something," Jon said, cutting him off. "Who has been our archrival in recent years?"

"Denver, of course."

"Of course."

"And why is that? What has always been their greatest strength?"

"Their defensive depth. They've always had—"

This time Tanner cut him*self* off. Then he went into an astonishing transformation. First, the grin he'd been wearing since he came in vanished. As it did, his mouth fell open, equally slowly, until it formed a neat little O. His eyes, usually soft and jovial, grew wide and trained on Jon in a look of both amazement and disbelief.

"You knew they'd lose a lot of defensive depth with any deal they made for McKinley, because Skip wanted a defense."

Jon shrugged. "Pretty much, yeah. It could've been us or it could've been them. Then Raymond came along and changed everything."

Tanner's mouth moved soundlessly as his words bottle-necked. It wasn't that he had nothing to say, but rather he had many things to say and couldn't figure out which should come first.

"I studied Denver's roster pretty thoroughly," Jon said. "I knew that little bastard would want McKinley more than ever after he found out we did, too. I factored this into the equation. So while I was studying the rosters of the other teams we'd be competing with, I studied theirs as well. And I realized the Broncos didn't have quite the depth on offense that we did. That meant they wouldn't be able to wheel and deal for other defensive players around the league like we could, so they'd have to give up some of their own. Maybe not starters, but from second and third teams. It would hurt them a lot more than it would hurt us."

Tanner, with a look of awe and respect usually only given to religious icons and elder statesmen, said, "So you rammed McKinley down their throat in order to weaken their defense?"

"You got it."

"So next year, they wouldn't be as strong defensively, and in turn they wouldn't be . . . my God, Jon."

"As much of a threat to us," Sabino finished. "That's right. They were our number one threat to making a third Super Bowl. Not anymore." Sabino laughed. "Yeah, they have Christian McKinley, but he won't do much good on that team for a few years. By then, hopefully, we'll have secured our place in history." Then he added, "*That* is how I've fulfilled my dream of playing—I wiped out a defense single-handedly."

Tanner was shaking his head now. "Incredible, Jon. Just in-friggin'-credible."

"Thanks."

Tanner laughed, too. A quick little hitch through the nose that somehow conveyed his incredulity.

"Connally was going crazy, you know," he said softly. "I thought he was going to fire your ass at one point."

"Yeah, me too."

"Now he's going to fall in love all over again."

"Let's hope it doesn't come to that."

Jon turned off his desk lamp and headed toward the door. When Tanner rose also, Sabino put an arm around his shoulder.

"Oh, and by the way, my friend," he said as they walked out of the office and began down the hall. "Cary brought us a new assistant coach on the team to help Raymond along. His name is Quincy Pressner. . . ."

Kevin Tanner was too punch-drunk at this point to be astounded anymore. Wearily, he simply nodded.

RAYMOND'S LAST VISIT TO THE ABANDONED FIELD AT GW high came just days after he signed his contract with the Baltimore Ravens. Jon had given him a fair deal, especially for an undrafted free agent. A modest signing bonus of $1.7 million, plus a two-year deal worth $3.4 million, some of which was based on incentives. But he knew he was within reach of all of them.

He tossed the ball to his father, who held onto it for a moment before tossing it back. Raymond got the feeling he didn't want to really let it go.

"I'm glad to see you and mom getting along so well," Raymond said after a while.

"Yeah, me too," Quincy replied. "You know, she's the only woman I ever really loved. I want you to know that."

"I know, Pop. I always knew."

"Yeah, well, I did a lot of stupid things with other women when I was your age, as you now know."

"Yeah."

Quincy heaved it back again, and Raymond was surprised by the velocity, the strength. After all these years, that arm was still in pretty good shape. *I wonder if it* ever *realy goes away?* he wondered.

"I guess it sounds like something out of a movie," Quincy continued, "but they didn't mean anything to me. None of them. I was thinking with my . . . well, you know." He still didn't feel it was okay to use that kind of dirty language in front of his boy. "But in my heart, there was only one person."

Raymond surprised his father with a laugh. "I forgive you, Pop, okay? If Mom does, I certainly can."

Quincy smiled. "That means a lot to me."

"You mean a lot to us," Raymond countered quickly. "And to Uncle Pearly, too."

"Oh, hell, what you did for him, son . . ." Quincy shook his head. "One of the most generous things I've ever seen. He'll never know what to do with all that money."

"He deserves it," Raymond said. "He's been through enough."

A few kids had gathered on the fringes of the field now and were watching them. They appeared to be unsure as to whether or not they should come closer. Raymond noticed this and was equally unsure how to react.

"Get used to it, Ray," his father said. "They used to come for me. Now they'll be coming for you. You'll get it every day."

Eventually the boys—a total of four—worked up the collective courage to approach the newest celebrity in sports, and a local figure at that. Even two weeks ago this wouldn't have happened. But the heavy rotation of the story on ESPN, and thus in every other sports-related media outlet in the country, had turned Raymond into an overnight sensation.

The boys only wanted autographs, which Raymond gave happily. His father watched from a comfortable distance, experiencing one of the proudest moments of his life.

After the boys left, father and son went back to their game of catch. The initial purpose of this visit was to run some basic drills that Quincy wanted to show him, but somehow that didn't seem appropriate anymore. There would be other days, other opportunities. For now, though, it was enough that they simply throw the ball around, just as they had when Raymond was a little boy; a wide-eyed child looking up to the capable father. And in many ways that was still the case. They had made their memories then, and they both knew the time had come to make some more.

They stayed until the sun dipped below the trees to the west. Then they headed for home.

EPILOGUE

WITHIN THE EERIE QUIET OF ARROWHEAD STADIUM, with more than seventy thousand Chiefs fans watching in disgust on an otherwise clear and beautiful autumn evening, Ravens quarterback Raymond Coolidge crouched down behind his center, hands open and ready, and began the count.

They ran another new play—a variation of their "Stem I Right Close Z Peel—P 82 F Arrow"; an action pass used in goal-line situations. Receivers on either side ran shallow crossing routes to create a rub and pick a linebacker. Kansas City's defense tried to break the line in their frustrating search for a sack, but they'd been unsuccessful all day. Only one so far, plus two hurries, and the game was almost over. Raymond, trusting his protection, ignored them and waited for Darryl Bailey—who was playing in only his third game of the season after a long period of rehabilitation—to get open. DB did, cutting a straight line down the right side, and Raymond lofted it effortlessly into his waiting arms. He was taken down at the two. On the next play, Raymond faked to fullback Paul Ellis and ran the ball in himself for the touchdown. With less than two minutes remaining and the score at 28–3, most of the Chiefs were thinking about next week's matchup against the Jets.

Jon, standing next to Quincy, said, "He's going to have one hell of a career."

Jon nodded. This was a Monday night game late in the season, and the Ravens were leading the league with their 11–2 record. Defensive coaches wanted to confuse, or at the very least rattle, Raymond into making typical rookie mistakes. But it appeared he had indeed inherited his father's legendary calm, transposing himself from an emotional young kid into a cold-blooded, steely-eyed warrior the moment he got on the field. His memory was also outstanding, to the point where Blanchard felt comfortable creating new plays just for him. Soon the media was raving over him. When word hit that he was the son of Quincy Pressner, and that Cary Blanchard had also been blown away by Quincy's natural leadership talents and hired him as Baltimore's assistant quarterbacks coach, there was a frenzy. The cameras couldn't keep away from the former legend and mystery man. Patti Sheridan had written the "welcome to the world" piece as a freelancer for *Sports Illustrated* and was promised the book deal, if it came to that.

The Broncos, with their depleted defense and their tepid 7–6 record, fumed but remained stoic. They knew they'd been had. The press wouldn't let that go, either. They constantly goaded Jon in the hopes of starting World War III, but he wouldn't cooperate. He knew the Broncos would get even with him eventually. That's how this part of the game was played. But by the time they exacted their revenge and McKinley was up to speed, it wouldn't matter as much. All he cared about was the current campaign—a third Super Bowl and on to history. And he knew they were on their way to both.

Baltimore got the ball back with less than a minute remaining. Raymond took it in hand and dropped to one knee, and Quincy went out to his son. Jon Sabino savored the moment because he knew it wouldn't last. Tomorrow he'd be expected to conjure a more miracles and record other victories. Such was the nature of his job, to which he knew he was hopelessly addicted.

As the team jogged off the field, their general manager went with them.